To Han... Best wishe-

Kingdom of Wrath and Embers
By V M Stiller

First published via KDP Publishing in 2022.
ISBN 9798839777163

Cover by @InkFae.
Chapter Title Images (Flame Paper) by Dawn Hudson,
used with permission.

DEDICATION:

To all those who feel lost or alone, and find a home in stories.

KEY TERMS: MR = Mage Ruled, that is the time period used in this fantasy world instead of BC and AD. Before MR, there was HR. This means Human Ruled. Before HR, there was SR which means Sorcerer Ruled. But neither the HR nor SR periods feature in this first novel.

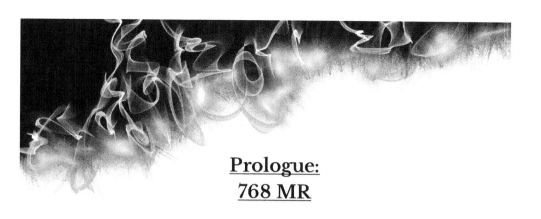

<u>Prologue:</u>
<u>768 MR</u>

*A*mbassador Rizwan Rasul nervously sipped at his cardamom tea, his thigh shaking, as he regarded the young Crown Prince of Azyalai. The Prince, a rather dashing youth of twenty years, had sprawled himself out across the black velvet sofa within his temporary apartments, absentmindedly playing with the garish knife his father had gifted him upon his instatement as Crown Prince.

It was not the careless, reckless way in which he handled the sharp object that was the cause of the Ambassador's tension. No, a near-fatal stab would be less worrisome than the topic of their conversation, the woman whose court they currently resided within: the Night Queen.

Corentine.

"Father thinks I don't stand a chance," the Prince bemoaned, his dark eyes flickered between his knife and the Ambassador he was addressing, "but imagine the renown I would earn as the man who tamed the Night Queen."

"Forgive me, Your Highness," Rizwan began delicately, wishing that it was the reasonable Prince Azaj he was dealing with, rather than his commendably ambitious but foolhardy older brother. "But I do not believe that one, ah, tames the Night Queen."

Crown Prince Afzal sat up suddenly, tossing his knife to a nearby sofa, denting the gold that lined the glossy leather.

Rizwan winced. Having grown up neither poor nor rich, the Prince's blatant disregard for opulence was something he had yet to grow used to.

The black-haired boy narrowed his eyes at his father's Ambassador to Galaris.

"They say whoever would hold her holds the continents, and I intend to become the greatest King Azyalai... no, that any of the continents has ever seen."

The Ambassador held back a sigh. A thirst for glory was a common trait within the Prince's bloodline. It was why his father, his grandfather, and great-grandfather before him had established themselves as the rulers of the second largest empire in the world, leaving Valark in the dust. But this goal would not gain him glory. In fact, it could kill him.

Wracking his brain for a way to sate the Prince without bringing the matter to his father, Rizwan decided to inquire, "if you don't mind me asking, Your Highness, what have you heard of the Night Queen?"

With Crown Prince Afzal only arriving in Galaris the night previously, he knew he was yet to meet the woman in question.

2

The Prince shrugged, "what everyone does. That she is beautiful and cold; that she is very old and a Dark Mage."

Rizwan nodded. All of those facts were correct.

"Yes," the Ambassador said, "she is. But she is also more than that. You say she is cold? She is arctic. You say she is old? She has been around for more than five centuries. You say her magic is Dark? It is near black and terrifying and she plays it like a fiddle."

Though Afzal did not appear entirely put off, a degree of trepidation could be seen within his eyes.

Thank the Gods, Rizwan thought to himself, *this I must build on.*

He knew that if anyone realised he both had knowledge of and went on to relay this information, let alone to a Prince of foreign lands, he would meet an unimaginably terrible end at the hand of the monster-Queen. So, tentatively he continued;

"The story of the Night Queen is a guarded one. A forgotten one. But some still remember parts of the tale, passed on through the generations or relayed in fraying diaries of people long dead. They say she was a hero once, before the Last Battle, sometimes simply called the Massacre, but its results destroyed her. It was not a hero that rose from those bloody meadows five hundred years ago, but a monster with nothing but wrath in her heart. Accounts differ; some say it was when she drove a knife through King Caradoc's heart that she truly fell into the twisted descent that led her to become who she is now. After all, she is said to have truly loved two in her lifetime. The very King she

3

murdered, and the slaughtered Commander Zarola."
He took a careful pause before he continued;

"My Prince, the one you speak of, that you desire, is a monster with the face of a woman; a demon confined to a flesh prison. If she had a heart, it blackened and died at the Last Battle as she held the rebel Commander in her arms, or in this very Palace as her dagger entered the Fire King's chest. All she has now is power. The power of the continents; the power of a conqueror. She will never share it with you. She will not share it with any creature. Let go of this wish to win her. Attempt to make a friend of her rather than simply an ally if you judge it so necessary, but always remember that, with her, you are not playing with fire – you are playing with darkness, for she is the Dark."

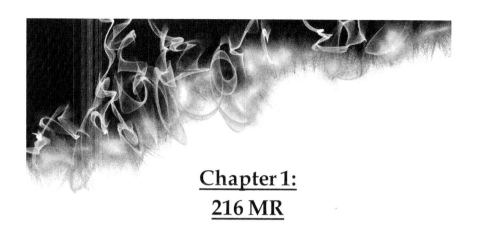

Chapter 1:
216 MR

$\mathcal{I}$t began with fire.

The day had started as it always did for the eighteen-year-old Corentine, with the crow of one of her father's cockerels.

She leaned up from the hard, splintered wooden floor on which she slept, stretching like a disgruntled feline, before stiffly rising and hobbling towards the small, rotting archway that led to the house's main room.

On the rickety, brown table, five bowls were already out; the one before Corentine's normal seat had the most within it, but that was not out of love or care, but rather out of fear.

Last night, she had lost control.

Ashamed, she could not meet the wary and condemning eyes of her father and eldest brother, both of whom were already awake whilst her other brothers, Aubin and Colden, slumbered on.

The first time Corentine had used her powers she had been five and frightened. Cornetine and her closest friend, Mina, had been sneaking into the woods to see the young willow mage tree, betting on who would be able to climb up the furthest, when bells had sounded announcing the presence of Snatchers.

Despite their efforts to sprint home as fast as their legs could carry them, they were far too slow.

A tall man with slicked-back blonde hair soon caught up with them. She could still remember his lecherous smile as he looked them up and down, reached out a hand for Mina and-

The Darkness reached out to greet him.

What appeared to be black smoke entered through his eyeballs and mouth and nose. His back arched; his eyes bulged; he fought desperately for breath as the Darkness continued its relentless invasion, choking and filling, his screams coming out garbled and limbs spasming. His hands clawed at his throat, leading to blood soaking his nails. He choked on pain, yet he didn't stop.

He ripped his own throat apart.

When he dropped to the floor, his eyes were as black as spilled ink, pupils no longer visible and yet they seemed to pierce into Corentine, cruel and accusing.

Demon, they seemed to tell the five-year-old.

Monster.

She had fallen to the ground crying. She hadn't meant for it to happen; she had just wanted Mina to be safe. She didn't want to hurt anybody, and she wasn't a monster. She wasn't, she wasn't, she wasn't, she-

Small, dark-haired, fearless Mina had clutched her younger friend to her chest as she cried. When the girl's tears had stopped and grey-green eyes blinked up at her, Mina had reassured her that being a Mage, being powerful, didn't make her a monster so long as she didn't use her power to do bad things. But, older and wiser, had added, "we can't tell anybody, okay, Coren?" Mina hadn't cared what Coren was; she never regarded her with suspicious or wary eyes.

That didn't matter now. Snatchers had gotten Mina eventually, and her sisters, and nobody ever returns once they're taken.

The next person to find out about Coren's powers had suffered a worse fate.

Her own mother, the previous night.

Coren swallowed and took a seat at the table. Small, shaking hands plucked up her wooden spoon and she lowered it into her bowl. As usual, the broth was filled with giblets.

While her father owned a chicken farm, they could not afford to eat the more luxurious pieces such as the thigh or wing, those had to be sold to the customers if they wanted to continue to get by.

Still, the young girl could not help but wince when chewing a particularly tough bit.

Despite the three people at the table, there was silence. A state that she thought would be maintained throughout the entirety of the meal, until it was broken by her older brother.

"Nothing to say today, Coren?" he asked.

Just his voice, his angered, condemning voice, made her want to turn tail and hide away somewhere no one could find her. Any strength she believed she possessed was gone in the face of Jolon and his grief. His righteous anger.

She eyed the dirt crusted beneath her fingernails.

He knew. There was no chance she could make up a story and retain her state of normalcy; no chance they would continue to love her as she loved them.

"You did it, didn't you?" he declared, loudly, afterwards; devastated and furious.

Her eyes burned.

"Tell me, you unnatural swine," he began dangerously before roaring, crashing his fist into the side of his bowl, sending his wooden spoon clattering against the left wall, "was it you?!"

Coren said nothing, guilt clawing up her throat, choking her as she had once choked that blonde man with her Darkness.

She nodded.

Jolon all but launched himself over the table, grabbing her pale neck and brutally slamming her against the wall. The poorly built shack shuddered at the movement. Coren clawed at his hands, her power awakening within her, desperately attempting to seduce her.

I'm here, Coren, I'm here. Use me. Use me. You can be powerful, you know, so, so powerful. You can make them beg. Coren, I'm here. Coren...

She shoved it down, and instead kicked out, her bare foot slamming hard into her oldest brother's gut, sending him backwards into the table whilst she held herself up against the wall, knees threatening to slump beneath her.

Her brother was nearly twenty-six and bulky. So much larger and more imposing than her, even when wearing rags. He looked upon her with such untampered hatred that it made Coren feel sick with fear and self-hatred. Tears leaked from his watery blue eyes as he pulled himself up, shakily telling his younger sister, "she was our mother. Our mother, who you slaughtered like some kind of runt! I've suspected you were an abomination for years, Ren, but this... You're not even human."

Defences fought against her closed mouth; words echoing around her head. *I loved her too. I couldn't control it. I'm so sorry. It's getting more powerful, I can't... If only father would permit me to go to the Mage educators. I never wanted this. I never asked to be born. I'd die if I could, I swear.*

That was the thing about Mages, the only thing that could kill them was a weapon of willow mage wood, and the King had long since had the willow mage trees – including the one of Coren's youth – burnt. Apart from that exception, they were immortal, locked to the age in which they reach the majority of their power. That is, except for being tied to a stake and burned for eight days. But she couldn't bring herself to do that. *Coward.*

So, it was eternity as a monster. The very idea filled Coren with hopeless dread.

Clearly, however, the knowledge of the Mage's immortality momentarily escaped Jolon, who lunged towards her heart with a wooden knife. Having gained much strength from his second job as a woodchopper, he would have the power to drive it home.

It didn't matter that it wouldn't kill her; her magic, having been growing more and more unpredictable with each day, gaining strength each time it was used, reacted.

Black smoke erupted from the small female, who cried out in warning, before it violently exploded outwards. The blast shoved her father and brother through the wooden walls of their eating area just as the shack itself imploded, roof and walls being thrown away. To protect her from the blast, Coren's Darkness encased her, taking on a physical form as it pillowed her from the impact of her back hitting the hard, dried mud outside. She heard a *SNAP* not far from her, and a scream with a responding shout. Even after her Darkness receded, feeling satisfied with itself, she kept her eyes closed until she heard her father screaming at her.

Opening her eyes eventually, she saw that debris had been scattered throughout their farm; sorrow filled her heart when she saw that several chickens had been impaled by pieces of wood, others injured. Looking towards her father, she saw that he was glowering at her whilst leaning over her brother's withering body.

She brought a shaky hand to her mouth.

Hearing a commotion to her left, she saw her other two brothers, bleeding and bruised, hurling pieces of wood off of themselves. Colden, just a year her senior with a rather low pain tolerance, was lightly sobbing as he cradled his injured wrist to his chest, whilst Aubin helped to get the rest of the fallen bed frame off of his right leg.

In the distance, she heard the villagers' cries of concern and knew that they would be here soon. Asking questions; wanting answers. Answers that would see her burnt.

"What did you do?!" her father demanded, desperately trying to help Jolon sit up.

"I-I," Coren tried. The villagers were getting closer. They couldn't know, they couldn't- she didn't want to burn, "please, father, *please*, let me leave. You'll never see me again. I'll go to Andern and catch a ship tonight! I can't control this, I know I can't but I'll leave, you'll never see me, I'll-,"

Her father laughed, the sound taking on a manic quality, "you think I'll let you leave? That I'll let you flee after you slaughtered my wife and... and nearly my boy too? You think I'll let you live, knowing you'll go out there and destroy more families, because that's all your worthless, murdering being is capable of? No. And you're not my daughter. You're not anything, to anybody. And certainly not to us."

Coren's arms, which had been trying to push her up from the ground so she could run and run and run, her injured fingers screaming under the pressure, weakened and collapsed at his words.

The villagers had reached them.

"It was her," her father got out, in between begging for Mrs. Krenz, a pretty, plump lady whom had worked as a Healer's assistant for many years in the capitol before moving to their village, to help Jolon, "she's a Dark Mage."

11

Nearly a hundred human eyes turned to her.

Her Darkness surged up, a black mist shoving those nearest to her away as she desperately scrambled backwards, tripping over fallen pieces of wood. *Away, away, away.*

What she hadn't seen, however, was the zealous son of the village patriarch who had leapt free of the Dark attack, coming up behind her to slam on the cuffs passed down from patriarch to patriarch, and worn at all times. He must have taken them from his father, knowing his faster and more lithe body would stand a better chance at approaching the Mage, hopefully unseen in her terror.

He was right.

Under those cuffs, one of a hundred pairs known as the Mage's Bane, her Darkness dissipated. She could no longer hear its seductive song, begging her to use it; to show the world its power.

The pain of being cut off from her magic brought a scream to her lips; it was like having a limb torn off. The patriarch's son picked up her writhing body, black spots already dancing in her vision.

Before she closed her eyes, she felt and heard as the grinning, brown-haired boy with dark, unstable eyes leaned his nose down to her neck and sniffed. Coren wanted to slap him. Smugness and a dark edge were present in his tone when he muttered to her, "you smell nice, witchy. I wonder what you'll smell like when you burn."

Coren tried to scream, but was helpless as her world faded into nothing.

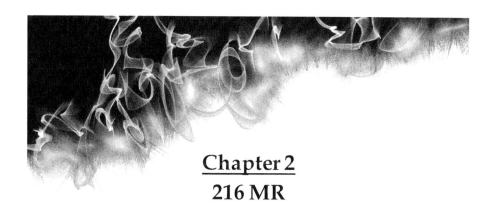

Chapter 2
216 MR

*W*hen light filtered in through her small cell window,

chasing away the comforting darkness of night, Coren knew that, soon, she would be dead.

The thought would be comforting, if not for the manner by which she would die.

Soon enough, a guard appeared at her cell door.

It was a small village, so she knew him. Amos, his name was, he'd had two wives and had three children. He enjoyed chicken wings the most, although, if his wife came in, she would always ask for a thigh and four legs. The oldest of his children was unpleasant, as was Amos himself.

"Last meal, witch," he said, revelling in the last word, a derogatory term for female Mages, as he chucked a bread roll into the cell towards her head. Coren moved her head out the way, watching as it bounced off the crimson coated wall and into a suspicious puddle in the corner, and snarled at the guard.

He looked at her with deep dislike, reeling back to spit into her cell, muttering, "animal," before he stalked off back through the tunnels underneath the village patriarch's house.

Coren looked at the bread and knew that she would not eat it, it was not as if she could reach it anyway. The chains that linked the Mage's Bane – and thus her – to the wall were short.

She hadn't drank any of the discoloured water they'd left for her last night either. Although thirst and starvation would not kill her, she hoped that it may at least lead to her losing consciousness, until the eighth day of flames burnt away her magic and then her life.

It was merely one hour after waking (an hour, two minutes and forty-two seconds if her counting was reliable) when four guards came to escort her out of her cell, towards the pyre.

Before they could come into the cell and grab her, she forced herself to rise. She had begged enough in the last forty-eight hours; begging the Darkness to stop, for her mother to wake up, for the Gods to bring her mother back, to die, for her father to let her leave.

There would probably be begging later too, as she was eaten away by flames for eight consecutive days.

The least she could do was approach her death with dignity.

It was not as if begging would move them anyway, not now they knew she was a Dark Mage.

Within the continents, all know that there are eight categories of Mages: Light, Elemental, Material, Body, Transformative, Mind, Dark and Death. Light,

Elemental, Material and Body Mages were all widely accepted by humans, and deemed as non-threatening due to being lower down on the Mage spectrum. They do not bring the same level or power as Dark and Death.

Light Mages were mainly seen as party tricks. They could manipulate natural and artificial light that already existed, but not to any great degree. The same could be said of the Elemental Mages, altering what is already there with little power, rather than summoning it from nothing. The only time Elemental Mages were a true threat was when a child was born of a same-element union, such as the King, who was born of fire. Multi-generational Mages were deemed by humans as dangerous.

Material and Body Mages were more powerful than the former two, though still to a lesser degree than Mind, Dark or Death, but deemed 'good' by the humans for their functions in society – Material Mages often became immensely skilled Blacksmiths, whilst Body Mages were often Healers.

Transformative Mages could be argued to be a form of Body Mage, but they were regarded more wearily by the humans as they could become fearsome animals such as wolves or bears. And there were a lot of bear and wolf attacks on human villages.

Mind Mages, meanwhile, were outright persecuted. After all, who wants somebody poking around in their head, especially when they wield the power to break it entirely or have complete domination over their thoughts and actions?

Then, there was Coren's category. Dark Mages. Well known to be immensely powerful beings who could, when strong enough, control the Darkness. Nobody knew where the Darkness originated from, or the extent of what it could do. If there was something humans feared more than anything else, it was the unknown.

Finally, Death Mages. There were only three Death Mages, triplets, born every two hundred and fifty years. This was because nature always demanded balance, thus less powerful Mages such as Light and Elemental were almost common, whereas Dark Mages were an extreme rarity and Death Mages were almost a celestial event.

So, for her power, for the way she was born, the humans judged that Coren must die.

Her legs were shaky, but she managed to hold herself upright.

The guards seemed slightly relieved at this, even the returned Amos. Spitting and insulting her from a distance, it seemed, was fine. But the prospect of having to touch a Dark Mage, even with the Mage's Bane cutting off her power, with all they knew of them... that did not seem to be a prospect any of them were fond of.

Why don't you take off my cuffs and come a bit closer, she thought at them, *and I'll show you exactly what my Darkness can do.*

Her sudden thirst for violence disappeared entirely, however, when she saw who another one of her guards was: Miriam. She had been her mother's friend.

The mother she'd killed.

Situated in the middle of the four guards, they started onwards; they marched her from the cell towards the intense light that seared at her eyes. Blinking to recover, she swallowed and addressed one of the guards, a man who had told her she looked pretty once when he came to their farm for eggs, "are my father and brothers here?"

The guard lookedat her. From the look in his eyes, he was certainly not thinking she was pretty anymore. "No," he responded shortly.

The young woman fought against the sob that threatened to erupt from her throat. They would turn her in, condemn her to death, and yet they would not even watch as their wishes were fulfilled?

They didn't condemn you, a voice whispered to her, one that sounded like her mother, *you condemned yourself. The moment you allowed the Darkness within you to meet my blows. This is your fault. You deserve to die this way. For the blonde man, for failing to save Mina, for me, for Jolon.*

Coren nodded at the voice's words, and kept on moving forwards.

Eventually, they exited the underground passageway to find themselves in the extensive fields at the back of the patriarch's luxurious property.

Any strength Coren had summoned left her when she was faced with the pyre. There was a long, sturdy pole of wood impaled fully in the ground; the grass beneath it had encompassed the bottom, holding the pole in place. No doubt this was made with the assistance of their resident Earth Elemental Mage, Garwyn.

Around it was a mass of wood; twigs of all shapes and sizes, even some pieces of wood so large they looked like trunks. With her brother being a woodcutter, perhaps some of this timber had been collected by him. The very thought made her want to wretch.

Beside the pile, the patriarch stood, holding a torch of fire. He was a man in his seventies, short with a bald head, wrinkling features and a protruding gut; he had a damaged right leg which forced him to lean on a cane. Coren had heard that this impairment had been caused by a Mind Mage the man had once almost caught; they said the Mage had mentally manipulated him into cutting into every tendon in his leg. It was only by the help of a nearby Body Mage after the Mind Mage's escape that had saved his life.

Despite his widely unimpressive appearance, his cruelty, hatred, and zeal shone through his dark eyes that were a mirror of his son's. He smiled softly at the guards, before gesturing one wrinkled, shaky hand towards the pyre.

Coren hadn't even realised that she'd become immobile until she felt wary hands grab onto her and begin to drag her forcibly towards the pyre. It wasn't a conscious movement, to try and implant her feet in the grass desperately, but she found herself doing so regardless.

There was no pathway through the piles of wood, so they simply dragged her over the top of it. Twigs and branches scratched and tore at her tender skin, but she refused to cry out. After all, the pain was only just beginning.

When they finally reached the pyre, two of the guards stood at her front whilst two went behind her to tie her hands – wrists still encased by the Mage's Bane, an article that was unaffected by fire – to the wood. They pulled on it several times, ensuring that she was secure, before all slinked off to the edges to the crowd.

She had an audience.

Mrs. Krenz was there with her husband and eight-year-old son. The boy looked between her and the fire with wide eyes and an open mouth as his father leaned down in his ear, no doubt telling him why they were there and what she was.

A monster.

It would be the young boy's first burning, she supposed, as the previous one had been a Mind Mage – not the one that the patriarch had failed to catch, a different one – six years prior. Coren could still remember the boy's screams.

He had been twelve years old at the time. But that didn't matter. To most, he wasn't even human.

Jolon, then twenty-one and already despising powerful Mages, as he had been brought up to do, had cheered whilst physically holding thirteen-year-old Coren's eyes open.

Nobody had interfered to save him, not even Coren. And nobody would save her either.

"This woman," the Patriarch declared grandly, flourishing his free hand towards where Coren was secured, "has been discovered to be a Dark Mage. She was born and has lived in this village all her life; a monster residing in a fleshy suit. This female, Corentine, may appear like one of us, but she is not. In fact, last night, she murdered her own mother!"

"Monster!" The crowd spat at her; people who had watched her grow up, had chatted with her and bought eggs from her. People who had smiled indulgently as she had prattled on about her dreams to visit Valark and Djor and Azyalai and all the countries dotted around their wide, intriguing world. People she had cared for.

More insults joined it: "murderer!" "demon!" "Dark creature!" "witch!" "traitor!"

The last one was shouted by the little eight-year-old himself, swept away in the adults' bloodlust.

The patriarch gestured placatingly towards the infuriated mob.

"Creatures such as this threaten the very foundations of our society. Already, we have a monster for a King, an abomination born of a line of fire Elementals, their good magic twisted into something threatening and evil." Here, miles and miles from the capitol, the people of this rural village in Galaris felt more than confident to shout obscenities about the King. Despite her situation, the irony struck Coren. They were more than happy to accept Elemental Mages, they had used Garwyn to stabilise the pyre and would have him put on shows to entertain the children, but not when they were powerful. Then they were abominations, like the Mages lower on the spectrum.

The patriarch continued, "as a result, we must do our duty to our country, and gain justice for Melrose,"

Coren flinched at her mother's name, "and compensate for the injuries inflicted on Jolon. Therefore I, Darius, patriarch of our humble village, hereby sentence Corentine, the Dark Mage, to die by eight-days-fire." As he lowered his torch to the wood, Coren attempted to move backwards, to escape. All it did was shove her back further into the hard wood of the pole she was bound to.

The wood began to light up, circling her and moving inwards.

Desperately, she reached out to her magic.

Helpmehelpmehelpmehelpmehelpmehelpme.

There was nothing there to answer her call.

The fire reached her feet, and Coren bit into her lip so hard she felt crimson blood drip down her face as her flesh began to sizzle.

Helpmehelpmehelpmehelpmehelpmehelpme.

The flames worked their way higher, reaching her calves. Her head tilted back and her mouth cleaved itself open; she began to scream.

Helpmehelpmehelpmehelpmehelpmehelpmc.

To her knees.

Helpmehelpmehelpmehelpmehelpmehelpme.

To her thighs.

Helpmehelpmehelpmehelpmehelpmehelpme.

Suddenly, the fire brutally burst outwards, abandoning her legs and instead fleeing towards the crowd and the Patriarch. A symphony of screams rose up all around her. A woman in a long dress, who Coren could barely make out through the spreading embers and unimaginable pain, was rolling in the grass trying to put out the fire of her dress, only to be consumed by it. The Patriarch's son was dropping to the floor, screeching in agony. Looking to her right, the Patriarch himself was already a picture of melted flesh and bone. Coren forced her eyes to rise above the flames, to try and find the perpetrator, but she saw no one. She saw and understood nothing, until she felt somebody close behind her, pulling at the rope that held her to the pole. *They're untying it*, she realised through the haze of pain.

When the rope was undone, Coren's knees gave in and she slumped to the floor, the Mage's Bane still locked tight upon her wrists. Her rescuer moved around her, the screams around them slowly dying out as villager after villager melted like wax candles.

He, she assumed from their physique, was wearing armour that was so deep a red that it was almost black, polished so thoroughly that reflected upon it were the flames – his flames? – surrounding them, wrecking chaos upon all they encountered.

The man cocked his head to the side as he regarded her, the burnt legs, the blonde hair that was so stained by the mud of the farm and blood of her cell that it appeared almost auburn, before slipping his helmet off. His hair was an exact mirror to the colour of his armour; his face long but sharp with aristocratic cheekbones and a harsh, clean-shaven jawline. The man's most striking feature, by far, were his eyes. They were a bright, burning amber. And a wildfire appeared to be confined within them.

There was no doubt as to the identity of the man who had saved her, and yet there was no world in which Coren believed she would be face to face with the infamous King Caradoc of Galaris; the Fire King.

The King must have seen the recognition within her eyes, as his lips quirked up into what was more a smirk than a smile. Amidst the dying screams of those who condemned her to death, he greeted her softly. "Hello, little Mage."

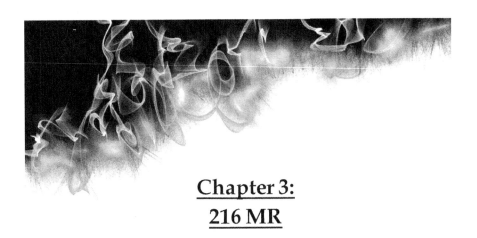

Chapter 3:
216 MR

*C*oren gritted her teeth against the pain as her black

mare continued onwards over a particularly rough bit of landscape, the movement making the constant, harsh rubbing against her sore thighs intensify. Her leg injuries, thank the Gods, had been healed by one of the King's guards, a Body Mage, after she had stumbled away from the pyre. Otherwise, she doubted she would have been able to bear the pain at all. Just remembering the feeling of searing flesh made her feel nauseous. Suddenly, the horse missed a step and the blonde barely managed to keep herself atop the horse, her wrists still held tightly in the grip of the Mage's Bane. Being saved by the infamous Fire King, a Mage, it would be easy to assume that he would free her of the barbaric cuffs, but one thing was for sure: this King was no Knight in Shining armour. In fact, she could have sworn she heard the man chuckle at her almost-fall. *Bastard.*

If she had not been so afraid that he would turn them around and give her back to the village and thus the fire, she might have thrown an insult or glare his way. As it was, she did nothing, a choice that irked her more than anything.

To righten herself, she grabbed onto the front of the horse with both of her hands. She winced harshly when applying such weight to her broken fingers; they were the last thing her mother had given her.

Disgusting murderer, she hissed at herself mentally, *you killed her, monster, you killed her.*

She bit her lip and blinked away any tears as she made a promise to herself upon that horse, her thighs chaffed, a King laughing at her near-humiliation, her power negated by archaic cuffs, that she would find a way to become gain a semblance of power and control in this world.

Coren didn't want to just survive as she had been, she wanted to live; she wanted to live without the constant fear of magical outbursts, that they would kill the people she cared about or that those people would discover her and see her for what she really was. An unnatural monstrosity. The question now was how to obtain that power, and how far she would go for it.

One of the King's Guard, who was at the front of their pack, a man in his early fifties with greying hair, a long beard and a rather fearsome looking wolf-hilted sword at his side, stopped suddenly. Everyone paused behind him, including the younger King's Guard to whom Coren's horse was attached by a long, thick piece of rope.

Staring at his back, she couldn't help but admire the younger guard's sapphire-encrusted twin swords.

"We should stop here for the night," the older man said, his voice gruff, before turning to the King who had left his helmet off, the soft, spring breeze permitted to caress his red-black hair, "if that pleases Your Majesty."

The Fire King nodded once, and everyone dismounted simultaneously. Coren stared at them in bewilderment, had they rehearsed that? Or was synchronisation a prerequisite for joining the King's Guard?

Her guard with the pretty swords came up to the left side of her horse and reached up to grab her waist, lifting her up and then on to the ground. She rather disliked being treated like a sack of potatoes, but it was better than burning.

The guard laughed slightly, and Coren immediately looked at him, brows furrowed, before realisation hit her.

Mind Mage, she thought, staring at him properly for the first time. He looked the kindest of the lot and far more youthful, with clear, unwrinkled skin and warm brown eyes set into a sun-kissed face, shaggy dark-blonde hair framing it. But, with Mages, appearances could be deceiving.

Yes, I am, he communicated to her through one of the Mind Mage's many abilities, known simply as Mind Speak, *and I would like to commend you for not actually calling the King a bastard, unless you wanted a singed arse that is.*

Know from personal experience, do you? Coren shot back.

I'm offended you would even consider that idea. I'm an angel.

Coren snorted lightly, before moving towards where other guards were setting up a fire. Resolved to not give them any reason to take her back on account of laziness, she went to follow the guards to help gather wood.

A hand encompassed her wrist, stopping her before she could even get to the treeline. Turning and moving her gaze up from the hand, she was faced with the Fire King once more. With narrowed eyes he inquired, "and where do you think you're going?"

Oh, me? With magically binding cuffs on, hardly any weight or muscle, no weaponry skills and standing at a formidable 5'3? I'm just going off to incite rebellion, you know, kill you all seize your throne. Surprise!

She said nothing. It was one thing to lightly tease a guard in the privacy of her own head, it was entirely another to anger the King. Onc wrong word and those flames, the ones that had threatened to devour her legs, her body, her magic, her being, could be a reality once again. Coren closed her eyes for a long moment, reminding herself that she wasn't in the flames any longer and that, so long as she did nothing to anger him, she hopefully never would be.

"To collect firewood with the other soldiers," she answered, her voice quiet.

For a long moment, neither spoke, before the King lowered his hand and nodded, amber eyes that held the promise of fire drifting from her to the pile of wood the soldiers had already begun to create. With barely a flick of his fingers, the wood became enflamed, embers swaying to the song of the wind. Then he turned back to her, and she felt as if those same eyes were burning a whole within her trying to see and see and see until her entire soul would become unravelled, "we have all the firewood we need."

With that, he stalked off to take a seat at the other side of the fire.

The next day, the day after that, and the day succeeding that, repeated themselves. Each time, her thighs grew more and more sore, so much so that simply walking to her tent and having her thighs brush together made her legs threaten to give way.

The Mind Mage guard, who she had learned was called Milo, had given her a salve for it that day, which Coren had yet to utilise. She hadn't seen much of the King during the rest of the ride, who rode at the front and often slept and ate far from her, though she didn't think it was an intentional move. In fact, she rather thought that the King had simply found her boring. She would be offended, if it didn't play so greatly to her advantage.

If he was bored of her, then why would he care if she fled the Palace and went to begin her peaceful life far away, somewhere like Valark?

It was perfect really.

Of course, Milo had to be the one to bring those dreams to a momentary halt.

Even if he is bored of you now, Milo told her inside her head, his voice similar to her own thoughts, but with an unnatural, invasive feel that allowed her to tell them apart, *then that won't last long. You're forgetting what you are. Dark Mages are only a result of 1 in every 334,000 pregnancies and you've already proven yourself to be powerful. The King felt your magic from the capitol. And the King likes rare and powerful things. Especially pretty ones.*

She ignored the pity in his eyes, and looked away from him.

So that's how you found me, my magic?

Milo nodded, *His Majesty said that he felt a magical disturbance, and we set off that night. Took us a couple of days but we got there in time for us to see... well, you know.*

A nicer way to put 'you being brutally burned to death', Coren answered.

The guard laughed slightly, turning upon his horse to grin at her. With that smile, Coren recognised his type. The troublemakers. She wasn't sure if that endeared her to him, as it usually would, or made her want to flee for the hills in order to ensure that he didn't rope her into some kind of mischief that would get her sent back.

No trouble you get in, with or without me, will get you sent back Milo told her, but he wasn't teasing this time, he was talking tentatively; delicate in a similar way to how one would handle a fragile object, *did you not see? Your village is gone, the people are gone. Everything went to the flames.*

Coren thought of Mrs. Krenz's young son. A child; a child easily influenced, as all youngsters are. His only crime was his parents' decision to drag him along to watch a woman burn from within a raging, murderous mob. It made her feel sick.

But what made her feel worse, what truly made the greeny, yellowy, burning, warm, putrid feeling rise up her throat towards the freedom of day, was the fact that she felt relieved.

Over a hundred people died. Her father and her brothers, both of whom she had loved greatly, likely died. And yet here she was, feeling grateful for their murders; feeling free.

Their words, the ones the villagers had shouted at her as she'd been tied to the stake, the ones she accused herself of being so often, started shouting within her mind once more.

She had no doubt that, if the cuffs were not on, her Darkness would be purring at her too. It's voice neither woman nor man, old or young, human or monster – just chanting; seducing.

Come play, she could hear, even though she knew it wasn't real due to the cuffs; it was just her memories, just her mind playing tricks on her, *come play with us. Coren. Coren. Use me, Coren. So much power. So much potential. Make them bow, Coren.*

The distractions of her own mind faded away when their group finally came to a halt. Coren strained herself trying to look past Milo's tall, almost gangly frame to see what all the fuss was about.

He moved to the side for her and she saw from the hilltop, for the first time, the Capitol of Galaris.

Carradora, otherwise known as the City of Gold.

Under the midday sun, Carradora glittered and glowed; every house, every street, all coloured in yellows and golds, with the exception of those decorated in tapestries of red or orange. At the very back of the city, separated by a long but narrow moat of fire and glowing under the proud sun, a Palace loomed.

The rumours were true.

The Fire King's Palace was made of real gold.

No doubt the Material Mages saw to it regularly to ensure it remained sturdy and never lost its shine.

On the two ends of the golden Palace were glowing turrets, connecting to lower Palace walls before they met up in the middle. The front centre of the Palace was higher even than the turrets were, with spires and balconies and a flag, with a red sun pierced by four red swords against a gold background protruding from it.

Windows, of course, lined the Palace walls too; Coren had no doubt that the inside of the Palace would be lit brilliantly.

Tilting her head further to the side, she saw how the Palace did not just have a long front, but also went incredibly far back.

Having grown up in a small, rural village that she had only left for the occasional food market in nearby

31

Aidiar, she had never been faced with such splendour. It was even more magical when one, like Coren, knew some of the history behind the great city. Mina, whose mother had been a scholar, had said how Carradora had once been called Karrdora, before King Caradoc took over and altered the name in his image.

Coren remembered giggling with Mina about the sheer arrogance of such a move, once. One of the last days before she was taken, in fact.

Mina had also reported, much to Coren's fascination, how the city seemed to change its colours depending on who was ruling. With the humans, it had been the White City and when King Caradoc had seized the throne, it had become the City of Gold.

There must be so much more to know as well. The idea of looking in the Capitol's libraries made her want to salivate. In her village, she possessed only three frequently reread books that Mina had once given her; now, the possibilities were endless.

Coren must have been gaping, as Milo gibed at her.

You might want to close your mouth, you don't want to catch Fae. I've heard they'll fly in and eat your brain.

She closed her mouth, and looked to the King.

He, too, was looking upon his city and smiling down at it. It wasn't a smile of joy, however, but one of satisfaction. King Caradoc looked at his city the way one looks upon a precious, desirable piece of jewellery that you own, rather than with any kind of fondness. With a growing sense of hopelessness, she was reminded of Milo's earlier words.

The King likes rare and powerful things. Especially pretty ones.

It was at that moment that the party began to move once more, spurring their horses to head down from the hillside and towards the city. Golden gates lay ahead, and Coren couldn't help but feel as if she were riding towards a gilded cage.

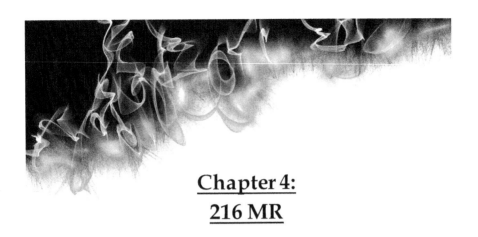

Chapter 4:
216 MR

*W*hen they arrived at the Golden Palace, having

walked across a fire-resistant bridge to get across the moat, there was no grand greeting for the returned Fire King. They had waited at the bottom of that hill, in the tree line, until dusk so that no one would see them. Milo explained that the King had wanted it this way, as he had made it so that nobody had known he had even left the castle.

The King doesn't like people knowing his whereabouts, Milo explained, *which is fair enough, really, when every other peasant and nobleman would like to see your head on a pike.*

My village would certainly have enjoyed that, Coren Mind Spoke back to him, *they probably would have declared it a village holiday and celebrated with a yearly Mage burning.*

Nothing beats a good burning, Milo returned with mirth, before physically wincing and looking back at Coren, who was immediately behind him.

She merely shrugged.

The Mage was trying her best to place it at the very back of her mind. Joking about it; treating it as something normal, was actually helping. Maybe, soon, her feelings about all the recent events would come crashing down on her and perhaps it would break her, but, for now, all she felt was a sense of removal from what had happened. It was as if it hadn't even happened to her, that it was some kind of bad dream and she had simply been a spectator, watching it all occurring to someone else from somewhere far away. Milo must have been listening to what she had been thinking, as he eyed her pitifully. She simply looked away and closed her eyes.

The Dark Mage wanted to live, but did she deserve to? Despite her sense of removal from her near death, there was nothing removing her from the murder she had committed.

"This is so you learn, Coren. You must learn."
Those had been the last words out of Melrose's mouth, before something Dark had awoken within Coren and the woman had begun to scream and scream and *scream.* The worse fact of it all, even worse than murdering her own mother, had been that she had enjoyed it. The screaming; the power that inflicting pain had given her. In fact, it made her understand her mother in a way that she never had before.

35

In that moment, Coren had become the teacher and Melrose the victim.

This is what I am.

The group halted. They were finally within the palace. Coren, exhausted from endless days on horseback, would barely recall the King's commands for Milo to take her to chambers in the East Wing in the morning. Nor the feeling of the guard dutifully grabbing onto her elbow and beginning to lead her in said direction. In fact, she did not even have the energy to gape at the stunning interior of the palace. That, she supposed, she could leave for another day. Even if she didn't exactly know how long she was spending, or what exactly she was even doing here, Coren decided she would be here long enough to be able to investigate a little.

"Certainly," Milo agreed out loud, "when your maids arrive tomorrow, I'm sure they'd be more than happy to show you around the palace if that's what you want. The gardens here are absolutely spectacular."

Maids? Well, looks like she certainly was going to be here a while.

"I've communicated with the King a few times on our walk," Milo continued on, ignoring the fact that Coren was practically asleep on her feet, "you'll be taking lessons with Izak and I on Mondays, Wednesdays, and Fridays, and the King on Saturdays. Before you ask me what your lessons with the King will entail, I have absolutely no idea – do I look like his confidant? – but I assume it has something to do with your magic. And myself and Izak – yes, that's the one that tries to look serious all the time but instead looks rather constipated

– will be teaching you how to actually defend yourself, since your little quip when you were faced with the King let on that you have absolutely no idea."

Rather than asking the more important question: why did the King want her trained to defend herself? Coren's worn out brain instead made her ask, desperately, "you didn't tell the King what I was thinking, did you?"

Milo grinned down at her, seemingly unbothered by the fact that he was now all but dragging most of her weight, "don't worry, oh Dark One, your sarcasm is safe with me."

Coren smiled up at him, letting him drag her all the way into her new chambers. Before he'd even left the room, Coren stumbled towards her bed and was out like a light.

Corentine, this is Akeros, God of Death. I command you to awaken, and do my bidding.

Coren stuffed her head further into her pillow, ignoring the wrists that ached unpleasantly from having been locked in the cuffs all night. She was used to it.

Get lost, Milo.

She heard a familiar laugh from the doorway. If she could actually use her hands, Coren would throw him the middle finger.

"Wake up, Princess," he joked, this time aloud, grabbing one of the pillows from her bed and hitting her on the back of the head with it. She growled, though she could admit that the sound was actually rather pathetic. He laughed again, "you absolutely reek of embers and horses and, well, shit, so unless you'd like to meet your maids smelling like a horse's ass then I recommend you get up and bathe before they get here."

Sighing, she swung her legs over the side of the bed, rolling her shoulders and glowering down at where her wrists were connected as she did so.

"Hold still," Milo told her, and then brought his sword up and down in an arc, smashing through the chains that held her wrists together and imbedding itself in the tile floor between her legs.

She glared up at him, though relished in being able to move her arms apart.

"You ruined my new floor."

The King's Guard shrugged, "I'll get the King to get you some new tiles."

Coren looked back down at her now-separated wrists, "are the actual cuffs not going to come off too?"

He offered her a sad smile, "sorry, the King says they have to stay on until the Saturday lessons."

Well, Coren supposed, *being able to move my hands more than 5 millimetres apart is at least something*.

Though, it was only now that she realised that she had absolutely no idea what day it was.

Thursday, Milo informed her primly.

Will you ever stay out of my head? She shot back without bite, he simply grinned at her, and motioned his arms towards where she presumed the bathing chambers must be.

Sighing, but relenting, she moved away from the bed – upon which she had stained the cream sheets so thoroughly with mud and blood that the servants would surely mutter ragefully about her – and made her way towards said area. It was only now, in the morning light and without exhaustion looming over her, that she began to truly take her chambers in.

The colour scheme appeared to be cream and yellow, with spotless, cream walls and beige curtains embroidered with gold lining the countless windows around the room. On the east side of her room, there was what she believed may be a balcony. When she was not reeking of her travels, and without Milo mother-henning her, Coren would be sure to take a look.

How dare you compare me to a chicken, came the guard's voice inside her head, even as she slid her bathing room door shut, *I most certainly do not 'mother-hen' anybody.*

She rolled her eyes at him, whilst marvelling at the off-white tiles on the floor of the room, each with a small sun painted upon them. One thing was for sure, the presence of the Fire King was emphasised within every part of his palace.

Coren moved to the tub, and found that it had been filled by the servants not long ago, the water was only just cool enough to enter. Suspiciously, she cast her eyes about the chamber and found a small door at the far side of the room.

Disgusted by the idea of people entering this room whilst she was bathing, she grabbed a cabinet and pulled it in front of the door so that nobody could come in. Satisfied, she got undressed before stepping into and then lowering herself into the tub.

It's glorious, she thought as she let out a small groan. The feeling of warm water caressing her aching body, allowing her to feel cleaner than she had in years. In her house, back when they had been able to afford to rent a tub every other month rather than relying on water out of the pump, bathing was done in age order. Her father went first, then her mother, then her three brothers. By the time that it was Coren's turn to bathe, the water was so brown and repulsive-looking that she'd rather forgo it and risk the river monsters of the River Ziqinor.

Of course, she wasn't allowed to do that. So, she had always reluctantly lowered herself into the water, staying there for all of five minutes before she practically jumped back out, her mother frowning at her.

"Defiance won't get you anywhere in a small village like ours, Corentine. I need to teach you that. Let me teach you."

Shaking off her mother's soft, haunting voice, Coren grabbed the sponge to her side and began to scrub and scrub and scrub until her skin was red and raw. Still, she felt tainted, vile, *uncleansed.*

Eventually, Milo knocked his knuckles against the door and asked, hesitantly, "are you done in there, Coren?"

Scolding herself, she answered, "just a couple more minutes!" before moving onto her hair.

She watched in satisfaction as the shades of brown and red abandoned her smooth strands for the water she resided within, allowing it to return to its natural, golden blonde. Looking down, the young girl made a disgusted face at the now murky water, and lifted herself up, grabbing onto a smooth length of material that was hung above the bath that she assumed she was supposed to dry herself with.

Wiping it down her body and over her hair, she mentally sent out, her cheeks heating, *can you grab me some clothes?* To Milo before repeating the action.

Coren couldn't help but laugh at the way the Guard opened the door, barely wide enough to fit one arm through, and all but chucked her clothes into the room before he rescinded his arm swiftly, closing the door with a slam.

Milo sent something that sounded like a grumble down the Mind Speak link, which only made Coren laugh harder.

She didn't want to leave, she thought to herself, which startled her due to the unknowns. The unknown place she was in, the unknown people around her, and the unknown reason as to why she was here.

But, she supposed, it was better than a known place with known people who longed to see her burned.

Placing her underclothes on, and then pulling a – surprise, surprise – golden dress over the top, she soon opened the door and waltzed out through it.

Milo gave her a quick once over.

"The dress clashes with your hair," he told her frankly, but when Coren narrowed her eyes at him he amended, "though you're still a sight for sore eyes, blondie."

She then rolled her eyes at him. *Flattery will get you nowhere, Mind Mage.*

On the contrary, Milo objected, *it got me into Duchess Ozielle's knickers more times than I can count.*

Coren was torn between being disgusted and amused at his reply, but was saved from reacting at all by a knock on her chamber doors. When the person did not enter after knocking, as Coren had expected them to, she hesitantly, to Milo's amusement, called out, "come in."

The guard, Izak, Coren faintly remembered, entered the room with three girls trailing behind him.

They must be her maids, Coren supposed as they all came bustling in behind the knight like little ducklings.

"The King hopes you like your new chambers, Miss Corentine," Izak stated, his face stoic, "and sends you three maids to help with your day-to-day activities, such as cleaning and dressing."

Coren would rather like to remark that she didn't need help with either, as she was not incapable of either, and had been doing both all of her life. But she didn't voice that thought. If the King wanted her to have maids then she guessed she would have maids. After all, she had come to the realisation that she actually might want to stay here.

"This," he gestured firstly to the woman on her far right, "is Nerah, a Light Mage," smiling at Coren, the girl brought her hands together and summoned the limited amount of light that first generation Light Mages could manage and Coren smiled appreciatively, "and this is Dahlia, an Air Mage," Dahlia's power was small as well, just jostling her own hair about lightly. The guard then moved a bright haired girl, who eyed the room in an unimpressed manner, his lip curling slightly in disgust, "and this is Zarola. She's human." Coren studied each of them in turn.

Nerah was a larger girl, curvaceous and unusually tall, perhaps approaching six feet, with long, curling brown hair and bright blue eyes. Despite the way she towered over the shorter Coren, her smile was more than friendly and so infectious that Coren could not help but return it. To her left side was a girl shorter and slighter than Coren, with dark skin and matching wide eyes, who offered her a shy smile. Coren offered her the same smile she had Nerah.

The girl on the far left, however, was the opposite of the previous girls. She was neither friendly nor shy. If anything, she appeared hostile. She held her lean, sun-kissed body with a kind of grace and confidence that many did not achieve within their lifetimes, her chestnut brown eyes narrowed upon Coren as if damning her for some kind of imagined slight.

The blonde's smile faltered the longer she regarded the fiery haired girl. Izak soon coughed in order to drive her attention away from her.

Seeing that she was focused on him, the serious-faced guard informed her; "Milo and I will be seeing you at seven in the morning for swordplay. Until then, you are permitted to travel within the palace grounds though not leave them."

Coren nodded, and Izak turned away with Milo soon falling into place beside him.

See you later, blondie, enjoy your new friends!

I hate you.

No, you don't!

Pulling herself away from the conversation she was having with Milo, she eyed the girls in front of her. They remained in silence for several moments, before the friendly Nerah let out an excited squeal that had the rest of them flinching back in surprise, before she bound over towards Coren.

"Oh, I can't tell you how relieved I was to be brought to Court just before the Spring Ball! I was so hoping it would happen, but you know what they say about hope. My twin sister, Stella, is already here so I would have been very jealous if she got to experience another ball without me! I can just tell we're all going to quickly become the best of friends!"

Ignoring the damper that the less-than-pleased redhead's presence placed upon her, Coren smiled genuinely at the excitable brunette. Perhaps the presence of a woman like Nerah was exactly what she needed right now.

So, indulging her, Coren inquired, "what exactly is this Spring Ball?"

Nerah gaped at her, before enthusiastically beginning to prattle away, and Coren allowed herself to become lost in the company of new people; trying, in vain, to forget the past she knew would refuse to stay behind her for long.

Chapter 5:
768 MR

𝒞omrade Hearne hated the throne room. He hated

how it was decorated extravagantly in great riches, with
four yellow-diamond chandeliers in each section of the
room, a fifth, even larger and grander than the rest,
residing in the middle. Diamonds mined by human
slaves, no doubt.

It was spring in Galaris, thus emeralds, rose quartz and
gold were all adorning the room. Additionally, green
tapestries lined each wall and nets full of fresh, green
leaves, and dotted with said emeralds were draped in
between the chandeliers. The rose quartz was used on
the tapestries in depictions of budding flowers, as well
as in the centre of the water fountains that mirrored
each other near the left and right walls. Gold was
present everywhere: gold thread lined the tapestries,
gold metalwork on the chandeliers, and a gold dais and
throne for Galaris' Night Queen.

They said the Queen's favourite colour was gold.
Flatterers often compared the rich colour to the

Queen's mid-length hair.

Hearne doubted that it was truly her favourite colour, considering that it had been King Caradoc's colour and he rather thought that light colours would repel a woman with a soul like hers. Still, he believed that the assumption suited the Queen regardless.

He remembered how the poor on the streets of Galaris' capitol, Kardorra, would paint brass coins with gold to make it appear as if they were *jarnas* rather than *cardars*. After having mistakenly accepted one of their so-called jarnas, shop keepers would be in for a nasty surprise when the gold would flake away to show the bronze underneath.

He wondered, if he scratched and pulled at the Queen's thick blonde hair, or at her golden crown and throne, if the colour would fall away and reveal only Darkness. The colour of her rule, after all, could be described as nothing but a blanket of midnight upon her realms.

Before King Caradoc, humans had ruled Galaris. Under their rule, humans had flourished and though many Mages towards the darker end of the Mage spectrum had been persecuted, there had been relative peace. Under King Caradoc's rule, humans had been treated harshly. The King had a Mage-exclusive Court and Council, only allowing humans in the Palace as servants and enforcing their position as second-class citizens within Galaris' major cities. However, in rural areas, he was largely disinterested and thus out-of-city humans still retained considerable freedom and peace.

Then came Queen Corentine. After she murdered the Fire King and took his throne, she extended her influence throughout the entirety of the lands. Humans had no power, be it in urban or rural areas. While Hearne did not necessarily agree with the eight-days-fire, the Night Queen's decision to have any human caught attempting to practice it held suspended by chains over a pit of fire and slowly lowered into it over the course of eight days appalled him. Water tubes ensured that the humans did not die too quickly for her tastes.

Hearne fought the urge to grimace just thinking about it.

Under her rule, all humans were able to do was be born, work and work and work, survive and die. But that was only if they were lucky enough to not be caught taking their understandable resentment out on Mages, because then they would suffer their own eight-days-fire and their relatives dating back eight generations would be induced into slavery; to work until they died. It was not a life worth living.

Humans are born to die, he had once heard the Night Queen remark to his Great-however many times-Aunt, *so let them.*

His gaze, which had previously been glowering not-so-subtly at the décor, switched to his Aunt Auryon: the Captain of the Queen's Personal Guard. His Aunt was an impressive and intimidating figure, tall and well-built with dark hair, skin, and eyes. She wore twin swords on her back, both with sapphires as large as fists imbedded at the hilts, and an array of silver daggers around her waist. Many described her looks as lovely, though one would rather dangle themselves in front of

47

a fully grown chimaera than approach the Queen's most fearsome protector.

Aunt Auryon was a Light Mage, and thus had very little magical power, but was arguably the best swordswoman, or man, in any of the Queen's realms. In contrast, her younger sister had been human, and it was from her line that Hearne descended and he, like his ancestor, was a human. He was the only human at Court, courtesy of his Aunt being in the good graces of the Queen, and yet he despised Aunt Auryon along with Queen Corentine.

Even though his Aunt was not anti-human, she stood by the Queen and did nothing. That made her just as guilty in Hearne's eyes.

He was more than thankful for her getting him a position at Court though, without it he never would have met Greer or Thaddeus. Both Mages, both fairly easy to manipulate, and both discontent with the current Queen's reign.

Greer was descended from a long line of earth Elemental Mages, and was bitter over being passed over by the Queen for the place of Earth Mistress on the Queen's Council. Thaddeus, foolish and brutish Thaddeus, was a Mind Mage, who thought himself to be powerful enough to gain the throne if the Queen was killed.

Hearne, of course, would not allow that to happen. Not that he could let himself think that in Thaddeus' presence. Instead, Hearne had to keep his thoughts silent and just listen as the utter idiot droned on and on and on about how all the court ladies would positively fawn over him in an attempt to become his Queen. *Arrogant prick.*

However, he was invaluable to his plan, the very plan that he would be divulging to them that night.

A plan to destroy the Night Queen once and for all.

As if summoned by his mutinous thoughts, the Queen rose from her throne.

Queen Corentine was, without a doubt, an incredibly beautiful woman. Her golden hair was styled in tight ringlets, with a black crown of ruby and onyx stones upon her head. The rest of her state of dress was crimson, with long, sheer sleeves that gaped around her slender wrists and a low neckline in order to show off soft, pale skin and the corners of her breasts; the material cinched at her waist and flared at her hips, the silken ends gently caressing the floor.

She stuck out like a sore thumb against the greens, pinks and yellows of the spring-themed room, but Hearne supposed that was her intention.

In her left hand, she held a golden chalice filled with crimson liquid. The liquid was likely wine, but Hearne could not help but wonder if she had finally decided to start drinking the blood of her enemies like the sadistic, insane monster that she was.

I'm going to kill you one day, witch, he thought at her, a smile tugging at the corner of his full lips, envisioning a future where humans could live in freedom and peace, *and I'm going to enjoy it immensely.*

"Now, now my dear rebel," came the smug, amused voice of Thaddeus, who had sidled up beside the dark-skinned man, quiet enough to draw no attention as people quietened down to hear what the Queen had to say, "you might want to stop announcing your plans to every Mind Mage present. If you want to survive, that is."

Hearne, wisely, stopped projecting out his homicidal desires.

The Night Queen drew her finger around her glass in a circular motion whilst the last conversations finished, before moving her gaze up from a red-painted nail to observe the crowd.

When she smirked, her grey-green eyes flashed with something so distinctly predatory that it made Hearne want to sink back. To use Thaddeus as a shield.

He refused to bow to his fears, but he did see several others shuffle back and fought an eye roll. *Pathetic.*

After another moment of invoking a tense silence, the Queen finally spoke, her voice sweet like honey, "I am glad to see so many of my subjects have made the journey to my wonderful spring ball, and I am especially sorry to see that Duke Ardan could not make it," no doubt the Queen would be sending men after him, not to deliver justice but to deliver death; attending to the Queen's every whim was not a request but a command.

The Queen continued, "However, this is no normal spring ball. This year, we are hosting the Crown Prince of Azyalai, Prince Afzal. Both the Prince, and his esteemed Ambassador, Mister Rizwan Rasul, are our guests of honour, and will be treated as such. So, I propose a toast: to the continuation of friendly relations between Azyalai and Galaris, for a war between such powerful nations, well, that could only result in Darkness."

They lifted their goblets up to her toast, including the Ambassador and the already drunk Crown Prince, but Hearne knew he was not the only one to hear the threat in the Queen's words; the Ambassador himself going rather pale.

She had all but announced to the room that should Azyalai displease her and a war begin, their realm would be bathed in Darkness and Queen Corentine would be the victor. The worst part was that Hearne had no doubt that this would, indeed, be the case. Other than her threat, the Queen spoke with all the strength and diplomacy of a true, stable ruler. If Hearne hadn't heard of the murder of the unborn Death Mage triplets 273 years prior, or known she murdered her first love, or seen the eight-day-fires and the subordination of humans and the beatings, the beheadings, the torture, the chaos beneath the surface, perhaps he would have believed it.

But, as it was, he could see nothing but a demon wearing a mask.

The Queen sat after taking a small gulp of wine, passing the chalice on to one of her servants. Despite her beauty, there was something wrong about her. Something so unnatural. It was in the way she sat so still, in the way her eyes were bright but empty, in the way that, under her fingertips, Darkness danced, creating little figures that were formed, faded and repeated that cycle again and again.

He turned to Thaddeus, and murmured softly, "the east exit of the castle, continue to the underneath of the south bridge where you'll find a small room burrowed out in the earth next to the bridge. Go in. Let no one see either of you, pass the message on to Greer through your Mind Speak."

Thaddeus offered him an enthusiastic nod, no doubt already tasting Kingship on his tongue.

Hearne silenced any thoughts on the contrary.

Ten minutes later, Thaddeus having already left, Hearne's guard shift finally came to a close. Before he left, he looked back at the grotesquely beautiful picture that was the Night Queen for a final time.

Let the games begin.

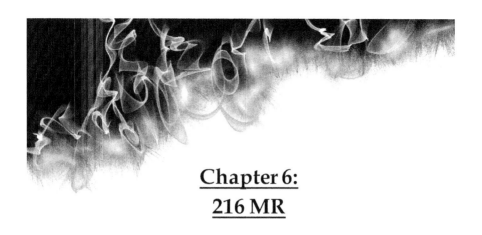

Chapter 6:
216 MR

*C*oren hated swordplay. It was a ridiculous sport that might as well be named 'in which Coren gets whacked onto her backside again and again' for accuracy purposes. The two guards had proclaimed that she was a natural, but she knew they were only saying that to help her bruised ego. And it was bruised. Very, very much so.

The next morning, her body littered in purple and black from the blunt edges of Milo and Izak's wooden swords, Coren didn't even want to move. She didn't know which of her maids was tasked with waking her up this morning, but she hoped it was Nerah. Surely the lovely girl would allow Corentine to wallow in self-pity and offer her own sympathy into the mix.

It was just Coren's luck that it wasn't Nerah who was waking her up, but Zarola.

She was treated to a rough shake of her shoulders and a snapped, "get up," by the red head. Forcing her eyes open, Coren squinted at the girl. With the early morning sun making its way past her balcony curtains, Zarola was a rather beautiful sight. Her hair was illuminated as if she had a head full of true flames, her sun-kissed skin a lovely golden-brown under the light. There was nothing beautiful or bright, however, about the way that her maid grasped onto the water cup from her bedside table and chucked it over her.

Coren gasped at the sudden cold.

Was she even allowed to do that?

Zarola didn't seem to care, "the King wants to see you in twenty minutes for your Mage lessons, I suggest you get out of bed and get ready, unless you would like to see His Majesty looking like a wild hag."

Okay, Coren was sure she definitely was not allowed to say that.

The girl, who looked about Coren's age, if a little bit older, cast her gaping face one final, unimpressed look before she whirled out of the room and was gone into the maid's chambers with a bang of the door.

Coren took some solace in the fact that she could hear Nerah berating her on the other side.

Take that, the blonde thought, though did get up from her bed and groggily make her way over to her extensive wardrobe.

What exactly was one supposed to wear when faced with a King? Her mind immediately went to a fancy dress, but that wouldn't exactly be very practical for training, which is what it seemed to be from what she knew. Never mind that Coren had no idea what exactly that training would entail.

Some kind of fancy tunic and trousers then, Coren settled on hesitantly, and began ravaging in her wardrobe for anything that was not gold. Milo was right, the colour didn't suit her. Not that it really mattered, she supposed.

Did it matter?

Before being saved from, well, death, Coren had never met a royal before.

With a frown, she just threw on a dark red tunic and black, lace-up trousers, though she was unable to escape the gold, decorative threads sewn into the black, and made her way towards the door. Either Milo or Izak, she knew, would be standing outside waiting to escort her. Coren hoped it was Milo, and barely refrained from sighing aloud when she saw that it was stony-faced Izak waiting for her.

Today really wasn't her day.

The other man was silent as he all-but marched down the halls at her side towards the King's chambers, making no attempts at conversation, and Coren returned the silence. She spent the time contemplating what exactly this meeting would entail.

The Dark Mage garnered a few curious looks as she made her way with Izak across the castle towards the West Wing, which was very busy. According to Nerah, this 'Spring Ball' was in a half-moons time so there would be a steady influx of guests in the lead up. Coren didn't know if she would be invited, but she hoped she would be. The Dark Mage had never attended anything like what Nerah had described before.

After what felt to be around twenty minutes of wandering the castle's extensive, glimmering halls, they seemed to have finally reached the King's chambers. Or his study. Or wherever it was that they were supposed to be meeting.

Two heralds, one old and bearded and the other not even out of his teenage years with a prominent pimple on his forehead, stood either side of the doors. The boy all but jumped at the prospect of announcing Coren whilst the other watched on in fond exasperation. Swiftly, he slipped inside the room and Coren could only faintly hear him announcing, "Lad- er, Miss Corentine has arrived, Your Majesty."

Then, the doors were opened for her.

It was, in fact, his study.

The room was circular in shape, with a mahogany desk in its centre and a fireplace, made of dark-coloured marble with eight figures perched atop it, immediately behind it. There were large windows to the immediate right and left of the desk though. However, due to the early hour and this room's position in the west wing of the Golden Palace, there was little light being let in. Unlike seemingly everywhere else in the palace, this room's colour scheme was far darker; made up of rich reds and dark browns and blacks. The rug below the desk that almost filled the entirety of the room was a particularly fearsome, crimson shade.

The King sat behind his desk that held three lit candles. There were papers in front of him that he was looking down upon; not sparing Coren nor the herald so much as a glance. With a careless wave of his hand, the herald was dismissed; Coren watched as the boy walked backwards out of the door before pushing it shut with a sharp click. Then, she looked back to the King.

For several moments, he continued to ignore her. His silence irked her, but she refused to show it. She remained standing, hands clasped behind her straight back and chin tilted slightly upwards.

When, at long last, King Caradoc looked up at her, all Coren saw was fire. The moment his eyes, burning infernos of golds and reds and oranges, met hers, every fire in the room leapt up under his silent command. The fireplace roared; the candles reached up and up and up.

Coren thought she should be afraid; that she should have wanted to take a step back. But she didn't. Coren didn't just see fire, she saw power. It wasn't fear that filled her but a sudden burst of envy and desire so strong that it startled her.

He smiled at her, as if knowing what she was thinking. The smile was not kind or cruel; it was victorious, as if he had already won a game that Coren hadn't even known they were playing. It left her with an unsettled feeling that she could not shake.

His champion's smile continued even after the fires had settled down once more. He moved his hands from where they had been holding onto the parchment upon his desk, placing his elbows on the table before folding his hands over one another and placing his head atop them.

It was then that he asked, "what do you know of the Gods, Corentine?"

About as much as you'd know about chicken farms, I suppose, she thought to herself.

She knew that he was asking of the Mage Gods, but her knowledge of them was limited to anything that Mina had known from rifling through her mother's books. In human villages, it was definitely not acceptable to worship the Mage Gods; It was even frowned upon to know of them. "I know the human Gods. Lexin, God of Light; Aliona, Goddess of the Elements; Minerra, Goddess of the Made; Venrin, God of Health; Rowtin, God of Lies; Nyata, Goddess of Premonition; Ysdar, Goddess of Chaos; Kalas, God of Life. The Mages also worship Lexin and Aliona as well as Venrin and Minerra, though the humans have changed their titles slightly. I'm not sure about the others, but the Mage version of Ysdar is the Goddess of Darkness."

The King removed his head from where it sat atop his hands and pushed back his chair. He moved around his desk in long strides; when he passed Coren, he was so close that it would have hardly taken a twitch of his hand to touch her. He didn't, of course, and simply continued walking until he was almost back to where he had started, but now leaning against the right side of his fireplace.

Taking that as a cue to follow him, she moved towards the left side of the fireplace.

He motioned to the figures she had seen earlier on the fireplace. Looking at them again, Coren realised they were depictions of the eight Gods, assumedly the Mage versions.

"As you mentioned, we share some Gods with the humans. The other Gods are simply renamed and repurposed by humans so that they could distance themselves from the Mages," the King explained patiently. Coren could feel his fiery stare upon her, but she continued to admire the small statues instead of returning it, "for us Mages, there is Lexin, God of Light; Aliona, Goddess of the Elements; Minerra, Goddess of Material; Venrin, God of the Body; Jakar, God of Transformation; Remi, Goddess of the Mind; Nias, Goddess of Darkness; and Akeros, God of Death." Coren nodded to show she was listening, trying to remember all the familiar and unfamiliar names being thrown at her whilst the King continued on, "depending upon which deity is responsible for your powers, they are your matron or patron God or Goddess. In order to have control of your power, you need to first form a connection with them. You have no control over your power now, because you only have a one-way connection with the Darkness. That is why it is ruling you rather than the other way around. It is also when you make The Connection that you fully come into your abilities as a Mage, becoming immortal for one."

With his final words, he offered her a large grin, as if the sound of immortality was supposed to be the most enticing thing she had ever heard. It wasn't.

For a moment, her mind flickered back to that one time, in her youth, when she'd tested the idea of a Mage's aversion to death. It had been four days since the Snatchers took both Mina and her sisters; three days of stewing over her awful powers, nightmares resurfacing of the man with the slicked blonde hair; two days since her mother had Coren sleep locked in a tiny chicken hut in the midst of winter; one day since Melrose had first began to hit her.

She had tried to escape her fate as a monster for eternity.

It had failed.

"If you can't make this 'Connection'," Coren asked, forcing herself out of her own memories. To dwell too long upon the past is to become lost within it. "Is there any way to still control your powers?"

He narrowed his eyes at her consideringly, leaning forwards, before replying, "yes. You can still learn to control them to an extent, which we will work on while you form your Connection to Nias, but your power will be largely unstable and unpredictable, as you've already experienced, no doubt."

Her entire body flinched. Yes, she remembered exactly what her power could do when it so desired.

"Let me teach you."

"What did you do?!"

Seeing her reaction, he pushed himself off of the wall and took a single, long stride towards her; eating up the distance between them. Coren barely refrained from moving backwards. One of his hands lightly gripped her forearm, tugging her closer. She was surprised at the heat she could feel from it, she could feel it even through the thick material of her tunic.

60

Would his touch on bare skin burn? The sudden thought had her looking away from his face quickly. This proved futile, however, when his other hand found its way to her chin – tilting her face back towards him.

It didn't burn her.

A slow, amused grin drew itself across his face as leaned toward her, hot breath ghosting her ear, "tell me, little Mage, what kind of trouble has your magic gotten you into, hm?"

At that, Coren did move backwards, wrenching herself out of his grip. She glared at him, "why even ask? You already know, you were there when they tried to have me *burned* for it."

He frowned at her, "you overestimate how long I was there. It's simple. I felt your power, I went to your village, I saw what they were doing, I burned them. I have no idea why they wanted you dead, little Mage, although I confess to being rather intrigued."

"I killed someone."

The words were so quiet they were practically whispered; a confession with enough shame in it to please the human Goddess Melette, whose domain of protection included truth and lies. As she spoke the words, Coren felt the heavy press of guilt in her stomach. To her shame, she felt it mixed with the heart-lightening feeling of relief. There would be no more shame or punishments; not with Melrose gone. But what did that make Coren?

Traitor! It was the voice of Mrs. Krenz's boy ringing inside her head. *Monster!*

61

However, the King simply dropped down into his study chair that had been just to his right, and said, "oops." Coren stared at him incredulously. *Oops?*

He rolled his eyes at her, swinging around slowly in the chair once, twice, before speaking again, "so what? It wasn't your fault; you had no idea what would happen or probably even what your powers could do. And it's not as if humans are useful for much."

"It was my mother," Coren snapped.

The King was quiet at that, assessing her with those unnerving eyes.

All the will to fight, to learn and control her powers, simply seeped straight out of her. She didn't care that it was probably some bizarre form of treason or something to dismiss a King, or that leaving was a sign of cowardice, Coren simply stated, "lessons are done for this week," and left his study in a rush.

It was not Izak or Milo waiting for her outside, but Zarola. The maid must have seen the tears threatening to leak from Coren's eyes, but she didn't comment, nor did she make any of her usual biting remarks. They simply walked in silence, with the other woman glancing towards her every now and again.

Concerned? Probably not.

Coren had no idea what she was doing or how long she would remain, having stupidly forgotten to ask the King about either while she had been so caught up in her own misery and anger and the man himself. The uncertainty made her sick.

When they reached her door, a walk that Coren barely recalled, she swiftly told Zarola that she'd be going straight to bed; no dinner was necessary. As if a murderous abomination deserved to eat.

"Jolon tells me you were very impolite to Mrs. Heindall's eldest boy today," her mother said to her softly as she placed the eggs she had collected from their many chicken coops upon the table that her daughter was just about to finish cleaning.

Coren didn't look up from her wiping, the familiar, hollow feeling of dread settling in her stomach, but her defiant words spilt out regardless, "he'd wanted to put his hands up my skirt and is apparently ignorant to the meaning of the word 'no', so I wasn't in a very polite mood. I'm sorry if I disappointed you mother, I-"

"That's not what Joshua Heindall says."

"Well," Coren said, moving onto the backs of the chairs, her voice growing frustrated and desperate, her eyes begging for her mother to believe her, "Joshua Heindall is a liar."

Melrose sighed deeply, dropping herself down into the seat at the head of the table. She placed her elbows upon it, and rested her chin atop her hands. Her green eyes, the same shade as her daughter's, trained on the young girl in front of her sympathetically, "you must know by now, Corentine, that what is said of you means everything in a small village like this. Here, defiance is not a valuable trait in a young woman such as yourself. Especially one that is of age to wed."

"Perhaps it should be," Coren bit back, ignoring the part of her brain that screamed for her to stop, as she always had, "perhaps defiance in young women should be encouraged, especially in situations like this."

Her mother got up suddenly. Her chair caught on one of the uneven stones on the floor of their dining area. It clattered to the floor with a sharp BANG.

Coren's entire body tensed.

The older female walked around her, so that she was at Coren's back, before she delicately ran her hands through the back of her daughter's hair, long fingers tugging at golden strands, "you can't be like this Coren; I can't let you be like this. It will be your ruin. I have tried to teach you, again and again," her mother sighed, "and now I must do so again for what I hope is the final time."

Melrose grasped onto her daughter's shoulders gently, turning her around with little hesitation. She was taller than her daughter, a fact that she rather enjoyed. After smoothing the hair away from the eighteen-year old's face and smiling at her softly, the older woman brought her hand up and, swiftly, back down across her daughter's face.

The sound echoed throughout the small house and the girl's face tilted sharply to the side.

A few tears began to trace their way down her daughter's face, so the mother frowned, shushing her daughter gently as she wiped them away.

"You need to learn, Coren. I need to teach you."

She repeated the motion almost mechanically, bringing her hand up, and then back down upon her daughter's cheek until the skin atop it was a blazing red and her lip split, blood welling in the corner.

Then, she told her to place one hand upon the table.

"It's for your own good, Coren," the woman told her, smiling softly once more, before bringing a pitifully-made cooking pot down on her fingers. The girl screamed at the collision, but her tears had already begun to stop.

Melrose did it again. This time, there was a snap.

"I need to teach you."

And again. Another finger.

"I want you to learn."

Another hand.

"Let me teach you."

Those were the woman's final words before Darkness erupted from its golden host, smiling and free and heading directly towards the pot-clutching woman.

In her canopy bed, Coren launched herself upwards, waking from her uneasy sleep. Her breathing was rapid as she desperately brought her finger nails up to her face, checking there for dirt.

Dirt from desperately burying her own mother's body. Shaking hands. A spade. Burning forearms.

"I'm so sorry, I'm so sorry, I-I,"

There was nothing there. It was over. But Coren could not forget.

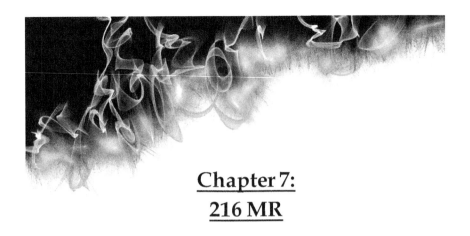

Chapter 7:
216 MR

$\mathcal{L}$eaving her chambers, unseen and unheard, had been

easier than she had expected. Clearly, her maids were
fast asleep and her only guard was a man in his late
thirties who, according to the empty flask at his side,
had drank himself into unconsciousness.

As a result, she swiftly crept away from him and down
the hall, distantly acknowledging the press of the
startlingly cool yellow marble against her bare feet. She
just couldn't find it within herself to care.

The Golden Palace was entirely different after sun set.
Without the sun shining through the open hall making
the gold of the walls glitter, the palace's interior could
almost be described as dull. Some places, some people,
thrived in the dark, but this palace was not one of them.
Even the tapestries that lined many of the halls seemed
less grand, especially in depictions of the War of Kings,
in which King Caradoc's flames that he sent racing
towards the mortal King's army looked to be a
forgettable grey-brown.

She stopped at the tapestry. It incited her curiosity, taking her mind off of her dream.

It was widely recognised that dark triumphed over light, after all, Dark Mages generally had well over a thousand times the power of that of the Light Mages. But would the darkness triumph over fire, she considered, especially a fire with the strength of the Fire King behind it.

As she stared at the tapestry, Coren could have sworn it *moved*, as if knocked by a breeze. When she looked around, however, there was nowhere for air to be able to get through. When she shoved the tapestry aside, there was nothing but a dull wall.

Shaking her head, she moved on, her feet beating lightly against the ground.

"Oi," Coren jumped, swinging around. She couldn't see where the voice had come from, so decided to hide behind another nearby tapestry, not fifteen feet from the one she had previously been regarding, in the hopes they had not seen her. Her hope was released when the voice continued on, "get a move on Jakan, the King will want a report on their progress, unless you want to appear before him without having a shot for confidence first."

The man appeared to be alone. Coren briefly wondered if he was insane.

"A shot isn't enough, I'd want the whole liquor cabinet," his companion, Jakan, mumbled as he, to Coren's utter bewilderment, walked through the wall opposite the tapestry she had been in front of.

The other man laughed lightly. He was a short but bulky man, older than the one beside him, and very merry. Jakan appeared to be half his age, taller than any of the boys from Coren's village with gangly limbs and messy brown hair. They both started down the hall, pausing when they caught sight of the guard outside Coren's rooms. She tensed.

The older man grabbed onto her guard's shoulder and shook him vigorously. Her guard came back to consciousness with a slurred, "whhaaa?"

"Honestly, Lan, are you trying to get yourself literally *fire*d?" The short man asked him, loudly. By the way he said fired, Coren assumed that there was more to it than simply losing your post, "you're meant to be guarding that Dark Mage, you know. The King would have your head if she got taken or left."

Her guard grumbled something back in response.

"Well," the short, burly man continued, "we might as well check."

Then, to Coren's horror, he gestured to Jakan to knock on her door. The younger guard did as was requested of him, bestowing three sharp raps upon the door.

As expected, there was no answer.

Just as Coren was about to reveal herself, pushing aside the tapestry so she was visible, lest they go in and start up a frenzy by finding her missing, the door was answered by a girl with a head full of red hair.

She regarded the guards first, and then looked past them to spot Coren. Coren's heart quickened as she shook her head at the other girl, desperately hoping that she would understand, and watched as the girl's brown-eyed gaze turned back to Jakan.

"Is everything alright with Miss Corentine?" the boy asked politely, and Zarola nodded sharply while Coren moved back to hide herself behind the tapestry once more.

"Yes," Zarola stated when it became clear that they weren't going to leave without a spoken response, "Miss Corentine is sleeping. Was there anything else that you needed?"

"No," Jakan said, "that was all. Thank you for your time, miss."

Zarola said nothing. She simply glanced at the tapestry Corentine was hiding behind, before retracting herself back into the room and closing the door with a sharp thud.

"She's a bundle of laughs," the older guard said, laughing at his own joke, "we'll be off then, Lan. Try not to drink yourself to death before the morrow. Come on, Jakan."

Then, he headed down the left corridor, Jakan dutifully trailing after him. Despite the other man's words, Lan slumped down in his seat once more, and soon began to snore away. After a moment, Coren finally allowed herself to expel a breath of relief and, once again, removed herself from the safety of the tapestry.

She considered going back to her room. It would be the safest course of action by far, considering what had just happened, but curiosity won out. Coren took several strides forwards, and moved into the wall.

It was a truly awful feeling. A chill embraced her from head to toe along with the feeling of being pressed down upon from every angle. Whether the wall was trying to crush her or make her a part of it she did not know. The squeezing, pressing, chilling, shoving feeling dissipated when she reached the other side, and was greeted with silence.

This hall was dimly lit, prompting Coren to squint her eyes, but there was nothing ahead of her. Just more stone walls. Despite this, every single one of her senses screamed at her to run. That there was something wrong.

She thought fleetingly of turning back, but didn't. She knew so little about this place, about why she was here, that any insight, even a frightening one, seemed worth the risk.

So, she moved forward, her legs reluctantly but dutifully carrying her onwards. Every time a bare foot hit the ground, it echoed within the silence and made her wince, but there appeared to be nobody here at all, unless one counted the drops of water that fell from the damp ceiling as company.

When she reached a corner, she pressed herself to the wall before tentatively peering around it. Luckily, there was not a guard in sight, which Coren found odd, but supposed the King was simply assured enough that nobody would find his false wall – no doubt created by a talented Material Mage – that he hadn't bothered. Following the tunnel around, left, then right, then left, then right again, she was only met with silence, stone walls and dripping ceilings. When she, at last, heard footsteps, Coren once again attached herself to the side of a wall, before peering around it.

The room was filled with who Coren assumed were Body Mages, they were wearing white coats with identical red symbols on their backs and were standing in front of horizontal glass tubes. To one another, they muttered about heart rates and hormone levels curiously, debating how to alter them, as if what was in front of them was a mere observatory experiment.

But it wasn't.

There were people *attached* those tubes.

In the one Coren was observing, a dark-haired boy was suspended, tubes surrounding him and a symphony of machine's beeping all around him. She moved her gaze leftwards towards a small, brown-haired girl who was several years younger than Coren's eighteen. After several moments, the machines surrounding her all seemed to stop at once.

The white-skinned man observing the girl gave out a sigh that displayed what an inconvenience he found the occurrence to be, folding over a brown clipboard before announcing, "patient 473, Group 2, has failed," he waved his hand carelessly towards a nearby youth, "have her taken."

A mid-height boy pressed a button on the tube in response that made it recline into a vertical position before beginning to push her away, "have patient 474 brought out to me."

The boy nodded and carried on moving.

Several moments later, he came back with the tube now filled with a different child. A boy, this time, and so young that Coren's heart clenched. He couldn't be more than ten and, unlike the girl, was very, very awake.

He screamed and pounded on the glass, grey-blue eyes glistening and wide, mouth open in a scream that was silenced by the glass. The man who had spoken merely opened a hatch at one side of the glass tube and roughly reached a hand within, grabbing the boy's arm hard enough to bruise, and kept holding him as he struggled for several moments. Soon enough, the child was unconscious.

A few other Body Mages had moved towards him, so the man began to speak aloud, grabbing a vial of crimson liquid from the several ones next to him, "Patient 474 is a part of Group 5 now, the first injection of 5 blood will be entering his system in three, two," Coren desperately tried to summon her Darkness to protect the boy, only to be met with silence and reminded of the Mage's Bane, "on-,"

Suddenly, Coren surged forward from where she was hidden by the wall, intent on stopping them, but a hand grabbed onto the back of her nightgown and shoved her against the wall, clamping a different hand over her mouth. When she opened her eyes, having briefly closed them from the pain of the impact of her head with the wall, she was greeted with a glowering Zarola. Blood was leaking from her nose, trailing over her lips, down her chin and beginning to drip onto her dark cloak. Her skin, usually a warm brown colour, was startlingly pale, as if someone had leached the colour from her. If that wasn't enough to tell Coren that something was very wrong with her, the fist that still held onto the back of her nightgown was clenched startlingly tight and was beginning to pull on it, as if she was trying to use it to help hold herself up.

"You're being a fool," the other woman hissed at her, before grabbing onto her forearm and beginning to drag her back down the halls towards the exit.

Anger swiftly replaced Coren's momentary concern as she demanded, "what the hell are you doing? They are injecting a *child* back there! Did you know about this?" The red-haired girl went to hurtle back a barbed response, but missed her footing and almost crashed into the floor. Coren quickly grabbed onto her arm, hauling her back up and trying to place one arm around her shoulder so she could take some of her weight. Zarola shook her off.

"What is wrong with you?"

"Following you is what's wrong with me," Zarola responded sharply as she grabbed onto Coren once more, continuing on her diligent march forwards, "humans are not built for travelling through walls. But I followed you anyway. You... you should be than-thanking me."

Her last sentence was separated by quick inhalations of breaths as they finally reached the wall by which they had both entered.

Coren scoffed, irritated. This girl had hated her since before Coren had even spoken a word to her, and now she wanted gratitude for stalking her? And dragging her away from a young boy getting seemingly *tortured*? Upon returning back to her chambers, she would have been more than happy to thank her for lying to the guards but for this?

They stopped before the wall, and Zarola turned to her once more, "listen, you don't have a clue about half of what is going on in this palace. Stay away from places like this and, if you can, stay away from the King. You're not just his guest, he intends to use you."

Before she could respond, she was dragged through the wall by Zarola. Upon reaching the other end, the girl collapsed. Coren barely managed to catch her before she hit the floor; with great concern she noted that blood wasn't just flowing from her nose now, but also her ears and eyes.

Coren grabbed the other girl's arm, and did as she had intended to do in the tunnels, wrapping one of Zarola's arms around her shoulders so that she could try to get her back to her chambers. When she'd adjusted her, Coren looked towards the red head.

She looked peaceful. A complete contrast to how she looked in the world of consciousness.

Sighing, Coren began to try and make both of their ways down the corridor, towards the still-sleeping Lan, with her resolve growing. Next time she had a lesson with the King, she was going to find out what he wanted with her.

And she was going to find out what was going on within the Palace walls, regardless of Zarola's warnings.

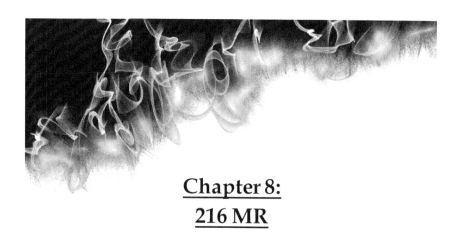

Chapter 8:
216 MR

𝒯he following morning had Coren awakened to a

knock at her door, which was much more favourable than Zarola splattering her with water. Despite the kinder wake-up-call, all she wanted to do was continue lying there with her head buried in her pillow. She hadn't managed to get to sleep until the light of dawn was filtering in through her curtains.

On the other side of the bed, she felt somebody shuffling and then a sudden release of weight. Coren jolted upwards, startled. When she finally managed to work her eyes open, squinting helplessly against the bright, invasive sun, she saw the back of Zarola's head as she went to answer the door.

It all came flooding back to her. The wall; the children and the Body Mages; Zarola following her; the blood coming from the other girl's nose and ears and eyes; lugging her back to her bedroom and, unwilling to wake up Nerah and Dahlia, dropping her onto the bed before all but passing out next to her.

When the other girl opened the door, the guard at the other side looked taken aback; practically gaping at her face.

Coren snorted. Zarola was very beautiful, but that was a little bit overdramatic.

"Were you attacked, Miss?" the guard inquired fiercely, looking around Zarola presumably to check if there was an intruder or if anyone else was injured.

Ah, yes. Zarola's face was still covered in blood. Maybe Coren should have tried to wipe some of it off before falling asleep last night.

The female in question brought one hand up to touch the dried blood under her nose and then her eyes. Coren could not see her face but she imagined she was grimacing.

"I'm fine," Zarola responded, before nodding to something that the guard was holding, "is that a letter for Miss Corentine?"

The guard affirmed that it was and handed the letter over, a concerned expression remaining on his face as he regarded Zarola. She clearly did not care, because she just turned around and shut the door in the face of the guard who still stood behind it.

She chucked the letter at Coren, who collected it from where it fell onto the bed sheets and stared at it curiously.

"I'm going to wash my face," Zarola told her shortly, moving towards the maids' chambers.

Coren, who didn't know how spacious their bathing room would be, briefly looked up from the letter and told her, "you can use mine if you want."

Nodding once, Zarola made her way towards them. She looked back to her letter. *Corentine* was all that was written on the front in an elegant, twisting script that must have taken years to perfect. Gleaning nothing from the front, she soon opened it up, scanning the words inside.

Since our lesson was cut short, I'll complete some of it in this letter. Izak will be along shortly to take the Mage's Bane from your wrists. I rather like my palace as it is, so I'd rather you refrain from any magical outbursts. As a safety measure, Izak and Milo will keep it on their persons at all times.
After Izak has released your magic, I want you to go to the palace library and find a book titled 'Connections of the Divine and their Chosen', which will detail how to begin creating a foundation for your Connection to your matron.
I have business to attend to concerning the north, so you'll have to survive without my presence momentarily. I know that will be difficult, but I will find you soon.

The letter was not signed, though it was not as if Coren needed clarification of who it was from. She allowed herself one last, longing glance at her pillow before getting to her feet and moving towards her dresser. As she didn't have lessons or training, she chose a dress this time if only so that those in the hallways would stop staring at her as she passed. It was cotton, burgundy coloured with a square neckline. She decided it would do, especially as she didn't wish to wear a corset and this was unremarkable enough for her to pass by unnoticed.

Swiftly, she shed her night clothes and put on the dress, which was actually prettier on than it had looked in her dresser. Mere moments after she had finished changing, Dahlia entered her bedroom only to see her already dressed.

Coren offered her an apologetic look, having still not grown used to the idea that she was not supposed to dress herself, but Dahlia merely shrugged it off, moving towards the bedsheets – bloody from Zarola – with a raised brow but no questions.

Just as Coren went to justify it, there was a knock at the door for the second time that morning. She opened it for Izak to stride hesitantly inwards. The brown-haired guard had on his usual clothing, slim, grey armour with a sword at his hip and a mild frown on his face.

The guard brandished a key in his hand as Coren moved aside to let him in. The Mage's Bane cuffs were extremely difficult to get off, if not impossible, without the Bane Key. Along with a hundred cuffs, a hundred keys were made, though many had been lost or stolen over the centuries. From what she knew of her village, they had the Mage's Bane but no Bane Key.

Not that they needed one. If they caught a Mage, they would be taking the Bane only from their ashes.

Izak took her left wrist into one of his rough hands, inserting the key and twisting it. Coren barely refrained from sighing in relief when the cuff fell and clattered to the ground. Despite its removal, she still didn't have access to her magic yet. Both had to be removed.

Then, he slowly took her right wrist in hand. A growing sense of trepidation filled Coren as he inserted the key and began to twist. What if she lost control again right away? What if she hurt Izak and Dahlia? They were both close, too close. What if-

There was a click.

The remaining cuff fell to the floor.

Regaining her magic felt, to her horror, like burning. Her very blood boiled with power as the sudden, renewed influence of the Darkness turned every vein in her body black. At first, the pain was unbearable; she wanted to scream and cry and tear herself apart until everything just stopped. But then came euphoria; her toes curling and head tilting. The pleasure that came with feeling indestructible, unbreakable. The sudden influx of power made her forget that it had both destroyed and broken her again and again and again. She could recall nothing. Not her name, her family, Izak or Dahlia or Zarola, for whom the door between the bathing chamber and the bed chamber had opened and shut. There was only her power, and what she could do with it if she just gave into it – let it in; let it complete her.

She felt as if she could bring an empire to its knees.

For a moment, she wanted to.

Make them bow, Coren came the tantalising voice of the Darkness, but, rather than tempting her, it brought her back to reality.

Coren didn't want to forget. She didn't deserve to forget. For her mother, for the blonde man, she deserved to live with her crimes.

When she tilted her head back down, the high diminishing, she found herself looking at Izak's wary face. Moving her gaze, her stomach dropped at the sight of Dahlia. Her dark eyes were wide, staring at Coren with unadulterated horror; she had seen, for the first time, the monster that lurked beneath the golden curls and pale face.

Coren blinked before either of them could see the growing tears.

She didn't even dare look over to Zarola, who she knew would be regarding her the same way she had when Coren had first arrived – with hatred and condemnation. Zarola was likely wishing she had left her to be discovered inside those walls.

"Well," Coren began, hating the way that her voice wavered. They were only seeing her for what she truly was (*monster!*); it shouldn't hurt this much, "shall we get going then?"

Izak only nodded, turning around to leave the way he came with Coren trailing after him, the weight in her heart heavier than all the gold in Caradoc's Kingdom.

Even though Coren had never before seen a true library, she knew that this one would have put any others to shame. Where one would have expected a ceiling, there was none; in fact, it seemed that this library took up an entirety of one of the palace's glowing turrets.

The room was large, larger than any other that she had been within, it could have fit her home in its width at least thirty times, and circular in shape. Books filled the room, organised by colour upon curved, golden shelves. Every now and again, there was a gap between the shelves where a ladder resided, giving access to the four different balconies that resided within the tall tower.

Tilting her head all the way back, Coren could see that the far-away ceiling was painted beautifully. It depicted dawn upon a sandy landscape; the sky was alight with golds and pinks and oranges. It made her think of hope. It was the most beautiful thing she had ever seen.

Coren turned to Izak, wanting to see if the novelty of this room ever wore off. Only, when she looked at him, he had his eyes on a different kind of beauty.

The guard from the other night, the gangly Jakan, was guarding a locked, golden gate through which Coren could see mountains of books. Forbidden books, most likely.

Smiling slightly as she looked between the two guards, Coren turned to Izak and asked, "do you know how the books are ordered?"

Izak snapped his gaze away, clearing his throat, before telling her, "it's ordered both by colour and alphabetically. The book you're looking for is by Attia Reed and it's silver, so it'll be on the third balcony."

When Coren moved towards one of the ladders, Izak moved with her.

"I'm more than capable of finding a book by myself without blowing the library up," she told him, before nodding towards Jakan, "maybe you could stand with the other guard. He looks bored."

Izak flushed but nodded and Coren made sure she had fully turned around before she allowed herself a small smile. Soon, she reached the ladder and grabbed onto it firmly. Last thing that she wanted to be doing was plummeting to the ground from ladders, especially considering the protective nature of her magic.

Pulling herself up, she passed the first balcony with books coloured pinks, white, cream and grey; next, she reached the second balcony that held more vibrant books – blues, yellows, purples and greens; finally, she reached the third balcony, climbing the ladder until she could push herself off to stand upon the balcony. This isle held reds, blacks and metallics.

Moving to where all the metallic-coloured books resided, she scanned the authors last names until she finally reached *R*. On the second to bottom shelf, she found her target. 'Connections of the Divine and their Chosen' by Attia Reed.

With the silver book in hand, she moved towards the edge of the balcony and gazed around.

The library, it turned out, looked just as spectacular from every angle. Though, Coren decided that she preferred the view from the balcony as when she looked up she was able to see the ceiling painting in even greater detail. From here, she could even see the initials at the top, right-hand corner.

A K.

Looking back down, she spotted Izak and Jakan standing together near the presumably forbidden books. Izak was smiling lightly at something the other boy had said. Now *that* truly was a rare sight.

Not wanting to break his happiness up, Coren scanned around the balcony for somewhere to sit so she could stay up here and not make Izak feel obliged to be with her by going down. There was nowhere, regretfully, but Coren had sat in far more uncomfortable places than this pristinely cleaned library balcony's floor. Moving down the length of the balcony, she sat against the wall next to the black bookcase. Then she looked at her book fully.

Upon the silver front, the title was written in an elegant black script that hinted that the book was considerably old, which was only affirmed by the yellowing pages within. The first couple of pages merely continued to explain what King Caradoc already had: that to become ageless and gain full control over your powers, you had to form a Connection to your matron or patron God or Goddess. When the opening came to an end, Coren went back a few pages to look at the contents page. Her eyes scanned down the page until she finally caught sight of *Nias, Goddess of Darkness, page 55.*

NIAS, GODDESS OF DARKNESS
Human Variant: Ysdar, Goddess of Chaos

The Goddess of Darkness is the matron of the seventh group of Mages: Dark Mages. This group is second only in power to the Death Mages. They possess the power to create and manipulate Darkness; under their control, Darkness can take on a physical form and it has been known both to kill for and protect its user. Regretfully for the wielder, the Goddess of Darkness is the most difficult matron to form a connection to and their powers the most... unruly. This stems from the Goddess' rumoured instability, which is why the human council named her the Goddess of Chaos. She is known to demand great sacrifice from her Connectors before allowing them full reign of her powers. Some Dark Mages have been unable to make the Connection at all, ageing until they turned to dust. Other times, the Goddess only forms a half-connection, otherwise called a Promise Connection, with her Mages. Many times, this is eventually fulfilled. But not every time.

It is recommended that the user begins to learn to control their powers whilst also attempting to reach for the Base Connection. The Base Connection can be found when one meditates, focusing their mind solely on finding what links them to their matron, which should appear alike to a line of black for Dark Mages. If you have a mental hold on this connection, your matron will hear your communications and elect whether or not to respond. The Goddess of Material and the God of Death are known to always respond though the others, especially the God of Light and the Goddess of Darkness, are known to often be unresponsive.

Coren shut the book, thumped her head back against the wall and sighed. That wasn't exactly what she had been hoping to read; she had been hoping for step-by-step instructions on how to create an immediate Connection so that, for once in her life, she could feel a semblance of control. Of course, she had known that wasn't going to happen – optimism was always doomed to die the cruellest of deaths. *But it had been nice to hope*, she thought, staring up at the dawn-depicting ceiling.

"Not good news?" came a voice to the side of her. She glanced away from the ceiling and towards Izak, whose cheeks were still slightly flushed.

"No," she told him honestly, wincing as she pulled herself up from the floor. She had spent so long recently lying on her feather-like bed that she had begun to forget what discomfort felt like, which was a prospect that more than unnerved her. She didn't want to become dependent on nice things, just in case the King did end up throwing her out. Which he might very well do, if she proved useless making the Connection. "The book just confirmed what I already know: that my powers are unpredictable. And then told me to meditate."

Izak laughed slightly, surprising her, and said, "I had to do that too. I had more trouble than most making a connection to Aliona, Goddess of the Elements. But, when I managed to get through to her, she truly helped me realise what she wanted from me; what I needed to do to prove myself worthy."

"Nias might never find me worthy," Coren confided quietly, thinking again to the mentions of the Dark Mages who had never made the Connection, slowly withering away.

The guard stared directly at her, speaking with such an earnest tone that Coren's breath was knocked from her lungs, "you are worthy, Coren. I haven't even known you for a half-moon, and I know that you have a good heart. And you don't give up, even when faced with things you're not all that good at," he let out a cough that sounded suspiciously like 'swordplay', "You'll *make* Nias see you as worthy if that's what it takes."

A startled laugh worked its way out of her throat and she offered Izak a bright smile.

The guard smiled back. It was a smaller smile than her own, but fuller than any other she had been given by him previously.

Coren had forgotten what it felt like to be seen positively; to be seen as something more than a nightmare.

"You're a good man, too, Izak," she told him, and, clutching the book, they both made their way back down the ladder, Izak offering a small wave to Jakan before they left. Resolved to visit the gardens, Coren, hope-filled, invited Izak. He agreed.

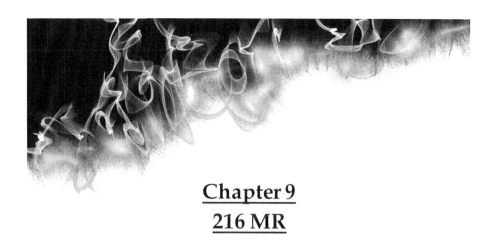

Chapter 9
216 MR

*S*trolling the gardens with Izak, it turned out, was not to be.

As they were making their way down the corridors of the south wing towards their destination, a comfortable silence between them, the King spotted her. He appeared to have been moving between meetings, several old council men and women scurrying after him like little ducklings, rambling no doubt about treasuries and territories and... whatever else it was that Kings had to concern themselves with.

He was dressed very finely, more so that he had been when they'd met in his study. He had on black breeches with a ruby-encrusted, crimson tunic. The tunic brought out the sheen of red in the King's dark hair, which was neatly arranged, wavy and parted.

When he saw her, one side of his rosy lips quirked up slightly and he broke away from the small hoard. His councillors frowned at his retreating form, but dared not reprimand the Fire King.

Caradoc jerked his head at Izak, and the bowing guard (by the Gods, was she supposed to curtsey?) left her side with an apologetic frown. Quickly, Coren decided to curtsey, hoping that he didn't see her hesitance as an affront. When she dared to look up, however, he was still smirking.

When he did so, the fire in his eyes seemed to glow brighter.

"Now," he commented in a light tone, offering her his arm as she dared to begin to straighten, "there's no need for that."

Coren nodded and took the offer of the well-muscled arm, allowing him to lead her towards the gardens.

In truth, she had no idea what to say and feared that if she opened her mouth, something stupid would blurt out. Such as, *are you experimenting on small children within your palace walls?* She was sure *that* would go down well.

The King's low voice soon cut through her concerns, his tone somewhat teasing as he said, "I take it you've recovered from the last time we met."

Coren refused to blush.

"Yes," she answered tonelessly, "thank you for your concern, Your Majesty."

The dark-haired man laughed, leading Coren down a set of stairs that delivered them from the main structure of the palace into the luscious expanse of gardens. When he stopped laughing and finally spoke, his voice took on a quality that was a mix of mocking and musing, "I sometimes wonder what it must feel like, to feel such guilt over a human death. I don't think I've cared about them for at least two centuries. All my family had been Mages."

"And where are your family now?" Coren asked.

To her surprise, he did not seem bitter or enraged when he answered. Besides perhaps a morsel of guilt, the King sounded detached, "long dead. The human King saw to that," he looked at her then, "they died the same way you would have."

"That must have been unpleasant," Coren said aloud with a grimace.

"Quite."

Turning away from him, she finally took in the gardens in front of her. They were gorgeous. Throughout the courtyard, various plants climbed up the palace walls such as ivies. In the centre, there was a large, white marble fountain adorned with what was presumably figures depicting the Gods. From north, south, east and west, a single path led in different directions with rose bushes at its sides.

Coren jolted when warm breath tickled her ear, having not felt the King lean towards her, "wait until you see the gardens on the north side of the palace, they're even more of a spectacle. It was said to have been cultivated by Aliona herself, who was a native of Galaris. After seeing the maze, most are inclined to agree."

The Dark Mage turned towards him. His long legs were still bent from his troubles to be level with her ear, so they were face to face when she did so. Sharp jaw, chiselled cheekbones, aquiline nose, glowing tan skin, bright, burning eyes. He looked every inch a King, and a handsome one at that. Gazing at him as she was, she couldn't help but finally ask, her voice quieter than she had intended, "what do you want with me?"

The corner of his lips picked up once more, fiery eyes darting to her own lips and back up before he inquired, "whatever do you mean?"

This time her voice was louder, and more assured, repeating, "I mean, what do you want with me? You saved me from my village, from the e-eight-days-fire, for what? I don't believe that you ride around your Kingdom aiming to aid any Mage in need. So, what do you want with me?"

His eyes seemed to assess her for a moment, deciding what secrets could or could not be spoken.

"I need you," he told her simply, not straightening nor moving away. He didn't seem in the slightest bit apologetic or regretful in his admittance. If anything, his eyes seemed hungry. "I need your power."

"You intend to use me."

"Yes," he confirmed, one hand reaching from his side to curl a strand of blonde hair around his index finger, "I intend to use you. But in order to do so, I need you to be powerful. What would you prefer, to be free and weak or used and powerful?"

Her initial instinct was to say free and weak. After all, she had dreamed for many years to run off to Valark or Novurum or some other far afield Kingdom. But, despite all her dreaming and the once or twice she'd actually set off from her village, she'd never actually left. Even when she'd gained the money to, by sharing her first kiss with the rich Billius Nohle so she could snatch a jarna or two from his pocket.

Why? Because what kind of life could she have if she did? It would be a life of weakness as she had no control over her powers. Coren would be bowing constantly to the whims of the Darkness. When it wanted to kill, it killed; when it wanted to play, it played. She would not have a peaceful or pleasant life as some kind of adventurer, she would have a fearful and lonely life running away from any connections she made to prevent herself from hurting them. The Mage tutors would never agree to train an eighteen-year-old; not when they thought five to be too old to begin training. But to be controlled? She didn't want that either. After all, she wanted to conquer her power so she could have control. She didn't want to take back control from the Darkness only to give control of herself over to Caradoc instead. And what did that even mean? What did he want to use her for?

When she voiced her last question, he simply smiled and shook his head, unravelling the golden strands from his finger slowly. With his other hand, a hand that radiated a startling warmth, he touched her cheek, before slowly moving towards her ear once again. Everything inside Coren tensed.

"That's my little secret," he whispered, a rough pad of a thumb caressing the skin of her cheek, before he pulled his hand and face away and stepped several strides back.

"Come find me with your answer at the Spring Ball," he told her, eyes still locked upon hers and lips ever-so-slightly raised. With one hand, he blindly picked a flower from the bush beside him, before offering it to her. Coren hesitantly took it as he finished, "I'll be waiting in the middle of the maze."

With that, he left, and Coren was alone, staring at the red dahlia he had handed her. She admired it briefly, then dropped it upon the floor before she turned on her heel and left the gardens, eyes darting the immediate corridors for any sign of Izak.

Meditating, it turned out, was much more difficult than it sounded. Coren supposed that it didn't help that King Caradoc's question was bouncing around relentlessly inside her head.

What would you prefer, to be free and weak or powerful and used?

Coren found herself unable to keep her mind silent for more than two milliseconds, let alone keep focused enough to search for a black line leading to the Goddess of Darkness.

Nias? She called out inside her head, deciding to forget the black line and simply try and get the Goddess to talk to her regardless, *hello, I know you're probably busy with... Goddess business but I would really appreciate a moment of your attention, if you can... please? Hello? Goddess Nias?*

Are you short of several marbles? That's not how it works. Of course she's not going to reply to you, you have to offer a human sacrifice first, Milo Mind Spoke to her from where he was guarding the front of her chambers.

Her eyes widened. *What?*

She especially appreciates juicy, handsome young men. Perhaps you should offer her me.

Coren could all but hear him snickering. She rolled her eyes. *Perhaps she would not accept you; there might not be enough space for all that ego in the land of the ascended.*

They'd make space for me, blondie. There was a small, blissful pause before the insufferable guard continued, *I wonder what would have happened if I'd told you she wanted you to flatten yourself to the floor and shout praises up to her. Oh, ascended Queen of my mind, body and soul! I hereby give myself up to thee-*

Next swordplay lesson, I'm suggesting to Izak we use you instead of one of the dummies.

So violent. It's not very becoming of a young woman such as yourself.

The Mage grinned as she sent back a *What can I say? You inspire violence in me*, before pushing herself up from the floor at last and grabbing a nightgown to change into. Just before she did so, Milo Mind Projected an image of his wounded face and she laughed aloud, earning herself a slightly concerned look from Nerah, who was plumping the pillows. Clearing her throat, Coren hesitantly asked her, "have you managed to find some dresses yet?"

93

After viewing Coren's less than stellar clothing choices over the duration of her time here, and not being overly impressed with either Zarola's or Dahlia's, Nerah had insisted that she be the one to find their ballgowns. Coren had readily agreed and so had Zarola; Dahlia had agreed more hesitantly, requesting that Nerah ensure hers was rather modest, to which the taller girl replied that if she wanted a modest dress, that's what she would get her.

When Nerah asked Coren if she had any requirements, the blonde hadn't given any. In contrast, Zarola had requested a darker coloured gown. Nerah had frowned somewhat at that, remarking that it was a *Spring* Ball, not a funeral, but said she would comply.

Her maid immediately brightened, "yes, I have. It took me a while to find a seamstress who could competently make dark colours look spring-like for Zarola, but I managed it! Don't tell her yet, but Zarola's is styled to look like black roses. I think it's very beautiful, but the others are too. Dahlia's is a lovely bright blue, like spring streams, and mine is a very spring-like pink and yours- well, you'll have to wait until the day to see your gown."

Coren gave a playful groan and reluctant nod that pleased Nerah, who soon bustled out of her chambers and towards her own. The taller girl almost knocked straight into Zarola as she did so, shouting an apology to her before she continued making her way inwards. Coren looked at the red head questioningly, but Zarola merely continued to stand there for a few more moments, bright hair wilder than usual and a bit of mud on her cheeks. None of it took away from how lovely she looked, even when frowning. Finally, the other girl spoke. "You're not planning on going back out into the walls, are you?"

Truthfully, but evasively, Coren responded, "not tonight."

Zarola's lips pinched together, but she gave a slight nod, retreating back towards the door. Before she could lay a hand upon the door knob, Coren called out, "wait!"

The redhead's hand paused, and her head turned.

"If you had to choose," Coren began, her voice far more vulnerable than she had wanted it to be, "between freedom and power, what would you choose?"

At her question, Zarola fully turned towards her and walked to where Coren stood in the centre of her room. She regarded her for a moment, her brows furrowed, before she inquired, "did the King ask this of you?"

Coren's silence was answer enough.

"I would choose freedom," Zarola told her honestly, "as having power but not being free does not make you powerful. When have you ever seen a prisoner that looked powerful?"

The Dark Mage nodded, looking down and swallowing the lump in her throat before she looked back up to Zarola's awaiting, dark eyes, "but what if being free without power means that you will never find peace or happiness? That even when you're theoretically free, you're a captive because of a power you can't control?"

Zarola went silent for several moments. Eventually, Coren began to think that she would never answer.

Then, reluctantly, she told her, "I don't know."

Coren nodded, and went to step back from the girl. That was until Zarola latched onto her arm and pulled the blonde towards her, close enough so that she could lean in and seal her lips over Coren's. And that's exactly what she did.

The blonde was so shocked that she just stood there, frozen. Before she could even think how to react, Zarola had wrenched herself away from her and stumbled backwards. The redhead's face, Coren would later think, looked like it was even more shocked than her own. Horrified, in fact.

Wide brown eyes looked at her apologetically, not breaking eye contact as she continued to stumble back and back and back.

Just before she turned and twisted the door knob, Zarola rasped out, "don't trust the King. And don't go into the maze," before she opened it and rushed through.

Coren remained standing there for many moments afterwards.

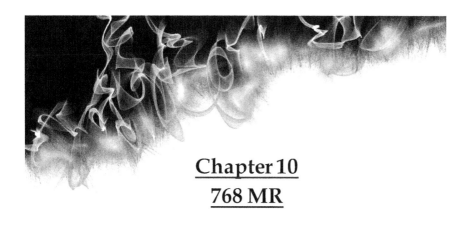

Chapter 10
768 MR

*U*nder the cover of the capitol's eternal darkness,

Hearne, head bowed and covered in a black cloak, made his way from the east exit and towards the south bridge. Drugging the guards had not been easy; the Queen enforced a state of constant vigilance among them, but they trusted him as a fellow guardsman, so he had managed it. When they awoke, they should be none the wiser.

Upon reaching the bridge, rather than crossing it he moved to the left side and lay down on the ground, forearms digging into the earth, and began to crawl his way under the small gap between the earth and the bridge, moving straight ahead and then turning to his left. Through the tiny gap where the bridge and the earth connected was a surprisingly large meeting room that Hearne had Greer create not six moons ago. There was a small drop when one finally managed to manoeuvre themselves through. When Hearne got there, he braced himself for the impact, covering his head with his arms. He swore when he landed, but dusted himself off and rose.

He had always thought of the process like posting a letter, only he was the letter. And it hurt.

Inside, Hearne, a man of six feet, could stand comfortably thanks to the fact that the floor went deep underground. In the centre, there was a table made of dry mud, and chairs of the same material. While Greer was no Material Mage, coming from a long line of earth elementals allowed her to manipulate existing earth into the shapes she so desired. Up to a certain level anyway.

Reaching into a hidden pocket he had created within his dark guard's uniform, he withdrew a thoroughly folded map and a creased letter. He set them down upon the table before taking a seat at the head, and awaited the arrival of his dutiful followers.

After two minutes, he began to tap his foot against the ground – the only show of nerves he allowed himself. Had they been captured? After three, he took the map and letter back off the table, tucking them into the well-concealed pocket. After all, if they had been captured it wouldn't take much for Thaddeus to break and tell them of this room.

When it reached five minutes, he heard people crawling towards the room. He grasped the dagger that resided in his boot, holding it up in front of him as he narrowed his eyes at the entrance. Hearne may be a 'mere' human, but he was not going to go out without a fight.

He discovered his reaction was all for nothing when Thaddeus, and then Greer, came tumbling out of the entrance way, both colliding with the deep floor as they did so and cursing profusely.

"Why is the entrance way this small? It should be bigger," Thaddeus complained, not for the first time, as he rubbed his fingers where his cheek had hit the floor, suspecting a bruise would soon appear.

Greer was similarly put out, all but pouting as she batted dust from her long, sandy brown hair before gazing at her admittedly very lovely, and now very ruined, outfit with great discontent.

Hearne raised an eyebrow at Thaddeus, "do you want to be discovered? If we make this hole any bigger and we might as well hang glowing lanterns up for the Queen and shout 'we're here! Come and kill us you homicidal maniac!' Don't you want to become King?"

Thaddeus muttered something unintelligible, but stopped his complaining, so Hearne turned to face Greer, "did anyone see you come in here?"

The brown-haired woman shook her head.

"Then what took you so long?" Hearne demanded, exasperated with them but unwilling to let his thoughts linger on his frustration for too long. When in range, Thaddeus was *always* listening.

"We were watching the guards you drugged getting arrested," Greer told him matter-of-factly, running her hand across the top of one of her dirt chairs before grimacing and deciding to sit, "it was assumed that they'd got drunk on the job. You know the Queen's views on incompetence. Pretty sure they're off to the gallows right now."

Hearne sighed. He'd liked some of that guard shift. Ana and Mattas had always been welcoming to him.

Oh well, some sacrifices were necessary. *Especially* for the betterment of the realm.

After a moment of silence for his, undoubtedly, fallen comrades, Hearne finally addressed the impatient Thaddeus and eager-looking Greer, "there has been a new development in our plan. This morning, I was passed on a note from one of my reputable contacts that was from Duke Ardan. There was a reason he wasn't at the Ball. He has decided to rebel against the Queen."

"What's his motivation?" Inquired Greer, sceptical. Being a member of the high society of Galaris, the brunette had no doubt met the man before thanks to their similar social circles. Hearne, too, had been surprised and sceptical when he had first received the letter, after all, why would a man as powerful as Duke Ardan wish to change a world that suited him so well? But, the information in his letter could change *everything*.

Thaddeus, who had clearly heard that thought, was all but bouncing in his seat, a rather unusual look for the broad man who was taller even than Hearne. Hearne sent him a firm look, and the man went still.

"The Death Mage triplets killed in the early 500s were his younger sister's children," Hearne finally told her whilst reaching back into his uniform to take out the letter and map once more, "and then he had a daughter. A Dark Mage, more powerful than most. Our beloved Queen must have felt threatened, because, during her visit to his estates, his daughter was found dead in her rooms. He believes the Queen poisoned her. So, revenge."

Greer nodded; concerns resolved. Revenge was a motivation that she understood.

"Though," Hearne continued, throwing the letter towards Greer and beginning to open the map up across the earth-made table, "with the information he gave us, I would have trusted him regardless of his motivation."

Having finished spreading out the map, he watched as Greer's eyes widened considerably, before she passed the letter onto the irritated-looking Thaddeus, who all but snatched it out of her hands. Once he had finished, his jaw was almost wide open.

"Better close that," Hearne said, grinning as he pointed to a small dot upon the map by the coast labelled as *Andern*, "or you'll catch Fae."

He moved his finger in a circular motion around the small marking, bringing both of the Mages' attention to it, telling them, "this is where they are. The brother is even on leave from the Queen's Army. Now is the perfect time to go after them, before the Queen catches wind of it."

Hearne settled back in his chair, watching as they glanced at Andern before rereading parts of the letter. Even Thaddeus looked contemplative about the possibilities.

"But how do you plan to subdue them?" Greer finally questioned, tapping her nails against the table as her eyes continued to flicker between Hearne and the map. The dark-haired man grinned at them both, "that's where you two come in. Thaddeus, you're a second-generation Mind Mage, are you not? So, if one of them is not expecting it and you enter their mind-,"

Thaddeus nodded, "I should be able to momentarily subdue them," before reluctantly continuing, "but, considering their power, I won't be able to hold them for long."

"And Greer, as a sixteenth generation Earth Mage-," Hearne fought a scowl when he was interrupted, yet again.

"Yes," Greer told him, looking back to the map, "I should be able to subdue one, but I won't be able to hold two."

He shook his head, his grin returning, "all we need to capture is one. I've been reassured that they are all very close to one another, they wouldn't dare risk a sibling's death through non-compliance, especially when, for a Death Mage to revive another Death Mage, it would cost their life."

They both stared at him in wonder. After a moment, Greer finally asked, disbelief coating her voice, "so we're really going to try this?"

"Like the Duke said," Hearne began, picking some of the dirt out of his nail, "we don't have any army and the people of this generation are far too afraid of the Night Bitch to ever dare to rebel. So, we need a new army, from a different time. And what better one to bring back than an actual rebel army from five hundred years prior? I hear Commander Zarola was an especially fearsome fighter."

Thaddeus looked up from the map, his voice slow and patronising as he reminded Hearne, "yes, but she was also in love with the Queen. And the Queen with her. Let's not forget that the Queen massacred a King and practically his entire Court because of Zarola's death. Who's to say she won't take her army and protect the Queen from us. Our aim is to *kill* the Queen. Resurrecting people who fought alongside her in the Winter Rebellion might not aid in that."

Suddenly, Hearne stood from his seat. He braced his hands against the dirt of the table, leaning forward until he was face to face with Thaddeus. "Do you truly think that the greatest rebel leader of her generation can love the greatest monster of ours? Do you truly think that noble Zarola will want to save a monster worse than the one she originally fought against? That any of them would? The Queen was a rebel, yes, and she *was* loved by their Commander, but the woman that she was died five hundred years ago, Thaddeus. All that remains is a beast that needs to be put down. Commander Zarola and her rebels will see that, or I will put them back where they came from. If you want that throne, Thaddeus, then this is the only way we will gain it."

The Mind Mage hesitated for a moment, before nodding.

"I want that throne," the lighter haired man told him, "if this is what it takes to get it, then I'm all in."

Hearne cast his gaze to Greer. When their eyes connected, she grinned, all teeth, "I'm betting that vengeance could be no sweeter than watching the Queen be stabbed through the heart by her second love."

Hearne grinned back, beginning to fold the large map back into its small square. Then, he took the letter from where it sat between Thaddeus and Greer, folding that too before placing both back into his uniform.

"We meet here at sundown tomorrow," he told them, already beginning to move towards the exit, "I have some items I need to collect before we leave. Send letters to your families, if you must, warning them only after we have already left. When we set off, we will ride as continuously as possible to Andern. Then, we will find the Death Mage triplets, capture one, and force them to group their powers together in order to bring back the Winter Rebellion rebels. We have one chance. If we fail at this, if even the slightest thing goes wrong, we're dead. So be prepared and, by the Gods, do *not* muck it up."

With that, Hearne pulled himself up to the ledge, muscles aching, and began to crawl his way out from their hideout.

It looked like he would be paying the royal vault a visit, as he would need as many Mage Willow Stakes as he could get his hands on. Especially, he thought as he made his way a safe distance from the Mind Mage, as the Death Mages weren't the only ones he'd need to put down soon.

It was for the betterment of the realm, he told himself, moving past the east entrance and onto the north entrance, his dagger glistening in the moonlight. When he got to the entrance, nineteen-year-old Linna and her seventeen-year-old brother, a guard in training, Axen, greeted him enthusiastically.

"Welcome back, Hearne!" She said merrily, the three other guards behind them offering him a small, friendly wave, "have you been off for a midnight str-." Before she could finish her sentence, his dagger was imbedded in her throat. She didn't even have a chance to use her powers. Yanking it out, he swiftly plunged it into the chest of her approaching younger brother. The three other guards, frozen in shock at their brother-in-arms' betrayal, had barely even moved before Hearne's sword, which he detached from hip, was swinging towards them, each arc swift and brutal. Blood sprayed down his cloak and over his face, he wiped it away, thankful for the dark colour of his cloak.

There could be no witnesses knowing he had left the palace. Not yet. Especially not when somebody could easily discover that the other guards had been drugged. Once all the guards had been slain, he went about hacking each of their heads off, crimson blood spraying and staining his dark skin. It would take the Mages at least a fortnight to recover, by then he would be long gone.

"Sorry," he told the head of the seventeen-year-old, grimacing at his vacant eyes and open mouth.

It was what was necessary, for the betterment of the realm.

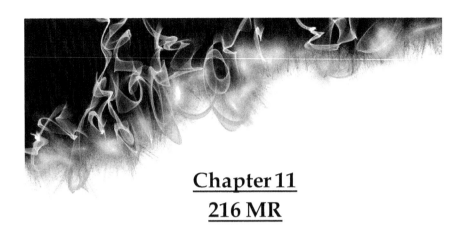

Chapter 11
216 MR

*C*oren stared at herself in the vanity, a large grin

overtaking her face; Nerah's choice in clothing was truly breath-taking. She twirled around in it, once, twice, and thought of that painting of dawn, of hope, that was depicted upon the library ceiling.

The dress was an array of colours, all mixed together into such a wonderful reminder of a sunrise; one that Coren was amazed could be captured on a dress.

At the top, it began with a dark blue that, at her waist, faded into stunning yellows, ferocious reds and sequin-adorned oranges. The dress was tight-fitting, and had a lower neckline than most would consider socially unacceptable, but Coren had gotten used to being stared at in disdain whilst wandering the palace halls in breeches and tunics to her lessons. The judgement of others mattered very little to her now.

In the vanity, she saw Nerah, Dahlia and Zarola coming out of the maid's chambers before moving to stand behind her. Coren turned to them, flashing the former two large smiles and then, when her gaze reached Zarola, her cheeks burned and she looked away. Neither had been able to meet the other's eyes all day.

"I hope you enjoy your night," Coren told them earnestly, "thank you again for sorting out the dresses," she told Nerah, before turning to Dahlia, "and thank you for doing my hair."

Nerah, to her surprise, stepped towards her and suddenly embraced her. Coren's arms floundered for a moment, before tentatively wrapping back around her. After that, Nerah retreated and, with a small smile flashed at Coren, Dahlia left with her.

Zarola remained behind.

The two girls stood in silence for several moments. In that time, Coren finally managed to force her eyes to Zarola's face, who was looking spectacular in her black-rose themed dress. Zarola did not look back at her, simply opened and closed her mouth several times before reaching under her dress and into her boot. From there, she retrieved something that glinted brightly under the light.

Coren's eyes widened when she realised that it was, in fact, a dagger. A rather lovely looking one, she noted with brief admiration, but still a killing-people-pointy-thing.

Reluctantly, Zarola thrust it towards Coren, stating, "for if you decide to do something stupid. Again."

Coren took the dagger from her, but, before she could respond, Zarola was gone.

With a frown, Coren brought her gaze down from where Zarola had been to the dagger. Taking off the dark sheath, she brought the weapon up higher so she could see it better. The sheath, the handle, the blade, were all black, reminding her somewhat uncomfortably of her Darkness.

Come play, Coren it sung happily, as if glad to be thought of, *come play.*

Shut up, the Mage responded sharply.

Slowly, she brought her finger up to the tip of the blade and pressed against it. She cursed when it sliced straight in, blood falling from the small wound, and realised just how sharp it was. Coren put the sheath back onto it and lifted up her own dress.

"By the Gods," she complained when she discovered how uncomfortable it was to try and stick an entire dagger inside her boot. After wiggling it a few times, and feeling as if she were about to break her ankle if she tried to walk with it in, Coren finally realised that the weapon also had a strap on it. Sighing, she tied it around her forearm instead. The large, puffed up nature of the sleeve there would conceal it. While she did so, she found herself muttering in victory, "got you, stabby."

Coren didn't hear someone else enter.

"Talking to yourself is the first sign of madness," chimed Milo, leaning against the door; his lips quirked when Coren jumped. If he had seen her placing a dagger under her sleeve, he didn't mention it, simply offering her his arm.

Even the guards were dressed according to the spring theme, their uniform taking on many a shade of green. "Nobody is completely sane," Coren told him, trying to subtly finish fixing her sleeve by also smoothing out the rest of her outfit, before walking towards him and taking the offered arm. "Everybody has a kind of madness lurking beneath the surface," she thought of her Darkness, and what it did to her, "sometimes, all people need is a little push for madness to reign." Something in his eyes seemed wary then. Not of her, necessarily, but perhaps he too had seen her words come to pass. He didn't say anything, however. Instead, the duo simply left her chambers in pursuit of the northern gardens.

Just like the library before it, the northern gardens put any other of its kind to shame, including the garden she and the King had strolled around. Like many aspects of the Golden Palace, the garden was circular in structure; this circular space, however, was so large that one could scarcely make out the opposite side of it. At the north side of the circle was an opening that admitted guests into the extensive maze which seemed to continue on for many miles.

Coren stared at it, bewildered, and wondered how she was going to find the centre.

Looking once more at the interior of the garden, Coren saw that all around it, couples were dancing, twirling in fine garments of golds, greens, pinks, yellows and light blues. Above them, supported by the occasional beam of wood, golden lanterns were strung up throughout the entirety of the circle. As a result, when one looked up, the lanterns lit up the dark sky like stars.

"Do you want to dance?" Milo asked. With one last look at the maze, she accepted his offer. They turned to face one another, Milo placing one hand on her waist and another upon her shoulder.

As they began to sway to the music, Coren spotted a woman in a dark dress at one corner of the circle, standing with two similarly dressed men, and was instantly reminded of Zarola. She quickly shut her thoughts down when they started to consider the very short kiss that Zarola had given her, before all but fleeing.

"I should warn you," Coren began, trying not to think of the redhead, "I don't know any of the difficult dances. The village would have the occasional small dance on Mayday, but nothing too intricate."

Milo twirled her away from him before pulling her sharply back in. A laugh burst out of Coren at its spontaneity and the man's silly expression.

"That's fine," Milo told her, grinning, "I've been told I have two left feet anyway. Also, just being this close to you is causing Lady Kandra to be positively seething."

Coren put on a mock-hurt expression, "so you're using me?" She pressed a hand to her chest, "that hurts, right here."

"You'll get over it," he told her, shrugging, before taking on an expression so devilish that Coren braced herself in preparation for what he would say next. He leaned in until his lips were almost touching her ear and paused, before he whispered, "or maybe you could get Zarola to kiss the pain away."

Startled, Coren suddenly pulled away from him. Milo didn't offer any explanation as to how he knew, but then it was obvious. It was easy to forget that you were dancing with somebody who was also reading your mind. The dark-blond simply offered her a wink, before sauntering off in the direction of a rather put-out woman that Coren assumed would be Lady Kandra.

Turning away from him, Coren spotted Izak. Seeing her without Milo, he broke away from the group of several guards that he had been standing with to come over to her, reminding Coren of how either Izak or Milo were supposed to be near her at all times.

But, Coren didn't want Izak to witness what she would be doing tonight; not after he had just begun to see her positively.

You have a good heart, he'd told her in the library. She did not wish to see his reaction when he realised that he was wrong.

So, Coren turned towards the maze. Picking up her skirt, she all but ran towards it, dodging dancing couples here and there, surging through the opening and down the first pathway, choosing left when she came to the first choice. Behind her, Izak was calling out her name.

Despite this, Coren continued on and on and on.

Left, straight on, left, straight on, left, straight on, left. The deeper into the maze she got, the further from the hanging lanterns of the circular garden, the greater the influence of darkness. With the dark, cold began to creep in. Spring in Galaris is often more so cold than warm, especially the nights, and this one was no different. Coren folded her arms over her front, hands running up and down her forearms in an attempt to warm them. Every now and again, her hand would brush against the lump that concealed the dagger. Each time it did, a feeling of danger overcame her and she found herself looking over her shoulder warily.

There were other people in the maze, quite a few actually. Groups of giggling girls, and older couples looking for a bit of privacy. At one point, Coren could have sworn she saw Zarola disappearing between hedge openings, her black-rose adorned dress trailing dutifully after her. By the time Coren had thought to call out for her, she was gone.

When she came to a choice once more between two different pathways, Coren decided to continue straight on. However, when she glanced at the pathway leading right, she noticed that some of the leaves upon the hedge leading in that direction were singed.

Abandoning her original route, Coren moved to the right. She doubted the singed leaves were from some kind of accident, as most fire elementals could not summon fire from nothing, so, unless they were walking around holding a stick of fire, it was likely a clue.

At the next choice, there were again singed leaves, so she moved right; then right again.

There were no other people in sight now, but Coren could not shake the feeling of being watched. Not by a person, no, but by the night, who held its breath in trepidation for what was to come.

When she got to the next choice, the singed leaves were there again upon the path that led straight on, but there was also something else guarding it.

A stone figure resided in the centre of the pathway, appearing alike to an elderly woman with a bent back and a fine, curved cane in her left hand. The cane had a snake's head at the top, around which the woman's frail, stone fingers grasped. The snake's eyes, Coren noted, were represented by two, small jewels known as *jikita*, otherwise called the sight, occasionally used by Mind Mages who wished to attempt scrying. Not that many succeeded from what Coren had heard.

The stone woman moved, tapping her stick thrice on the ground.

"If you want to enter the centre of the maze," the woman spoke, a smile tugging at her stone lips, grey wrinkles creasing as she did so, "you will answer a riddle."

Oh Gods, Coren thought to herself, *please be simple.* The woman's voice was deep and quiet as she rasped out:

> *"They who see all,*
> *But none shall see.*
> *They who rule all,*
> *Yet are ruled by none.*
> *They who can ascend,*
> *But should never again descend.*
> *Who are they?"*

Coren could have kissed the stone woman, barely needing to take a moment to think before promptly responding, "the Gods."

The stone woman nodded, but did not yet stand aside. Instead, her cold, unnerving eyes seemed fixed upon Coren; the jikita glowing beneath her harsh grasp. Finally, she told her, "five hundred and fifty-two years."

"What do you mean?" Coren asked, frowning at the woman.

"Blood and death and pain and descentation, Malva. The consequences of today, and the consequences of love," the stone told her. Coren repeated her question, but the woman paid her no mind. She simply closed her eyes and returned to her inanimate form – lips stilling, body freezing, jikita dimming.

With a final, contemplative look at the statue, Coren continued past her and down the path. Did she mean the consequences of her agreeing to Caradoc's terms? Or the consequences of something Coren had already done? Or was she just trying to frighten her with further riddles? All thoughts of the woman's words were pushed to the back of her mind when she, following the maze, saw light coming from around the corner she was about to turn, her own silhouette a figure of darkness within the bright, echoed light. Taking the turn, Coren found the Fire King.

His back was to her as she stepped out from the hedge and into the confined, circular centre of the maze. Around him, fires were raging; torches were dotted about the area and even the floor was alight, with lines of fire circling around the centre. The only opening was the small path from which Coren had entered. Sucking in a breath, she followed the path that had been outlined for her; towards him, towards her decision, towards her future.

Slowly, he began to turn.

When he was fully facing her, Coren could see that the King was dressed almost entirely in gold; the colour dominated his breeches and jerkin, though he had on a scarlet undershirt, with rubies decorating the jerkin. Upon his face, gold glitter lined his cheekbones, making them appear all the more cutting.

Upon seeing her, his lips tilted upwards. Coren expected him to immediately ask if she had made her decision; to pester her and ensure it was the one that he wanted.

Instead, he offered his hand to her.

After a moment of hesitation, Coren took it.

And then it began.

They were dancing with fire, Coren observed, as the King guided them between the raging embers, twirling her so close to one torch that its warmth licked her face, before pulling her back in closer than she had been before. Every flame in the area seemed to reach towards them – towards her – but she remained out of reach, twisting to the left, to the right, twirling in, pushing away. Dancing with the King felt like being chased, and caught, and chased all over again, and she wasn't sure that she wanted it to stop.

But it had to.

It was Coren that stopped dancing, her sudden pause halting the King in his steps. He tilted his head down towards her, burning eyes inquisitive with one side of his mouth forever raised.

She did not allow herself a moment of hesitation or guilt before she told him, her voice strong and assured, "I want power."

The King nodded, appearing unsurprised, but Coren wasn't finished, "I want power, Your Majesty, and I understand that it comes at a cost, but you cannot have my freedom forever. You can have three months of it, to use my power how you wish."

Between her lashes, she studied him. Discerning whether or not she could bargain with him would not only benefit her in regards to freedom, but it would also tell her how desperately he needed her.

At this, he did seem surprised, though he soon caught himself. He began to barter with her. "Two years."

"Three months."

"A year."

"Three months."

"Nine months."

"Three months."

"Six months."

"Three months."

"Five!" He barked out, losing his patience.

Coren shot him a serene smile, "done," and offered him her hand to resume their dance.

So, he needed her. Rather desperately. That gave Coren more questions than it answered. If she was so valuable to him, what happened to the other Dark Mages? Coren had never personally met one before, but she knew at least two were born each century.

That would be a question to consider at a later point, along with what was going on in the tunnels. Instead, she focused on her deal.

She had survived eighteen years with a lack of freedom, whether that be from her power or from her mother's punishments, she could survive another five months.

Despite appearing displeased, the King took her hand regardless, and the dancing resumed. Once again, the King was leading, with Coren moving swiftly to keep up with the more complicated moves, all the while trying not to stumble into a circle of fire.

Coren pushed away, twirling her body around as he extended his arm and was pulled back in. This time, the King did not twirl her back to their original dancing positions. Instead, he placed both of his hands upon her waist, tugging her in further so her back was against his warm, solid chest. He leaned down, stating, "you strikc a hard bargain, little Mage."

"I aim to please, Your Majesty," Coren told him dryly, hints of a smile pulling at her red-painted lips.

He huffed out a small laugh before telling her, his fingers expanding and tightening their grip on her hip and soft lips brushing her ear, "now we're in business, you should call me Caradoc."

It was then that several twigs snapped. Both Coren and Caradoc whirled around, his hands still clutching her close, to see a group of what must have been nearly thirty darkly clothed individuals standing before them.

One figure stood forward, their face obscured by a black mask with a hood concealing their hair and a cloak to hide their garment. Their voice was veiled by the way they severely deepened it as they proclaimed, "we are the rebellion, and your reign is over."
Then, raising a dark coloured dagger, the figure launched it straight towards the Fire King's head.

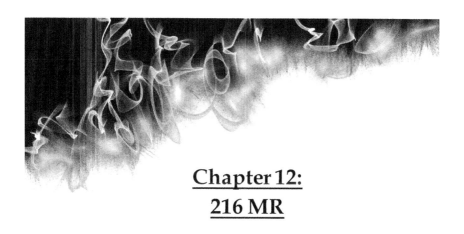

Chapter 12:
216 MR

*C*haos reigned.

From the rebels, arrows were being fired at Caradoc, aiming for the head or heart, daggers were flying and cries were heard as they charged towards him. The King summoned his fires upwards, cutting off the rest of the rebels from joining the sixteen that had already made their way into the inner circle. Waving his left arm, he brought across a fire shield of such intensity that most of their weapons burned before they reached him. The only weapon that managed to reach him was the dagger of whom Coren assumed was the leader, which the King caught in his right hand, before flinging it back towards the rebels.

He struck one of the sixteen in the heart, and they dropped to the ground.

Coren's left hand grabbed for the dagger hidden up her sleeve. Seeing what she was doing, the figure closest to her told her, "you should step aside. This is not your fight, Coren."

Coren and the figure seemed to realise their mistake at the same time; the dark-cloaked assailant recoiling whilst grey-green eyes narrowed at them thoughtfully. "She's with me now," Caradoc told the figure, cocking his head to one side as he carefully considered them. It appeared he had noticed the slip too, "so yes, it really is. How about you show me what you can do, little Mage?" *This is what I have chosen,* Coren told herself resolutely, adjusting her stance, *I chose power. So now I will have to fight for it.*

"Very well," a different figure told her, sending their own dagger sailing towards her. With her Mage reflexes far out-shining their human strength, it was easy to bat that dagger away with her own. Her Darkness, however, was not content with simple protection; it wanted vengeance, it wanted them to scream while repenting to each and every one of the Gods every decision that they had ever made leading to them raising an arm against her.

And what the Darkness wanted, it received. It surged towards the figure like a flood, regardless of the resistance of its host, entering through his eyes and nostrils and mouth and ears and watched in satisfaction as he choked on it; screaming, wailing, thrashing, tearing his own throat apart with his nails.

There was no sound or movement for several moments, all staring at the black-veined corpse of the person Coren's Darkness had just slaughtered, before tossing the corpse carelessly to the side.

Monster! The voice in her head, Mrs. Krenz's boy, screamed at her.

I am what I need to be, Coren told it in response, too high on the Darkness to repent.

When they launched their next attack, nine surged towards Caradoc and six towards her, and Coren's Darkness took full reign.

Two figures choked on the Dark before they even reached her, whilst another aimed their dagger at her neck. Once again, Coren batted it away whilst ducking as a sword swung over her head and stepped right to avoid an attempt to kick her legs out from underneath her.

Straightening up, she launched her dagger at one of the assailants, and cursed when it missed. She had begun to be trained in swordplay, not dagger throwing, but Coren had thought it was worth a shot. Instead, her Darkness created a black fog around them, taking away her assailants' vision, while she scrambled to get her hands back on the dagger. When she managed to, she, after a moment of hesitance, slit the throat of a stumbling figure. Before she had time to process what she had done, another figure stumbled into her back. Hooking her leg around their ankle, she attempted to shove them to the ground. Only, the figure caught themselves before they hit the floor, turning around swiftly and raising their sword high.

Coren clenched her fist, and the Darkness formed around it; she raised her fist to meet the swiftly approaching sword. When the sword met her fist, it broke into a thousand small shards. Both Coren and the assailant stared at the shards for a moment in bewilderment, before looking back at each other.

Neither had a moment to attack before the fourth figure, who Coren had forgotten about, fisted the back of her dress. Faster than Coren could react, the hand was gone and instead she felt her back hit the hard ground and the weight of somebody else was atop her. Distantly, she heard the screams of burning rebels, but she was more preoccupied with the blade kissing the soft skin of her throat.

Even at this angle, Coren could not determine the identity of her assailant.

The person atop her hesitated, and that was all Coren needed to use her strength to flip them over, grasping for her own dagger and shoving it to the throat of the rebel while theirs dug into her corset.

Looking down at them from this angle, Coren could have sworn there was something so familiar...

A scream of pain tore out of her throat as a dagger was thrown from one of Caradoc's attackers, piercing her side. At the same time, another rebel tugged her off of the familiar one. Looking to the side, she could see that, in one hand, they were holding several castor beans; their veins were a leafy green as they transferred some of the poison from the beans to her. Distantly, she noted that they must be a rather powerful, generational earth elemental to be able to achieve this.

Immediately, she felt drowsy; bile rising in her throat as the pain from the dagger burned.

Her Darkness, however, was not to be outdone. All of the rebels, two of whom had just gotten to their feet and joined the one poisoning Coren, were propelled backwards. The Darkness threw them so hard, in fact, that they sailed over Caradoc's ring of fire into the distant reaches of the maze.

One assailant remained. They, curiously enough, were also a Mage. A water elemental with considerable fighting skill, hence Caradoc's troubles. Unfortunately for them, they were so distracted by the dance of fire that the King displayed, flamboyance and a kind of murderous, morbid beauty to his every movement, that they never saw the Darkness before it was too late. Coren brought her hands together and Darkness congregated before shooting out like a spear, impaling the man who'd barely managed to turn towards her straight through. His mouth dropped open into a small 'o' before his legs gave out and he slumped over. Sweat dripped from her forehead, and she felt her legs shake. The King called the fire that encompassed him away, straightening and looking towards her. Soon enough, he was sauntering over.

Coren straightened up.

The dagger, she believed, had not hit anything major. So long as she did not remove it, she could momentarily live with it. The poison... Well, hopefully she would be fine.

Coren didn't realise Caradoc had finally reached her until cool hands were on either side of her face. That's odd, she thought with a frown, he's usually obscenely warm.

"The poison is acting fast, as it has been transferred straight into your bloodstream," she thought he told her, though maybe she was imagining it, he did seem a bit fuzzy, "we need to get you to a Body Mage."

Coren nodded faintly, vision unfocused and
blackening. She felt an arm circling her waist, steadying
her; that was strange, did she stumble?

She had to swallow the urge to break into hysterical
laughter when the King's guard finally showed up. Real
saviours, the lot of them. In a haze, she thought she
heard Milo call out her name in concern as a hand
grabbed onto her shoulder. She flinched away,
believing it to be the poisoner, but someone was
murmuring something about a Body Mage?

Surely enough, the poison was suddenly taken from
her system. Coren still felt unbearably warm, but the
nausea and dizziness mostly subsided. Still not feeling
well enough to speak, she nodded in thanks at the Body
Mage.

Now there was only the matter of the dagger
protruding from her side.

As if her thoughts had been heard, the dagger was
pulled out of her side suddenly and replaced with cool
hands. Coren let out a harsh gasp, and bit down upon
her lip. It felt as if her flesh was being sewn back
together. Perhaps it was.

Then, the Mage moved over to the King, who only then
released her waist. He shrugged off his jerkin with a
wince, displaying the deep slice to his shoulder he had
been dealt. The Mage placed his other, clean hand over
the King's wound, staining his skin crimson while he
healed the King to the best of his ability.

"We should go to the infirmary, Your Majesty," the
guard who must have also been a Body Mage informed
the King. Coren noted with interest that he seemed to

have Mages of every type within his guard, and powerful ones at that. A first-generation Body Mage would have struggled to achieve that without breaking a sweat. "You both need to get your wounds cleaned up and to-,"

"We can do that ourselves," the King interrupted, dismissing the majority of his guard until there were only two remaining, both of whom Coren had not formally met.

She noted that no guard was holding the Mage's Bane, and wondered if the King truly was powerful enough to contain her darkness. Which, Coren suspected, had only obeyed her today because she was doing exactly what it wanted; wrecking havoc and murder. She began to wonder if the King was simply too arrogant to realise that this chaos would not be easily contained, or perhaps he just did not care.

He offered Coren his arm, and she readily took it. As he began to lead her out of the maze centre, she glanced back at the area. What had meant to be a quick glance caused her to pause in her tracks.

In the very centre, where she and the familiar figure had fought with the dagger, lay a single black rose. Zarola.

For a moment, the world around her seemed to freeze as she stared at the spot, her mind running faster than she could catch up; question after question begging for attention.

"-tle Mage?" She finally heard, breaking through her stupor, "Coren, are you alright?"

She turned to see Caradoc staring down at her, brows furrowed.

Though the King had done nothing against her, Coren was not a fool. He was a dangerous man, no matter what kind of power she may or may not have over him in regards to how much he needed her for his little plan. If she told him about her suspicions surrounding Zarola, the redhead would be killed.

So, thinking swiftly, she plastered a smile upon her face, "I'm fine," she told him, before unwrapping her arm from his and moving back towards the scene on slightly unsteady feet, "I just wanted to grab my dagger."

She retrieved her dagger from the ground, and discretely took another lying in a dead rebel's body near it too. It looked like a twin to the one Zarola had given her, which must have been the one thrown at Caradoc, which he propelled into a rebel's body. Turning back around, she walked back over to the Fire King and took his arm. This time, he truly led them away and there was no glancing backwards. They manoeuvred through the gaping crowds of guests, who eyed their bloodied garments and whispered suspicions of what had occurred and into the palace, moving through corridors that were unfamiliar to Coren. *Zarola*, Coren thought, dread and concern coiling in her stomach, *what are you doing?*

Their destination, it turned out, was the King's chambers. Upon arrival, Caradoc slammed the door shut before either guard could think to try to follow them inside, and Coren took a moment to take in the interior.

It was yet another circular shaped room, with a large, canopy bed that possessed enough space to fit five comfortably in the centre. Unsurprisingly, the colour scheme was red and gold; with rich crimson furniture and gold drapes adorning the room. In one section of the circle, a door resided, leading to what she assumed was a bathroom. Caradoc tugged on her arm and she followed him towards the room.

After they entered the bathroom, which was massive, being at least half the size of his chambers, Coren hesitantly perched on the edge of his bathtub while he rifled through supplies.

Considering the similar structure of the room once more, she inquired of him, "what's the meaning behind all of the circles?"

His back still to her, Caradoc answered, "I'm sure you've heard how the city changes according to who is ruling?" Coren nodded, not that he could see it, "well, that is the same of the structure, too. Circles are supposed to represent the sun, I believe, and are present in all the major areas of the palace – in the great hall, the north gardens, my chambers, the library and others."

"So, if someone was to usurp you-," Coren had barely began before Caradoc, who appeared to have finally gotten his hands upon the supplies, turned back towards her.

He proceeded to move forwards, pausing only when he was standing directly in front of her. He set the materials down at her side, with Coren tracking each movement with her eyes. Her distraction, however, caused her to wobble precariously from where she sat on the lip of the tub. Caradoc caught her, leaving him bent over her.

One lip tilted, Caradoc inquired, "planning a coup, are we, little Mage?"

The Fire King offered her a sharp grin, and Coren responded with one of her own.

"Perhaps," she told him teasingly, their faces so close that she could feel his hot breath upon her cheek, "who's to say that when I gain my freedom, I won't stay in Galaris and see what kind of colour the city might turn for me?"

Though his grin remained, Coren could have sworn she saw a flicker of something in his eyes. It was not desire, despite what their current position might suggest. She realised what it was when his response did not appear as light-hearted as it was intended to be. He remarked, "after what I've seen today, with your full access to your powers, and control, perhaps you could."

It was only a small amount of something akin to fear, but it was still there. It made Coren's brows furrow. Didn't he know that the last thing she would want was a crown? To be responsible for the safety of millions when she couldn't even keep her own family safe from herself? Even with full control over her powers, she didn't believe that she could ever trust herself enough to want a throne.

Still, if Caradoc was not going to acknowledge his brief concerns, then Coren would not address them either. In the time that she had been lost in her thoughts, the King had knelt before her. Coren was momentarily frozen by the image, but soon relaxed. He knew that she would not harm him in any way, not when she needed him as much as he seemed to need her. And even kneeling, they both knew who held the true power. Coren would not allow herself to be fooled into believing otherwise.

"So," Coren continued, deciding to keep to their little game, "why are you assisting your future rival then?" Smirking lightly, he looked up at her through dark lashes; the only barrier between her and the eternal flame of his eyes, "I protect what's mine," he said.

Coren frowned, reminding him, "five months."

The King did not bother to respond, simply telling her to lift up her shirt. She did so, watching as he carefully cleaned the blood away from the still tender area. The concentration on his face, the gentle touch of his hands on her bare skin, it incited a rather peculiar feeling within her. It was something akin to fondness, but... stronger.

Biting her lip, she wondered how she could be so foolish as to be attracted to the Fire King.

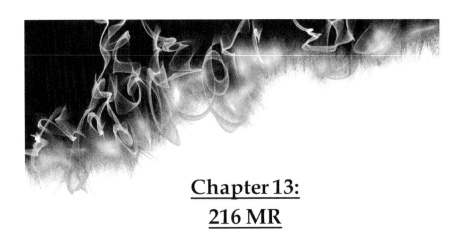

Chapter 13:
216 MR

*A*cknowledging her attraction to the Fire King, even

if it was only in the (hopefully) private realms of her mind, made their one-on-one lessons much more tense for Coren. Each time his skin brushed her own, even in the most innocent of ways, she felt herself grow tense and would even flinch away. Most of the time, he ignored it, however she had caught sight of his furrowed brows on occasion.

Coren's face burned and her heart thumped heavily at the prospect of him discovering that secret. Briefly, she recalled his laugh when she had almost tumbled off of her horse on the way to his palace. Would he mock her? Most definitely, she decided. Would her pride survive it? Certainly not.

"You're not concentrating," he stated, irritation seeping into his tone. Coren opened her eyes, looking to the King who sat opposite her, his crossed legs mirroring her own pose, "meditation requires a clear mind."

"It might be clearer if I wasn't stabbed and poisoned by unknown assailants less than forty-eight hours ago," Coren grumbled. An attack which the King would offer her no more information on, and one that she hadn't had the opportunity to confront Zarola over yet.

When Coren had gotten back to her chambers after helping to clear the blood away from the King's shoulder wound, all the while desperately attempting to appear utterly unaffected by the sight of him shirtless, she had looked for Zarola everywhere, screaming her name like a mad woman.

Zarola, however, had been nowhere to be seen.

Just as Coren had closed her eyes again, heaving out a sigh at the prospect of spending another hour fruitlessly attempting to contact Nias, who was probably too busy having a wine and dine with the rest of the Gods to bother to answer her, she felt two hands grasp onto her ankles before suddenly pulling her forwards.

By the time Coren's eyes were opened wide, she was face to face with Caradoc, her legs either side of him, leaning on his crossed legs. Looking up at him in surprise, she noticed that his fiery eyes even captured smoke, grey rising within the amber embers.

If this was him trying to get her to concentrate, it was not helping.

For a moment, he didn't say anything, just stared at her. Coren swallowed, and thought fleetingly of scooting back, but that felt too much like defeat.

He raised a hand towards her face, as if to touch her

cheek or tuck hair behind her ear, but dropped it before he made contact. Instead, he said, "a cardar for your thoughts?"

"My thoughts are worth more than a cardar," Coren told him, leaning back onto the heels of her hands to keep her balance, her legs still laying limp over well-muscled thighs.

His lips twitched, "a jarna then."

Well, she couldn't exactly tell him that she was admiring the presence of smoke within his fiery eyes and thinking about her growing attraction towards him. No, his head would grow so large that it would hit the ceiling and give him a concussion. And the floor beneath her felt pretty solid, so it, unfortunately, wouldn't be able to swallow her whole afterwards. Instead, she spoke aloud the first alternative thought that came to mind, "the fight in the gardens."

He sighed, his head falling back to allow spectacular eyes to look up to the ceiling in exasperation.

Coren scowled. She had every right to want to know why her life had been threatened that night, so cared little that he didn't want to talk about it.

He placed his eternally warm hands just above her knees, thumbs slowly beginning to sketch out shapes, as he finally responded, "they're part of a rebellion that has begun in the north of Galaris. It's not a very large rebellion, but it's a passionate one. They wish to destroy all I've built, take away power from the Mages, whom they see as mindless monsters," Coren flinched at the word, and the King's hold on her legs tightened, "and place a human on the throne once more. They even have Mage sympathisers," he spat out that part, and the fire in his eyes leaping with hatred as their fuel, "but I'm slowly rooting them out."

And slaughtering them like the pigs they are, his light smirk told her.

Coren nodded, though privately considered why any Mage would support a movement that saw them as inhuman and wanted to completely displace them from power. It didn't make any sense. There must be more to it, but she was definitely not going to ask the King; not when her freedom was less than five moons away.

She had more sense than to push him, or face meeting her end at his hands

This time, when he lifted his hand, he didn't drop it before it made contact with her face, softly brushing a blonde strand away from her light eyes and tucking it behind ear. She sucked in a breath when his fingers grazed her ear.

Desperate to not let herself get lost in all of this, especially as there was no way the King felt the same kind of attraction to her, Coren found herself asking, "what did it take, for you to make the Connection to Aliona?"

He stilled.

The long silence soon made Coren believe he would not reply to her, and she would not push him. She cursed herself for asking a question that was clearly personal, but she had just felt so tense and-

"The Gods are cruel beings," he told her suddenly, his

voice quiet and bitter in a way she had never heard before, "never forget that they haven't been on the continents for more than a millennium. They've forgotten love. And they certainly don't care about us." In an attempt at comfort, Coren placed her hands atop Caradoc's, but he immediately pulled away. He withdrew from under her and lifted himself up from the ground, beginning to walk back to his desk in the centre of the room.

Before he got to the chair, fists clenched into tight balls at his sides, he looked back at her, and said, "I'm sure you've already read about the Goddess Nias and how she demands greater sacrifices from her Connectors than most. Whatever the price is, pay it. There is nothing crueller and more vengeful than a Goddess' wrath."

Coren took an unfamiliar route back to her chambers, content to get lost, ask a servant for directions, not follow them and continue the whole cycle over and over. She needed time to think about everything that had been occurring as of late, and things that she knew were to come, such as the Goddess' price, should Coren even be able to contact her. Her walk, however, gave her no answers, and more questions entered her mind. By the time she had passed the sleeping Lan and gotten back to her chambers, the moon high in the sky, converting her normally bright chambers into a realm ruled by shadows, Coren had decided that she was going to begin to answer her many inquiries one by one.

Starting with what was going on within the palace walls. Softly padding over to her wardrobe, she wrenched the doors open as quietly as she could, pushing various garments aside until she found a dark grey cloak. Pulling it out, Coren rolled her eyes when she saw the typical gold embellishments, but placed the garment on.

Securing the golden clasp, she moved to her bedside table and then kneeled, flattening her hand upon the cool flooring before reaching underneath it and pulling out one of Zarola's daggers. She doubted she'd need it, but Coren thought she'd feel safer with it secured beneath her cloak regardless.

Despite the lack of necessity this time, Coren decided to secure it to her arm once more. It would give her easier access than trying to reach up through the folds of her cloak.

Drawing up her hood, the Dark Mage gave her silent chamber a last, fleeting look over before slowly opening up her chamber doors and slipping through. Soft snores came from her right, and Coren looked down at her incompetent guard. On one of the arms of the chair in which he sat was a Mage's Bane. Knowing what she was doing was dangerous and harbouring a lack of trust for herself, Coren gently picked up the key from where it resided upon the floor and then took the

Mage's Bane. Then, she placed both into one of her large cloak pockets.

If everything went to shit, she'd place the Bane on herself. It would be difficult, knowing the pain that it caused, but it was better than the alternative: losing control and killing. She chose not to remember the people she had killed alongside Caradoc.

Stalking down the corridor on light feet, she moved her head from left to right, scanning for the tapestry depicting the War of Kings. Finding it, Coren turned to face opposite the tapestry and strode forwards, straight towards, and then through, the wall across from it.

Taking out her dagger, she began to cautiously move through the tunnels; stopping, as she had the first time, at each corner to look around the side. But all was silent, so she carried on.

When it came to the last turn, Coren did not see a well-sized, grey stone on the floor. Her foot kicked it, and the stone went sailing towards the opposite wall, clanging off of it with a loud echo. She desperately attempted to grab onto the wall to keep her balance, wincing at the feeling of the hard stones cutting into her palm.

Footsteps hurried out into the tunnel just one turn away from Coren. Swiftly, the Dark Mage flattened herself as well as she could against the cool wall.

"Who's there?" A woman's voice called out, cautious and slightly terrified, "… Jakan? Larson? Izak?"

Coren stopped breathing for a short moment.

Izak had been down here. He knew what was going on. Incredulity filled her. *How could you?* She wanted to shout at him, but forced herself to think clearly. Izak, solemn-faced and resigned, *Izak,* had exchanged kind words with her once, it didn't mean that she knew him or should have any kind of expectations of the things he would or would not allow to happen.

Still, he had told her she had a good heart, and seemed to think well of her as a person. Such words were not so comforting against the symphony of cruelness within her own mind, especially with new found knowledge that he was the type of person to condone the torture of children.

The woman's footsteps began to get closer and closer to the turn in the corridor that would surely lead her to Coren. Raising her dagger up, her mind was running wild with what she should do should the woman turn the corner and discover her.

Hesitantly, but desperately, Coren called out to her Darkness: *hey, you wouldn't mind... covering me? Or something?*

In response, her Darkness lashed out, crashing into the ceiling above her. Coren stifled a scream as several parts of it fell down opposite her.

Very helpful, she told it in frustration, hearing the other woman yelp yet continue surging forwards. Closer, and closer.

Coren's mind whirled quickly. So, the Darkness wasn't going to respond to hesitance or desperation. It always responded on its own terms when powered by emotion. Lack of emotion and no hesitance, she could try this.

I command you to shield me in shadows, she told it,

uncertainty still lingering. Nothing happened. Coren wanted to shout in frustration, but quickly dispersed the emotion.

Clouding herself in apathy, she mentally ground out, *I command you to cover me. Now.*

The shadows shifted slightly at her sides. Areas that had previously escaped the brightness of the torches lightened up, as the dark pulled towards Coren like a magnet. In and in and in. Her heart leapt in victory, she had done it, she had controlled them, she had –

As quickly as the shadows had been gathering, they fled away from her.

While she had succeeded in calling them to her; she had failed to keep them.

It was too late now to attempt to control her Darkness once more. Instead, Coren grabbed a large rock from the ground and waited, baiting her breath. Just as the woman turned the corner, Coren leapt, bashing her hard in the head with the rock.

The woman dropped to the floor.

The Dark Mage grimaced as she looked down at the woman, hoping the hit hadn't killed her. Though Mages, which Coren was now certain this woman was thanks to the uniform she shared with the other Body Mages, could not be permanently killed by anything but the eight-days-fire and willow mage stakes. Dying temporarily hurts still and leaves some nasty after effects, such as extreme fatigue.

Despite wishing that she hadn't hit hard enough to kill her, Coren did hope that it had been ferocious enough to give her some kind of memory loss. If not, then she

would likely be in more than a little bit of trouble.
In hindsight, she really should have thought this plan
through better.

Moving past the woman's body, Coren rounded the
corner and could see into the room she had previously
observed, before Zarola had made her dramatic
entrance.

It appeared, from this angle at least, that the woman
had been working alone, with only her patient for
company. Before stepping into the room, Coren
pressed herself to the wall outside the door, peering
around so that she could have a full scope of the room.
Empty.

Swiftly, she slunk into the room, all but racing over to
where the patient was contained. Looking down at a
young girl who possessed dark, wild curls and ghost-
like skin, Coren opened one side of the tube to feel for
a pulse, and tightly shut her eyes when she found none.
"I'm sorry," she whispered to the girl, who could have
been no more than eight, "I'm so sorry."

As she wiped away at her silent tears a thought hit her,
one that hadn't even crossed her mind last time. Her
entire body stilled. Were these children all Mages? If
they were, how were they dying? There were no stakes
or fires...

Coren's gaze moved to the left of the tube, where she
again saw the vials of various, dark liquids. Walking
closer to it, she realised that the colour of the vials was,
in fact, a dark red, and that they were numbered from
one to eight.

Cautiously, she picked up number seven, spinning

around to observe it closer to the lab's only light.

Eight. A very specific endpoint, and one that had a lot of significance within the Mage world. Eight days aflame to kill a Mage, eight Gods, eight Mage groups... Coren looked sharply back towards the vials.

An idea began to form within her mind, one that surely could not be true... No. *No.* There was no way that somebody could be mad enough to try that.

All but slamming the vial back into its holder, Coren fled the room, heading back the way she came from at a startling speed. Turning the corner, she almost tripped over the woman's body but kept on going and going.

Somebody was trying to find a way to change human children into Mages within the palace walls, and if they succeeded, Coren shuddered to think of the consequences for Galaris.

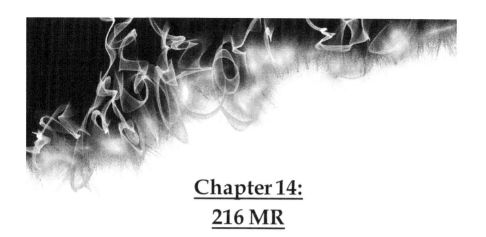

Chapter 14:
216 MR

*R*eaching her chambers for the second time that

night, Coren slipped past Lan with ease, remembering to place the Mage's Bane and key back, before entering her chambers and slowly shutting the door. Once it was fully closed, she slumped back against the door and tried to catch her breath.

Someone was trying to create more Mages within the palace walls. Someone was trying to create more Mages within the palace walls. Someone was trying to create more Mages within the palace walls. The words kept on echoing around her mind but she could still barely believe them.

Was it the King? Was he trying to raise an army against the northern rebels? Though he said to her that the rebellion was not large, he could have been lying but... Why? With his kind of powers, and with his guard filled with Mage legacies, destroying that rebellion surely wouldn't be difficult enough for him to create an entire Mage army to try to best them with?

What if it wasn't the King at all? What if it was the rebels, or some highly ranked guard striving to overthrow the King?

What if-

"You've certainly been out late."

Coren startled at the familiar voice penetrating the darkness of her chambers, before moving over to her bedside table and dropping the dagger atop it.

"Zarola," Coren greeted.

All the things that Coren had wanted to say to her had somehow flown out of her head at the sound of her voice. There had been so much she had wanted to shout and ask but now, nothing.

Frustration seeping into her voice, Zarola ground out, "I can't believe that you would go back out into the walls after I warned you not to."

Ah, there it was. The anger that she had felt when she had been screaming Zarola's name after returning to her chambers from Caradoc's; it burned in her veins alike to how the Darkness had when it had been released from the Mage's Bane.

But this time, it wasn't fire burning in her veins, but ice. Coren gritted her teeth together, but did not respond. Instead, she knelt to the ground by her bedside, and reached her hand under it. From there, she pulled out a dagger identical to the one that she had kept on her arm.

Carefully, she chucked it sideways towards the end of

the bed, where Zarola sat. The Dark Mage's voice was cold when she informed the redhead, "I believe this is yours."

"I gave it to you. You can keep it."

"It's the other dagger."

Zarola was silent. Squinting in the harsh darkness, Coren could just about see the other girl pick the dagger up, holding it in her lap. When she continued to not say anything, Coren laughed harshly, the anger from today's failures, Zarola's previous words, and now her silence pushing her over the edge, "what, no more reprimands? No more 'I can't believe's from you? You want to know what I can't believe? That one day you're kissing me and the next you're holding a dagger to my throat. How dare you come here and reprimand me for my actions when-,"

Before Coren could finish, she was no longer standing. Having sprung from her place at the foot of the bed, Zarola had grasped onto the back of her cloak, sending her tumbling onto the mattress. Coren didn't have the time to react, before Zarola was straddling her with the twin dagger held to her throat.

"Like this, you mean?" The other girl spoke, their positions mirroring that of the night of the fight. Coren swallowed, and the dagger dug in slightly, nicking at pale skin. Despite the pressure, Coren continued to glower at the girl.

"I wouldn't be reprimanding you," Zarola told her harshly, the dagger biting into Coren's throat more cruelly now, "if you weren't making such foolish decisions. Running off into palace walls, then trying to charge to the rescue of children whose death certificates were signed the moment they were caught by Snatchers, all but signing yourself over to a King who doesn't give a crap about you-,"

Zarola's words came to a halt, a short, thoughtful silence breaking through. Then, Coren could make out a smile forming on her lips. It wasn't kind.

"Is that why you signed your freedom over to the King? Because you like him," Zarola laughed slightly and humiliation surged up in Coren. It was only half-true. She certainly did not give Caradoc five months of being able to control her powers because of her attraction to him, it was for power, but such an attraction was still there. Zarola continued; "I bet he already knows that, that he's begun to be more physical with you," at this, Zarola's free hand moved to Coren's face, where she stroked her cheek, "inciting your fancy further. What better way to control the one you need, than by making them need you?"

Rageful, Coren hooked one foot behind Zarola's leg, flipping them over and ripping the redhead's dagger from her hands, so that now she was the one trapped and unarmed.

Coren made no move to put the dagger she now possessed up to the human's neck. Instead, she observed Zarola. Her eyes simmered with rage and... jealousy? Well, that was certainly an emotion that could be used against her.

Lowering herself down onto her elbows so she could reach Zarola's ear, she told her quietly, "and that just fills you with rage, doesn't it? That I might need and want him, instead of you? You're tormented by the image of the King, the horrible King that you're rebelling against, together with the one you wish you didn't want."

Coren pulled back from Zarola's ear, instead keeping her face hovering just above Zarola's own. She didn't spare a single thought for her actions, the only thing she cared about right now was her rage and need to know. With Zarola unwittingly watching her lips with dark eyes, Coren asked her, "what's going on in the palace walls?"

Zarola's eyes flickered up to Coren's own, filled with wrath and humiliation, "get off of me."

The blonde swiftly retreated, moving aside so that Zarola could pull herself back up. Both were silent, individually stewing in their own emotions, before Coren finally asked, "did you know that they're trying to change human children into Mages down there? Is this for your rebel army? Is it for one of the guards to take over the throne?"

"Of course, it couldn't be your precious King that's to blame," Zarola told her bitterly, standing up from the bed and smoothing out her skirts, before tugging her slightly bloodied dagger out of Coren's grasp, "and you're not even correct about what's going on down there. The children aren't humans, they're Mages. Maybe you should try out your pathetic seduction attempts on your King, and find out the rest for yourself."

Zarola waited for a moment, no doubt expecting a barbed response shot back from Coren, but the blonde was already deep into her own thoughts.

As far as Coren had known, the only way to kill a Mage was with the eight-days-fire or with a willow mage stake, so what in the name of the Gods were they doing to those poor children down there that actually killed them? It shouldn't be possible.

And yet it was happening.

Finally breaking out of her thoughts, Coren asked the question that had been harshly pressing at her ever since she realised that Zarola was a part of the rebel group. "Why are you rebelling?"

The redhead, who had already almost reached the maids' chamber by that time, looked fleetingly back at her, one hand already atop the door knob, "if I told you, you wouldn't believe me."

Coren went to protest, but Zarola had already passed through the door and closed it with a firm but quiet *click!*

The next morning was Sunday, and Coren had no lessons from the King nor Milo and Izak scheduled. It was a relief, considering yesterday's discoveries.

Despite this, Coren did not stay in bed past dawn. Instead, before her maids had the chance to enter her chamber, she ventured into the palace in search of an empty room to try and practice controlling her powers. Even if she hadn't fully succeeded yesterday, the shadows had momentarily moved according to her whim, and she wanted to investigate further to see if a state of apathy was, indeed, a way to keep her powers under control before achieving the Connection.

Unfortunately for her, Coren's attempt at having a quiet morning of practice was shown to be futile when she saw a rather tired looking Izak waiting outside of her chambers. When he saw her, he attempted a small smile but it didn't quite reach his eyes.

Looking past him, Coren froze when she saw a cluster of guards opposite the tapestry depicting the War of Kings, with the woman she had knocked out yesterday in the centre of them, looking so frightened it was as if her life was in jeopardy.

With a sinking feeling in her stomach, Coren wondered if it actually was. Would whoever was controlling what was going on down there have her killed for this? For something that Coren had done? But that woman had been hurting children, so should she truly care what becomes of her?

Quickly trying to control her expression, Coren asked Izak, attempting to make her tone one of confusion opposed to horror, "what's going on over there?"

"A woman was attacked last night in this hallway," Izak told her quietly, "they're trying to get her to identify her assailant, but all she keeps on muttering is green and dark."

"How awful," Coren murmured, and watched as Izak nodded to her words.

She would have been thankful to leave the conversation there, if Coren hadn't seen one of the

147

guards grab onto the woman's wrist in a tight, bruising grip. Coren didn't think before she started towards the group, Izak desperately calling out her name from behind her.

Suddenly, Coren did stop. But it was not because of Izak.

"Where are they?" The guard gripping onto her wrist interrogated roughly, towering over the smaller Body Mage in an attempt to intimidate her, "where are the blood vials?"

The blood vials?

A meek, shaking voice answered him, "I-I-I don't know. Something, someone, knocked me out and I can't remember anything," the woman began to sob, "please, he has to believe me, I don't know who took them! All I saw was green. Green. Green!"

Coren looked back towards Izak, whose expression was grave and regretful.

Just then, Milo appeared, sauntering down the hallway, frowning lightly when he saw the woman, before maintaining his approach towards Coren. He looked at Izak, who was only a few paces behind Coren now. Milo must have communicated with him mentally, because Izak nodded and left soon after, handing over his Mage's Bane and Bane Key to Milo.

Where are you off to today, blondie? He inquired, pointedly ignoring the guards behind him, who were now taking the near-hysterical Body Mage away.

Desperately, Coren attempted to make sure that no thoughts of last night's activities made their way into her head, lest Milo discover that she was there, and for her to be accused of stealing the blood vials. Or learn anything about Zarola.

As much as she liked Milo, she hadn't even known him for one moon cycle, so she wasn't going to put her complete trust in him.

I was looking for somewhere private to practise my magic, the Dark Mage informed him, *as far away from the majority of the palace's population as I can get. And away from any rooms the King's particularly fond of. Do you know a place?*

Milo nodded at her, turning around and gesturing for her to follow. Coren frowned slightly, it was very unlike Milo to be so quiet. Regardless, she followed, noting that they were heading towards the northern areas of the palace.

They walked in silence for a bit, Milo leading and Coren enjoying the scenic views outside of the Golden Palace's large windows. Eventually, Coren glimpsed the maze at the end of the northern gardens, and fought a shudder as she recalled the feeling of poison rushing through her system. With a furrowing of her brows, she suddenly recalled the stone lady, her encounter with whom she had forgotten amongst the chaos of that night.

She briefly tried to recall all of the strange mutterings of the woman, before asking Milo, "do you know what Malva means? It is not Galarian."

Milo looked back at her with his face scrunched up in thought, "I don't think so. Why do you ask?"

"A dream," Coren told him with a careless shrug. If she didn't know its significance, then she was not about to tell someone she didn't entirely trust about it, "and also something about a descentation to do with the Gods?" The Dark Mage was more than a little bit startled when Milo appeared to burst out laughing, stopping his long strides to turn around and playfully flick Coren's nose. She frowned at him. "I think someone has been reading one too many folktale stories before bedtime."

Ignoring his jibing, Coren questioned, "folktale stories?"

"Yes," he told her, turning around so that he could continue walking. Coren ran a little to catch up with his long strides, "you know, the folk tales of Mad Marion the Mind Mage? Every Mage child has heard of them." After a moment, he shot Coren an apologetic look, clearly having remembered that she had not been raised as a Mage.

"Can you tell me about them?"

Milo frowned in thought, but nodded, "I can't remember much now, it's been about a hundred years since I've read them, or had them read to me. Most just centre around 'the end of the world'," he said the last part dramatically, wiggling his fingers at Coren and laughing slightly, "crazy, the writer was. Lost her mind trying to scry. Anyway, she would mutter about the Malva and the most terrible war the continents had ever seen. She called it the War of Realms; I think. Apparently, the Gods would descend, the First Mage would be freed and, well, everything would go to shit. There are loads of different versions and translations."

Well, Coren had definitely never heard about that. The only fear-evoking bedtime stories she had ever been told were about the evil God of Death, who grew horns from his head and had spider's legs, and his Mages who liked to eat small children. Mina, before being taken by the Snatchers, had always found those stories particularly amusing, requesting Coren's father tell her them over and over.

"Are there any books about this in the library?" Coren asked. Milo offered her an amused look but nodded, calling a servant over and asking them to request for the librarian to have books on Galarian folklore be sent to Coren's chambers.

This just made Coren more confused than she already was, "we have a librarian?"

"Yes, pernicious Peta," he let out a shudder, eyes full of dramatic warning as he turned to her, placing both hands on her shoulders and bending so he could look her straight in the eyes, "hurt one of his books and he shall hurt you."

Coren's lips quirked up, "what did you do to him?" Milo's faux-innocent expression was fooling no one.

"I may or may not have accidentally tripped and doused some of the white books in hot chocolate," Milo told her, "but it was an accident! It's not my fault that the chair simply moved into my path! If you want my opinion, the chair was trying to sabotage me."

"You're a hazard," Coren told him, laughing. They both continued to move down the hallway, Milo casually pointing to various tapestries and telling her stories of what was depicted upon them; stories that grew slowly more and more outlandish.

Once they had finally arrived at the room, Milo bowed deeply, before opening the door to allow her through.

151

As she walked through, Coren stomped on his foot. Hard. And grinned at his sound of pain.

Being with Milo reminded her a lot of how her relationship with her brothers used to be, all teasing and play fighting and cheeky smiles. It made her wistful for a moment, before she recalled the feeling of Jolon's hands around her neck and how he'd looked, bleeding in the midst of the wreckage that had once been their home.

Milo, knowing her thoughts, put a hand upon her shoulder. Smiling in thanks at his attempt at comfort, she gently took his hand off of her shoulder, telling him *I'm here for training, not pity. Trust me, I give myself enough of the latter.*

Or maybe not enough, Milo countered as Coren surveyed the room, amazed that it was rectangle shaped for once, *calling yourself a monster every other hour-*

"Don't," Coren cut him off aloud. Milo nodded, though harboured a displeased expression, retreating to a cream leather sofa at the far side of the room.

This room, Coren decided, observing it in a quick sweep whilst choosing where was best to train in the hopes that her powers wouldn't go surging for Milo, was far more to her preferences than the rest of the palace. It was less clustered, with just some cream furniture, a brown, fluffy rug, and an unlit fireplace. Coren loved beautiful, intricate decorations as much as the next person, but disliked too many objects surrounding her; confining her. It reminded her of the time her mother had locked her in the small chicken

152

coop for talking to Mr. Deiri out of turn. All night, she had lain on her front in chicken droppings, legs and arms bent to accommodate for the small space. There had been only darkness.

Something slammed onto the floor, and Coren winced, remembering Milo. She didn't look at him, simply retreated from her memories and moved to the opposite side of the room.

Coren-

Please, stop.

Closing her eyes, she focused on trying to get to a state of apathy that she could maintain. Internally, she imagined a wave of calm travelling from the top of her head all the way down her body, sinking past her stomach and down her legs.

I care for nothing. I care for nothing. I care for nothing. I am in control. I am in control. I am in control.

She repeated the process several times, opening her eyes only when she felt a sense of indifference take over her. Nodding to herself, she brought both her hands out in front of her, ignoring the unnerving feeling of Milo's eyes upon her.

I command you to rise up, she told her Darkness, *to create a ball of Darkness in my hands.*

It was daylight, so there were only a few shadows in the room residing behind the sparse furniture. Despite that, a few of them moved to join her eagerly. In her hands, she had a small ball of darkness, half the size of a child's ball.

Looking around the room, Coren saw that other shadows still remained, such as the ones behind Milo's sofa. She frowned, indifference giving way to irritation, and the Darkness immediately abandoned her, fleeing to hide from the harsh sun behind the furniture once more.

Ashamed, she didn't want to meet Milo's eyes. She hadn't been a good example of a daughter or a sister or even a friend to Mina, who she failed to save, and now she couldn't even be a good example of a monster. Despair hit her hard, filling her throat, but she refused to choke upon it. She refused to drown in failure when she could live in eventual freedom, in success.

Closing her eyes, she imagined a wave of calm travelling down her once more, sweeping the despair away with its slow but powerful force.

I care for nothing. I care for nothing. I care for nothing. I am in control. I am in control. I am in control.

Her inner voice was as cold and demanding as any wartime Commander as she hissed at her Darkness, hands out in front of her, *you will come to me. You will form a ball of Darkness within my hands, for me to command as I see fit. You will come because I am Darkness, thus you are me.*

This time, every shadow in the room came towards her, their approach as swift as they filled her hands with their essence. In her state of indifference, Coren offered the Darkness a cold smile. The Darkness did not smile back.

You will shoot towards the door, but you will not destroy it. You will simply crash harmlessly against it, and then disperse.

The Darkness did as she commanded, hitting the door

before fleeing away from her as if she were diseased. To the Darkness, Coren supposed, she probably was. After all, she had not yet made the Connection.

"Impressive," came Milo's voice, Coren whirled around, having forgotten he was there, "I've only met a couple of Dark Mages, so I always forget how powerful they are. That they can somewhat control their magic even without the Connection. But that's as much as you'll be able to do without it. You'll only be able to call shadows and darkness that already exists to you, rather than creating it from nothing; the Darkness will never truly respect or accept you as its wielder and you'd maybe be able to take down a hundred humans with the power you could grow to Connectionless, whereas I've seen a Dark Mage kill thousands with a single bout of magic."

The idea of having the power to kill thousands sent a bolt of fear through her, though she quickly reassured herself that she'll have learnt to control her powers by then; she'll have made the Connection. She won't hurt anyone.

Coren would never admit that there was a small, small part of her that liked that idea. That she would have that kind of power.

"I've created Darkness from nothing before," Coren told him.

"Was your life in danger? Were you being hurt?" Coren thought back to those few times, with the blonde man, her mother and her brother. In those instances, there had been shadows around but not enough to make up the entirety of the ruthless attack. Milo didn't even need her to nod, reading her mind, before he

155

continued on, "that's why. Mind Mages, Dark Mages and especially Death Mages are known for having their magic react very violently when threatened, achieving heights of their power that they aren't supposed to be capable of. Many think it's because there's a lot fewer of us. In the last five hundred years, there's been only eighty-five Mind Mages, twelve Dark Mages and six Death Mages."

Coren nodded, deeming the prospect as reasonable enough, before she asked, "are there any other Dark Mages alive? I haven't ever met any, and I haven't heard of any whilst at the castle."

"None in Galaris," Milo told her, his voice tense, "not for a while."

Observing him, his frown, tension and refusal to meet her eyes, Coren said more than asked, "Caradoc killed them all, didn't he?"

Milo didn't say anything, which was answer enough.

"If he killed all the other Dark Mages, then why has he left me alive?" she asked, her mind already whirling through all the possibilities. It was obvious why he had killed them: their power posed a threat to him. But why, then, was he encouraging her to grow more powerful? Why is he trying to get her to make the Connection and promising her freedom?

Milo looked at her gravely, "you'll have to ask the King all of that, I can't give you any answers," Coren nodded, and Milo swiftly began to change the subject, "also, by your thoughts when you were trying to summon your magic, I'm guessing you were trying to feel cold or indifferent?"

Indifferent, Coren informed him.

Milo continued on, "although it will be a lot more difficult, if you want to try to get to the full amount of power that you can control Connectionless, then I'd recommend trying to lure the Darkness with a very strong emotion. But you have to have full control over this feeling, or the effects will be disastrous. Magic with emotion is magic given more power. But, the fact that a recognisable feeling can be manipulated by us, rather than simply a hollowness, gives us a better hold on it." She thanked Milo for his information, but, remembering the times her emotions had fuelled her magic, Coren decided to stick with apathy for now. So, the Dark Mage moved back to her position in the corner and began her calming process once more.

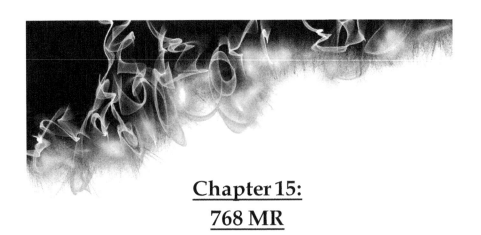

Chapter 15:
768 MR

*A*uryon, Captain of the Queen's Guard, remained
stationary in the corner of the room; silent as death.
Her expression did not so much as twitch as she
watched one of the Queen's Guards, her guards, be
hoisted into the air, vines of Darkness wrapping around
his throat and squeezing so harshly that the man's face
began to turn blue.

Like a vengeful wraith, her Queen approached the
young guard, the train of her deep black dress sliding
behind her like a serpent's tail; her golden head
crowned by the Darkness that smiled back at her.
When Coren was finally in front of the man, she had
the Darkness lower him down somewhat, allowing her
to place her hands either side of his face.

She drew so close to the man, if he could even be called
that yet due to his youth, that it was almost as if she
were going to kiss him, but Auryon knew that was the
last thing she would be doing.

"Are you telling me," Coren hissed at him, grey-green eyes alight with cold fury, dark red lips clenched in an unyielding line, "that, under the supervision of you and your fellow guard unit, a pathetic *human* man managed to get into my vault, steal three willow mage stakes, destroy every document we have on human rebels and kill not one, but *two* of my highest-ranking Mage guards?"

Auryon kept any pity far from her expression as a wet stain darkened the front of the man's breeches. The last thing she needed was the Queen's ire directed at her, especially when it had been her nephew who had committed such thievery and deception.

"Answer me," the Night Queen screamed at him, striking the man when he would not answer. The Captain of the Queen's Guard suspected the man wasn't choosing not to speak, but rather couldn't thanks to Coren's chokehold upon him.

Suddenly, the Queen released him.

The man fell to the floor with a crash, sobbing and clutching his throat. Snot was dribbling down his face by the time he had recovered enough to crawl from where he had been lying in a heap towards the Queen, thanking her and apologising with every breath he could spare. He went to kiss her feet but she kicked him, hard, in the stomach, as if he were nothing more than an inconvenient object in her path.

Those bright, furious eyes lifted to Auryon, and the Captain swiftly moved forward, dropping to a knee before the Queen. She didn't dare raise her head. Not after what Hearne had done.

159

"Have this man, and every other guard that was on duty last night taken to the cells. With one of the few mage stakes that *your nephew* did not manage to get his filthy, human hands upon, they will all be executed immediately," Coren told her, looking down in disgust when the man, who could not be more than twenty-one, carried on sobbing and repeating 'no', trying to move towards her feet once more. Her lip curled up as she continued, "there will be no mercy for incompetence."

At this, Auryon hesitantly looked up, "the guards from last night are, indeed, incompetents, my Queen, and you are right to punish them harshly... But we do not have enough guards, I-,"

"Then I will employ some more!" The Queen shouted, one hand shooting out to send a surge of Darkness towards a lamp in the corner of the room. Upon impact, it exploded, glass sprinkling against the wall behind it. Upon the Queen's head, the crown of shadows thickened from a dark grey to black. Auryon barely retained a flinch. "You're lucky I'm not throwing you in the cells like the rest of them. Don't think that I haven't considered it."

Auryon nodded, and the Queen turned her back to her. Now out of the Queen's line of sight, the Captain sent her once friend a desperate, piteous look; her heart sinking. Shaking her devastation away, she quickly moved about to set the Queen's demands into motion. She began by carefully lifting up the hysterical man and hauling him to the doors, where she commanded one of the guards standing out there, who looked

160

rather close to creating his own wet stain beneath his armour, to carry him to the cells. Then, she returned to round up the rest.

The Captain knew that the Night Queen, High Ruler of the Galarian Empire, would have killed or severely punished anyone else for a family member's betrayal. Most who went against her had their entire family line butchered, or worse. But not Auryon. It gave her hope, too much hope for her to bear, that the Coren she once knew was somewhere beneath the surface. Even after all these years.

Tears that she had already cried, over and over, threatened to resurface as she thought of her friend; her sister in arms.

Still, every time she went into battle, the image from five hundred and fifty-two years ago played in her head. A hand had been offered, raising the tearful Auryon from the ground, as bright, kind eyes offered her the courage, the belief, that she needed.

"It doesn't matter what anyone else thinks. It doesn't matter whether or not he thinks you can do it. I believe in you, Auryon, and if you begin to truly believe in yourself, then I think that fight today was the last sword-fight you will ever lose."

It was then that Auryon had decided she would fight to her last breath alongside this woman.

The Captain hadn't fought to her last breath, of course, but many others had. The dark-haired guard shut her eyes and desperately swallowed down the bile that rose in her throat as she recalled Coren, crawling through hot, thick blood and over torn limbs to Commander

Zarola's body. Her screams of anguish would forever echo within Auryon's head, and she didn't think that she would ever forget the Darkness that followed.

The Darkness that still reigns now.

No, Auryon would never leave Coren. She was her friend, no matter what she had become. One day, she hoped, she pleaded to any God that would listen, her friend will come back to her once more.

The female guard knew that Coren would never be the exact woman she had once been, five hundred and fifty odd years in Darkness and despair would leave their mark, but some of her best qualities – her ability to love, to care, to see those who were overlooked – Auryon wanted to see those come to the surface once more.

Some of the men and women cried as they were staked, others yelled out in anger, and some simply sat there, staring death in the face and patiently awaiting its claim.

The Queen watched every single one of them die, her expression still. In the beginning, Auryon had hated that expression; its lack of a small quirk of the lips and determined glint of the eyes. There was nothing.

Now, the Captain had become used to it, her apathy towards death, even if she would still check the other woman's face for any sign of feeling each time.

Once the last guard had died, a woman, one of the patient ones, Coren turned to Auryon. The glint in her eyes was nearing manic as she commanded of her, "I want you to send your best riders after your nephew and his companions. Tell those who ride out that they can kill them however they like, but I would appreciate their hearts and entrails brought back as gifts. And maybe a head or two."

When she grinned, the Queen showcased her gleaming, milky teeth. The Captain swallowed harshly. Hearne was one of the last reminders she had left of her sister. There was only him and Jesalin from her line left now. She couldn't... She couldn't order his death.

Closing her eyes, Auryon prayed she wasn't singing her own death warrant at last, when she said, "forgive me, Your Majesty, but would it not be wiser to have them watched first? To take the risk of breaking into your vault to get the stakes... They must be planning something. Something large. We should learn of it, to ensure that no others will think to follow in their footsteps."

It was shaky reasoning, but the Queen was not always completely... *there* in the mind department, if Auryon were to be blunt, so she was hopeful that she would listen.

The golden-haired woman looked thoughtful for a moment, eyes narrowed, before she turned to Auryon, displaying their suspicious yet pleased gleam, "a fair point, Captain. I still want all the best riders you have going after your nephew, but they will not kill him or his companions, not yet. I want to know exactly what he is planning before I have them all slaughtered. Anything that they do, anyone that they interact with – dead or alive – I want them brought back to me."

Auryon nodded tightly, gesturing for her guards to leave the room and begin preparations. The Captain went to follow them, but the Night Queen's voice sounded from behind her, and Auryon turned to show that she had her full attention, "do not fail me, Auryon. Your nephew may have stolen three of my stakes, but, as you have seen, I still have five left. And the urge to redecorate."

She swallowed. The Captain knew exactly what she was alluding to. Upon each turret of the Black Castle, four heads of traitors resided, along with one in the main hall, where the Queen often had everyone feast so that her Mind Mages could use such dinners to search for traitors. The one in the main hall was beginning to smell, thus the Queen would be having it replaced with a new one before tomorrow's meal.

And Auryon certainly did not wish for it to hers.

"I will not fail you, Your Majesty," Auryon told her, bowing (curtseying, in her heavy armour, being rather impractical) before leaving. She would like to think that the Queen's threat was empty, that she would continue to spare Auryon as she had for the past five hundred years but, as of late, the Queen's mental state had been deteriorating at a rapid rate. More outbursts, more cruelty. It was as if the Darkness had been slowly taking over her for the past half a millennium, its grip growing stronger and stronger each day that passed in a world without Commander Zarola.

Despite this, Auryon thought back at the Queen, who was now staring indifferently down at the body of the last woman, *I'm not giving up on you, Coren. I've stood by you for five hundred years, and, if you don't kill me first, I'll stand by you for five hundred more.*

As far away as their relentless riding could get them, the three traitors to the Queen dashed through woods and fields of corn, the one in the centre smiling widely. At this pace, they would be at Andern after just two nights. Then, his world-rightening rebellion could truly begin.

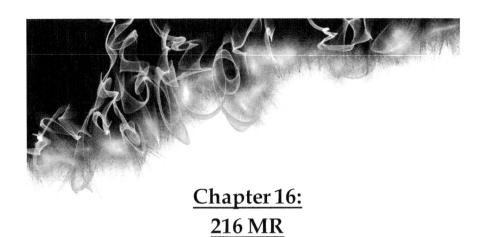

Chapter 16:
216 MR

The floor beneath her feet was familiar in its

roughness, as was the shuddering, hastily made wooden walls that surrounded her. In the centre of the room was a small, rickety table with wobbling chairs pushed in beneath it. In one corner was a small stove, and the rest of the room was bare; empty with the exception of the memories it confined. Memories of lessons, of hurt, of desperation.

When Coren had begun to carefully craft her mind landscape, this had been the last place that she had expected to take form. But take form it did. At the sight of it, she hadn't been able to hold back the hysterical laugh that bubbled out of her throat.

Even when it was no longer standing, that room, that shack, still haunted her.

"The black line," a voice prompted from the outside, echoing around the fragile walls, "do you see it?"

Looking to one of the many chairs, her chair, she could see a small thread tied around it, right where she used to grip it as the bones in her fingers were brutally snapped. It was also the

same place where her back became her mother's canvas of pain, Coren's fingers going white from the tight hold she had maintained. Walking towards it, she placed one hand on the table – not on the chair, never again on the chair – and she wrapped a pinky around the black line.

"Yes," she breathed inside her landscape, hoping that it projected to the outside world. To Caradoc.

"Good," the voice told her, and she could imagine his contented smile, "follow it."

She hooked her finger around the line. It was hard and thin like wire. Step after step, she continued on her journey, soon meeting the wall of the small shack. When she got to it, Coren knew that if she walked into it, she would simply go straight through it.

So, she did.

On the other side of the unpleasantly familiar shack, was the Darkness. No light managed to wade its way into the endless nothing, thus each step Coren took was navigated only by the wire, now no longer visible, that her pinkie was still latched onto.

Most people associate Darkness with cold, but Coren felt nothing. No warmth, no coolness, no breeze; there was only stillness and an anticipation that settled low in her stomach and slowly began to stir itself.

There was something waiting for her in the Dark.

One step. Another. They were no longer hers, no, something else had seized control of her, marching her down the path of nothing towards... something.

Towards her, the Darkness whispered, and Coren felt her throat swell with nerves.

Left. Right. Left. Right. Left. Right. Left. Right. Left. Right. Left. Right. Left-

She stopped.

From all around her, the Darkness appeared to be being sucked away. Something, someone, was pulling it towards a certain spot, directly in front of Coren.

The blonde was surprised to discover that waiting behind the Darkness, reclaiming its space, was light. By the time the figure had fully formed, the place the Darkness had occupied was illuminated by the colour white so intensely that Coren's eyes closed and squinted in an attempt to acclimatise to it.

When her vision was fully returned to her, she could do nothing but stare at the figure before her. A woman.

A Goddess.

Nias, the Goddess of Darkness, though not what Coren had been expecting, fit her role perfectly. The Goddess was not classically beautiful; her face was not perfectly symmetrical, her skin not flawless, her lips thin and lacking the coveted bow structure. But her eyes were the most beautiful that Coren had ever seen.

The Goddess' eyes were so dark a brown they were almost black; the dark swirls were unusually expressive, speaking of Nias' keen intelligence and the blazing fire that lay beneath her cool exterior.

For a moment, the Goddess simply watched Coren with a kind of stillness that no mortal would ever possess. Soon enough, her thin, pale lips curved downwards in displeasure, before she reached out a hand towards Coren.

Warily, Coren reached out her right hand in response, which the Goddess swiftly latched onto, yanking the blonde forwards with a force that sent her stumbling. This appeared to amuse her.

With Coren in her grasp, the Goddess, taller than her, yanked her chin up to meet those soulful eyes.

"Not yet," Nias said as a thrum of power seemed to transfer from the Goddess' fingers into Coren's wrist. Her veins went black as the Dark power travelled towards her chest, "you don't have anything to offer me; anything to lose. But soon, my Mage."

With that, the Goddess dropped her wrist, and began to move away from her with several long, backwards strides. As she did so, parts of her began to fade away, becoming Darkness once more.

Before she could fully disperse, Coren called out, "wait!"

To her surprise, the Goddess paused, raising one dark, finely crafted brow in her direction.

"What will I have to lose for the Connection?"

Nias smiled at her. "Everything."

Then, the Goddess disappeared entirely, and Coren was left with nothing but Darkness.

She waited. Her mind was paused upon the one word from the Goddess; dread began to settle in her stomach, pushing bile up towards her throat.

Everything, she had said.
Closing her eyes, Coren reassured herself that it was
nothing worth despairing over. After all, how high was
the price of everything to someone who had nothing
worth losing?
At last, she said, hoping the King would hear her, "I'm
ready to leave, Caradoc."
With that, he began to help guide her out of her own
mind, coaxing her from the Dark and back to reality.

Soon enough, Coren was opening her eyes with a sharp
intake of breath. Grey-green eyes took a moment to
adjust to the change in lighting, before she looked over
to the Fire King who was hovering over her, brows
scrunched together as if in concern.
She didn't allow herself to believe it was actual concern.
She couldn't.
A large, warm hand placed itself on her back, helping to
move her into a sitting position as a glass of water was
placed in her hands. When she opened her mouth to
drink it, she was surprised at how dry her throat felt.
Quickly, she downed nearly the entire glass.
Caradoc allowed her a couple of moments to gather
herself, before he inquired, "what happened?"
"I saw her," Coren blurted swiftly in response, still
taken aback by the fact that she had seen an actual
Goddess, "Nias. Her eyes, they're so-," she cleared her
throat, deciding that Caradoc probably didn't want to
hear her gush about how fascinating the Goddess' eyes
were, "she grabbed onto my wrist and I felt something,

like some of her power moved into me or something. But she told me 'not yet', and left."

Coren didn't want to tell him about what the Goddess Nias had said she was waiting for. It felt too personal. Observing him, she saw that the Fire King's jaw clenched slightly, perhaps in frustration, but he nodded, telling her, "that feeling, the power moving to you, that was the Promise Connection. Did you read about that in the book I told you to find?"

Thinking back, Coren could briefly recall the term, she nodded and explained, "the book didn't really go into what it was, but it was mentioned."

"It's not a true Connection," he said, placing his fist under his chin, elbow leaning upon his left leg, "it's like... how before one gets married or even betrothed, they enter a courtship. The Goddess Nias is suggesting that she is interested in fulfilling her claim on you as one of her Mages, but isn't assured of the commitment just yet."

Trying to ignore spiralling into fear and self-doubt, Coren grinned at him and said, "so, you're telling me that a Goddess is interested in me? How dreadful for my admirers, none of them would ever be able to compare!"

The King leaned his face towards her, "what if one such admirer had a castle, and a throne? How may he compare then?"

Coren scrunched her face up in thought.

"A castle, a throne or a place in the city of the Ascended with a Goddess possessing the most striking of eyes?" She questioned aloud, turning to look at him fully,

171

"you'll have to tell that admirer that they've got a challenge on their hands, but," Coren's lips pulled up into a smirk, though her heart was beating heavily with nerves as she stared into a different pair of stunning, fiery eyes, "I could still be convinced."

At first, Coren thought that she was imagining the way that Caradoc appeared to be leaning in towards her, his lips inching towards her own. Soon enough, however, when his face was but centimetres away from her own, she could not deny it.

Her eyes became fixated upon his lips, plump and soft looking. With more than two hundred years under his belt, she had no doubt that the King would be a wonderful kisser. It would certainly be a better kiss than the sudden peck that Zarola had bestowed upon her just six weeks prior.

Thinking about that sort-of-kiss saw the redhead's words echoing around her head: *"you like him. I bet he already knows that, that he's begun to be more physical with you, inciting your fancy further. What better way to control the one you need, than by making them need you?"*

Coren pulled back, away from the King.

As much as she would like to believe that he truly returned her attraction towards him, she was unsure, and it was a bad idea to become involved with him even if he was attracted to her. In what way could it end positively? He wanted to use her for reasons still unknown, and she was determined to leave him for some far afield land in less than three and a half-moons.

At her retraction, the King blinked in surprise, but both were spared any awkward conversation by a sharp knock upon the door. Coren heard Caradoc sigh irritably, before he pushed his tall form off of the sofa and moved towards the door.

Sharply, he pulled it open, and Coren was greeted to the sight of a very nervous looking messenger. The poor boy physically recoiled when the Fire King demanded, "out with it, then."

The messenger was just tall enough to see over one of the King's broad shoulders and, when his large, brown eyes caught with Coren's bright ones, he hesitated. That second of hesitation must have brought an expression of ire upon the King's face, because the messenger soon began to talk rapidly, "the Captain of the King's Guard wants to see you at your earliest convenience, Your Majesty, he says that he has a lead on the northern rebels."

"Finally," Caradoc muttered, before the Fire King turned his burning eyes towards Coren, offering her a shark-like grin, "we'll have to resume our conversation at the feast, little Mage, duty calls."

Coren nodded in response, and the King swiftly strode out of the study; the door clicking shut behind him. The Dark Mage waited for several moments, to see if he'd return or ask a servant to see her out. When nobody arrived, she got up from her position on the sofa and moved to his desk.

This, considering her suspicions and curiosities as to what was currently occurring inside the castle, was an opportunity that she could not ignore.

Silently, she spent several moments observing the placement of everything upon his desk, so that she would know exactly how to put it back, before she lifted up some of his correspondences, flicking through them. Most were invitations; to luncheons or weddings. Coren frowned. How dull.

Then she moved onto the next few letters, sighing aloud when she found that it was more of the same. So was the next pile, and the next, but, as Coren was scanning a letter in the following pile, she caught the word 'rebellion' and hurriedly put the other correspondences aside.

Your Majesty,
As we had discussed, I have attempted to place several spies within the ranks of the northern rebellion. Of the spies, one has been able to report back to me at the meeting point. I do not know of the status of the others, who Leon claims have been sent to other encampments, but I will inform you should I hear from them.
Leon has been able to report that the Commander's name is Alyxan. He is a human of around forty years, and is a farmer's son. Very proficient in battle, especially with a bow. I will have Leon search for more information on the Commander, but he says it was Hylla who was sent to the Commander's encampment.
In terms of the rebellion's structure, there are five encampments within the north. One is under the Commander, and the other four under his Secondaries.

Leon has reported that the leader of his encampment is Secondary Cilla, who is, in fact, a Mind Mage; a Mind Mage who has a human family which she has told her encampment about in one of her regular speeches.
Apparently, they are who she is fighting for.
Her family, I have found, live in Gwynythal, not far from the Great Northern Rock. She has three sisters and two brothers, all humans, as well as six nieces and nephews. If you command it so, I can have them seized so that we may lure her out and interrogate her.
Your humble servant,
Maxwell, Duke of Dorcern

If that letter was all the King had previously had on the rebellion, then Coren was not surprised by the lack of patience he had shown the messenger boy. Closing her eyes for a moment, she allowed herself to hope that Caradoc had not taken the Duke up on his offer to seize the Mind Mage's family, but she knew that he would have.

This could lead to a war, she told herself, *what other choice does he have?*

Despite her attempt at rationalising it, an uncomfortable feeling still settled her stomach as she flicked through the rest of the correspondences. There was nothing else of interest, so she began carefully settling them in the slightly askew way they had been when she'd first picked them up. As she was doing so, Coren picked up on the sound of heavy footsteps coming in the direction of the door.

Quickly, her eyes darted towards the sofa, but she knew she would not have the time to run to it and get into a casual position. So, instead, she quickly adjusted the last piece of paper before dropping herself back into Caradoc's study chair.

When the door opened, she was swinging in it. Spinning herself around fully, she saw that it was a tall, slim shouldered man with straight brown hair and brown skin that had entered. Izak. He arched a fine brow in her direction.

"What?" Coren asked, forcing a sheepish expression onto her face, "I wanted to see what kind of seat was deemed fit for a King."

Izak's brow remained raised as he questioned, "and what do you think of the seat?"

Coren looked down at it for a moment, pursing her lips, "a perfectly suitable seat for any royal ass."

The guard rolled his eyes at her, motioning for her to get up and join him at the door. As she moved towards him, she sent one final, fleeting look towards the pile of papers, looking away when she decided that she was content with their arrangement.

It was disappointing. Coren had wanted to be able to rifle through his draws too, but she hoped there would be other opportunities. Maybe he had information on the walls in there.

Once both herself and Izak had left the King's study, the Dark Mage forced her thoughts away from her curiosities. Having been in the castle for nearly two moons, Coren was keenly aware of the fact that the

King had Mind Mages in his employ. Instead, she turned to the guard, inquiring, "how's Jakan? Will he be at the feast tonight?"

She delighted in the dark red tinge that took over his cheeks and the mumbled response, the small laugh she let out earning her a small shove to the shoulder by Izak.

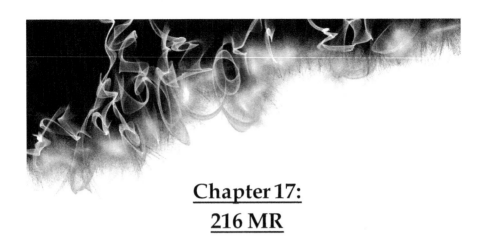

Chapter 17:
216 MR

$\mathcal{P}$erched in front of her vanity with long, thin fingers combing through her hair, pulling at this strand and that, Coren opened up the crimson-coloured book before her for what must have been the twentieth time in the past seventy-two hours.

Kir Melra Diansos fyr Caxien, the title read. Beneath it was the translation: *The Tall Tales of the Continents* and the name of the author who was, as Milo had alluded to, simply called the 'Mad Maid'.

How delightful.

Opening it up to the page that held her fascination, Coren once again read the few sentences that concerned the 'Malva'.

On this paragraph, the Mad Maid's writing was almost unreadable in all its slants and curls and blotches of ink. Some of the writing could not even be read, the translator forced to substitute an ellipsis for words.

When eternal darkness reigns the skies, the Mad Maid
had written, *and desire takes life thrice, order... (1) bow
to chaos. No prisoners (2) will be held; no realm left
untouched. Malva... warned... and be the bringer of the
end.*
(1)   *Very likely to be 'will'*
(2)   *Likely alluding to the First Mage, the infamous
'realm prisoner'*

Malva warned of what? Coren found herself stewing
over. As well as, *is desire a person or an emotion?* The
lack of capitalisation would suggest it was merely an
emotion, but it was a translation of the ancient
language, and Coren did not know how differently
language was structured within it. The bringer of the
end of what? That had so many possibilities. End
tyranny? End of the continents? End of magic?
Additionally, why had the stone woman called her
'Malva' when this had been written centuries ago? If,
for some strange reason, Coren was the Malva, then she
decided that this book was useless anyway. It didn't tell
her what she should be warned of, or what she may be
the bringer of the end of. Very unhelpful. If she saw the
stone lady again, she would be sure to introduce her to
the sailor's tongue this 'Malva' could possess.
Her stewing was interrupted by a sharp pull at her hair.
Coren winced, leading Dahlia to quietly mutter,
"sorry."
"It's fine," Coren told her, shooting her a reassuring
smile in the vanity mirror, which Dahlia swiftly looked
away from, and placed her book down on the wooden

179

surface before her, "where did you learn to do hair like this? You always make it look so intricate."

Dahlia's tan cheeks reddened and she ducked away slightly, dark hair reaching around her shoulder to shield her face somewhat. Despite her apparent embarrassment, the Air Mage told her, "my mother taught me, she was from Azyalai and would travel to the houses of many nobles to do their hair for them for fine Balls. They demanded perfection, and my mother always delivered. She taught me everything I know, including many cultural hair styles."

Coren smiled, "do you often do your own hair in the Azyalain style?"

Dahlia turned around to show her the hair style she currently had; her long, dark hair being placed into intricate braids.

"It looks amazing," Coren told her honestly, and Dahlia gave her a large, but still tentative, smile back. Coren would have gone on to ask if there were specific hairstyles for different religious occasions, and if Dahlia practised such. After all, while the Continents all worshipped the same Gods, the way they worshipped and their perspectives of the Gods differed.

Ceremonies for the Gods, she believed, were more common in areas such as Valark than in Galaris, with Azyalai being somewhere between the two.

However, her thoughts were interrupted by the opening of the maid's chamber to emit a certain redhead. Coren caught her eyes through the mirror and watched as Zarola's lips tightened into a thin line before she walked straight out of Coren's chamber doors.

Not once in the past six weeks had either of them spoken to one another. It was an accomplishment on Zarola's part in all honesty, considering her job. But each day that went by, the redhead's silence made Coren feel more and more bitter and, truthfully, a little bit hurt. But she wasn't going to be the one to give in.

"Do you know where she's going?" Coren asked of Dahlia. The other girl shrugged, seemingly more at ease now, offering up the theory that Nerah had demanded Zarola go and bring Coren some refreshments.

The Dark Mage had lightly snorted at the idea. Honestly, it was more like Nerah was the lady they were all serving, always being the one to call for food and ensure they were all organised for any upcoming events.

Coren didn't mind in the slightest, her mind had been far too occupied by the writings of the Mad Maid, the walls, the numerous questions she had about her relationship with Caradoc, and her trainings in both magic and swords play, to waste any time thinking about refreshments and making sure she had everything sorted for the next feast. It was a relief that Nerah took the incentive to keep everything running smoothly, really.

"Almost finished," Dahlia informed her, bringing Coren out of her wandering thoughts. Instead, she watched in the mirror as the short, dark-haired woman stuck her tongue out in concentration as she finished pinning up the last piece of golden hair. Supporting the first grin Coren had seen her wear since the Dark Mage had arrived, Dahlia proudly proclaimed, "done!"

Coren took a moment to study her hair now that Dahlia had finished, turning her head from side to side. Unable to see the true masterpiece, the Air Mage handed her a mirror so that she could see the back, and Coren's face lit up upon seeing it.

Half up and half down, a fair amount of her hair was laying as it usually did but, at the very back of her head, Dahlia had braided some of her hair before twisting and pinning it into three, intricate, twisting buns that had jet black flowers woven into it. It was certainly the most beautiful hair style that Coren had ever worn, if not one of the loveliest she had ever seen.

Slowly getting out of her chair so that she would not disturb her hair, Coren turned around to grin widely at Dahlia. She moved to hug the shorter woman, before remembering how uneasy she had seemed when she had witnessed Coren releasing her powers. Hesitating, the Dark Mage asked, "can I?"

Dahlia understood what she meant, and gave a small nod.

Swiftly, Coren embraced the girl, telling her, "thank you," before releasing her. It was only during the hug that Coren realised how long it had been since she'd embraced somebody of her own volition. The sudden feeling that accompanied the realisation, bizarrely, made her want to cry, but Coren pushed the feeling away. Coren, with Nerah's guidance, had put on her cosmetics barely an hour ago and she was determined not to ruin it.

Just after Coren had moved away, Zarola came back in. Sure enough, she was scowling and holding a tray full of cakes and tea. Dahlia gestured an arm towards Zarola, her expression slightly smug, as if saying 'see? I was right'. Coren laughed, probably harder than she should have, earning a scathing look from Zarola and a reddened face from Dahlia.

"Finally!" A voice called from the doorway of the maids' chambers. They all turned to see a smiling Nerah bustling in, "I was beginning to think you'd gotten lost, Zarola. Now, who's up for a cup of tea and some treats before the feast? I hear it's good luck."

"I'll never say no to a lemon tart," Coren told her, moving towards the table. Nerah beamed at her, before turning to Dahlia in the hopes of tempting her with a slice of strawberry pie that the Air Mage was known to like.

Zarola, however, could not be tempted in the least. For the first time since their... night all those weeks ago, she addressed Coren. "Am I dismissed for the night?"

Coren regarded her for a moment, hoping she would say something more and cursing the way that her heart hammered just a little bit harder when she finally spoke to her. But Zarola did not add anything, so Coren simply nodded at her and Zarola was soon sweeping out of the room.

At the red head's retreating form, Coren saw Nerah aim a deep frown and picked up some muttering of how she would be in a better mood if only she would try the raspberry shortcake, but Coren didn't offer an opinion.

Instead, she placed the plate holding the lemon tart that she had just picked up back down, offering Nerah and Dahlia apologetic looks.

"I'm sorry," Coren told them, "thank you for the thought in getting us tea and cakes but I think I better get to the feast."

And with that, Coren turned around and moved towards her chamber door. She took a deep breath, before plastering a smile on her face as she opened them to see Izak on the other side. With a slightly awkward expression, he offered her his arm and Coren took it, mentally preparing herself for the night ahead.

Rather brutally, Coren stabbed her fork into the slice of meat in front of her, tired of acting as if she didn't hear all the whispers going on around her.

Upon her arrival, a servant had led Coren to her seat which happened to be at the King's right-hand side. The place of honour.

Coren had barely restrained herself from laughing at the irony of the name. A place of honour. Her position didn't feel very honourable when she was surrounded by courtiers who were currently speculating about whether or not she was warming the King's bed.

"Poor girl," she heard a narrow-faced woman mutter to a much younger, but very eager, looking man on her left. He appeared to be groping her thigh beneath her long, white dress, "doesn't she know that the King would never take a peasant whore as his Queen, Dark Mage or not. I'm humiliated on her behalf."

Personally, Coren thought to herself, now stabbing her fork into a particularly villainous potato, *I'm humiliated on your behalf for thinking that your Gods-awful black and white hat was suitable to leave the house in. You look like a cow. But you don't see me voicing it.*

She heard a small chortle from behind her, and smiled to herself.

To her left, Caradoc leaned over, whispering to her, "ignore Cassandra. She's simply envious. The Dowager Countess is the daughter of a Light Mage and a Dark Mage, but inherited the very limited powers of a Light Mage."

The King was dressed very finely tonight. His jacket was black in colour, with marvellous gold embellishments that swirled up his long sleeves, creating two, large suns just below each of his shoulders, along with possessing shoulder pads made of golden thread.

The colours of his outfit mimicked her own. Coren's dress was mostly black, the fabric reaching up to her neck before continuing down only one arm. It was upon that one arm that gold embellishments had been placed. There were no suns depicted by the golden thread, but there were stars which looked very similar at a distance. As a result, Coren and Caradoc appeared to match.

She wondered if that had been intentional, and hoped that it was not as their state of dress only served to inspire the whispers. Under some people's breaths, like the Countess', she was a common whore reaching above her station. To others, she was a lonely, pitiful Dark Mage who was helplessly in love with the King, destined to get her heart broken.

After a moment, Coren's brows furrowed as she fully processed his words, asking quickly, "are they still alive?" Before clarifying, "the parent who was a Dark Mage?"

Did you kill them too? Was her unvoiced question. Coren didn't think that the King knew that Milo had all but told her that he had slaughtered the former Dark Mages, and Coren didn't exactly feel like it was a conversation to have in the middle of a feast, surrounded by snobbish nobles and Mind Mages.

"No," Caradoc informed her, sending what would have been a secretive grin her way if she didn't know the truth behind it, "Garris, tragically, lost his life during a tavern brawl. Impaled straight through the stomach by a falling willow mage beam. He continues to be missed."

At his undeniably untruthful words, Coren didn't know whether to frown or laugh. By the Gods, she was an awful person.

Suddenly, hands were reaching beside her and taking her plate away. Coren looked around in surprise, but saw that everybody else seemed unfazed by it. Looking to her left, she realised that Caradoc had finished his meal, which, according to what Nerah had told her when the feast was announced, meant that everybody else's meals were to be taken away too.

So, Coren was left awkwardly holding her fork, which had been poised to stab yet another vegetable.

Caradoc, who had been facing her way when he had finished the last bite of his meal, offered her an amused look, taking the fork from her hands and placing it on the table in front of her. Then, the King offered her his hand.

"Do you want to dance?" Caradoc asked her.

In response to his question, her heart raced. She could remember dancing with him in the gardens, before she had even realised the extent of her attraction to him, and how wonderful it had felt. However, she knew all too well that the two of them dancing together would only increase the horrid whispers.

She didn't really have a choice though. Caradoc was the King; she could not turn him down.

So, Coren nodded, reluctantly taking his hand and allowing him to lead her towards the centre of the feast hall. Seeing their King's intentions, the musicians began to play a slightly faster tune.

Caradoc turned her to face him, hands upon her waist, and Coren took that moment to mutter to him, "nothing too complicated please. I don't want to embarrass myself."

With all of her training and snooping, the Dark Mage did not have the time to work on her dancing skills, not that they were of that great concern to her regardless. Still, it would be nice to not give the courtiers anything more to mock her for.

With one lip tugged upwards, Caradoc took another step towards her, pressing them close in a way that bordered impropriety. Leaning down, he breathed into her ear, "just follow me."

He brought his hand up to hers, twirling her away before pulling her back in, swaying one way and then the other. Soon, they were spinning from place to place. Though she tried not to, Coren's gaze frequently strayed down to her footwork to ensure that she was matching his steps. If not for the intensity and violent beauty of the Fire King's eyes, perhaps her eyes would have been permanently fixated to the ground.

Conscious of the courtiers that would be attempting to listen in, Caradoc whispered, "you look beautiful."

Coren quirked a brow at him as he spun her once more, whispering as he pulled her back in, "you know you're just complimenting yourself by saying that, considering how well we match. One could wonder if that was intentional."

She wanted to know if he had coordinated their attire intentionally.

"One could," he hummed in response, and Coren's earlier suspicions were confirmed. He moved to the left and then the right, in and then out, turning them slowly as he did so. Soon enough, he added, "I wanted to match with you. It makes a statement."

"What kind of statement were you trying to make?"

"A statement of power," he told her, the flames in his bright eyes rising, "I am the Fire King and you are the only breathing Dark Mage. Together, we wield forces that they could never dream of. Or, we will, once you have made the Connection."

Coren continued on her inquiries, though, this time, more hesitantly, "and who are you making this statement to?"

He grinned down at her, like a dragon who possessed all the treasure he needed, "everyone. Azyalai. Novorum. Valark. Taniasburg. Soon, to question my power will be akin to questioning the power of the Gods."

"A bold claim," Coren remarked, noting how many courtiers were joining them now, partnering up as the music drew to a close. Soon enough, a new song began. Coren's feet stilled, before she said, "I don't-,"

It was too late.

Ignoring her protests, Caradoc spun her away into a noblewoman's arms with a grin. Nerves clawed at Coren's stomach as she desperately looked at the other woman's feet, trying to mimic her movements. By the time she was comfortable enough to look up, the brunette before her was giving her a condemning look, before looking most pleased when a dip in the music prompted a change of partners.

On and on she was spun, desperately trying to keep up with each partner and not injure their feet. That was with the exception of a man whose hands dipped far too low. His feet were squashed, just like her hopes to be loved.

When the song ended, Coren all but leapt from the dancing area towards where the refreshments were. There, she was content to be alone and simply observe the room, sipping on a rather delicious sparkling drink that tasted of elderflower.

Caradoc, she noted from her eagle-eyed spectating, seemed to adore the dancing. Grinning as many a partner twirled into his arms before departing with a flourish; eyes shining as all the courtiers appeared to gravitate around him, as if he were the sun and they his humble planets. It made him happy, and her heart felt lighter watching him.

"That's the Dark Mage everyone's been talking about," Coren heard someone say. She barely stopped her head from snapping in their direction, instead forcing herself to continue on sipping at her elderflower drink, "the one they say the King spends so much time with." Despite not looking in their direction, she could feel herself being assessed, and knew that they weren't impressed by what they found. The person – a woman, Coren was sure by her voice – remarked to her companion, "she's pretty, I suppose. But have you heard about what the Countess has found out about her?"

The Dark Mage's body tensed as the companion responded negatively, but seemed eager to hear what it was.

"Well, the Countess heard from her maid, who had heard from the Baroness' maid, who had heard from the Baroness ,who had been told by one of the King's guards, that the girl had been living in a shack before being brought to the palace! On some kind of farm!"

"Oh my!"

"And that's not all," the woman continued on, and Coren's hand began to clench around her glass. Hard, "he said that she was being tied up for the eight-days-fire when they found her! For murder!"

Helpmehelpmehelpmehelpmehelpme.

Her legs. Her thighs.

No.

Coren shut her eyes tightly, feeling phantom pains. She couldn't... She couldn't let herself remember. It hurt. It hurt so much.

"Traitor!"

It was Mrs. Krenz's boy.

Never one to miss an opportunity, her Darkness soon began to sing to her. That horrible, terrifying, tempting song. *Use me, Coren. Make them suffer. Nobody should be able to belittle you. You are the one with the power of the Goddess of Darkness. Make them bow, Coren, make them bow.*

No, she told the Darkness firmly, her voice commanding as she tried to send a wave of calm down her body, *you will not hurt anybody. They can say what they wish; it doesn't matter.*

"Who did she kill?" Continued the first one, her voice filled with morbid fascination.

"It was her own human mother," the woman told her, revelling in the suitably large gasp that her associate emitted, "I mean, what kind of monster-,"

"Monster!"

A pulse of her Darkness struck out, throwing the lady and her companion backwards with such a force that they slammed into a refreshment table many metres away from them, glasses smashing as plates slammed against the cool, stone floor.

Anybody else within an eight-metre radius went too, sounds of solid flesh colliding echoing around the feast hall.

The music stopped. The dancing stopped.

All eyes turned to her. In fear, in anger, in horror.

"Monster!"

Coren did the only thing she could: trying not to hurry, and keeping her head held high, she walked out of the hall.

Nobody tried to stop her.

Coren had barely managed to turn around the corner of one, golden hall before sobs racked her body. Back colliding with the wall, she slid down it, body shaking, until she was sitting with her knees pressed into her chest, her arms hugging them to her.

"I'm so sorry mum," she got out in between cries and violent gasps, "I'm so, so sorry. I n-n-never learn."

She had tried. She had tried so hard these past weeks to learn to control it; had spent more than six hours every day, regardless of training or her investigations, in that room Milo had first taken her to, working to a place where she was comfortable with her powers.

For once, she had felt like she was in control. Like she was something more than some murderous, monstrous, pathetic cannon that could go off any moment, unleashing pain and death upon all those around her.

Desperately, she brought her hand up to her mouth, even going so far as to place her knuckles into her mouth to try to quiet the loud sobs that just kept coming and coming no matter how hard she tried to stop them.

Pathetic, she hissed at herself, nails brutally digging into her forearms. Once they were sufficiently deep in her skin, she began to scratch, deeper and deeper until blood and skin was caught in her nails, the former dribbling down her arm, *pathetic, stupid monster! You should have died. You should have found a way. You should have let the eight-days-fire take you. You don't deserve to live.*

Jolon, her mind began to chant, as her nails scratched and scratched and scratched away, *Melrose, Mina, the Blonde Man.* All the people she'd hurt, failed or killed. *Papa*, she thought, and she lost the strength to keep on scratching. The way that he'd looked at her; the way her throat was so sore from sobbing but it just intensified.

"You're not my daughter. You're not anything, to anybody. And certainly not to us."

"I'm s-so sor-ry," she managed to repeat between cries, "I'm s-so sorry. I'm-,"

Coren heard heavy footsteps approaching, and tried in vain to stifle her cries. She wanted to get up, to show no weakness in the face of those who would tear her down – but she had no strength left.

She watched through obscured, watery eyes as the Fire King crouched before her. With a hesitant hand, he gently reached out to brush a strand of hair behind her ear.

"I'm sor-ry," she told him, hiccupping between her words as the tears still streamed. *Pathetic, murderer, traitor, monster*, "I-I lost control. I-,"

Carefully, he tilted her chin up so that she would meet his eyes, his beautiful, burning eyes, as he told her in a voice softer than she had ever heard him use, "you're not a monster. Not to me."

Before she even knew what she was doing, her arms had winded themselves around the back of his neck and she pulled him towards her, pressing her lips to his. For a moment, he didn't respond, arms hesitating and mouth stiff, but, before she could retract in shame, his large palms grasped onto her waist, pulling her closer, and his lips pressed more firmly against hers.

Honestly, Coren had thought about kissing him before. Many times, in great detail. Though, she had never quite imagined it happening when fat, salty tears were sliding their way down her face with both of them crouching unsteadily upon the floor, but he didn't seem to mind in the slightest. His tongue ran across her bottom lip, requesting entrance, she opened her mouth for him, holding onto him more tightly as their lips moved against one another's and his hands ran up and down her sides.

"Coren!" A voice called from not far away, before jogging footsteps turned the corner, "are you o- woah! Uh, you're definitely okay then... I'm just going to-,"

The two Mages broke away from one another, turning to face a floundering Izak whose hands were flying all over the place and a grinning Milo right on his heels. Swiftly, Izak turned away and moved around the corner, dragging the more reluctant Milo with him. Once they'd gone, the King's gaze dragged back to hers, and Coren felt unsurety settle in her stomach.

After regarding her for a moment, Caradoc stretched out of his crouch and offered a hand towards her. Hesitantly, Coren took it, enjoying the warm feeling of his hand in hers just as much as she had loved the feeling of his hands on her waist.

Finally back upon her feet, they both just stood there for a moment; Coren looking up at him with something akin to awe painted in her green eyes, and him returning her stare with a grin.

"Let's get you back to your chambers," he said at last, turning away from her before they began to walk together down the hallway.

He didn't let go of her hand.

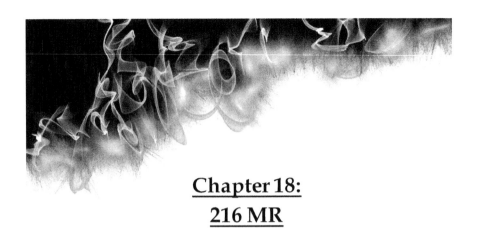

Chapter 18:
216 MR

*H*is hands were everywhere all at once; his mouth a

constant presence upon her own, kissing, exploring, ravishing. Before long, his large, warm arms were underneath her legs, one moving away from her to swipe his papers aside before she was placed atop the cool desk.

Caradoc pulled away from her slightly, grinning as he observed Coren's swollen lips and tangled hair, before he surged back in to find her lips once more.

His hands travelled up, one remaining on her waist whilst his right hand found its way into her hair. Grasping tightly onto the golden strands, he pulled her head back, giving himself better access to her mouth. A moan tore its way out of her throat, and she wrapped her legs around his waist, using them to pull him in closer.

Boldly, she bit into his bottom lip, and revelled in the sound of enjoyment he made before the Fire King pulled away from her lips, instead moving his attention to her neck; his hold on her hair allowing him full access.

As he licked and sucked on a sensitive spot where her neck met her shoulder, Coren tightened her legs around him, desperately attempting to pull him closer to where she wanted him. It had the opposite effect, instead, he pried her legs from around him and stepped back further than he had the first time, offering her his usual smirk.

"Not now, little Mage," he told her, retreating back even more, as if distancing himself would quench the urges that they both felt, "I want to see you in my bed first." Ignoring the heat his comment incited within her, she questioned, "who's to say that I'll let you take me to your bed?"

"I think you'll find me very persuasive."

"Perhaps I need a demonstration," she returned, leaning back onto her palms. The King's lips tugged back into a grin, but he didn't move any closer. Instead, he retreated back to his long, leather sofa and threw himself down upon it.

After a moment, Coren pushed herself off of his desk, fixing her tunic before moving over to the sofa as well. Before she could sit beside him, his hands grasped her hips, and pulled her backwards so that she was sitting in his lap. The Dark Mage turned her head towards him. Looking at him as she was now, Coren couldn't help but stare in admiration. Sun-kissed skin, tussled red-black hair, bright, burning eyes; her King truly was a creature of the flames. She was allowing him to lead her to the fire, to burn alongside him in the desire he ignited.

With him staring down at her, his arms cradling her, butterflies pranced about her stomach and she couldn't help but let a wide smile light up her face. Without even noticing it, her right hand had lifted from her side, reaching up to his face. Caradoc tensed for a moment, but allowed her to touch him; to trace the sharp cheekbones that looked as if they could cut more finely than any Material Mage-created tool.

"Tell me something," Coren breathed, not even realising how breathless she had become just from his stare, from the feeling of his arms around her, "tell me something nobody else knows."

He studied her for several moments, silence reigning the room as an unseen queen. Then, he took the hand tracing his face in his own, moving it to his lips so that he could kiss the back of it before dropping both of their hands down, intertwined.

The Fire King took in a long breath, eyes moving from Coren's to the door in front of them. At last, he admitted, "I had a sister."

Coren stayed silent, watching as a small smile lit up his face.

"Her name was Febronia. We," he paused, and Coren hesitantly began to run her thumb across the back of his hand to try to bring some comfort, "we all called her Ronnie. She was wonderful; so full of life, of love. Despite his cruelties, she still loved Brax, which was," he let out a breathy laugh, but she could sense the underlying anger through his hardened voice, "an achievement to say the least."

Caradoc swallowed harshly, and then his eyes darted from the door back to Coren's. There was something so raw within them that Coren could barely believe that the person in front of her was actually the King; the one who was usually all teasing and games and control. "She was the price," he told her, "and I paid it."

"What do you mean?" Coren asked, speaking up for the first time.

It was as if a switch had been flipped. The emotion in his eyes was gone, one side of his mouth was, once again, tilted upwards.

"Nothing," he said, the other side of his lip quirking up too so that he could smile down at her, "nothing at all."

Coren went to open her mouth to speak, but was silenced by the hard press of his lips upon hers; by his wandering hands. The fires of desire lit within her once more, and the conversation slipped away from her mind almost entirely.

On her way back to her chambers, Coren grinned at every passing servant, chirping a merry 'hello' at any who's gazes lingered. They all gave her looks of surprise in response, which the Dark Mage supposed was warranted. Her conflict with Zarola and struggles with the Connection had not exactly put her in the best spirits of late.

Now, those concerns were far from her mind. Caradoc, *the Fire King*, seemed to genuinely like her! He had opened up to her!

She felt as if nothing could break her spirits.

Was this love? She wondered. The feeling of it made her want to cry. For one of the first times in her life, she felt like she wasn't alone anymore. Like she had something that was hers.

After greeting the still slumbering Lan, Coren dramatically shoved both of her chamber doors open, waltzing inside to where her maids were still bustling about. At her entry, all of them looked up, and not even Zarola's harsh frown could bring her spirits down.

"Good afternoon everyone," she told them, flopping down atop her canopy bed, "do you need any help with anything?"

"Well, it would be helpful if you weren't throwing yourself around on the bed I just made," Nerah complained. Coren quickly jumped off the bed guiltily, but the damage was already done. The larger girl batted away the Dark Mage's apology, rolling her eyes in fond exasperation.

Then, Nerah's eyes lit up in recollection and Coren watched in interest as she bustled over to a cabinet near her wardrobe. From on top of it, she grabbed a letter before moving back over to Coren and handing it to her.

"This came for you," she told her cheerily, before moving over to where a tray of snacks lay in order to bat Dahlia's reaching hand away, telling the smaller girl, "you've already had three of them! Leave one for

Coren."

When Nerah had fully turned her back to them both, Coren shot Dahlia a mischievous smile, gesturing for her to take the last one. Dahlia grinned, grabbed it, and stuffed it into her mouth quickly before Nerah could turn back around, her tan cheeks protruding outwards like a hamster.

The Dark Mage then turned her attention to the envelope, frowning slightly. It was unusual that messages were distributed about the palace in envelopes, normally they were just scrawled onto a piece of paper and sent with a servant. So, it must be private.

Perhaps it was from Caradoc.

Her heart felt as if it could fly out of her chest in its lightness.

Could it be a love letter?

Eagerly, she tore the envelope open, taking the letter out and folding it open. Swiftly, she realised that it wasn't a love letter, it was far too short for that. When she started reading, Coren discovered that it was something else entirely.

Move aside the tapestry of the burning woman on the sixth floor of the palace, walk through the wall there. Take the left corridor, then the winding steps downwards. Go alone; tell no one. There lies the truth. A friend.

"Are you alright?" A soft voice inquired. Coren's head snapped up to look at Dahlia, the other woman's words bringing the attention of Nerah and Zarola to her. She hadn't even realised she was frowning, but quickly rectified that.

"I'm fine, Dahls," she told the dark-haired girl, who nodded, though did not look convinced.

Once both Dahlia and Nerah were looking away, Coren made sure to catch Zarola's eyes before she could look away.

Did you send this? Coren mouthed to her, holding the letter up.

The redhead's brows furrowed and she shook her head. After a moment, she mouthed back, *what does it say?* But Coren did not answer her.

Her earlier contentment fled from her as she looked down at the letter once more, replaced instead by curiosity. Could this letter from a mysterious 'friend' truly be the answer to all of the questions that had plagued her since arriving at the palace?

Coren wasn't positive that it would be, but she was sure of one thing: she was going to find out.

But, until night time fell and she had the opportunity to sneak away, she would continue about her day as normally as she could.

"Don't you have sword fighting lessons this afternoon?" Nerah inquired of her, and Coren jumped out of her chair, cursing. Dahlia and Nerah's, both of whom already felt like true friends, laughter followed her running form out of her chamber door, where she found an impatient looking Milo waiting for her.

202

When the moon had chased the sun from the sky,
Coren left her chambers, letter clutched in one hand.
Carefully, she passed by Lan, following the corridor
that led straight on, passing torches and tapestries, the
former of which giving the palace walls some of the
usual sparkle that they possessed during the day.
Glancing from side to side, her eyes lingered on the
wall that she had disappeared into regularly, but she
carried on and on. At the end of the corridor, there was
a set of light, stone steps that would take her to the
fourth floor. She took them, and then the next set, and
the set following that.

On each floor, she would occasionally catch eyes with a
servant. They, however, were far more occupied with
going about their business than what a young woman,
even if she was the Dark Mage, was doing wandering
about the hallways. And if one of them were to report
her travels, then Coren would simply say that she
couldn't sleep, and needed to wander about to clear her
head.

When she finally reached the sixth floor, she made a
show of pacing in front of a large window, before
sitting herself on its ledge and staring out of it. Using
the reflections in the pane, she waited until the corridor
was cleared before she stood and began to scan each of
the tapestries.

One depicted eight figures – a platinum-haired man

bathed in light; a narrow-eyed woman with green, red, blue and silver bursting from her fingertips; a tall woman holding wood in one hand and metal in the other; a hulking man with the claws of a beast; a dark-skinned man with a mischievous smile; a grey-haired woman holding a *jikita*; a woman with soul-capturing eyes, embraced by darkness; a man crowned in horns, his shoulders gripped by the hands of skeletons.

The Gods.

Coren quickly moved on, her eyes having lingered on Nias, to the next tapestry. It turned out to be another depiction of the War of Kings, this time capturing the human's perspective. Within it, Caradoc stood upon a hill, his cavalry behind him, raising his arms up to the air as the human army before him scorched.

She shuddered slightly at the pure power of the movement, though she didn't know if it was in fear or want.

Four tapestries further down, she found the one she had been looking for. It was a massive piece of cloth, outmatched in size only by the one that displayed the Gods, and predominantly featured a young girl. She had blazing red hair and shining, golden eyes. From those eyes, fat tears leaked and dribbled down her face whilst fire began to consume her from every angle.

Helpmehelpmehelpmehelpmehelpmehelpme.

Coren closed her eyes tightly, trying to shove away the feeling of fire licking at her, her hands bound behind that stake, from her mind.

Finally opening her eyes, she, with a sorrowful look at the sewn girl, pushed the tapestry aside and walked straight through the wall, the uncomfortable feeling of being shoved from all angles overcoming her.

Unbeknownst to any but the Gods, outside of the palace walls, deep within the northern maze, the stone woman blinked; jikitas glowing.

Then, Coren came out the other side. Taking in several heaving breaths, she straightened herself up from the slight crouch that she had fallen into and grabbed her dagger from its now usual spot up her sleeve.

There were three different corridors that she could follow. The right was lit by burning torches, displaying to her the dripping, dark stone walls, yet the straight and left ones remained within darkness.

Checking the letter, she took the left corridor, clutching her dagger so hard that her palm protested, but Coren's grip did not relent. There was something wrong here, she knew it in her heart and in her bones. It made her want to shake, to back away and leave for the security of her chambers.

But she would not.

Coren forced herself to take step after step, her footsteps the only sound; a sound that was echoed so loudly by the tunnels that it made her wince each time. When she walked into a wall, blind thanks to the darkness, she yelped and scowled, before telling her Darkness in a state of forced indifference: *I command you to come to me, and to stay with me.*

The shadows of the room all reluctantly trickled towards her, wrapping her within its cool embrace, and Coren berated herself for not thinking of it earlier. Now, she could see almost as clear as if there were daylight.

Looking to her side, she saw that the wall she had walked into was leading around a short corner, after which there were twirling, rotting, descending steps. Just as the letter had directed, Coren stepped down onto them.

With her sight, Coren was far less unnerved, so allowed herself to laugh over thoughts of what Zarola would say if she could see her now. *You fool*, she imagined the redhead would seethe, *the letter could be a trap; you should have at least brought someone with you!* Maybe she should have, but the opportunity for that was long gone.

Bracing her hand against the wall, she continued moving down and down and down. Despite the fact that it was summer in Galaris, Coren began to shiver. After the last step, she was faced with a large, metal door. The Dark Mage went towards it, her movements fast to try to stave off the cold, and attempted to open in.

Surprise, surprise, it was locked.

The truth, Coren supposed, sighing inwardly, *is never easy*.

Closing her eyes, she murmured her mantras over and over; *I feel nothing, I feel nothing, I feel nothing, I am in control, I am in control, I am in control.* With a state of cool calm settling within her, she addressed her Darkness: *I command you to attack the door quietly, to destroy it.*

Thrusting her hand out in front of her, the Darkness sped towards it, hitting the door with a series of loud bangs, before filling the room and taking away her vision once more. Immediately, Coren called it back to her.

When she observed the door, she frowned. It was a prime example of the limited control her Darkness allowed her. The attack had been loud, and had clearly not destroyed the door. Its hinges, however, did appear to be weakened.

Instead of trying to control her Darkness once more, Coren ran at the door herself, slamming into it with a high kick like Milo and Izak had taught her when they had been working on combat.

Her leg hurt like a bitch, but, with the door having been weakened by her Darkness and then subjected to Coren's Mage strength, it fell with a resounding *BOOM!*

If there was anybody else within this tunnel or the ones that resided near them, then they certainly knew she was here now. The thought made her hurry to the door.

Once she stepped through the empty gap, she had to call the darkness of that room to her as well and what the shadows unveiled made her breath catch in her throat.

A thin corridor lay in front of her, with cells residing on either side of it. Turning her head to her left, she saw a boy with long, dark, matted hair being reclined in a grey, metal chair. On either side of him, his wrists were secured to the chair in single Mage's Bane and a gag had been forced down his throat. His eyes, Coren noted, were watery and distant, flitting about the room with purple bags beneath them. At one point, she could have sworn his brown eyes caught on her, but, if they registered her presence, he certainly didn't show it.

The restrained, distant appearance of the boy was by no means the worst part of it. No, it was the tubes that connected to the veins of his upturned wrists, dark red liquid being transported from him to a large, circular contraption that was slowly being filled with it.

They were forcibly draining him of blood.

Coren shook desperately at the bars that separated her from him, wanting to help the boy, but they wouldn't give. Instead, they left her hands with harsh burns upon them. Moving back from the bars, which were, rather surprisingly, made of a type of wood, she saw that there was a sign upon the stone wall to his left.

Mage Group 1: Light
Source 28
Lucian

Glancing between the sign and the boy, Coren crouched before the cell, shaking it once more. Her voice was tight and fearful as she told him, "I'm going to get you out of here, Lucian. I promise."

Before she could try her luck at prying open doors with her Darkness again, Coren heard a low groan from the other end of the narrow hall. After promising Lucian that she would be back, not that he appeared to hear her, Coren began to move forwards, past more cells.

Mage Group 3: Material

Source 19
Farrah

The girl in that cell was similarly placed in a chair, her blood being forced from her body, but Coren could have sworn that there were tears tracking their way down her vulnerable face.

Mage Group 4: Body
Source 22
Lyssia

Whilst Coren had taken a moment to stare at this girl piteously, she heard the groan arise again, and hurried past the next few. The signs moved quickly in and out of her vision, *Mage Group 5: Transformation, Mage Group 6: Mind.*

When she went to move past the cell labelled *Mage Group 7: Dark*, Coren's legs forced her to stop.

The cell was empty.

Swallowing the bile rising in her throat and forcing down that horrible, certain feeling that the cell there was meant for *her*, she finally arrived at the source of the groaning.

The inside of that cell was different. There was no chair, no blood being stolen through tubes, no Mage's Bane. Instead, there was simply a woman, her knees clutched to her chest; dark, messy hair obscuring her face from view.

She appeared to be whispering words under her breath; names, Coren believed, but she was too far away to hear what she was saying.

"Hey," Coren called out delicately, crouching before the cell in the hopes that she wouldn't scare her, "are you okay?"

When the woman looked up, Coren knew that had she still been standing, her knees would have buckled beneath her. As it was, she still fell out of her crouch, hands tightening around the painful bars as something like a sob forced its way out of her body.

"Mina?" Coren questioned, her voice breaking.

Why was she here? Mina had been taken by Snatchers over eleven years ago. She was the only person to have known about Coren's powers; to have comforted her about it. Mina was human! Why was she down here being drained of blood? Blood that Coren assumed was being injected into the children in that lab.

Coren pushed herself far enough away from the cell bars to be able to read the sign, her heart beating harder than any drum:

Mage Group 8: Death
Source 3
Mina

When Coren's teary gaze moved back to the cell, she fell backwards. Mina had rushed to the bars, holding them with whitened knuckles, ignoring the fact that her hands were physically *burning* at the contact, as she scanned Coren's.

"Coren," her old friend whispered, her voice hoarse and disbelieving, "no, no, no. Coren. How did they get to you? How did they find you? I didn't tell them anything. I didn't tell them anything! Didn't-didn't-didn't-," sobs overtook the young woman's body, fading into something that sounded more like howls. Looking at Mina like this, Coren wanted to be sick. Had she been locked up for all eleven of the years she had been gone? Mina didn't even look human anymore; she was closer in sound and appearance to a rabid animal. "What did they do to you, Mina?" Coren asked desperately, placing her hand atop Mina's on the bars. The Death Mage, if the sign was to be believed, startled at the contact, as if she had not felt the kind touch of human flesh in years.

Mina's beautiful grey eyes were utterly broken, "he killed them," she told her, tears falling down her face, "he killed my sisters. D-drained them of so much blood. D-drained one, and t-then moved onto the next source. They're dead! They're dead! They're dead!" Her final words were screamed as she took one hand from under Coren's and began to punch the bars so hard that crimson began to pour down it. Mina's eyes then tracked the drip of her blood down the bars, "they want this. They take this."

Triplets. Death Mages were always triplets. Coren had never even considered it before, after all, Death Mages were only born once every two-hundred and fifty years.

Mina, Kyra, Doria. They'd all been Death Mages. Mina had never told her what she was, even after finding out Coren was a Dark Mage, but she didn't blame her for that. After all, by telling Coren, Mina wouldn't have only been putting herself at risk but also the lives of her sisters.

Coren shut her eyes for a moment and then swallowed tightly, dread rising within her, before she asked, "who did this to you, Mina? What happened to the Snatchers?"

"The King," Mina told her, her eyes alive with determination, "the Snatchers work for the King. But I won't let them take you too, Coren. They can drain me like a blood bag but they won't lay a hand on you. I won't let them take you like they did m-my sisters."

"Mina-,"

A scream tore through the air as Mina fell to the floor, eyes wide, clutching her head desperately and throwing it forwards and backwards, rocking, as if she were trying to get something out of it.

Get someone out of it.

Coren's heart squeezed painfully as she turned her head to the side, and saw Milo standing by the entrance to the tunnel of cells, his hand outstretched towards Mina.

He lowered his eyes to her and gave her a smile, small and regretful, and said, "I'm sorry, Coren," before he extended his other hand to her. An invisible grip clutched her head in its hands, and she descended into darkness.

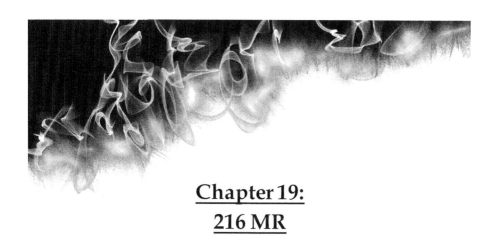

Chapter 19:
216 MR

*S*lowly, Coren eased her eyes open, her body jolting

as if someone was walking and carrying her with them. When her eyes had fully adjusted to her surroundings, she realised that that was, indeed, the case.

As soon as the memories of earlier surged back towards her, Coren shut her eyes tightly, faking sleep as she wondered whether or not it would be futile to launch herself from Milo's strong arms and try her luck at sprinting away.

I know you're awake, Coren, he told her, *and the only thing that you would gain from running is humiliation.* Cold, consuming rage filled her. She stiffened in his arms and resolved to say nothing back to him.

Milo, it seemed, couldn't take condemnation of silence. *Don't you want to know where you're going?* He asked, his Mind Speak making her throbbing head pulse further, *normally you're asking me a billion questions and I can barely keep up.*

Her silence continued.

Please, Milo begged, and Coren felt nothing, *please say something.*

You're just as much a monster as me, Milo, she told him. She then went silent once again, the harsh quiet punctuated only by his heavy footsteps, *those are children in the labs. Those are people in those cages. People that mean something to somebody.*

Finally allowing her eyes to look up to Milo, she saw that he was clenching his jaw, his eyes glassy. Both knew that there was nothing that Coren hated more than herself, and now he had become an equal in her eyes. Alike in being a fellow monstrosity.

I believe in him, Milo told her, and she knew exactly who he was talking about. Caradoc. The Fire King. Coren turned her face from him. *And I believed in you.* The corridors around her were familiar; she knew exactly where she was being taken. With a surprising amount of detachment, Coren wondered if these were to be her last moments. It would be a cruel way to die, to have a person she had seen as her friend hand her over to the man she might love, like a pig to be slaughtered. Then, she remembered that they wouldn't be killing her. No, they'd be locking her in a cell and draining her blood away.

She didn't care. As Nias had told her, Coren had nothing worthwhile to lose; not now that her love for Caradoc meant nothing. It had all been a farce. A farce to use her and then lock her away in a cage.

At least she'd spend her last moments next to Mina.

For a short time, Milo hesitated, but then pulled open the door to Caradoc's study, moving them both to the centre of the room. Coren pushed herself away from his chest, wrenching her legs from his grip.

If these were to be her last moments as an uncaged woman, then she would be standing for them.

To her surprise, Milo helped ease her to the ground, and Coren willed her knees not to buckle as she turned slowly towards the King.

Fully facing Caradoc, she allowed herself a moment to take him in. He was reclined in the chair behind his desk, no emotions evident upon his face as he studied her as if she were a piece of furniture that he was deciding where to best place.

"Coren," he greeted at last, and the Dark Mage wanted to weep at both the familiarity and the foreignness of it. His voice was still deep, still made her heart beat faster, but there was no warmth to it. Even his fiery eyes, she noted, appeared colder than usual; stationary.

She wondered if the ability to close off and mask one's emotions was something that came naturally after centuries, and if she would ever be able to do the same. If she survived the Fire King, that is.

He seemed to be waiting for her to say something. A petty part of her wanted to force him to be the one to break the cruel silence. The stronger part of her, however, needed to know.

"What's happening, Caradoc?" Coren questioned, trying to keep the desperation that this was all one big misunderstanding out of her voice, "what are you doing to the children?"

He placed both of his elbows upon the desk, resting his head atop his hands, and the silence continued. At last, just as Coren was ready to shout, he said, "nothing that doesn't serve a greater purpose."

"What does that mean?"

"It means power, Coren," he told her coldly, "something you're very familiar with the desire for." His truthful, cutting words made her flinch and take a small step backwards. Noticing this, the King sighed, letting his head fall forward once more, but not before she saw a glimpse of something like regret upon his face.

Coren shook the idea away. He was probably faking the emotion, like he'd clearly faked so much. Raising her chin, she found the strength within herself to bite out, "so, when will you be locking me away? I saw that cell seven was available. The stone walls and metal bars certainly look homely and I love the grey colour scheme, very torture-esque."

"Nobody will be locking you away," he informed her strongly, running a hand through his red-black hair, "locking you away wouldn't even be useful until after you've made the Connection."

"How comforting."

He said nothing.

A hysterical laugh bubbled out of her throat as she hopelessly demanded, "what is going on, Caradoc?"

"What do you know of the First Mage?" He inquired instead, lifting his head. When his eyes came to rest on Coren, he must have seen the disbelief and anger upon her face by answering her question with an inquiry

216

over a folklore take, so added, "just humour me."

"That they're locked in some prison world and have something to do with Mad Marion's prophecy," she responded, a harsh frown pulling at her lips despite her compliance.

The Fire King inclined his head in agreement, "that is all true of the folklore, but what I'm interested in is his origins. Nobody knows for sure how he came to have his eight powers of light, the elements, material, the body, transformation, darkness, and death. There's some speculation about it from the ancient sorcerers and curious humans, but nothing concrete. Something that is written about with surety, however, is how he was defeated by the Gods. Do you know how that happened?"

The sheer frustration at his lack of a solid answer made her want to shove him off of one of the palace balconies. Closing her eyes, she tried to rationalise that he had to be telling her this for a reason. So, she played along, sharply responding, "no."

"Some woman, allegedly the last of the ancient sorcerer line that came before the Mages, said that she had foreseen that he could be defeated. So, she travelled the continents to try to find the people that she had seen defeat him; the people that we now call Gods, who were then mere humans. In the end, each of them took a power from the First Mage. Unfortunately for them, the sorcerer no longer trusted anyone with these kinds of powers so, as they were more vulnerable than the First Mage had once been by having only one power each, she was able to banish the first seven to a realm holding the Ascended City, the God of Death to the Realm of the Below and he whom had once been the First Mage to a prison realm of eternal frost and torment.

"Now," he continued, his eyes glazed and far away, "the object of my interest is how they took his power. Most sources seem to believe that the Gods each drank a certain amount of the First Mage's blood. So, if it is possible to take away powers through drinking the blood of he who possesses them-,"

"Then it should be possible to gain powers by drinking the blood of different people who possess the powers," Coren cut in, horrified fascination glazing her tone. Caradoc did not seem in the slightest bit disturbed, the beginnings of a proud smile tugging at his lips, "exactly," he said, pleased, "I knew that I would need to trial my theory, after all, it would not be pleasant to accidentally murder myself. How would the continents cope? It is regrettable that I've had to use Mages to see if it would work, but there was no other way, and children disappearing is far easier to explain and less fear-inducing than full-grown, adult Mages being taken."

It is regrettable that I've had to use Mages, Coren repeated in her mind, the idea that he wouldn't have cared at all had it been human children he was experimenting upon and torturing making her feel sick.

"Why did you kill the other Dark Mages then? You must have needed them as sources," the like you need me now, was left unspoken.

218

This time, Caradoc did frown, "it was before I realised that I needed them. I've killed many a Dark Mage, and a few Death Mages too. Even some Mind Mages, if they were too powerful or disobedient," Coren's mind momentarily went to Milo, who was still standing stationary by the door to the study, "that is the way of Kings, we put an end to potential opposition before they can become threats. Maybe you'll learn that one day."

No, Coren thought viciously, *I could never do something like that. I could never be like you.*

Seeing the condemnation upon her face, Caradoc's frown deepened and he began to walk around his desk, towards her. Coren refused to allow her feet to move backwards. Instead, simply waited there for him to reach her.

When he was in front of her, the Fire King placed a warm hand upon her cheek and leaned into her ear. At the feel of his breath against it, her whole body tensed. He began to mutter softly, "there's always a price to power, Coren, you know this. You're paying yours; I'm paying mine. When all of this is over, I'll be the ruler of empires and I'll be powerful enough to make that Goddess bleed. For your blood and full cooperation, perhaps there could be a throne in it for you. I hear that you can experience all four seasons in a day in Novorum."

Coren's brows furrowed, "the Goddess?"

She'd heard him talk about the Goddess' before, with great disdain and warning.

He pulled away from her ear, but left his face hovering

close to hers. Now, there was something hollow in those fiery eyes, something that screamed to her of years of pain and regret and loneliness.

Rather than quickly disguising such emotions as he normally did, the King seemed to let them burn, the embers in Caradoc's eyes dancing to his song of sorrow. Slowly, he said, "another price of power. One much higher, and much dearer."

That raw look seemed so familiar now, reminiscent of this morning when they had talked about his-

"No," Coren breathed out in disbelief, and Caradoc closed his eyes against her realisation, "you killed her. You killed your sister."

His eyes opened wide, now glimmering with rage instead of devastation. Harshly, he gripped onto her forearms, fingers digging in so hard that she knew they would bruise. "It was a punishment, for killing Brax. If I hadn't done it, if I ha-hadn't killed Ronnie, I would have had nothing! I would have been powerless. Aliona," he spat the Goddess' name out like it was a curse, "wanted me to prove how much I deserved my power. So, I did it. I earned it."

The sick feeling within her worsened. Many times, Coren had thought Caradoc and herself similar in some ways, but not in this. Coren would have surrendered her powers in an instant if it would have kept her family safe, yet Caradoc would sacrifice the person he loved the most for it.

She shook herself out of his grip, moving shakily backwards.

There was no doubt in her mind that should she stand

between Caradoc and his thirst for power and vengeance, he would sacrifice her too.

"Don't look at me like that, Coren," he told her softly, though didn't try to move any closer to her, "I'm looking for justice; I'm looking for power. Surely, you can understand that. If I hadn't burned them, wouldn't you have wanted vengeance against those that were prepared to watch you die? If someone killed the person you loved the most, wouldn't you destroy everything in your path, even yourself, for justice?"

Coren said nothing. Yes, she would have been tempted to do so, to go after them and make them pay, but she had deserved what they did to her. How can she go after justice when no foul was done?

For his second question, she couldn't answer. There was nobody that she loved the most in the continents. Her family, alive or dead, hated her; the King she thought she loved was somebody else entirely; the friends she had made at the palace she had barely known for a couple of moons, and death would be a kindness to the haunted and tortured Mina.

The loneliness of it all made another hysterical laugh demand to be let out. She swallowed it down.

Caradoc let out an exaggerated sigh, "of course, before I deal with justice for my sister, I have to tend to some pesky rebels."

He was immediately the centre of Coren's attention. Looking at him, she could see a great, triumphant glint in his eyes. Desperation filled her, but she wouldn't allow herself to think about the person she was worried about, not with Milo here, not when it could get her discovered. If she wasn't already, that was.

"To think," Caradoc continued, "one of my highest-ranking guards!"

Coren startled.

"Oh, so you didn't know about him then. Only the redheaded servant girl. A spy of mine was kind enough to inform me of all of Commander Alyxan's Secondaries. One of them was named Zarola, and he found out she was on a mission in the capitol. Foolish and arrogant, really, to not alter one's name."

The surge of fury that rose within her at his words took her aback. Coren didn't care if he planned to drag her down to cell seven or burn her on the spot. As Nias had so kindly pointed out, she didn't have anything to lose. Nothing to live for. At least if they dragged her to the cells, she could spend her last moments next to Mina. But there was no way that she would let them kill Zarola.

Whilst Coren continued to silently stew in her rage, Caradoc said, "Izak hid it well, must have had training from that Mind Mage Secondary in Alyxan's camps, otherwise Milo would have discovered him far before he decided to steal those vials of blood, I thin-"

"-you're lying," Coren interrupted in disbelief, thinking of stoic, strait-laced Izak, "you're mad!"

"I'm many things, my dear, but mad isn't one of them," he told her smoothly, before gesturing one hand towards the doors. Dutifully, Milo followed his command and had them opened, letting in a pair of guards. Between them, they held a body.

Coren's throat constricted, convinced it was Izak.

When they set the bloodied corpse down upon the King's sofa she heard Caradoc mutter complaints about how expensive it was, but her eyes were fixated on the face of the corpse. He must have died recently, eyes still puffy from crying beneath the still weeping wound that read *FOOL* upon his forehead.

It wasn't Izak.

It was Jakan.

"Boy should have been more careful who he gave his heart to," Caradoc commented idly, "all Izak needed him for was a way into the walls, so that he could steal the vials."

Her mind went straight back to the day following the theft, recalling noticing regret upon Izak's face as the woman pleaded her case to the guards. Not, perhaps, out of mere sympathy for the woman, but because he had been responsible for her predicament.

What was it that the woman had said? That all she had seen was dark and green, Coren suddenly recalled. The dark had likely been Coren knocking her out, but the green? It was the colour of the magic of an Earth Mage. The rebel that had poisoned her had been an Earth Mage, their magic turned their veins green. She closed her eyes tightly, cursing her own foolishness, as she remembered what he had said to her in the library: "*I had more trouble than most making a connection to Aliona.*"

Not only that, but Coren had known the King only employed powerful, generational Mages into his service and only a powerful Earth Mage could have poisoned her as he did.

It was Izak. He had been in the maze, he had poisoned her, he had used Jakan and stolen the blood vials from the King.

"What are you going to do with them?" Coren asked quietly.

Caradoc's brows furrowed and he turned to Milo, asking in disbelief, "does she care for them? Does she not think that they deserve to face justice?"

Her hands balled into fists at the frustrating feeling of being talked about as if she were not there, but she kept her lips sealed shut, wanting to see if Milo would betray her yet again.

After a moment, Milo responded, "she cares for them, especially the maid, quite deeply."

It felt like somebody was swinging an axe towards the sheet of glass that was her. All along, every time he had guarded her rooms, escorted her to lessons, comforted her or spent time with her, he had been spying for the King. Defiling her mind so that he could run back to his master with any dirty, dark little secret he could find.

Her face flushed in humiliation at the idea of Milo telling the King about the punishments her mother had given her. She could just imagine them now, laughing over how weak and pathetic she was, before they'd go about their day – the King giving her soft kisses and lingering looks, Milo taking on the position of the brothers she'd lost.

Neither had meant anything; she was still as alone as she had always been.

Coren, I didn-

Shut your mouth, Milo, before I show you what my

Darkness can really do.

They both knew that it was an empty threat. Even if he had betrayed her trust, she still cared for him. Despite that, he went silent.

"What," Coren began again, more demanding this time, "will you do to them?"

Now, Caradoc approached her, wrapped his arms around her and held her close. Coren offered no resistance. Not yet.

"Why, I'll make a nice, big bonfire, my little Mage," the Fire King told her, a slow, cruel smile crawling onto his face. He kissed the corner of her mouth, before moving to the side so that his lips could brush her ear "and, together, we can watch them burn."

Coren allowed herself a moment to enjoy the feel of his warm skin against her own for one last time, discreetly beginning to call the shadows of the room to her, before allowing a joyous smile to take over. Having moved his face back, Caradoc saw her smile and surprise and confusion quickly worked their way onto his face.

Exactly the momentary distraction she needed.

Before Milo could think to warn the King, Coren grasped onto the feeling of utter desperation; the need to save Zarola and Izak. Outwards, she commanded the Darkness, and it complied. Amplified by the use of her emotions, the Darkness seemed to explode in every direction, sending the King, Milo, the two guards and Jakan's body colliding harshly against the wall, emitting sickening *SMACKs*. Blood was protruding from their heads and she prayed to the Gods that they were both momentarily dead. It would buy her more time. Adrenaline coursing through her, she slammed open Caradoc's study door and began to sprint through the halls at a pace so rapid she hadn't realised she was capable of it. On the way, she mowed down several servants, but she didn't stop. The clock was ticking. They all needed to get out of the Golden Palace. Now.

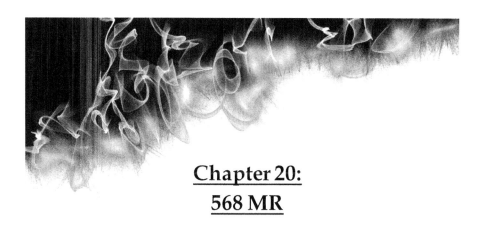

Chapter 20:
568 MR

$\mathcal{T}$he small, port town of Andern was not much to look

at. Pitiful, really, compared to the sprawling, dark
capitol or even the smaller city of Lorister, where they
had restocked supplies a day past.

Their senses had been assaulted miles back by the
strong, repugnant smell of gutted fish, pitch and tar,
and waste. Thaddeus had complained about it
reverently, before Greer had told him that by opening
his mouth, he was tasting the air as well. Then he'd shut
up.

Hearne had silently agreed with his complaints, it was
disgusting, but, for the opportunity that lay within that
ramshackle town, he would smell and taste a lot worse.
Briefly, he wondered if this was how the Death Mages
had remained hidden for so long; that the smell of this
town was so shitty, it had left any royal searchers with
the choice to turn back or cut off their noses.

"Dismount," Hearne commanded when they were just
outside the town. It was midday, so the streets were

empty whilst the dock, no doubt, was overflowing with workers, "having fine horses will attract attention. Last thing we need is them running before we can acquire one of them."

"And by acquire, you mean force to resurrect hundreds of people and then slit the throat of," Greer commented idly, slipping off of her own bay horse before rolling her eyes at Thaddeus' brief resistance. "Exactly."

Once Thaddeus had finally dismounted his horse, Hearne grasped the reins of the Mind Mage's mare and his own, moving over to a nearby fence to tie up their horses. Greer followed just behind him, mirroring his actions.

Hearne then faced them, staring seriously at Greer and Thaddeus in turn. Finally, he asked, "are you ready?" His plan rested entirely on their ability to momentarily bring down one Death Mage. If they couldn't, all of them would be dead by the Death Mages' hands or worse, he considered with a shudder, the Night Queen's. And Galaris would remain in eternal torment.

Do you ever lighten up? Thaddeus asked of him, but Heanre's dire expression did not falter.

"We're ready," Greer told him, nose scrunched up from the smell as she worked on getting the peasant clothing they had brought with them out of the horse bags, throwing one to Thaddeus and another to Hearne. Then, she faced him again, her expression determined, "we won't let you down."

Hearne gave a curt nod before he grabbed the hem of his finely spun guard shirt, tossing it over his head and moving to replace it with a much rougher, brown-stained one.

Once they were all dressed, he looked forward into the town's small alleys and hazardously built shops, most supporting a fish logo made of rotting wood, and nodded towards it. Tersely, he said, "let's go then." And began to lead the way.

One step closer to destiny, he thought to himself, *one step closer to a freed Galaris.*

When they reached the port itself, the smell became nearly unbearable. Even Hearne could not keep his nose from scrunching up, whilst Thaddeus wretched and Greer's face went more than a little bit green. They had almost reached the first pier when a laughing voice called out to them, "you strangers are always so entertainin'. It's just a bit o' fish."

Hearne turned towards the source, and saw a man sitting on the stone behind them, two buckets of fish at his feet. He had clearly put his heavy winnings down so that he could laugh at their expense, but Hearne didn't mind. In fact, it suited his plan perfectly.

Letting out a quick laugh, Hearne charismatically answered, "is it that obvious?" then, as if he were nervous, he ran a hand through his thick, dark hair, "I've come all the way from Kaiidir with my friends to visit my cousins, but I can't seem to find them anywhere."

The man's eyes lit up with understanding, and he curiously inquired, "is it true what they says about the fish there? I 'eard they 'ad big trout!"

"Very big trout," Hearne enthusiastically agreed, despite having no clue if it was actually true, "the largest you've ever seen!"

The fisherman hummed in interest, eyes going slightly glassy as if he were imagining the trout for himself. After taking a moment to appreciate the vision, he finally asked the question that Hearne had been waiting for, "who yous lookin' for, boy? Maybe I can 'elp."

"My three cousins, Tana, Ayla and Kaldon."

A large smile overcame the other man's weathered face, "aye, I know 'em all! Great kids, most o' all Ayla. She's a sweetheart, tha' one."

"Do you know where they'd be right now?" Hearne asked, relief filling him. The first part of his plan was going perfectly.

The man nodded and told them he'd take them there, but only if they would help him carry his fish buckets home. Irritation bloomed within Hearne, but he did as the man had asked, he and Greer each holding the fish whilst the older man limped his slow way back.

Hearne had wanted to simply deposit the fish upon his porch, but the man insisted that they be left within his house, if it could even be called that. Honestly, it was a shack that was ready to keel over at the earliest opportunity.

As soon as he passed the unsteady door frame, he all

230

but dropped the bucket on the floor, and the man chirped a happy "tar" when Greer deposited hers alongside it.

It wasn't until Hearne leant back up that he felt the tip of a knife piercing the dark, muscled skin of his back. He tensed, and used his thoughts to relay a command to Thaddeus that neither he nor Greer intervene. Not yet.

"Tell me," the fisherman asked, his voice low and protective, "what do yous want with those kids?"

Now, he instructed Thaddeus, and he felt the man behind him crumble from the invisible weight of having a hand crushing his mind. The knife clunked to the floor, so Hearne could finally whirl around.

The man was crying out, withering in pain. Hearne told Thaddeus to loosen his grip. Even after the Mind Mage complied, the man's legs still spasmed from phantom agony.

Harshly, Hearne reached down and yanked his chin up to face him. The knife the man had used was now in Hearne's hand, which he brandished in front of him. Leaning forward, Hearne asked him, "where are they?"

The older man's eyes shone with defiance.

With a frown, Hearne turned to Thaddeus and repeated, "where are they?"

"They live here. It used to be a boarding house for orphans before the lovely Royon bought it. He allowed them to stay," Thaddeus informed him, and the poor man's eyes went wide with horror, "they'll be back when the hour strikes for a lunchtime break."

Hearne looked over to the clock and saw that it was only five minutes to, and smiled. The old fisherman had begun to cry, devastated at having betrayed the ones he cared about.

I'm sorry, Hearne thought at the man, despite knowing that he, unlike Thaddeus, could not hear him, *but it's for the good of Galaris. You'd understand, if you knew.* After a moment, Hearne inquired, "do they all get back at the same time?"

The fisherman shook his head from side to side rapidly, gazing at Hearne through hateful, tear-stricken eyes. However, he hadn't been trained to protect himself against a Mind Mage, and when someone asks you a question, it is only natural to automatically think of the answer, even if you don't intend to give it.

"One of the girls, Ayla, sometimes gets back a minute or two early, as she works at the nearest pier."

Watching the fisherman break was a rather pathetic sight, Hearne decided, steeling himself against any further guilt. He was doing what had to be done, for the sake of the humans of Galaris. If he lost his nerve…

Hearne closed his eyes at the mere idea of things continuing as they are now.

"Gag him and take him quickly to a closet or cupboard somewhere and lock him in," Hearne said to Thaddeus, stepping back towards the door, "then get back down here. We'll need for you to listen out for their thoughts to know when they're approaching."

Hearne could see Thaddeus' jaw clench at being ordered about, so, keeping his thoughts far away from what he really believed, Hearne created an image within his head of how happy he would be to see Thaddeus become King, and of him dutifully kneeling in front of his throne. The Mind Mage then smiled, his eyes hungry and did what was commanded of him. All the while, the fisherman fought desperately, clawing at the Mind Mage's shoulders.

It only took several moments of thought from Thaddeus to knock him out.

Watching it occur reminded him of why he was doing all of this. Against Mages' tyranny, against the Night Queen's tyranny, humans stood no chance. The Mages were stronger than them, their senses sharper; they could burn humans with a thought, or kill thousands with a sweeping Darkness.

Humans wouldn't be safe without all the Mages gone. He locked that thought far away, waiting for the sound of Thaddeus' steps coming back down the uneven, creaky steps.

Soon enough, the tall Mind Mage was descending and then moved to stand with Hearne and Greer next to the door.

Hearne opened his mouth to speak, but Greer cut him off, "yes, for the four hundredth time Hearne, we're ready."

"Shut up," Thaddeus hissed, "someone is coming."

"Are they one of the Death Mages?"

"I'm a Mind Mage, Greer. I can tell you what they're *thinking*, not their fucking species."

Then, after a short pause, Thaddeus managed to confirm from her thoughts, "it's Ayla."

Barely a moment later, the rotting door began to swing open, and Hearne saw a glimpse of a beautiful, dark-haired girl's face before her knees buckled, and she fell to the ground screaming. Worried shouts sounded on the other side of the door, and Hearne cursed when he realised that the siblings had come home together today.

Swiftly, he ran to the door, pushing at it with all the strength he had. Almost as soon as he had placed himself in front of it, two people attempted to enter. When they realised it was blocked, they were running at the door shoulders-first, making Hearne fall back before quickly recovering and pushing back again against the door. He thanked the Gods for his extensive guard training, but, even with that advantage, he would not hold out against Mage strength for long.

"Have you got her?" He asked, and tried to turn his head around. Briefly, he saw the girl's dark veins and knew that if Thaddeus or Greer touched her, they would die instantly. She was writhing around desperately, trying to get into contact with them or fight them off. However, he could also see the way that she desperately gripped onto her head and cried, vines rising from the dirt floor of the pitiful house, wrapping around her ankles and up and up.

"Now Hearne!" Greer shouted, and he knew she must have secured the vines around the Death Mage's whole body.

Hearne did not have the opportunity to move away from the door. Instead, the wood shattered to pieces under their strength and Hearne became airborne, his back colliding with the opposite side of the shack. Ayla's siblings surged into the room, falling to the floor with their veins the colour of ink. Before they could righten themselves, Hearne was behind Ayla, one arm wrapped around her waist with no fatality thanks to the vines that acted as a barrier between his skin and hers. His other hand was grasping the old man's knife, which he held to her throat, the only part of her, bar her eyes and nose, that was not within Greer's earthly grip.

The two Death Mages got to their feet, eyes not leaving their sister's presumably large and terrified ones. They both had the same dark brown hair as the other girl and were around the same height, in addition to having the same unnaturally pale skin that Death Mages were famed for. Hearne marvelled at how young they looked. The boy hadn't even had his final growth spurt yet, appearing to be around sixteen, but Hearne knew that they must be nearing seventy by now.

At least it confirmed the fact that they'd already made the Connection.

"Let go of her," the female Death Mage, Tana, demanded with a growling voice. She went to move forward towards Hearne and Ayla, but Hearne tutted lightly and stepped back, increasing the pressure of the blade against her sister's throat. Her brother grabbed onto the back of her top, yanking her back towards him.

With his sister back by his side, the boy, who Hearne recalled had spent the last six months in the Queen's army, as most sixteen-year-olds, or those pretending to be sixteen, did, asked, "are you here to take us to the

Queen?"

Hearne laughed lightly, startling the siblings, "no, I'm the last person who would deliver you into *her* clutches," the boy seemed to relax slightly, until Hearne finished his sentence, "I have my own agenda."

Ayla began to squirm against the grip of the vines, jostling Hearne. The man responded by increasing the pressure of his knife once more. This time, blood began to trickle down from her neck. The girl's siblings watched her movements mournfully and desperately, but knew that they could not get to her nor kill Hearne before he could slice her throat. Not unless they wished to massacre the entire village by summoning armies of the dead and buried, ones that only Death Mages with centuries of experience could control. Would they do so? Hearne did not know how attached they were to these people, but hoped whatever relationships they had formed would be enough to stop such actions.

"Pretty simple agenda, really," Hearne continued onwards, ignoring their inner turmoil and his own uncertainty, "I want you to bring some people back from the dead. More specifically, Commander Zarola and those that fought in the Last Battle."

Unexpectedly, Tana began to laugh, prompting Hearne to narrow his eyes at her and hold Ayla tighter. She didn't stop for several moments. Finally, the girl got out, "you want us to bring people back from the dead?" she continued to giggle lightly, though her eyes were furious, "you're mad! You think we don't know that to bring back that entire rebel army, it would cost us all our lives? Tell you what, why don't you just start killing away right now, because I will not be using my last breaths to help you!"

"Tana!" Her brother sharply reprimanded, eyes still fixated on the writhing Ayla.

Hearne just smiled.

Of course, he knew all about that small... *issue* with Death Mages. Whilst they were the most powerful of all the Mages, able to kill someone with a mere touch and raise the dead, the latter came at a high cost. Especially when they were trying to bring souls back from the Below, not just bodies.

Everything must be balanced, as many a philosopher preached. So, to bring back a soul, the Death Mages would lose something comparable to the strength of said soul in comparison to theirs. A human, Hearne remembered rather bitterly, would cost them no more than a fingernail; a Light Mage would cost them a finger; a Transformative Mage would cost them a hand or a foot; a Dark Mage a full arm or leg; a Death Mage their life. All the rest, somewhere in between depending on wherever they were on the Mage scale. Of course, they knew this; he'd planned accordingly.

"I'm well aware," Hearne said, and was given surprised looks from Greer and Thaddeus. He reached into his pocket, having transferred them from his guard uniform pockets to his peasant ones, and revealed three glittering silver necklaces with large, purple stones in the centre, "these are very rare Mage Channelling Necklaces. Wearing one of these means that it's not you that will bear the brunt of your magic, but the necklace. So, rather than you losing body parts as the price for bringing back the more powerful Mages and the numerous humans, it will simply be that the necklace shall break."

The two siblings not being held at knife point looked intrigued, but sceptical.

"Greer, if you would," Hearne said as he handed a necklace over to the Earth Mage.

She put the necklace around her neck and gestured her arm towards Ayla. Around her, she made the vines slither. Whilst she did so, the necklace pulsed a bright purple. After she felt the demonstration had gone on for long enough, Greer took off the necklace and handed it back to Hearne.

"See? Works just as I said," Hearne explained, "and, if you do this, obviously I won't kill Ayla here and I promise you that I'll get you out of the country, no questions asked, to somewhere you'll be safe."

Tana and Kaldon exchanged a glance, one full of bright hope.

To get out of Galaris, one was subjected to harsh border controls where any Mage abilities would easily be discovered and documented. For Death Mages, trying to leave the country was a suicide mission as the Queen would kill them upon discovery.

"What do you want us to do?" Kaldon asked, and Hearne rewarded them with a bright grin.

He handed Greer two of the three necklaces, which she passed onto the two siblings, whilst Hearne quickly loosened the position of the knife so that he could swiftly place the necklace around Ayla's neck, before reclaiming his threatening position.

"All you've got to do is form a connection together, keep your eyes closed and focus on bringing back the Winter Rebellion. Just them. Focus on the intent," Hearne told them, jerking his head at Greer and Thaddeus, the former of whom loosened the vines so that Ayla's arms would be released, and the other who gave each Death Mage a piece of paper. "On that paper is the command to have the Winter Rebellion rise from the dead in Ancient Galarian, you will-,"

"We know Ancient Galarian," Tana said, cutting him off somewhat irritably, "it's one of the first things our patron God taught us."

Hearne swallowed as he thanked the human Gods that the ability to call on the Connection between a God and their Mages was one sided. If the God of Death, Akeros, had the opportunity to warn them... well, everything would go to shit.

"Good," Hearne said, not letting any of his momentary concern show on his face, "well, if you want to get that passage and your sister back-,"

Before he could finish, Kaldon interrupted him, "you can let go of Ayla. We will all go through with this without the threat of her life. After spending our entire lives hiding and running, your opportunity of freedom is enough."

Hearne glanced at Thaddeus, who nodded and amusedly informed him: *they are so desperate for freedom, I think they'd believe anything.*

So, Hearne let her go and the siblings, with only a moment of hesitance, formed a circle, connecting their hands.

"Eyes shut," Hearne reminded them, "and the necklace will not stop you from feeling phantom pains but, be assured, it will only be the necklace that pays the price." The boy offered him a sharp nod, and the triplets all began to close their eyes. Tana was the last, eyeing Hearne with the distrust that the others should have shared.

"Njt adir un kir hys Akeros God, kir Dahjir fyr Kyster un Below fyr kir Paza, jhar yslen sacra un lyfe kol fyiir ahdir. Kir lyfzes Vadir Fyal soldi fyr kir."

It was first chanted by Kaldon, then Ayla, then Tana, becoming a symphony of voices connecting themselves to the Below.

Though it was midday outside, the sun was forced slowly downwards, bowing to the power of Death, sending the land of Galaris into a blackness that was reminiscent of the Night City. Despite having lived in said Capitol his whole life, it made Hearne shiver. It was a different kind of darkness, not of shadows, but nothingness.

What are they saying? He asked of Thaddeus who, due to his rank as a noble's son, knew Ancient Galarian and had been the one to write the chant out for them. Not that the Death Mages were using his chant, mind you. Thaddeus replied promptly, *we call on the power of our God, Akeros, the Master of Death and Ruler of the Below, to accept our sacrifice and, from it, let old life bloom once more. The lives of the Last Battle soldiers.* Hearne nodded, and grimaced when the first piercing scream hit the air as three of Kaldon's fingers dropped to the floor with soft clunks. Luckily, Ayla, who had been holding that hand, didn't seem to notice. Hurriedly, though, Hearne once again told them, "keep your eyes shut! It will not work if you break focus by opening your eyes. These are only phantom pains." Another roaring scream hit the air as one of the sisters lost some of their own fingers, blood now oozing down from all of their noses; from Tana, blood was pouring out of her ears.

"Njt adir un kir hys Akeros God, kir Dahjir fyr Kyster un Below fyr kir Paza, jhar yslen sacra un lyfe kol fyiir ahdir. Kir lyfzes Vadir Fyal soldi fyr kir."

The shack began to quake under the pressure of their magic, and Hearne heard screams rise up from all around. He had Greer poke her head out of the door. When she returned, it was transferred from her to Thaddeus and then to Hearne that the sea was rising. She seemed to think that a tsunami was on its way. They needed to go faster.

"What's happening?" Ayla questioned whilst her siblings continued to chant around her, "is everybody out there okay? I heard screaming."

Swiftly and soothingly Hearne assured her, "there's no screaming; it must be the screams of the dead you are hearing."

The young girl hesitated for only a moment, before she continued chanting with her siblings.

It was then that the rain began to pelt down upon the shack, the wind thrusting it this way and that; screeching as it launched its attack. The siblings' knees buckled simultaneously, forcing them towards the ground as they continued to chant.

The window broke. The air came in, throwing Hearne, Thaddeus and Greer off of their feet and into the nearby walls. Still, he roared for the siblings to continue, tempting them with promises of a free life, and so, desperately, they did.

Their facial features began to tear themselves off; noses, ears, skin, eyes. Still, they were told that it was phantom pains and diligently continued their chanting, thinking of the freedom they would have when Hearne helped them leave Galaris; of the warm feeling of safety that would then blanket over them, of the idea of not having to look over their shoulders every day.

Hearne startled when Kaldon's body slumped forward. Eyes wide and open. Dead.

"Kal?" Came Tana's voice, and Hearne ran over to the boy. He wrapped his arms around the waist of the corpse and lifted it up, making it so that he no longer pulled at the sisters' hands.

His eyes, however, grew wide and panicked when he saw the almost faceless Ayla swaying back and forth rapidly. No doubt, she was about to slump into death too. He tried to meet Greer's eyes, but she was too busy screaming as the roof caved in. Hearne lifted the corpse up slightly to protect his head, but no debris fell within the circle that the siblings had made.

"Ayla?" Tana's voice questioned, before growing hysterical and desperate, "Ayla!"

When Hearne rose his head from beneath Tana's brother's corpse, he saw that the final Death Mage's eyes were wide and open, the rest of her face a bloodied mess, filled with indescribable grief.

She turned her gaze to Hearne, whose arms were still wrapped around her brother's body, and let out a wail, dropping her crimson face to the floor. Tana seemed to be rocking back and forth. Hearne realised far too late that she was whispering some kind of chant in Ancient Galarian. Of it, there was only one word that he recognised.

Caradoc.

Then, her body seemed to lose all tension and slumped forwards. Before Hearne could reach towards her, to check if the last Death Mage was truly dead, the town was ripped apart, the cleaving of the shack sending him tumbling through the black, black air.

It was a rip that seemed to echo throughout the entirety of the universe.

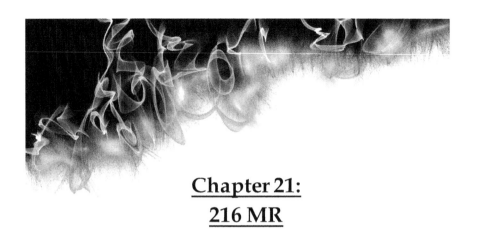

Chapter 21:
216 MR

"*He* knows!"

Coren had burst through her chamber doors like a
tempest, slamming them violently into the walls
behind. Her breath was coming out in short pants, her
words shouted wildly and desperately, her whole-body
trembling.

Zarola and Nerah had been inside, both startled by her
sudden, aggressive invasion. The brown-haired maid's
brows furrowed, her mouth opening to question the
frazzled girl, but Zarola's eyes swiftly hardened.

"Nerah," the redhead began, though her eyes did not
leave Coren's, "I think Coren might need some water.
And maybe a few of those lemon tarts."

The other girl went to protest, but Zarola cut her off
with a rather fearsome glare. So, with a final concerned
look at Coren, Nerah vanished out of the chamber
doors.

As soon as the door had shut behind her, Coren rushed

straight over to Zarola, grasping her arms tightly, "we need to go. We need to run. I've incapacitated him for now, but he knows about you and he knows about Izak and, oh Gods, what he's doing to those children. Did you know Zar? He's mad! He has to be! Oh Gods, oh Gods, what did I do? Oh-,"

"Coren," the rebel cut in firmly, her expression betraying none of the concern and surprise that she knew Zarola must be feeling, "you need to tell me exactly what has happened. Quickly."

As fast as she could, Coren began to tell Zarola everything she thought was notable, beginning with the letter and ending with her Darkness exploding outwards. All the while, her green gaze continuously moved towards the door, knowing that any minute King Caradoc or his guards would come bursting in. The uncertainty of it all made her shake even more violently, but Zarola did not falter.

"Pack your things," she said to Coren, grimly, "quickly and lightly. Go into the maid's chamber and grab my dagger and cloak as well. When you've got them, go to your bathing room and take the servants door out. Keep to the left the whole time. I'm going to go and get Izak, and we'll meet you there."

Coren had to force herself to stop nodding after a moment, tremors still raking through her.

The redhead did not spare another moment for her, darting towards the door. But, when her hand was on the handle, she murmured so softly that the Dark Mage almost didn't hear it, "I'm sorry, Coren," and then left. Coren did not allow herself to fully process the words, and the events that had led to Zarola saying them. She couldn't. She could not afford to shut down. Not right now.

Her shaking lighter now, she rushed towards her closet and pulled out a cloak similar to the one she had been wearing just last night – oh Gods, it was growing light outside of her windows, how long had she been down there with Mina? How long had she been staring at and listening to Caradoc in utter disbelief, like some dumbstruck idiot? – sobs began to wrack her body, as she pulled it out and placed it around her.

"You're not my daughter. You're not anything, to anybody. And certainly not to us."

Her father had told her that, and yet she'd been so quick to forget it, so swift to hope that she could be somebody to someone. That she could mean something. That somebody could love a monster like her.

That she wasn't worthless.

But she couldn't; but she was.

Despite the violent cries erupting from her throat just as Mount Ipyrcas had to end the last of the sorcerers, she did not stop. Luckily, her dagger had been tucked securely into her undershirt sleeve, not her cloak sleeve, and thus she still retained it. Though her mind was muddled, the Dark Mage also had the foresight to grab the smallest vase in her room – as a bottle could not be found – apologising to the very beautiful orange lilies as she threw them out, and then filled it with two water glasses left on her bedroom table.

They'd be needing some water when running away like

the fugitives they'd become.

Coren cast such thoughts swiftly from her mind. Then, the woman with red-rimmed eyes charged into the maid's chamber, prepared to grab Zarola's things and get out as swiftly as she could, only to be met with a bleary eyed, still-dressing Dahlia. They both stared at one another for one moment, and then another. Coren's mind whirled momentarily. She knew that Zarola would no doubt berate her for this, but it wasn't as if she had the time to truly consider her course of action.

"If you trust me," Coren told the Azyalian maid desperately, her voice croaking and breaking, "then, please, get dressed as quickly as you can, and follow me."

Dahlia observed her for several moments, her dark eyes widening and then narrowing, but she nodded, moving to her wardrobe and gathering her own cloak out of it.

"Thank you," Coren said, and the need to sob re-emerged, but she shoved it down relentlessly, rushing over to where, from its spotless appearance, she assumed Zarola's bed was and repeated, "thank you." Rummaging in the side draw of the thin, uncomfortable-appearing bed, Coren found Zarola's dagger tucked between two books and discovered a flask on the side. Grabbing both, she climbed over the bed to the wardrobe and grasped onto a dark grey cloak, tucking Zarola's dagger and flask into its pocket. Then, turning towards the exit of the maid's chambers, she told Dahlia, who was standing just to the side of it, "we're going out through the servants' door in the bathroom, to meet Zarola and Izak at the bottom." Dahlia nodded in acknowledgement, so Coren led her dark-haired accomplice through her chambers, and then into the bathroom, where she pushed open the door in the wall before pausing.

Mina.

She was still all alone in the walls, gone half-mad and being used as Caradoc's blood bag. As his experiment. She closed her eyes tightly.

When Coren opened them, she pushed Zarola's cloak with affects into Dahlia's hands, who was eyeing her curiously.

"Go, run! You have to keep left, Zarola and Izak will be there," she gently but urgently, pushed Dahlia towards the door.

Dahlia refused to move willingly, eyeing Coren with alarm, "where are you going?"

"Tell Zarola that I went back for Mina, and that if I don't find a way out, somehow," Coren paused for a moment, trying desperately to keep the shattered pieces of her together, "to go on without me. Don't wait. It's not worth it."

I'm not worth it.

Before Dahlia could respond, Coren gave her a much firmer shove and closed the servants' door behind her, swiftly dragging over a cabinet so that Dahlia could not come back for her, which, from the way the cabinet was pushed back somewhat, she tried to do.

Spinning on her heel, Coren exited her bathroom and

all but launched herself from her chambers, desperate to get to Mina and get out before the Fire King and his followers awoke.

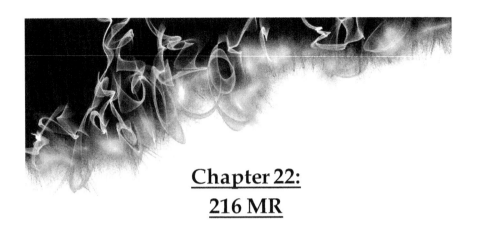

Chapter 22:
216 MR

*W*hen Coren finally reached the sixth floor of the palace, she could not help but pause for a moment in front of the tapestry of the woman with the fine red hair, who cried as Caradoc's flames consumed her from all around – there was no escaping from him.

Coren swallowed.

That may be her fate too. After all, she, like Febronia, made the mistake of trusting and loving Caradoc, even if it was in an entirely different way.

With that thought, Coren carefully pushed the tapestry aside, and took several steps forward, allowing the wall to embrace her, before it pushed her out to face a familiar darkness.

This time, the Dark Mage did not proceed with caution, but rather garnered an alarmingly fast pace, keeping her hands out in front of her so that she would not find herself nose-to-wall with any of the corners.

Fleetingly, she had thought of calling the Darkness to her to make the inside of the walls lighter and therefore easier to navigate, but her emotions felt far too out of control to ever hope to claim dominion over darkness. Clamouring over the door that she had broken down not even a day before, the Dark Mage found herself in a pitch-black version of the Mage prison.

Silence embraced the area, the only sound that ever pierced it being the shallow breathing of Caradoc's victims, irregular and harsh to the ears. Coren's throat swelled with sickness and with sorrow.

When she moved to take a step forward, a low, throaty whisper pierced the room, seemingly bouncing from one wall to the next. "Kill me," it requested.

Coren whirled around, but she could not see anything. Her entire body tensed, bracing for an attack, but nothing ever came.

"K-k-kill me."

This time, Coren followed the voice to the bars of one cell. Determinedly, she told the darkness – trying in vain to shove down the fear, shock, embarrassment and devastation that the past day had brought on – *come to me.*

Briefly, it did.

It was only a moment, after which the darkness used her mental instability to swiftly escape her clutches, but in that moment Coren was greeted by a pair of intense amber eyes gazing up at her. Their face was pressed tight against the bars, causing the fragile skin to blister at the contact, but a small, unstable smile still resided upon crimson lips.

"Kill me," he said again, eyes unfocused, and Coren realised his body was splattered with blood, "Kill. Beg I-

I."

The Dark Mage wanted to cry when she heard the thump of the child's knees hitting the floor of his cell. Though Coren could not see him, she knew that he would be slumped on the floor, staring imploringly up at her. A boy, likely no older than eight, begging for death when he had not even lived.

"Kill," this time, the voice came from behind her, and to the left. From cell four, where the Body Mage resided. Another voice chimed in from near it. The same word, the same plea: "k-kil-l," from cell three.

"Don't," Coren began, having to pause to swallow, "don't you want to live, to escape?"

"'Ren," a voice called. That voice was familiar and originated from the very end of the corridor. With great hesitance, Coren removed herself from the front of Lucian's cage and began to trek towards it, hands extended before her, hissing when they came in contact with the cell bars where Mina was.

Coren knelt by the bars of the cage.

"I-I can get you out of here, Mina," Coren told her, her knees cold against the stone floor, "I can save you all. I *will* save you all."

A hand touched her face, Mina's hand, wiping away a tear that the blonde didn't even realise had fallen down her face.

"Sweet Coren, kind Coren," Mina cooed softly. Even when being tender, the Death Mage did not lose the unstable edge to her voice, "you cannot save everyone. Sometimes, you have to let go of what is lost. Otherwise, you will lose yourself instead. T-the only liberation you can give us is death."

"But none of you are already gone! I can hel-,"

Footsteps sounded, and Coren's body froze.

"Coren," a voice whispered out. Milo's.

He'd come for her; Caradoc would come for her.

"Kill," echoed three voices down the hall, accompanied by the harsh breathing of those who were unable to bring themselves to the world of consciousness. Children who had never lived; children who were tortured and used and abused at the Fire King's whims, ripped from their families. Children who had no hope of a life without ghosts.

They couldn't live like this any longer; Mina couldn't live like this any longer; Coren couldn't live like this any longer.

And now Caradoc and his supporters had come for them.

It was too late.

"Kill, Coren," Mina begged, "please. I want to see my sisters again."

The only liberation you can give us is death.

And so Coren let go, and the Darkness embraced them all.

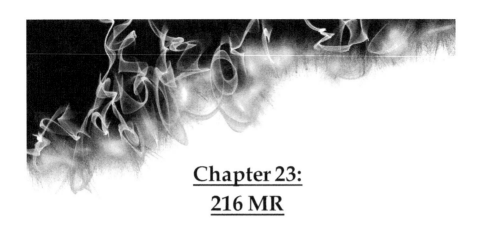

Chapter 23:
216 MR

*B*lack. Pitch. Coal. Night. Ink.

So many words associated with the darkness, so many words associated with the familiar, plain-faced woman who stood before Coren.

A burning, cold hand settled upon her chin, lifting two green eyes – almost lifeless, and wholly defeated – to meet her endless ones.

Gently, the woman, looking almost exactly as she had upon the tapestry of the Gods, tutted before smiling widely. It was not a joyous smile. It was a predatory one.

"Next time," she told her delicately, caressing her cheek. "Innocence, my sweet, was not the loss I was waiting for."

And so Coren opened her eyes, and met reality. From every side, the waters attacked her brutally, pushing and shoving, choking and embracing. With all the energy the Dark Mage had left, she fought against the current, not even realising the pain in her arm until half of the wood was brutally snapped off by the strength of the water whilst it was still buried within her flesh.

The pain made her scream; the water made her choke. By her side, another body was being pulled away by the water's undercurrent, pieces of the same wood that pierced Coren's arm embedded within their chest. The body was smiling, their eyes fixed wide and open for eternity whilst piles of matted dark hair delicately floated about her pale body.

Mina.

Coren reached for her, but the water pulled the Death Mage into its depths, leaving Coren to fight alone.

The wood that burned Mages, the wood that had surrounded each of their cages, Coren had not put nearly enough thought into it.

It was Willow Mage.

And so, Mina was dead for good. She was with her sisters, hopefully, at peace.

When the water desperately attempted to tug her through a gap between two rocks, Coren grasped onto them. Though her nails were forced from their beds, she still held on and on and on. She just needed to figure out how to get up to the surface of the water. If she could just get a foot on the bed of the water perhaps, she could-

An object collided with her hard, dislodging her grip and sending her tumbling through the passageway between the rocks. This sent her careening into a larger area once more, striking down any further hope of escape.

In her desperation, she had hung onto the object that had hit her, but soon found herself crying out as she got a better look at it. Directly facing her was the amber eyes of a boy of perhaps eight years, his mouth and eyes opened wide, his neck gaping and bleeding where Willow Mage wood had struck him. Coren pushed the body from her, and watched in horror as his head wobbled, held on by only a few tendons.

With great relief, Coren welcomed the embrace of darkness.

When peridot eyes opened themselves once more, it was to face the moon, which benevolently shone down upon her, as it had each and every night of her life. *Why?* Coren wanted to ask, wanted to rail against it, as she lay motionless whilst her senses returned to her. *Why are you the same when my entire world has changed? How can the world simply go on?*

The moon didn't answer her, it never would, for nature cared not for human suffering. The world would not stop simply because you had loved and lost. No, it would continue on the same as it always had, a constant in a world of inconsistency, no matter how much you needed some kind of acknowledgement of your pain.

She had killed again. She had become a monster again, a murderer again.

Young lives had ended.

Yet nature did not care.

Turning her head to the side, Coren stared at the now seemingly glowing wood that stuck out from her arm, pinning her soul down with the deeds she had committed with other wood of its kind.

In the explosion, the wood would have hit many a prisoner, possibly all of them. Mina was dead. Lucian was dead. Perhaps the other children were dead too. Even Milo.

Why was the idea of Milo being dead the part that made her hurt the most? Why couldn't she have eradicated all care she had for him the moment he had betrayed her? It would have been so much easier.

Reaching her right hand over to her left arm, Coren wrenched the wood out of her forearm, grunting at the pain of it. Then, she brought the wood closer to her face, all the while the wood burned away at the flesh of the palm in which she held it.

She had never seen Willow Mage wood up close before. It was light in colour, just as ordinary willow wood was, but had a decidedly unnatural glow to it. One that was made even brighter by the influence of the moon.

It was beautiful. It was deadly.

Just like Caradoc, Coren thought bitterly.

Then, she lowered the Willow Mage wood from her face, and closer towards her heart, until the sharpest end was only millimetres above the skin of her chest.

You'd be so proud of me right now, mum, Coren thought with a small, ironic twist to her lips, *I don't need you to teach or punish me anymore. I can do it all by myself. I'll tell you about it, if I see you again.*

And then Coren extended her hand higher, prepared to take the final plunge, until a scream pierced the forest to her right.

"Dahlia," Coren gasped out, her voice hoarse from choking over and over upon water. She scrambled up from the dirt floor and into the woods, the stake still held tightly within her grasp.

She tried to shout out her name, scream it, but nothing would come out of her throat any louder than a whisper.

Still, Dahlia's screams persisted, allowing Coren to follow them until they sounded not even two hundred feet away. When she broke into the clearing, she saw the back of a redheaded woman and a dark-haired man, both knelt down and lifting Dahlia up from where she must have missed her footing, slipping from the grass hill and almost into the lake a long drop below. When they got Dahlia to her feet, the tan woman fell to her knees, taking in breaths in large pants, before her eyes went wide as she connected eyes with the scared Dark Mage.

"Coren?" Dahlia questioned, her eyes roving up and down the soaking wet, muddy, deranged looking blonde.

"I-," Coren began, as Izak and Zarola whirled around to face her. Both appeared to eye her with great relief, though Coren did not know if that was just her mind being too hopeful, and Izak took a small step towards her.

Without even knowing why she did it, Coren took a long step back. Izak stopped in his place.

"What happened to you?" Zarola ordered harshly after a moment's silence, "you were supposed to meet with us, you were supposed to be here!"

Coren didn't, couldn't, look at her.

"Jakan's dead," she said instead, though when she stared at Izak's red-rimmed eyes she realised that he already knew, "I'm sorry."

Izak's smile was one that should have made that dastardly moon mourn. "Not as sorry as I am, for everything. For you and for Jakan. I-I sent the letter, I-"

"We don't have time for this," Zarola cut in, looking west as if she had heard something that not even Coren nor Izak's Mage senses had enabled them to hear. Not that they were exactly in the greatest state to be using said senses, "we'll have half of the royal army, if we're lucky, after us by the next sunset. We need to head as far north as we can. You can mourn later."

Coren nodded, reaching around for the pocket of her cloak, having realised her throat was parched during her brief exchange of words, only to find that the water had stolen her make-shift water bottle away from her. Of course it had.

Realising her dilemma, Zarola thrust her flask into Coren's chest, making her stumble slightly. Then, the redhead grasped her arm and reached up her sleeve. Looking down at it, Coren realised that the crimson colour of blood was staining all of her undershirt beneath that forearm. From it, Zarola grabbed her twin dagger, which had thankfully survived the moat, even if it had made a mess of her arm.

Then, Zarola eyed her equally bloody left arm with a look that Coren recognised as both concern and irritation, grabbing Coren's hand and tugging the Willow Mage stake from it.

"I'll be taking both of those, for now," Zarola told her, before marching past her to lead the way.

Coren nodded, and made a decision swiftly.

She would stay with Zarola, Izak and Dahlia until they reached the rebel camps up north; she would protect the people that she had grown to care about with everything she had. Then, and only then, would she liberate the world of one of its greatest monsters.

A monster capable of falling in love with the Fire King. A monster who, no matter the circumstances, had killed children; had gone so far as to allow herself to lose control. Had become a danger to everyone around her.

Coren herself.

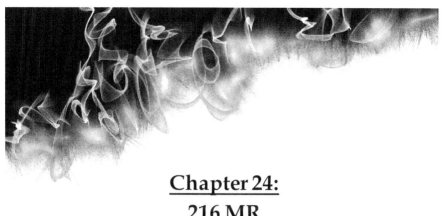

Chapter 24:
216 MR

$\mathcal{T}$he journey northward through the forests within the
riverlands of Galaris was an overwhelmingly
unpleasant one. This was largely because, for the sake
of navigation, they followed closely to what was widely
known as the 'River of the Dead', Zarola having
decided that when the King's troops came after them,
they would be more likely to track the Golden River
and Alyda River, both of which also headed towards the
northern mountains.

The problem, however, with following the
unfortunately named river was that the terrain was
very muddy, as well as a lack of food supply and the
repugnant smell.

From what Izak had told them, likely in an attempt to
get Coren talking through the offering of knowledge,
the river had gained its name during the War of Gods,
in which the God of Death – newly having gained his
powers – was said to have tricked the hybrid's troops

into entering what was then known, rather ironically, as *Lyfe fyr Galaris*, meaning 'Life of Galaris'. Once the troops had entered the waters, the God Akeros was said to have risen skeletons from the ground beneath it, having them pull the troops down and drown them in its depths.

Even to this day, the smell of death – of rotting flesh – still surrounded the river and, as was common of many sites where Death Mages exercised their powers, no life would grow there.

Normally, this topic of conversation would have intrigued Coren greatly, prompting questions of how many died? What happened next? But her mind was occupied upon a Mage that was not the God of Death: Nerah.

You cannot save everyone, Coren, Mina had told her, but, for Nerah, Coren hadn't even thought to try.

Unbidden, the image of the Light Mage returning to an empty room, a water jug in one hand and a plate of lemon tarts in the other, only to realise that everyone had left – that they'd forgotten her – made Coren close her eyes, pained.

Perhaps the room wouldn't be empty. Perhaps Caradoc's guards were waiting for her, ready to drag Nerah off to be tortured for a location she didn't know, or maybe-

Coren faltered in her steps.

Maybe, now that Coren had killed Caradoc's blood source for Light Mages, Nerah would be used in Lucian's stead.

She would be reduced to someone hopeless. To

someone who would beg for death.

The very idea had Coren prepared to retch, but she swallowed it down. The entire journey so far, Dahlia had been standing by her side, giving her concerned looks every time she thought Coren wasn't looking. The last thing she wanted to do was worry her more. Instead, bitter at her own powerlessness, all Coren could do was pray. And she did. She begged that Nerah's patron God – Lexin – would keep her safe. It was all she could do now, when the stern-faced Zarola would be more likely to tie Coren up and have her carried over Izak's shoulder than allow her to go back to the palace, if the lecture she had gotten over bringing Dahlia and going back for Mina had any bearing on it.

"She could have been a spy, Coren," was one phrase that Zarola had hissed at her, gripping onto her shoulders hard enough to leave imprints of her fingers, *"she could have taken you straight to that bastard! What would you have done then?"*

"Uh, if it helps, I'm not a spy?" the Elemental Mage had cut in tentatively.

Zarola had fixed Dahlia a dead look, and told her, *"that's exactly what a spy would say."*

Nobody could really argue with that.

Not that Coren would have anyway. She had not spoken a word since reuniting with her fellow runaways, all of her energy was focused upon trying to push away the image of Mina's dead body, of the way that Lucian's corpse had felt beneath her hands, of the images of the other children she had likely killed, of

263

the carvings in Jakan's forehead, of the explosions, of Milo's betrayal, of Caradoc and all that he once meant and had now become, of the imagined scene of Nerah being dragged away, kicking and screaming and blaming Coren all the while.

Gods, she longed for that stake.

Without Coren even realising, dusk had settled, and they'd begun to veer off into the forest that ran along the river. Dutifully, she had followed, barely noticing when she tripped, only to be rightened by the firm hold of Dahlia.

Coren nodded in thanks, before continuing onwards.

"We'll set up camp here for the night," Zarola announced, scanning the faces of her accomplices as she did so. If her eyes lingered longer on Coren's face, nobody was prepared to point it out, "autumn is approaching swiftly, and we've travelled northwards, so we'll have to have sleeping partners to combat the cold. I'll stay with Coren; Izak and Dahlia, you two remain closely together. Izak, tonight or tomorrow, you'll also need to catch Dahlia up on everything that's occurring and why."

It was now that Coren recalled some of Caradoc's words from their final meeting. Zarola was one of the rebel Commander's Secondaries. She was a leader, and certainly acted like it.

The redheaded woman inclined her head at Coren and then towards a nearby tree, and the Dark Mage followed without complaint, which, for a reason foreign to Coren, made the leader frown.

Neither spoke as dusk faded to night, not even as the sun rose the next morning, and the long trek began all over again. Izak led the navigation, offering a flimsy excuse of how he was more familiar with these forests than any of them, though, by the way Zarola occasionally corrected him, it was not true. However, if being in charge of the map and compass took his mind off his role in Jakan's death, then neither Zarola nor Coren were prepared to intervene.

For the rest of them, but especially Dahlia and Coren, neither of whom had even seen a forest of this size before, it was a long day of stumbling over roots, slipping in mud and exhaustion. Though, there were no protests to be heard.

"So, the Fire King was torturing children?" Dahlia asked, in shocked repulsion, on the second day. Her words sent a flinch through Coren. *Lucian. Farrah. Mina.* She couldn't even remember the names of the others, which made guilt settle even heavier within her stomach. "And was trying to use their blood to make himself into some sort of God?"

"Hybrid," Izak had corrected.

It means power, Coren. Something that you're very familiar with the desire for.

"He's mad!"

Jakan's body. His forehead. FOOL.

"Perhaps," the Earth Mage had agreed, the look in his eyes grave, "and that just makes him all the more dangerous. He won't see sense. He won't stop."

"Coren," the Dark Mage could see her now, Nerah, with tubes stealing the crimson life from her veins, tears

265

tracking down her bruised, beaten face, *"Coren, why did you do this to me? Why did you leave me?"*

Coren had fallen to her knees and thrown up in the hollow of a half-fallen tree, and all mentions of the Fire King had ceased.

By the fifth night, Zarola had grown tired of Coren's eternal silence. The days that she spent in a place far from reality; the nights that she spent with her gaze fixated upon the moon, searching for any secret acknowledgement of all that had befallen them. There was nothing, there never was.

On the four previous nights, when Zarola slept, Coren had found it comforting to study the other female. The redhead's face was long and thin, with high cheekbones and a finely crafted jaw. It made her look sharp, in the day at least. Whilst she was sleeping, she still appeared somewhat haughty in appearance, yet so much more relaxed. Like the stake had, Zarola also seemed to glow beneath the moon, brown skin gleaming beneath curling red hair.

But Zarola, unlike the moon, *had* changed. There was an anxious twist to her mouth, one that Coren did not recall being there when they had both slept in her bed after that night in the walls. Even her hair appeared on edge, treading the barrier between curly and frizzy.

One time, Coren's left hand had twitched, as if to reach out and curl a twirling strand around her finger, but the Dark Mage swiftly put a stop to that.

Tonight, however, the rebel did not appear eager to sleep. Instead, Zarola seemed to be waiting for something – and Coren braced herself for whatever it may be.

"You never sleep," she spoke to the blonde after many moments of silence, and Coren supposed that it was not a ground-breaking revelation. Although she had not seen her reflection since leaving the palace – with Zarola still holding the twin dagger captive and the river water being so murky that one would be lucky to see a shadow in it – the Dark Mage had no doubt that bags had appeared beneath her eyes.

"Every time I close my eyes," Coren responded for the first time in over five days, voice laced with pained candour, "I see them. I see him."

Zarola's deep brown eyes stared into her own, imploring her to go on, but Coren reverted back to her previous state. Silent as the river; sombre as those in their watery graves below it.

There was a flash of something within Zarola's eyes, which soon darted to the recently redressed injuries on the Dark Mage's forearms. Coren had always found the other woman difficult to read, as if she were a sentence without punctuation, or a book without vowels.

Coren continued to observe her as the other woman looked away and reached into the pocket of her cloak, bringing out the Willow Mage steak. Coren's eyes tracked its every movement with a kind of desperate hunger, and Zarola's eyes tracked hers.

"Once," the rebel began, poking the sharp tip of the stake against her finger. The wood's power had no effect upon her, its edge merely causing a red bud to form on the end of her finger, "you asked me whether I would choose power or freedom, for that was the question the King had posed to you."

The rebel's eyes searched her own. "You've tried power, so why don't you give freedom a chance?" *Because my liberation causes others pain,* Coren wanted to respond, *because if I let what is within me out, even for a moment, it will carve a path in the world of destruction and death that I won't be able to control. And I don't want that.*

But what was the point of saying any of that? Zarola could not help her and the only person who had seemed to be able to, she had fled from.

But what of Nias?

It was only in that very moment, after the confusing, horribly fast-paced rush of the past five days had come and gone, one which had flung Coren from one moment to the next with only the words 'save' and 'survive' able to break through the intense barrier of fear, that Coren recalled the words spoken during her unconsciousness in the lake.

"Next time," Nias had told her.

What if Coren tried to contact her again? Would she even be able to reach her?

Maybe, if Nias could tell Coren how to form the Connection, then she wouldn't need to die. Instead, the Dark Mage could become more stable, and take that boat to Valark, finding somewhere to live far away from others – just in case – after she had delivered Zarola and the others safely to the rebel encampments.

But did Coren deserve to live after all she had done?

Did a monster deserve to be released from its cage?

Alternatively, she considered, did she deserve the

liberation of death? Wouldn't it be far crueller to have her continue living and remember their faces every time she closed her eyes? Perhaps-

"I don't even know why I'm saying any of this," Zarola laughed out bitterly, her voice one of frustrated puzzlement as she cut through Coren's thoughts, rolling over to face the dark sky, "you know, when I first met you, I hated you."

Despite herself and her life-shaping contemplations, Coren found her lip quirking up slightly. "I know."

The human woman glanced over at her in surprise.

"Your hostile glares were not exactly subtle," Coren said, "plus, you held a knife to my throat, remember?"

The Dark Mage could have sworn the redhead blushed at the reminder of that night, but she turned her head from Coren before she could be sure.

Despite Zarola facing away, the blonde continued. "If I were you, I probably would have hated me too. After all, not all Mages are good people," Zarola snorted, as if to say *that's an understatement*, but Coren just rolled her eyes with a small smile, "and some of us, we have these powers, these strengths, that outweigh what humans are capable of so unfairly. So, whether we deserve it or not, I understand your fear and contempt. You want to protect yourself. I'm sure that if ants could hate, they would not look kindly upon humans, who can easily take their lives away with a single stomp of their foot."

Almost immediately, Coren grimaced, "I'm sorry, I didn't mean any offence by comparing humans to ants. It's just... I think hate is just another form of fear."

269

"It's fine," Zarola told her, looking at Coren rather strangely. Her eyes were narrowed, but not hostile. More like contemplative, the Dark Mage supposed, but... not.

Gods, someone really needed to write a manual of how to read this woman. Coren would give them everything she owned for it, which only consisted of the clothes on her back... but still, the sentiment remained.

She shook that thought away, and focused once more on the woman across from her. The light-haired woman did not know what possessed her in that moment but, with Zarola, beautiful and fierce Zarola, staring at her like that, Coren could not help but breathe out, "what-what do you think of me now?"

Zarola's eyes dipped towards a lower part of her face, but quickly drew back up to the tentative green eyes that were staring at her; fear in their depths. The rebel swallowed.

"Goodnight, Coren," was her answer.

Coren stared as Zarola turned over to face the opposite direction. As she did so, several orange-red curls spilled onto Coren's right hand, which had resided between the two. Quickly, as if the contact had burned her, the Dark Mage moved it.

"Goodnight, Zar," she responded, unable to keep the resignation from her voice, and turned her back upon the rebel.

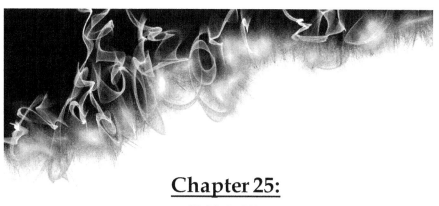

Chapter 25:
768 MR

𝒯he Queen was bathing.

Auryon, who had just arrived back at the Night City's Black Castle, her face stained with blood, sweat and mud, paused at the doorway. The tub was facing towards her, greeting the Captain with the rare sight of a relaxed Corentine, or, as much as she would allow herself to be.

Her head was inclined back towards the ceiling, with splendid grey-green eyes hidden away from the world beneath heavy lids; both arms lay outside the confines of the tub, unhealthily pale skin glistening from the aftermath of being submerged. Around her, red petals had been scattered and the water glimmered the kind of blue that could only be created by a Water Elemental Mage who had seen the waters east of Kokurun.

Auryon wanted to look away, but could not. She had always thought Coren to be beautiful, even when she

271

had first seen her at Commander Zarola's rebel encampment, bloody, haunted and hated by all. Even by Auryon.

Startling the Queen's Guard, a voice from the tub spoke, "If you keep staring like that, you're going to make me blush."

If she had not been suffering from mild humiliation, the greatest swordswoman in Galaris may have scoffed at such words. The Queen, blush, as if. Instead, the dark-haired woman brought her eyes back down to Coren's glistening, pale skin with a frown, "you need to sleep more. It's making you ill."

The Queen hummed in disagreement, having moved her arm so her fingers could lightly trace the illuminous bath water, leaving small ripples in their path, before lazily inquiring, "are you considering a career change from Captain to nursemaid? If so, I'm afraid to inform you that I'm not hiring."

"Coren-,"

SLAM!

Auryon barely retained a flinch as the door behind her shut with an ear-splitting amount of force, Darkness having materialised from nothing to form two, strong hands that sent it flying home to its frame.

When the Captain looked back to her Queen, she had propped herself up in the tub using her elbows, her now open eyes revealing light irises circled by a pitch-black ring. One side of her mouth gradually lifted.

"Now, now, dear Auryon, enough with the chit chat," the Dark Mage told her firmly, before she all but purred out, "I believe there are some guests in need of a warm greeting. Escort me, will you?"

Knowing that the Queen liked to see her adversaries on their knees, Auryon had arranged them accordingly. They were all lined up next to each other, heads bowed, knees aching, with their hands locked behind their backs in either mortal cuffs or in the Mage's Bane, depending upon their species.

Before them, Galaris' ruler stalked her way over to the slight podium where her throne resided. After rising from her bath, the Queen had pulled on a lightweight, chiffon black gown with a plunging neckline and high leg slits. It was a style of dress that had been worn by the Nithians – now a part of Galaris – centuries ago, with the Queen bringing it back into fashion. Around her waist, a low, dangling belt of pure gold resided.

A creature of luxury, Auryon's Queen was.

From her vantage point, now firmly seated within her onyx-adorned throne, Coren scanned what she could see of the faces of those before her, her lips pulling into a short, unpleasant grin as some thought crossed her mind.

One of the fifteen's head snapped up, eyes blown wide beneath long, brown hair, as he breathed out, "you're one sick bitch."

Despite his offensive words, earning him a harsh kick to the back by one of Auryon's zealous guards-in-training which sent him crashing face-verse into the marble floor, the Queen looked rather delighted. Propping her chin up on her palm, she smiled unkindly and stated, "you're the Mind Mage. Thaddeus."

The Captain frowned heavily as the tall man looked up, nothing having been reported to her about the fact that there was a Mind Mage, and a powerful one at that, amongst the prisoners. He didn't even have a Mage's Bane on. But Coren's smile simply widened.

"Only three nights ago, your parents were in this very room, begging me to spare you; telling me that you were just a foolish, ambitious boy," the Queen continued, the eyes of all upon her. Then, she cocked her head. "But I don't think I will."

Without so much as a flick of her fingers, the Mind Mage was suspended in the air, black, shadow-like claws clutched around his throat and tugging brutally at his face and limbs. Screams of pain and horror filled the audience room. Several of the others lined up tried to crawl away in vain, but the swords of guards were there to swiftly put a stop to any kind of retreat.

The Dark Mage continued talking, as if she were blind to the sight before her, to the blood being sprayed, "I bet you were hoping, when my guards caught you, that if you kept the fact that you were a Mind Mage hidden then maybe you would be able to get close enough to break my mind. Sorry darling, but I have protections in place for pests like you."

Without warning, the Queen dropped the man onto the cold, stone floor with an echoing *THUMP!*

When the brown-haired man struggled his way back onto his knees, whimpering like a dog in pain, Auryon grimaced. While his throat, to her momentary surprise, was not torn, his once handsome face was a canvas of blood and exposed flesh.

"Not quite so pretty anymore," the Queen commented in faux-disappointment, grey-green eyes still portraying utter disinterest, "unless one has some kind of a blood fetish, I suppose. Maybe I should introduce you to one of my beloved torturers; he'll like you plenty... Don't you think, Auryon?"

The Captain nodded dutifully, ignoring the warm, unpleasant churning of her stomach. She knew exactly who Coren was talking about. "Yes, Your Majesty."

With surprising swiftness, Thaddeus launched himself from the ground and towards the Queen, hands outstretched as if to throttle the woman. *This boy is a death-destined fool,* Auryon thought with pity as Darkness formed to hold him back, one piece of blackness lifting his chin up to give Coren a generous look at his disfigured face.

The Mind Mage secure, the High Ruler of Galaris descended from her throne, moving to stand not two feet away from the male Mage. The Darkness altered itself to keep the man facing her, his chin now tilted downwards.

The Queen leaned further towards him.

"Now," she breathed, smiling lightly, "why don't you start telling me whatever your master has done and plans to do, and maybe I'll treat the rest of you with more kindness."

Instead of answering, the Mind Mage, who towered over the Queen's short form, spat on her face.

She lifted one hand and wiped the spit away. Even from afar, Auryon saw the now familiar hunger for violence, for retribution, shine in her eyes.

"I'm going to find him," Coren, more than five hundred years younger, grits out to Auryon in her memories, *"and I'm going to kill him, slowly, painfully. And the last thing he will hear is Zarola's name."*

Auryon shuts her eyes as Thaddeus is suspended in the air once more, screaming, yelling, crying, floundering as claws defile the smooth skin of his chest; as they tear his nails from their beds. Eventually, the Mind Mage starts to beg for mercy, and promise that he will tell her anything and everything, but still, the Queen does not stop.

The Captain hears him choke, hears the screeches of those watching him from the ground. She opens her eyes to see the Queen, joyous, as she watches Thaddeus bend and break to her whim; revelling in the power she has; in the vengeance she can take.

"My Queen," Auryon interrupts hastily, watching as black fluid begins to leak from Thaddeus' eyeballs. She can't help but step back when the Queen's eyes – which were now pitch black – shoot to her, "you still need information from him. If he temporarily dies, it could be nearly a fortnight before you obtain it."

After several more moments, Coren commanded the Darkness away, and Thaddeus was left to fall to the floor once more.

It was a miracle that the man was still conscious, which

could be seen from the slow blinking of his eyelids, though he no longer had the strength to lift himself up. Rolling her eyes, the Queen seemingly decided she wanted him to face her, as she used her Darkness to prop him back up onto his knees once more.

"What do you say, Thaddeus?" The Queen questioned after a moment of silence, eyes shining with satisfaction when they briefly flicked over to a mortal man who had fainted during the brutal display, "do you want to start talking?"

"H-h-h-he-e," Thaddeus desperately gasped out, his eyes widening and resolve desperately strengthening when he saw that the Queen had begun to lightly tap her fingers against her bare thigh. A sign of her impatience, "b-broug-ht t-t-them ba-ba-ck."

"Brought who back?" Coren questioned further, but Thaddeus had begun a coughing fit, wheezing and retching. Green eyes flickered over to where two guards, one who possessed healing abilities and the other being a Mind Mage, were stood. They, hesitation stark on their faces, made their way over to the Queen. The healer leant down to Thaddeus. Though he did not have the ability to heal the imprisoned Mind Mage's wounds completely, with Dark Mage magic being something too complex for a Body Mage to entirely overpower, he could staunch the bleeding and lessen the pain, if only momentarily. Having been prepared by the Captain for this occasion, he also poured some water into the prisoner's mouth from the flask on his hip to make it easier for him to talk.

Coren's Mind Mage, on the other hand, grimaced after

briefly outstretching her hand towards Thaddeus' head, fearful, watery blue eyes darting to the Queen before reluctantly informing her, "his mind shields are too well enforced for me to pull the details out of him. However, I will be able to tell if he is telling the truth or not."

The Queen did not bother to acknowledge her words. She merely waited for a moment, before allowing Darkness to build up beneath her hand for Thaddeus to see. At the threat of it, his eyes went wide once more and he whimpered out, "s-st-stop, s-stop, stop! I said I'll tell you ev-everything I k-know! Hearne," Auryon flinched, "h-he used this ritual! An-an ancient one in the old language, w-whi-which required the sacrifice of three D-Death Mages to complete."

"And what did this ritual do?" Coren asked him, though her mind was already working away at the details. She had a good idea of what – just not *who*. For the first time in centuries, her blood ran cold.

Thaddeus looked even more terrified than Auryon thought to be possible, and she knew that the Queen would not like his answer. "He brought them al-all back," the Mind Mage responded, with the other Mage of the same category nodding along to each of his words, confirming it all as the truth.

"All of who?" Coren spoke through gritted teeth, her eyes glinting dangerously. When Thaddeus delayed answering, she took another step closer. "All of *who*?"

"The Winter Rebellion," the Mind Mage finally gasped out, his eyes following the Queen's every move as one would a predator that was destined to strike, "e-everyone in the Winter Rebellion."

Auryon stumbled, her legs giving out from the shock. On the other hand, Coren's cold expression was entirely unreadable.

"There's something else," the guard told Coren, her eyebrows furrowed. Her words caused Thaddeus to tremble, "something he's holding back."

The Queen marched straight up to the kneeling man, using the Darkness to wrench his head up by his hair to face her. She bared her teeth as she gritted out, "what is it? Tell me!

Thaddeus still hesitated, and so the Queen's arm rose. Clearly anticipating another wave of Dark torture, the man raced to get out, "r-right before everything collapsed, r-r-right before the eclipse I heard the last Death Mage say something! She sa-said a name!"

"Who's name?" Coren all but screamed at him, her hand clenching, her face filled with a desperate horror that Auryon had not witnessed in centuries. Her Darkness shook him. "Who's name?"

"K-King Caradoc."

As if his words had been heard by more than those in the room, a terrifying boom was heard in the distance, the force of it shattering the windows in the audience chamber, sending those within hurling towards the floor.

When the inhabitants dared to look out of the great windows, they could see his presence clearly for themselves.

The entire east wing had burst into flame.

Beneath the dark sky, two sets of boots trod upon crimson flowers; born in the place of the blood that had been spilt half a millennium earlier. After the boots were removed, the compressed flowers rose up once more; flourishing.

None had ever forgotten what had happened here.

The Bloody Massacre. The Battle of Crimson Floods. The Last Battle.

Kir Byrdir fyr Nygt. The Birth of Night.

"It was said," one of the hooded figures recalled to the other, tall and muscular in body structure, "that, in the place where Commander Zarola perished, it is not just crimson flowers that grow but ones of darkness."

His shorter companion nodded, though startled when, from in between the crimson flowers beneath her feet, a hand shot out. The hand was covered in blood and earth, and searched around blindly for any foothold above.

At her side, Hearne looked down at the hand and smiled.

"Help them, Greer," he commanded, "I have somebody else to find."

And so, Hearne continued on, the sounds of grunts, earth giving way, and desperate gasps for breath sounding behind him as more and more crimson-stained beings reclaimed their spot on the worldly plain. Their new place by Hearne's side.

As he began to approach the centre of the blood-flower field, hands reaching upwards visible into the far, far distance, the blossom began to grow darker, leading him, at long last, towards a small, circular area.

Within the circle, the flowers were as bright a red as the others. Surrounding it, however, were flowers the colour of the night sky, exploding brutally outwards. At that very spot, Hearne stared, and he waited.

He waited and waited until finally – a light brown hand shot up from the earth. With a grin, he extended his own to her, and pulled. From the ground, more of an arm was slowly revealed, and then a mud-caked head, beneath which bright red-orange strands could barely be seen. The slow retrieval of the woman continued, until even her legs were free, and she was left panting upon the ground.

It took several moments, but, finally, she rose her head to face his.

Even after five hundred years, her brown eyes shone with the same sorrow and love the bards sang of.

"W-w-wh-whe-where's," the redhead began as she struggled desperately to fill her lungs that, before now, had been filled only by the dirt, "C-C-Cor-Coren... Where's Coren?"

Comrade Hearne forced a faux-sympathetic expression, reaching out a hand to help the woman from the floor, but she batted his offer away, fierce determination for news of the Night Queen providing fuel for her refusal.

"You've been asleep for a long time, Commander," he told her, "but don't worry, I'll tell you everything you need to know."

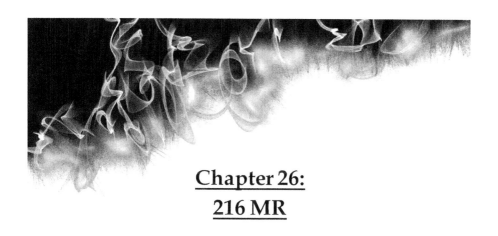

Chapter 26:
216 MR

$\mathcal{I}$f the Goddess of Darkness could sense Coren's

desperate searching, she did not care for it. Each day
that Coren tried to reach her, scouring her mindscape
– which took the form, as it always had, of the shack of
her past – there was no answer. Not on the first day,
nor the fourth, nor the eighth, nor the twentieth. There
wasn't even a whisper; not even a glimpse of dark,
emotive eyes.

Coren was dead to Nias, or so it seemed.

Instead, the Dark Mage was condemned to suffer from
a lack of purpose. Her only aim had been to ensure that
Zarola, Izak and Dahlia arrived at the camp safely,
which they appeared more than capable of doing on
their own, if the way that Zarola had bought and
coerced merchants' silence had anything to say for it.
If not for the fact that the redhead concealed and
protected the stake at all times, then Coren would have
considered removing herself from their small group
days ago. She could have followed at a distance,

protecting them from there, before putting her wooden possession to valuable use. But, prying that stake from fortress Zarola would probably take two whole invasion forces.

"We're almost there," Izak called back when they neared their thirtieth day of travelling. As they moved throughout Galaris, the thought had struck Coren that her agreement with Caradoc – for her compliance to him using her for power – would have still been ongoing, though the days left were minimal. It didn't mean much now, with Coren entering the northern mountains and Caradoc, if their plans of waylaying him by use of silenced merchants were successful, likely having his troops patrol the south coast of Galaris and the waters between it and East Rozante for them.

It should waylay him by at least a fortnight. A month, if they were lucky, as, despite sending him all the way down to the south, the King could have an army of generational Transformative Mages. They could alter themselves to birds and, taking into account rest time, Coren supposed they could get to the far north in eight days. Though, their exhaustion would incapacitate them for at least another five to ten.

"We'll get to that when it's necessary," a frowning Zarola had told Coren when the shorter girl had whispered such approximates, ones that she had garnered from the mage books she had read in the King's library, *"Commander Alyxan has been planning to take a true, combative stand for the past several years. Bringing the Fire King to us can be used to our advantage, I hope."*

Coren looked up from where she had been staring at her own footprints in the snow – she had never seen snow before; it was distractingly beautiful – and witnessed the truth to Izak's words.

Two white, towering mountains stood together, so tall in the sky that their stretching peaks were hidden away by obstructive clouds, with a narrow pathway in-between them. Either side of that pathway, high-reaching, muscular guards stood, their faces stoic as they watched the small group approach, hands on the grey hilts of their swords.

Neither Zarola nor Izak seemed surprised or unnerved by their presence, so Coren simply continued walking towards the guards at their side, lightly pulling Dahlia along by her hand when she hesitated.

"That path does not look safe," her former maid said, her hold on Coren's hand tightening, "it's very... restricted, and the snow on those lower peaks look as if they could topple off at any second."

Claustrophobic, Coren privately acknowledged, so squeezed the other girl's hand in reassurement.

Looking up to the lower points of the mountain, the Dark Mage grimaced. Dahlia's concerns about the snow were more than warranted, it looked as if it were baiting its breath, preparing to launch and bury them all.

It filled her with uneasiness.

"Identity," was all that one of the two, intimidating guards said when the group had, slightly reluctantly on Coren and Dahlia's part, reached the base of the mountains where they stood in wait.

"Secondary Zarola," Coren's redheaded companion said, displacing her dark hood from where it had covered her bright terrasses, "and Sector Leader Izak. We have two companions with us; new recruits."

There was a moment in which one guard assessed Zarola, who never shrunk beneath his cold, investigative gaze, until the other spoke up. "I recognise her. I was a recruit under Secondary Zarola when she was a Sector Leader two years prior."

So, the original guard nodded, and said, "go."

With long, confident strides, Zarola and Izak started on their way between the mountains. Behind them, Coren and Dahlia followed little hesitance, past verges of precariously placed snow; between icicles that extended out their fingers in search of something to feel, to tear; over a lake that threatened to swallow them whole with sharp *CRACK*s that echoed beneath their feet.

Looking back, Coren saw one of the guards with their hand extended towards the group of four.

An Elemental Water Mage, Coren supposed, who was likely using their capped powers almost to their full extent – particularly if they were only first generation – by controlling the temperature of the water.

The other side of the mountain-gap pathway was still hidden from view for a further fifteen minutes, at which point their entrance could barely be seen in the distance. However, when Coren was able to see the exit, the sight of the camp at the opposite side took her by surprise.

Her preconceived notions had been that the rebel

camp would be small and dreary, with patchwork tents and people walking around, backs bent from hard labour with melancholic eyes, but that did not appear to be the case at all.

Bright tents were littered around in the distance, taking on the colours of joyful yellow, loud purple and playful blue. Around the tents, Coren could make out what appeared to be a small number of young children running around, with adults dodging them in order to continue on their daily business without being bowled over. The sounds that were reaching her ears, small squeals and shouted greetings, even appeared... happy. Coren's brows furrowed. Looking left, she could see that this was not what Dahlia had expected either, who was staring at the sight before her with something akin to wonder. Moving her gaze forwards, Coren could see one side of Zarola's smile, which was carefree in a way that she had never seen.

To Zarola, the Dark Mage realised as she continued to study one side of her face, *this is home*. Such sentiments also appeared to be echoed by Izak, though his delight was dampened by shadows of the past – or, more specifically, Jakan.

You and I were both fools in love, Coren thought to the memory of the dead boy as she ventured closer and closer to the camp, fiery eyes haunting her every movement, just as they had this whole journey. And probably always would.

By the time they'd reached the end of the slim path between the mountains, finally ready to step out into the light, people had begun to notice them. Some gave them a passing look, and then continued onwards; others paused, staring; few had the name of 'Izak' on their lips; more called out 'Zarola' and a couple eyed Coren and Dahlia with suspicion.

Despite the people calling out to her, Zarola did not stop, only offering a few, short smiles and nods, continuing to lead them on a twisting route between children and tents. During the walk, Coren found herself looking up at the sky, which was clear and bright, and featured dark feathered birds squawking and diving between the low clouds. When a breeze began to play with her hair, the Dark Mage allowed herself a small smile, which grew as her eyes tracked one particularly vocal bird.

Freedom. What a feeling it must be.

The blonde lowered her eyes when she felt herself being watched. Though still strolling forwards, the redheaded Secondary had turned her head to her with an odd expression, which was quickly wiped off of her face when Coren noticed her.

Do I have something on my face? The Dark Mage wondered, bringing her hand up to wipe at her mouth, frowning when nothing showed up on her hand. Beside her, Dahlia snorted just as they all came to a stop.

In front of them was a tent identical to the others, square-shaped and purple-coloured, its flap left partially open to welcome the fresh, biting air that belonged to Galaris' mid-autumn. In spite of the open front, Zarola still knocked against a plank of wood that had been lent up against a bucket. A voice, whose owner was obscured somewhere inside the tent, called them in.

Entering, Coren saw that the interior was unusually clean and bare, without a single speck of dust in sight, and neatly folded clothes residing in three small piles in the left corner of the room, dirty ones folded in the right. On the far right of the tent sat a humble desk, behind which a tall, dark-skinned man poured over what appeared to be a map of the continents.

After a moment or two, the man looked up, his previously serious face breaking into a small, warm smile at the sight of Zarola.

"Secondary," he greeted, the smile remaining, before turning his eyes to the rest of the group, "and Sector Leader Twelve. I see you've also brought some friends with you."

The man's tone was hard to read, with his latter statement being said with neither displeasure nor contentment. His mouth, however, did settle into a thin line, so Coren would guess his emotions around the matter were closer to the former.

Zarola stiffened slightly at his words, before moving aside to give him a full view of Coren and Dahlia. Then, she informed him, "Commander, I would like to introduce you to Coren and Dahlia. They are both against the King and his cause, and are a Dark Mage and an Air Elemental Mage respectively."

At her words, the man's gaze sharpened considerably as he stared at Coren, who Zarola had gestured to as the Dark Mage during her introduction.

Condemnation, dislike and fear, those were the emotions that his startling blue eyes shone with, and

Coren fought to not allow it to affect her. After all, it was the normal reaction; it was the reaction that Dahlia, Izak and Zarola had when she took off the Mage's Bane. "Last I heard, the Dark Mage was firmly on the King's side. Involved with him, even," the man who Coren had come to realise was Commander Alyxan said. By the way he stared Zarola down the entire time, Coren knew that he had garnered such information from her. Humiliation threatened to drown the Dark Mage. Did everyone here know how much of an idiot she was? How she had been so pathetically desperate for freedom and control and a chance at love that she played directly into the Fire King's hands?

She felt Dahlia squeeze her hand in support, but it didn't stop her entire face from flushing.

Zarola stepped back in front of the two Mages. "Well," the redhead informed him, "that's not the case anymore, Commander. Also, Izak and I discovered what you asked. The King potentially has a force of 14,000 generational Mages, but, if he chooses to utilise less powerful Mages as well, then one of up to 30,000. For military camps, most are based within the west of Galaris, and there are a few in the conquered East Rozante. If we were to start marching down towards him, he would have his army of generational Mages ready in less than four days, as most are based near the capitol, and an army of up to thirty thousand gathered and marching in just about four moon cycles. He also has over seven hundred generational Transformative Mages in his force, which Coren has estimated could be in the north and ready to fight us in just eighteen days at the most. Though, marching down the country is no longer necessary, as the King will be coming to us."

"For her," the Commander said bluntly, eyes darting over Zarola's shoulder and back to Coren.

It was not as if the Dark Mage could counter his claim and she didn't believe that the stern Commander would want her apologies, so she simply agreed, "for me."

"And she'll be our greatest asset," Zarola said, causing both the Commander and Coren to stare at her, one in a combination of interest and discontent, and the other in surprise, "Dark Mages, even without the Connection, are capable of killing a hundred people, Mages or no. I wrote to you of how she'd fought in the maze-,"

"When she killed our men," Commander Alyxan interrupted, but Zarola ignored it.

"-when she took down twice as many as most of our rebel fighters would be able to in the same time. If she makes the Connection, then that's even better for us. If not, so long as the sword training that she began under Izak is continued and her powers remain under control, then she may become the greatest advantage we have."

What are you saying, Zarola? Coren wanted to ask, *I never planned to stay!* But swallowed her words. She'd talk to her later. For now, she was left to stare back into the hard, evaluating eyes of the Commander, whose assessing eyes ran up and down her as if she were an object he was deciding whether or not to buy, based upon how much he would use it.

Coren stared, silently and unflinchingly, back at him.

"You will train her," he said to Zarola, though he continued to look at Coren. The redhead nodded at his words, though looked displeased when he added, "and, when the Fire King's men reach us, she will fight in the front lines."

Despite her own feelings, Zarola curtly said, "yes, Commander."

"She will have to stay with you in your tent. All the rebels know who she is and what she's done, they won't want to stay with her as they don't trust her and neither do I. But I trust your judgement, Secondary."

Zarola did not seem at all put off by the arrangement, simply nodding again. There would be no reason for her to be upset anyway, considering the fact that the two had slept together in the woods, almost cuddling for warmth, for around twenty-eight nights. Though, the rebel leader did ask, "what about Dahlia?"

Commander Alyxan turned his eyes to the dark-haired Air Mage, "can she fight? Is she powerful?"

Out of the corner of her eye, Coren could see Dahlia's lips thin in displeasure. Before the Air Mage could think to say something to displease the Commander, Zarola cut it, "Dahlia is a good shot with a dagger, and we'll work on the rest."

The only response Commander Alyxan gave was a short grunt.

"She'll also be going to your camp, Secondary Zarola," he decided, "and I believe that there is space for her to share with either Riah or Auryon, the Gods know those two daughters of mine have done nothing to deserve the privilege of their own tent. Unlike you."

Zarola did not seem to agree, but nodded her head again regardless. The Commander then informed her that a war council would be held tomorrow, which he was going to inform the other Secondaries about. With that, the four were dismissed from the tent, Zarola beginning to lead them out, before Coren turned around.

"Your camps are compromised," she informed Commander Alyxan shortly, "I saw letters on the King's desk. Secondary Cilla has a spy in her camp, Leo.. no Leon and he knows the location of her human family. They know about you and your skills with a bow through the informant in your camp: Hylla. There are others the letter did not name, based in various camps." The Commander's brows furrowed together, accentuating the lines on his face. He must be edging towards, if not having already entered, sixty, and yet the man still looked ready to enter battle within a moment's notice. When his gaze met hers, Coren offered him an unfriendly smile. "Perhaps, instead of distrusting me based on stories you've been told, you should take a look at your own camps, Commander Alyxan. Thank you for your hospitality."

When the Commander neither berated Coren nor stopped them, Zarola continued on leading them outside, her own expression serious and thoughtful as she no doubt considered who in her own camp may be a spy for the King. The four walked for a short while with no conversation, before they stopped in front of a large stable.

"Zarola's camp is just over twelve miles north-west of

this one," Izak informed them as Zarola went up to a male that Coren assumed was a stable boy, "we won't be able to walk it before dark."

Soon enough, two stable hands were heading their way, each holding two horses. Though Coren was not a proficient rider, she was more than relieved to get atop her dark-coloured mare. Her legs were just about ready to give in. Dahlia and Izak must have been feeling the same, if their expressions of something alike to bliss were any indication.

After angling their horses in the right direction and ensuring everyone was ready to embark, the soft clip clop of horses' hooves filled the air, and they departed the main camp.

Darkness had just seized control of the sky when Coren, Dahlia, Zarola and Izak rode into camp. A few people were sitting around campfires here and there, which were settled in front of another array of colourful tents. With her hood now pulled up, no welcomes were offered to Zarola, who took them all firstly to the stables.

Then, they moved eastwards between tents before Izak bade them goodbye and entered a particularly atrocious green coloured tent. Zarola stopped two tents further down, in front of a vibrant red one. She gestured towards the tents to the right, telling Dahlia,

"Rhia and Auryon reside in those two tents. Rhia's directly next to mine, and Auryon's the next after that. Rhia is a human and Auryon is a Light Mage, so if you would feel more comfortable with another Mage then head to hers."

Dahlia nodded but didn't appear to mind whether or not she stayed with another Mage. So, she made her way tentatively into Rhia's tent after knocking at the same bucket-and-wooden-plank combo as had resided in front of the Commander's tent.

Seeing Dahlia had successfully gotten to a tent, Zarola then led Coren into hers, which possessed the same almost obsessive cleanliness as her side table had in the maid's chamber. There was only one sleeping bag in there, but Coren didn't particularly mind, after all, she wouldn't be staying long – if at all.

Should I leave now? The Dark Mage wondered, turning her head towards the tent flap. *Should I tell Zarola? And ask for a horse?*

"You can't leave," Zarola told her as if she had read her mind, though had probably just observed the direction of her gaze.

"Why?"

"I-," Zarola hesitated, turning her body around from where she had been placing her daggers on her side table, "you can't."

Coren frowned at her, "it's better if I do leave, Zar. I'm putting everyone in danger just by being here and I don't even have a Mage's Bane, and if I did have one, then I'd just be forcing the problem to go away for a short while and not actually dealing with it. Also, if

Caradoc learns that I've left the rebel camps, perhaps he'll split his forces, giving all of you more of a chance-"

"And how will you 'deal with it' Coren?" Zarola interrogated, before grabbing the stake from the pocket of her cloak, holding it up in one hand, "with this? I won't allow it."

Coren laughed at the absurdity of her words, "won't allow it? Won't allow it? Zarola, can't you see that is the best opportunity for everybody? You know that I killed my mother with my powers, don't you, Zar? Did you know that I first killed with them when I was *five years old*? The day we left the Palace, I permanently killed at least six Mages, one of whom was a child under ten. Ten! Everybody with half a brain calls me a monster, Zarola, and if you know what's good for you, you'll join them."

For several moments, the redhead didn't say anything at all. Then, she took one step towards Coren. That step was followed by another, and another and another. Eventually, Zarola was close enough to reach out and touch the Dark Mage should she want to, but she did not.

"I... We need you, Coren," the redhead told her, brown eyes looking down into ones of green-grey, "we need you because the Fire King is coming for us, and he isn't going to stop. With or without you coming here, he was going to be upon us by the end of the year, he was making arrangements, which is why Izak and I – two that had been trained to illude Mind Mages by Cilla – were sent to scope out his armies. He's going to try to destroy us, and then there will be nobody to stop him in his tyranny; nobody to stop him from hurting more young Mages and humans alike. So, stay, Coren. Stay and help us. Stay, at least until the battle is over. Just... stay, please. At least for now."

Under the usually stoic Zarola's imploring, desperate eyes, Coren's resolve crumbled. Even though every single instinct within her screamed at her to go now, that she was making the wrong choice, the Dark Mage found herself murmuring, "okay, I'll stay until the battle. But then I have to leave, Zar, I have to."

Zarola nodded but did not move for several moments. In that time, Coren found herself studying the subtle shades within her eyes – how, around her pupil, their colour was a light, almost golden brown, which darkened slowly to something almost akin to black around the outside. Finally, it was the redhead who broke their eye contact. She stepped away, looked away, and then swallowed harshly.

Moving to a draw, Zarola rustled around for a short while before offering Coren some nightwear and, to the Dark Mage's surprise, the willow mage stake. Wide eyes stared up at Zarola, and the rebel leader offered her a small, hesitant smile. In her right hand, she grasped Coren's left, before placing the stake delicately in its clutches.

"I trust you," Zarola told her in explanation, before she turned away to sort out her own nightwear, leaving Coren to gaze – cheeks red – at her back.

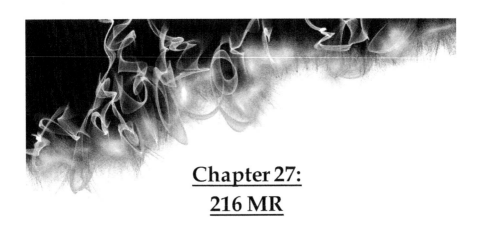

Chapter 27:
216 MR

$\mathcal{B}$y the time Coren awoke the following morning,

Zarola was nowhere to be seen. In her place on the right side of the sleeping bag, there was a short note telling Coren that she had left for the training area and that Coren was expected to join them.

So, reluctantly, she pushed herself off of the sleeping bag with a groan, standing up still for a moment whilst she waited for the world to stop blurring around her. Seeing bread on the desk before her, she eventually wobbled over to it, eating several slices before scanning her surroundings in a way that the Dark Mage had neglected to do the previous night.

The interior of the tent was rather cramped, barely managing to fit a long wooden desk, an accompanying chair, a sleeping bag, a side table and an armchair, in addition to thin wooden poles that resided within the tent to help hold it up in poor weather conditions.

There were also several lamps littered about the tent, wherever one could be placed, along with an assortment of neatly displayed weapons, the sight of which, for one reason or another, made Coren smile. Casting her eyes onto the peeling arm chair, she saw that a pile of neatly folded clothes had been placed on top of it, along with another short note that simply read: *for you.*

Pulling the basic, darkly-coloured clothes on, Coren soon found that they were definitely not a perfect fit. While the Dark Mage was on the tall side of five foot three, she estimated that Zarola was closer to five foot seven, making the top slightly baggy and the bottoms reach for the base of her foot. Rolling the latter up once, and tucking the former in, the Mage grasped the single twin dagger that Zarola had left by the side of the pile and then walked out past the tent flaps.

When Coren left the tent, it took a moment for her eyes to adjust to the harsh sunlight, but when they did, she swiftly scanned the area in search of the training grounds. In the end, it wasn't her eyes that found it, but her Mage hearing by which the harsh clash of swords greeted her ears. Bypassing Zarola's tent, the Mage moved towards the sound at a fast pace, conscious of the fact that she was – undoubtedly – late.

Coren had never been a particularly early riser.

Upon arriving at the training area, she took a moment to watch those within it. At one corner of the grounds, Izak and Dahlia were lightly sparring. Every now and again, Izak halted their swordplay, moving to the Air Mage's side so he could instruct her on her stance and attack. In the opposite corner, two dark-skinned women – whose features and height looked similar enough to be sisters – fought rather spectacularly. Though both were good, it was evident that the taller one was even more proficient, and was actually hindering herself to allow the fight to continue. Around the rest of the training area, other pairs were battling with various skill levels, and Coren was surprised to see some only appeared to be around the age of twelve. She also noticed, rather ashamedly, that they were probably better at swordplay than her.

"So, the mighty Dark Mage finally decides to grace us with her presence then?" a voice called out, telling Coren that her time for silent observation was over, "took a while, didn't it? What, could you not dress without the help of all those maids your lover provided for you?"

Coren pushed her blonde hair from her face and looked over to the man who had spoken, as did most of those fighting, and saw nothing but malice shining in his watery blue eyes. When she didn't respond, the brown-haired man grinned slightly, and mouthed 'King's whore'.

Though her veins threatened to blacken, Coren merely looked away. He was inconsequential, and clearly compensating for something.

The crunch of gravel beneath heavy feet told her that he was heading her way, but he was soon stopped in his path.

"One more step, Monrow, and you'll be on stable duty for the night," a voice that Coren recognised well – Zarola – informed him, "got it?"

Personally, Coren did not believe that the man had

enough brain cells to be able to compute such a simple sentence, but he backed off, leaving Zarola in his place. Having gained Corne's attention, Zarola made the rest of her way over to her. Conscious that the eyes of everyone in the training grounds were on them, the redhead muttered softly, "thank you, for not... *you know.*"

Coren raised a brow at her articulate phrase, smiling lightly, and told her, "attacking him even with words would just make everyone here dislike me more, if that's possible, which is the last thing that I need."

Zarola frowned at her before turning to face their audience, snapping at them to get back to practising. Then, she proceeded to lead Coren through the training grounds and towards a rack of weapons, from which she chose two wooden swords opposed to steel ones.

"We'll start with these," Zarola said, "considering the stories that Izak has been telling me."

Affronted, Coren turned to Izak, who looked at Zarola beseechingly before facing the Dark Mage. "Well," he began, his voice tight, "you did almost cut off Milo's manhood when we decided to move onto steel. I'm pretty sure he's got a scar now."

"That was one time, and he was being an ass!"

"Telling you to lay off the lemon tarts when you fell on him does not mean he deserves to get his dick chopped off, Coren."

"Unfortunately for you, I'm fond of all my body parts," Zarola cut in, something akin to a grin crossing her face, "so it'll be wood for now."

I wouldn't cut any part of you, Coren grumbled inwardly, *you're too pretty for that.*

The Dark Mage's thoughts made her pause. What was she thinking? Zarola gave her a weird look when Coren hurriedly accepted the sword, a vibrant red taking over her cheeks.

Desperately looking away from Zarola and her overwhelming feelings for her, she caught a pair of dark brown eyes watching her. It was the tall, skilled woman that Coren had seen fighting with her sister earlier. Hesitantly, the Dark Mage decided to offer the other woman a small smile, but all that she got in response was a scowl.

"Sword in position," Zarola told her, making Coren turn back to look at the rebel leader instead. Obeying, she prepared herself for the inevitable hours of fighting and losing, then losing some more, that were ahead of her.

Halfway through the day, Zarola had to leave to attend Commander Alyxan's war council. For some of that time, Izak alternated between Coren and Dahlia, the latter of whom was improving at a generous rate. Most of the time, however, Coren spent sitting on a rock behind the weapons rack, a cup of water – that she rather wished was wine – in her hands. From there, she would occasionally glance between two steel swords to assure herself that Izak was yet to find her hiding spot. At one point, another person joined her. Her partner in hiding from the godforsaken art of sword-fighting had wildly curly black hair, kind blue eyes and was easily recognisable as the less-skilled of the two sword-fighting sisters. When Coren turned her grey-green eyes upon her in surprise and inquisition, the younger woman merely offered her a silver flask, so the Dark Mage decided that she could stay.

"I'm Riah," she said, and Coren immediately recognised the name. Riah, one of the daughters of Commander Alyxan, who he had all but called a disappointment when Coren had been in his tent, "and that's my sister, Auryon."

The bright-eyed woman pointed towards the one who had glared at Coren earlier and now was engaged in a spar with the rude man from earlier, Marlow. *Maybe they can bond over their mutual hatred for me,* the Dark Mage thought idly, before turning her face away from them to offer Riah a small smile.

"Coren," she told her, though she had no doubt that she already knew her name. The whole camp did. Coren supposed that it shouldn't have surprised her, after all, she had observed how close knit they seemed when she entered the Commander's camp. No information appeared to be kept from the masses, including what Zarola and Izak's letters to the rebel leader must have contained about her.

However, Riah didn't tell her she knew, instead she directed a bright smile at her and declared, "nice to meet you, Coren."

Between them, the two women passed Riah's flask back and forth in a companionable silence. Coren hoped that the liquid would help her feel less uncomfortable with all the hostile stares.

That was until the atmosphere changed.

The clanging of swords, the shouting of voices, the cursing of the mildly injured; all of it had stopped. The two glanced at one another before moving out from their hiding place, and were greeted to the sight of the returning Zarola with Commander Alyxan at her side. Unlike Izak, it barely took Zarola a minute to find Coren. The redhead urgently widened her eyes and inclined her head at her, and Coren quickly gathered the meaning. Undoubtedly, Coren would not be very popular with the Commander if he saw her slacking off, even more so when she was accompanied by his daughter.

So, when Zarola pointed the Commander's attention towards his other daughter and Marlow's battle, Coren latched onto Riah's wrist and the two moved away, grabbing swords as they did so.

Facing one another, she was offered a grin. "Are you any good?" Riah asked her.

"I'm nowhere near as good as your sister," the Dark Mage told her honestly, "but I won't poke your eye out. Hopefully."

The dark-skinned woman nodded to her words before she, without any warning, lunged towards Coren with what the other woman only just realised was a steel – not wooden – sword.

Shit.

Coren stepped back, then brought up her sword to bat the end of Riah's away. She was not deterred, quickly lunging back towards Coren, aiming blow after blow. Coren was forced onto the defensive, unable to get a single blow in herself, but the delight in Riah's eyes as she fought made her smile regardless.

"Just as clumsy movements as ever," a voice that Coren had forgotten was there cut in, prompting all the joy in Riah's eyes to completely dissipate. The Commander then moved his critical blue eyes – ones that mirrored his daughter's exactly – onto Coren's, "as for you, that was only one step above pitiful."

That's actually a compliment; I must be improving, Coren thought to herself as Commander Alyxan then looked back to Auryon and Marlow.

There was absolutely no doubt that the former was the most skilled, defending and attacking with a fervour and agility that Coren could only dream of. However, she must have felt her father's gaze upon her, because Auryon turned her face to look at him for just a moment, faltered, and was sent crashing to the ground by a particularly cruel hit of Marlow's sword.

At the back of his throat, the Commander made a sound of disgust and began to walk away. The look in his fallen daughter's eyes was pure devastation.

From beside Coren, Riah moved towards her sister, offering her a hand to help her up, but Auryon batted her hand away and lifted herself to her feet. Then, she turned on her own heel and hurried away from the training ground.

Coren's eyes tracked her as she left, before she was

distracted by Zarola placing a hand upon her shoulder. "We should get back to practising," the red-headed human said, "our informants believe that the King has figured out our ploy and is assembling his force to move northward. At best, we have eighteen days before the Transformative Mages will be fully operational in the north, and thirty before Caradoc's entire force could reach here. And you're supposed to be in the front lines when, with your current skills, you'd be lucky to defeat one of our ten-year-olds."

Coren brought her sword back up to the position that had been drilled into her by Izak and Milo. Before, she had always been of the mindset that her powers would defend her, that she didn't truly need to be a proficient sword fighter, but now Caradoc's army was nearly upon them and her powers were still temperamental. Inside of her, she felt as if a sand glass had been turned. Time was running out.

The latter part of Coren's day of sword training had gone faster. Though, in the last hour, her stomach had begun to rumble,rather unfortunately loudly . When Zarola had finally dismissed them all for dinner, eager anticipation had filled her.

Unlike the Golden Palace, the rebel encampment sat around several different campfires for dinner each night, cooking meat on skewers and – if any had been found – vegetables to be placed in a small bowl at its side. Today, they ate wild rabbit with mushrooms that the younger children had found under the watchful eyes of the elderly.

Though Coren had eaten far nicer food in far grander places, she favoured the atmosphere here. Everyone now knew that Caradoc's armies were heading straight towards them but, if anything, this only seemed to spur them on.

Several couples by Coren's campfire chose to dance around it whilst another member of the rebel camp played a well-used violin for them. Those who remained seated were treated to stories of generations past told by a much older woman. Eventually, however, she retired to bed and another much younger person took her spot.

Like those around her, Coren enjoyed his tales of sorcerers and their magic, the ones that had existed before the Gods and Mages, and listened in awe and sorrow as he vividly described the death of their race. "As they did every year," he told them, "every magical being made the long trek to *Fyrdeer* – which is now known as 'the Black Isle' – where they would remember all that their Goddess had sacrificed to allow them to live harmoniously. How did they thank her, you must be wondering? Why, by transferring a set fraction of their power to a small stone, which they would then drop into what was called 'the mouth of the Goddess'. This was in the hopes that, one day, with their power rejuvenating her, their Goddess would be able to regain the power she had sacrificed for them, and take vengeance upon those who had threatened her.

"Though every legend surrounding the Goddess depicted her as having died for her children – the sorcerer race – they still had that hope. It was this hope that killed them. The 'mouth of the Goddess' was, in fact, an inactive volcano. Instead of rejuvenating their Goddess, who was long dead, they were providing what had once been known as Mount Ipyrcas with the energy it needed to bring ruin to them all. And ruin them it did. The sorcerer race was wiped out in its entirety, except for t-,"

"What can you tell us about the Evil King, Mister Seer?" A young girl asked him eagerly, only to receive a swift scolding from her mother for interrupting the man. Coren's gaze, which had wandered slightly towards the fire, snapped straight back to him. The man, who didn't look a day over twenty-three, felt her stare and inclined her face towards her. The Dark Mage could only stare at him in wonder when she recognised his eyes – they were the exact same colour as the *jikita* stone; the exact same shade as snakes' eyes upon the stone woman's cane.

He was almost unheard of, a Mind Mage with the ability to see both the future and past alike. For some reason, that filled Coren with trepidation as he seemed to stare through her – into her very soul. He, undoubtedly, knew too much; far more than Coren would ever want anyone to know about her.

After several long moments, in which the Mind Mage's

face had morphed into a rather obscure expression of intense pity and disgust, both of which made Coren squirm slightly in her seat, he turned to the young girl who had spoken. "I can tell you that the Fire King wasn't always so evil," he said, "I can tell you that he once loved and lost, like you and I."

"He's nothing like us," a particularly venomous voice informed the man, her entire body tense, "he's a monster!"

"Monster!"

Coren flinched harshly at the word, the back of her shoulder hitting a warm body. Her hands clenched tightly as she attempted to keep a better hold upon her Darkness than she had managed to the night of the feast.

Let us play, Coren! Let us play!

Around her fist, a somewhat calloused hand wrapped itself, not allowing her to struggle alone. Coren glanced to that side to see Zarola, though the other girl made no acknowledgement of her comforting action. So, Coren did not either, waiting it out as the Darkness' song gradually grew quieter and quieter.

Zarola then went to move her hand away but Coren chased it, entwining their fingers. With the Darkness so close to the surface, she didn't want to feel alone right now.

Zarola allowed her to do so, and this time it was her who turned to Coren, but she continued to stare at the Mind Mage.

"Once, King Caradoc was no more than one of two forgotten children born to powerful Elemental Fire

Mages," the man began to narrate, pushing his long, blonde hair away from his jewelled eyes, "those Fire Mages favoured their eldest son: Braxian, who was far more powerful than his twin brother Caradoc. They also had a daughter, Febronia, who had inherited not a single drop of power, which is a rare phenomenon that occurs to only one in every forty thousand Mage-born children born to parents of the same power group."

As the Mind Mage spoke, Coren recalled Caradoc's own words.

"I had a sister. Her name was Febronia."

"Braxian, who was raised by his parents to believe in his own superiority above his siblings, was cruel to them. For every deed he committed, his sister forgave him, whether he burnt the hair upon her head, scarring her scalp or killed the animals that she tended to whilst she cried. When angry, he would beat her until every limb bled, and leave her tied up until Caradoc came home to untie her and treat the young girl's wounds. Still, Febronia held no malice in her heart for him, but the King did."

"Despite his cruelties, she still loved Brax, which was... an achievement to say the least."

"Every night, young Caradoc would desperately try to reach out to the Goddess Aliona, patroness of the Elemental Mages, to beg her to bless him with powers greater than Brax's, so that he may protect his sister from him by earning their parents' love. One night, the Goddess answered and told the boy of a long-forgotten secret of the Mages. Identical twins, you see, are a far rarer occurrence in the Mage race than the human one,

310

due to the power balance that all Mages have to adhere to. They're like a mutation. This is because if one identical twin kills the other, they can absorb their powers as it is so similar to the signature of their own. "So, after Braxian beat Febronia for the last time, Caradoc did exactly that. He slaughtered Braxian before drinking some of his blood, claiming his twin brother's powers for himself. With that, Caradoc became the most powerful Fire Mage alive – a seventh generation Elemental, with double the fire they were born with. And he was positively drunk upon it. The boy of sixteen did not yet know, but this was no victory. That very night, he sought out Aliona to make the Connection, to consolidate control over his power, but she would only offer him a Promise Connection until he paid her price."

Every child around the fire was engrossed in the story, whilst adults differed between disbelief – scoffing at any moment that they believed Caradoc was being portrayed too kindly – and reluctant intrigue. Coren, unknowingly, had been squeezing Zarola's hand harder and harder as the story continued.

"'You have taken from me one of my strongest Mages,' the Goddess, Aliona, said to Caradoc, 'now you must pay my price.' The boy protested, of course, telling her that he had only done as she had directed. But the Goddess simply smiled. Gods, you see, are not like us, they were devoid of their own humanity long ago and often get bored in their Ascended City, so look for entertainment on the mortal plain. Therefore, the Goddess orchestrated another's misery for her amusement.

"She told Caradoc to kill all those in his village, bar his family. He refused. Then, the Goddess told him to kill only his parents. Still, the Fire Mage refused. Finally, she told him to kill his sister, and Caradoc refused that most adamantly of all. So, she denied him his powers. The boy went back to the mortal plain no better than a human, hated and feared by his village for killing his own brother, subject to the disgust and shame of his parents, and loved only by Febronia. Though he had that love, it was never going to be enough for Caradoc. He'd been given a taste of being one of the most powerful creatures in existence, of making people see him after years of neglect, and he refused to lose it. On the tenth day of being human, Caradoc killed his village, poisoning the water supply before seeking out and killing any who survived one by one. Then, a bit of his power returned to him, but not all. On the fifteenth day, he killed his parents. More power returned to him, restoring him to the usual amount of power that any seventh generation Fire Mage would have. Still, he wanted more.

"He begged and begged the Goddess but, in her rage, she refused him more power – unless he killed Febronia."

"Whatever the price is, pay it. There is nothing crueller and more vengeful than a Goddess' wrath."

"Fifty days passed, and each one made the King more and more desperate for power. Some would even say that he went mad in his desperation, being taunted by the Goddess by night and with a sister who couldn't even look at him by day. On the forty-ninth day, Caradoc killed Febronia, and truly became the King of Flames that we know today."

Silence embraced the world around Coren, whilst her heart cracked a fraction for the image of that young, fiery-eyed boy. The quiet did not last, however, as a rebel scoffed, informing the Mind Mage, "you've had too much to drink, Ahren. Nobody could believe that kind of shit about the King, even if you're usually right. Some people are just born evil, and I have no doubt that the Fire King came out with horns and a serpent's tongue."

With that, the rebel who spoke left the campfire, calling out that he was going to bed. Many others followed him, especially after an older woman looked up at the positioning of the moon and declared the time to be approximately one in the morning.

Zarola moved to leave as well, tugging at Coren's hand, but the Dark Mage simply muttered, "I'll be there in a minute."

Zarola shot her a look of concern, but left nonetheless, clearly sensing that Coren wanted a moment in solitude to gather her thoughts. However, the Dark Mage was not allowed such time.

"Malva," the Mind Mage spoke from across the fire, his cool gaze piercing into her. Swallowing, Coren resigned herself to look up at him. Seeing he had her full attention, Ahren said, "he will come to you."

"I know," Coren informed him, thinking of how Caradoc's armies were already marching up from the south.

"No," Ahren disagreed, offering her a small, secretive smile, "you really don't."

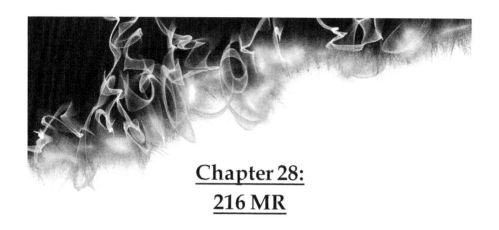

Chapter 28:
216 MR

*W*hen Coren awoke on the fourth day, exhausted after

having spent the entirety of her third day training with
her powers, Zarola had not yet left the tent. Instead, she
was standing behind her long, oak desk, palms flat on
its surface and shoulders hunched as she stared holes
into whatever was atop it.

Slowly detaching herself from the confines of their
sleeping bag, Coren got to her feet and lightly stumbled
towards Zarola. The redhead looked up from her map
to fix the blonde a look of amusement, before she
looked back down and anxiety took over her features
once more.

Coren reached Zarola's side soon enough, and looked
down at the piece of paper that was sprawled across the
desk. It was a huge map of Galaris, upon which red
arrows were drawn to show what Coren assumed was
Caradoc's progress so far and black dots to signify the
rebel encampments. What was most concerning upon
the map, however, was the short red arrow that was

making swift progress towards them.

"Are they the Transformative Mage group?" Coren asked quietly, watching as Zarola made a circle of red ink within the northern mountains. Zarola nodded at her before pointing to the newly made circle.

"That's where I expect them to set up camp," she explained, "there's a water source nearby and it's within a day's walk of the only major northern city – Rynook – while still being on a direct path towards us."

"Have you decided on a plan of action yet?" Coren inquired, studying the map for herself.

The human woman shook her head, sliding into the chair behind her to cup her forehead in her hands. "We don't have nearly enough people in condition to fight a force of nearly fifteen thousand. Across our encampment, we can perhaps gather nine or ten thousand, and if the King calls in the rest of his armies... Unless we fight the two separately, which could work as Caradoc and his army would be around twelve days behind them. But that only takes seven hundred out, he still has a host of fourteen thousand men as he wouldn't have had the time to summon his wider armies."

"It's not much, but it's a start," Coren agreed, trying to bring a degree of optimism to Zarola's despair. After taking several moments to scan the map extensively, Coren thought back to a battle formation that she'd read about in history books detailing the War of Gods, and told Zarola, "you should send three quarters of your force to where you think they're situated."

Zarola moved her head up to frown at Coren, offended, "three quarters? That's around seven thousand to fight seven hundred. Transformative Mages may be one of the stronger groups, but I think you're underestimating our warriors. We'd only need about four thousand to take them out."

"I know you don't need that many to defeat them," Coren said, taking a quill and dipping it to blue ink, then making small dashes on the map surrounding Zarola's red circle after she had received the leader's permission, "it's so that you can arrange your position for the battle. After your army of seven thousand have defeated the Transformative Mages, they'll split into three groups. One will head east, another south and a final one west. They'd need to keep out of sight of Caradoc's forces and then, when his forces reach the encampment that the Transformative Mages will have set up for them, you attack at all sides. From the north, east, south and west."

Zarola's eyes were fixated on the map as she added, "then we could expand outwards into a circle formation and close in on them. So long as we keep formation, we could push them back into such close proximity with one another that they couldn't hope to use their own mage skills without risk of injuring their comrades, whilst our Mages' would have a clear target."

"Exactly," Coren told her, looking towards the rebel secondary with a large grin, only to find that Zarola was already staring at her, eyes shining, before she all but leapt out of her seat and towards Coren. She let out a yelp as she was grasped onto, before the normally serious leader bestowed a quick kiss upon her cheek. "You're brilliant sometimes," the Dark Mage was told.

317

"Only sometimes?" Coren teased, trying and failing to fight away the blush that threatened her cheeks.

Zarola held Coren's face in her hands in a tender way that the Mage had never experienced before. Looking down at her, the redhead's grin softened to a smile. "All the time, 'Ren" Zarola said gently, before turning to swiftly roll up her map.

Coren had yet to recover by the time the redhead darted out between the tent flaps.

When Zarola returned, she was devoid of the rare smile that had been gifted to Coren that morning, her cold expressions even more frosty than usual. At her side, as had occurred at the end of the previous meeting, the Commander walked in long strides.

Across from Coren, her sparring partner – Auryon – scowled at her distraction, thrusting her sword forward none-too-gently into the Dark Mage's stomach. Slightly winded, Coren stumbled backwards and frowned at the other woman.

"You're dead," the daughter of Commander Alyxan told her, "let's go again."

Though Auryon was neither as sympathetic nor as considerate as her sister had been when Coren had fought against Riah earlier, she was a fantastic teacher. So, Coren readjusted herself without complaint, this time taking the initiative to lunge towards the skilled swordswoman.

"Sloppy, and guard your left," Coren was instructed, Auryon hitting her left side with the blunt side of her sword in demonstration. The Dark Mage altered her positioning and lunged again, whilst keeping herself in a suitable position to be able to easily switch back to a defensive positioning if need be. Auryon soon tested her defences, muttering, "better."

Just when Coren thought she was truly holding her own, a small flash of white light momentarily blinded her, and the Dark Mage found herself falling to the ground. Hard.

When she regained her sight, a hand was offered to her. Coren took it.

"Never be so arrogant as to assume you're the only Mage in a fight," Auryon lectured, "and, just because you're the 'all powerful Dark Mage', don't underestimate the effect a momentary distraction from someone *beneath* you can cause."

Auryon definitely doesn't like me, Coren thought to herself as she watched the Light Mage spin on her heel, preparing to march off to find someone else to practise with. Her steps faltered, however, when she noticed her father there. Though he wasn't even looking at her, preferring to scowl over at his other daughter, it was as if something within the other Mage changed – had become smaller.

"I want everybody to stop what they're doing and listen to me," Commander Alyxan called out after he tore his eyes from Riah, "this is about the upcoming battle."

Soon enough, all clashing of swords had ceased, the inhabitants of the training ground all swarming towards him, eager for news. Coren followed after Auryon, who was hastily pushing her way towards her father.

Seeing that he had everyone's attention, the Commander informed them, "some of you will be heading south-east, towards Rynook, in two days' time, but not all. For the upcoming battles, I have decided to separate all rebels into four groups, these groups have been decided to ensure an equal distribution of power, skill and leadership within each. I will be leading the western group, Secondary Zarola will lead the southern group, Secondary Cilla will lead the eastern group and Secondary Xian will lead the northern group.

Secondary Zarola will be informing you which one you are a part of by this evening. Now, back to training." Obediently, most rebels took up a partner once more and began to settle back into practising, though some made their way out of the swordplay area, choosing to move onto archery.

Zarola, however, did neither, marching past the Commander and back towards the tents. For several moments, Coren contemplated following after her, before deciding to give her some time on her own. She did not strike Coren as the type to want to discuss her feelings, especially when she was clearly still frustrated. "Again," she heard a voice call out roughly, and she turned her attention towards the Commander.

He was observing a battle Auryon and another female were having. Normally, it was always obvious that the

Light Mage possessed superior skill to whatever partner she took, harbouring the kind of ability that could only be reached by pure talent accompanied by hard work, but it was not now. Just like several days previously, she faltered beneath her father's stare, her normal fluidity turning tense.

Under his gaze, Auryon lost the fight.

With heavy, frustrated strides, the Commander marched himself in front of the kneeling Auryon. Then, he tore the steel sword from her opponent's hands, barking at them to leave.

"Father-," the Light Mage attempted.

There was not an ounce of kindness upon his face as he barked, "get up!"

Coren, along with anyone else who was not practising, all watched as Auryon rose on shaky feet, tentatively getting into an appropriate stance. Then, the Commander attacked her fiercely, displaying his method of swordplay to be one of brute strength compared to Auryon's more agile tactics.

Her chest, her head, her shoulders, her arms, her legs. There was no part of Auryon that the Commander did not try to maim, swinging his sword as his daughter shrank in upon herself, all confidence dissipating.

"Father-," the young woman tried again, only to have the blunt edge of his sword connect with her head, sending her hurtling to the ground.

Coren flinched at the smack of flesh upon the gravel. She went to move towards the fallen Mage, but Izak, who had moved behind her during the Commander's quest to humiliate his daughter, grabbed her arm.

"Don't," he told her, "intervening only makes it worse for Auryon; it makes her appear weaker in his eyes." So, the Dark Mage simply watched as the towering leader of the rebels crouched before his daughter, lifting her bloodied head up to whisper something in her ear. If the look on Auryon's face was anything to go by, his words were not kind.

After the Commander left, the Light Mage remained upon the floor for several moments, shaking her head to Riah when she started to make her way towards her. Not wanting to make her feel like a spectacle, Coren turned away, anger on the other woman's behalf blackening the veins of her hand. So, she clenched her fists, forcing herself into a state of apathy to give her more control, before positioning herself to fight with Izak.

Zarola did not appear for the rest of the day. Not during their lunch break from training, nor by the campfire for dinner where the children insisted that everyone join in singing rhymes that the elders had taught to them.

Though Coren's presence was still not welcomed by most, she couldn't help but begin to feel the slightest bit at home here.

Still, she retired early in search of Zarola, after shooting a surprised smile Dahlia's way when she displayed her vocal skills to the entire camp. The Air Mage grinned at her, whilst those around her applauded and sang along. It didn't take her long to find the bright red tent that she and Zarola rested within each night, swiftly pushing past the entrance flaps and emerging on the cramped other side. There, Zarola could be seen sitting at her desk, knees up to her chest as she idly played with her dagger, spinning it in circles, balancing it, throwing and catching it.

Coren knew that Zarola would have heard her come in, but the redhead showed no signs of acknowledgement, choosing to launch the dagger up in the air by its hilt, before catching it on her pinkie finger and leaving it there to balance.

The Dark Mage allowed the silence to stretch for several moments, before she finally gave in and asked, "what's wrong, Zar?"

Still, Zarola said nothing. Coren was convinced that she was going to be ignored, until, finally, the redhead stated, "they're placing us in separate groups for the upcoming battle."

"Why?" Coren immediately inquired, taken aback. When the four of them had first met the Commander, he had all but made Coren solely Zarola's problem, why was he suddenly changing his tune?

"Because," the rebel Secondary began, eyes still fixated upon the dagger that she had now begun to spin, "he thinks I'm too attached to you."

Are you? Coren wanted to ask. But she didn't. Instead, her cheeks merely reddened at the idea that the

Commander had been assessing their relationship to one another. She was soon distracted, however, by Zarola rising from her place behind the desk, making her way towards Coren.

Unintentionally, the Dark Mage took a step back. Zarola followed her, raising her dagger up to trace Coren's face so lightly that not a mark would be left. Nonetheless, the coolness of the metal and her proximity to danger made her shiver.

"Maybe he's right," the leader seemingly muttered to herself, though her dark brown eyes were fixated upon Coren.

In this moment, the Dark Mage would swear by every God that she could hear her heart pounding, whilst her throat seemed to constrict, taking away any hope of being able to respond, not that she could think of anything to respond with.

"I just," Zarola began tentatively, bringing her spare hand up to Coren's chin and tilting it upwards, "want to try something."

The Dark Mage didn't dare move as the human rebel brought her lips down to her own, connecting them. As she did so, Zarola tugged Coren towards her, holding their bodies flush together, moving her hands to settle upon Coren's hips.

After her surprise passed, she found herself responding enthusiastically, arms winding their way around Zarola's neck to pull her as close as she could, hands weaving themselves into the curling red locks that she had always admired.

Kisses shared between Coren and Caradoc had been of

two types: ones of sorrow, and ones of heat. And though there was heat in this kiss, it felt different. Each brush of Zarola's lips made Coren feel as if the other woman was trying to commit the feeling to memory; every movement of her hands, up and down the Mage's body, made her feel desired, almost worshipped.

When Zarola's tongue requested entry to Coren's mouth, the Dark Mage happily permitted it, pulling just a little bit harder at the redhead's hair in response. Zarola moaned into her mouth and faltered in her stance, the back of her foot hitting the desk.

The sharp bang was a wake-up call to both, shoving them back to reality. Zarola pushed Coren away, causing her to stumble back a step or two, and turned around so that her back was to her.

Coren was left to stare at the other woman's red curls, ones that her hands had just been buried within, hurt filling her heart.

"I-," the Dark Mage attempted, faltering in the aftermath of the rebel secondary's rejection, "I need to go."

She manoeuvred her way out of the tent, pushing past the tent flaps and then beginning to stride away from the tent as fast as she could. When Zarola called out to her, she was ignored.

Though Coren had no destination in mind, she found herself heading towards the training grounds, hoping to find solace there. And maybe a dummy to beat up. That, however, did not appear to be an option as a shadowy figure stood within the area, beating up a dummy of their own in a way that made it easy to tell that they were pretending it was someone else.

The Dark Mage decided to wait, in the hopes that they would soon leave. Instead, another figure joined them. "Your anger is foolish, Aurie," a voice that Coren recognised as Riah spoke in frustration, "he's always disliked us; he's always favoured others above us. When are you going to stop begging for his attention and praise?"

The one fighting against the dummy, Auryon, did not answer her, simply slicing off its left arm.

"Aurie! Are you listening? Aurie! Auryon!"

The right arm went next.

"He will never love you, don't you understand? Father will never think you're good enough! Wake up, Auryon, wake up!"

The head went next, toppling onto the gravel and rolling away as Riah's voice cracked whilst she tried to get through to her sister. Auryon, however, refused to acknowledge her, now hacking at its legs, as if – were it a person – it was not already long dead.

Her sister made a sound of frustration, before she brushed past the back of the Light Mage to, Coren assumed, make her way back to hers and Dahlia's tent. After the young woman's footsteps had travelled out of earshot, Coren watched as Auryon brutally buried her sword in the dummy's chest, a cry of defeat forcing its way out of her throat as she fell to her knees, head hanging low.

For a moment, Coren considered turning around and leaving. The Light Mage was clearly a prideful person, and Coren did not want to humiliate her further by letting her know that her moment of weakness had been seen. But, as Coren stared at her – looking as defeated and hopeless as Coren felt in her every waking moment – she knew that she couldn't do that.

Instead, the Dark Mage took slow steps forward, Auryon unable to hear her approach over her sorrow. When she did reach the other woman, Coren did not offer her a hug nor powerless, piteous words.

She offered Auryon her hand, as the other Mage had done earlier that day, and watched as the Light Mage looked up at her through conquered brown eyes.

"It doesn't matter what anyone else thinks," Coren told her, "it doesn't matter whether or not he thinks you can do it. I believe in you, Auryon, and if you begin to truly believe in yourself, then I think that fight today was the last swordfight you will ever lose."

Something within Auryon's eyes changed. Perhaps it was due to the confidence that an almost stranger had within her; perhaps Coren's words had solidified a conclusion she had already come to, or perhaps she had simply found a greater resolve within herself. Either way, she took Coren's hand and pulled herself up from the ground.

Chapter 29:
216 MR

$\mathcal{T}$he three rebel groups marched south-east for twelve

days before they reached Kodyn, a small town eight miles from Rynook. From there, the south-bound group, led by Zarola, separated into six smaller groups and left to scout for where the Transformative Mages were situated.

Coren had watched them leave longingly, catching sight of vibrant red disappearing into the distance, before electing to wander in search of an isolated area in which to practise her magic. There was a battle upcoming, after all, and the last thing that Coren wanted to do was lose control and harm the rebels. Harm Zarola.

Distantly, she could hear Secondary Cilla's frustrated shouting; no doubt she was continuing to lecture those who had failed to put their tents up. Luckily, Coren had asked Auryon – who, along with Riah and herself, was in the eastbound group – to be her partner, thus their tent had been erected within a matter of minutes.

So, Coren continued onwards, past a barrier of tall, fir trees and into the darkness of the woods ahead. One step, then another and another until she decided that she had created a suitable distance between herself and the east camp.

Amongst the darkness, the young, golden haired woman stood. Alone.

She closed her eyes and breathed in, stifling any sense of emotion, and then called it to her.

Come to me; come to both of my hands and form a ball of darkness in each, ready to be fired at will.

Dutifully, the Darkness rushed to the apathetic girl. With it obeying her tune, she brought her hands up, before – with an overarm swing – throwing a ball of Darkness into a nearby, richly green fir tree. At the impact, the thick-trunked tree toppled over, emitting a crash that could be heard for miles as it hit the ground. The ball in her left hand, she threw upwards into the sky.

Explode, but silently and only within a six foot radius, she whispered to it, and so it did. Somewhat. If one decided to call a thirty foot radius six feet, and a bang loud enough for all the camps to hear silent.

The Dark Mage tilted her head at it as she looked between the explosion of Darkness and the fallen fir tree, awaiting the slow return of her emotions.

Over the months that she had practised with it, firstly at the Golden Palace, then on the thirty-day trek to the rebel encampment, at Zarola's camp, and now here, one thing remained the same: the Darkness would obey her, gradually growing a fraction more submissive each time she practised, but always followed her orders more violently than intended.

She would have to account for that, when the battle occurred.

"By Akeros," a voice harshly swore behind her, and Coren desperately hoped that her veins were not still black, "are you trying to deafen us all?"

It was Riah who had spoken, and Coren heard a sudden 'hmph'. Turning around, she saw that Dahlia had accompanied her – the two having seemingly formed a fast friendship when sharing a tent together – and had elbowed her in the side for her profanity.

Coren's brows furrowed at the sight of the Air Mage, half-stating and half-asking, "I thought you were in the western group?"

"I am," Dahlia responded, before shooting Riah a sharp look, "and I was happily getting accustomed to my new tent when a certain somebody all but kidnapped me from my camp."

"Kidnapping is a bit far," Riah disagreed.

Dahlia shot her a dead look, "you put a hand over my mouth and dragged me out of my tent."

"That's just how we greet people in the north."

Coren snorted, prompting Riah to turn and grin at her, "so, what do you say to a little celebrating, shadow lady? I even managed to rope my surly sister into coming, and I'll go and grab Zarola and Izak too when they get back."

"Will you give them a northern greeting as well?"

Coren asked dryly as she brought her hands down, moving over to the other women.

Riah hummed in thought as she began to lead them from the woods, "maybe not Zarola. She'd probably cut off my hand before I managed to get it around her mouth. But Izak, probably."

"Riah here has also invited a certain somebody to our little celebration," Dahlia told her, wiggling her eyebrows about.

Riah's face turned bright red.

Coren shot Dahlia a conspirator's smile, and asked, "who?"

"A certain tall, handsome Secondary," Dahlia began, "his name is *hmphmm.*"

Riah had clamped a hand over the Air Mage's mouth, and Coren laughed loudly at the death stare the Azyalai woman shot Riah.

"Don't look so put out, she's just greeting you, Dahls." This time, it was the Dark Mage that received an elbow to the side.

Their small party – which had grown into a much larger one throughout the night – was in full swing by the time Zarola and Izak, with dirty tunics and even dirtier boots, were brought over by a more than slightly inebriated Riah.

Coren, who had been dancing with the reluctant Auryon, was able to walk over to them without stumbling at all, which was more than could be said for most of the people there. She wanted to resume her interrupted practice with her Darkness tomorrow, and that would be difficult to do with a hangover.

"Zar, Izak," the Dark Mage greeted merrily, high on the fast-paced violin music being played, on the dancing, the laughing, the atmosphere. When drunk, the other rebels that normally feared her appeared to forget that they had a monster in their midst, "could you not find them?"

"No," Zarola informed her tightly, the thinning of her lips and tenseness of her shoulders displaying her anxiety at that fact, "there are three groups that have yet to return though, so hopefully one of them will have found the camp. Then, as scheduled, we can depart tomorrow night. If not then-,"

Riah put a shaky finger to the redhead's lips, who looked at the appendage as if it had done something to personally offended her.

"Stop stressing! It's a party!" Riah told her, "one of the other groups will find the Tranfo... Transfer... Transformative Mages, that's it! And everything will be finnneee for tomorrow!"

The Commander's daughter began to sway, wobbling in a way that suggested her entire world was tilting.

Izak jolted forwards just in time to catch her before she hit the ground, picking her up into a bridal carry with a fond roll of his eyes.

"I'll go and get her some water to drink," he said, before disappearing through the crowd, Secondary Aldric's eyes following the duo the whole way.

Smiling a little at the sight, Coren wondered how long it would be until the fourth Secondary and Riah got together, considering the fact that he was clearly wrapped around her little finger.

When she looked back to Zarola, however, Coren's smile swiftly vanished. The redhead was still frowning, her fingers tapping against her thigh in a show of nervousness. Brown eyes eventually looked up and noticed the attention upon her.

"What's wrong, Zar?" Coren asked, almost reaching out towards her before thinking better of it. They still hadn't discussed that kiss, nor Zarola's subsequent rejection of her.

The rebel secondary's eyes were grave as she stated, "something doesn't feel right."

Just as she said that, the fourth group arrived safely back, the fifth group immediately behind them. Now, they were only waiting on one more group. But Zarola's eyes never lost their trepidation.

"I'm going back to my camp," she eventually informed Coren, after several moments of careful consideration, "I need to be there if things do go south."

Coren watched as, not for the first time, Zarola turned her back upon her, and Coren experienced the same, excruciating, stabbing pain in her heart.

On impulse, she shouted out, "Wait, Zar!"

Zarola turned, and Coren felt as if her throat had swelled up in its entirety. Zarola allowed a couple of seconds of silence to pass, before she called back, "what is it?"

"Nothing," Coren eventually got out, a bitter smile

working its way onto her face. *Gods, I'm a coward.* "Nothing at all."

And so, she continued to walk away from her.

"Want to dance?" A voice chirped from behind Coren. Before she turned around, she forced a grin onto her face.

"Lead the way, Dahls."

At what, according to the most sober person at the party, was around three o'clock in the morning, they all dispersed. Some were more reluctant than others, but they knew they needed to be energised for tomorrow. Tomorrow, after the last southbound group hopefully returned with the location of the Transformative Mage camp, they would set out at nightfall, intending to take them by surprise by attacking before sunrise.

Halfway to their tent, Coren lent down to one of the tapped-trees, pushing the metal device further in before filling a flimsy cup that had once been filled with alcohol with water instead. Firstly, she washed it out, then filled it again.

As she watched the water trickle in, Coren was startled by a loud squawk, and looked up to see a white-faced, darkly-feathered bird sitting on one of the tree branches, staring down upon her. A vulture.

"I'm not dead yet, I'm afraid," the Dark Mage told it, giving the tap a sharp whack when the volume of water coming out of it started to decrease, "so maybe come back in a couple of weeks."

Then, she turned around and gave the cup of water to Auryon. The Light Mage, whilst Coren had been talking to the bird, had fallen to her knees and begun to violently gag. Coren had barely managed to pull her thick, dark hair away from her face before the female warrior was throwing up.

Coren offered her the cup of water with a sympathetic look.

"I'm never drinking alcohol again," Auryon groaned.

The Dark Mage rolled her eyes and helped her up, placing one of Auryon's arms around her shoulders to keep her steady.

Before Coren could take another step underneath the not inadmissible weight of the Light Mage, shouts rose up from her left, and Coren turned – startled – to view a wild frenzy.

People were running between tents, grabbing weapons as they went; screaming out for their friends to awaken; they shoved and jostled and fought their way around the camp to where they needed to be.

The Dark Mage took Auryon's arm off of her shoulder and told her to stay where she was, before rushing over to one of the frantic figures. When they resisted Coren's attempt to stop them, she grasped them by the shoulders.

"What's going on?" She demanded, icy fear finding its home within her stomach, but all that the other person offered before forcibly prying themselves away and running off to another tent was a finger pointed upwards.

When Coren looked to the sky, it was as if a blanket of black had been thrown across it, with irregular white dots being the only other colour in residence. The blanket screeched and dived and, as they did so, a group of eleven or twelve dropped something. Something heavy. Something that rolled for a while, before laying sprawled out not five feet from Coren.

It was a body.

A body that had no eyes, no tongue; its face brutally skinned with both arms and one leg cut off.

Staring at it in horror, Coren realised that she recognised the clothing, hair colour and the remnants of its face.

Even disfigured, she knew that the corpse lying at her feet had once been Marlow, the arrogant man who'd insulted her at Zarola's camp. Coren could recall seeing him leaving camp earlier that day when she went to see Zarola off, as part of one of the six groups.

The group that had yet to return.

The message was clear.

Today, the rebels had not found the Transformative Mages; the Transformative Mages had found them.

The vultures then proceeded to drop another body, about twenty-five feet from where the last one had fallen, and Coren's legs threatened to give way when she recognised it.

This corpse was different from the last. Its face had not been maimed, nor were its eyes displaced or limbs removed. It was a whole; it was untouched, bar from the single, neat line across its neck, from which red blood continued to seep – marking it as a recent victim, opposed to Marlow whose long torture was evident. Bright blue eyes stared to the side of her, in the position of their last view of the mortal plain.

It was Commander Alyxan.

Coren's horror-filled eyes looked up to where Auryon was still standing, just as Coren had asked. The dark-haired girl's wide eyes were staring down at her father's body, hands shaking, legs slumping down to the ground.

All of a sudden, the birds began to plummet, flying closer and closer to the group. Dread settling in her stomach, Coren rushed over to a rack of swords that was only around fifty feet from her, grasping two of them before sprinting back over to Auryon and pushing one into the fallen woman's hand.

Time was a cruel mistress; it would not stop for a daughter's misery.

On Coren's side, Auryon had pulled herself up. Sparing a look to her left, the Dark Mage saw something different in the other woman's eyes. Something savage. Around them, the vultures continued to nosedive, before the colour yellow embraced Coren's vision, forcing her to shield her eyes. When it dimmed, it was not vultures that were flocking the camp but people. Mages.

"We're not ready," Auryon stated, looking to where two drunks fumbled over swords, one cutting their arm in the process. As she spoke, a group of four Transformative Mages spotted the two of them, and broke into a run.

Conscious of those approaching, Coren swiftly followed her eyeline and grimaced, "we don't have a choice. We have to be."

Then, she watched as the Transformative Mages grew fangs and claws, their smiles more animal than human as two raised their swords.

I feel nothing. I feel nothing. I feel nothing.

In one hand, Coren lifted her steel sword, positioning herself as she had been taught. She opened up her other hand, palm facing her opponent.

Ball. She commanded, and it obeyed, before Coren directed it to hit the stomach of the Transformative Mage on the far right. She did not even spare them a glance as she then turned to the second of the right-approaching two.

Now placing her available second hand upon her sword as well, Coren brought it swiftly down upon the Mage as he reached her. To her surprise, the man managed to catch it with his claws. Between her sword and his claws, the two stared at one for a moment – he, taller than the blonde by more than a foot and three times her size, displayed a predator's grin.

The Dark Mage offered the same grin back.

Roughly, she kicked him backwards, forcing him to stumble back a little. Then, she swung high, which he blocked, darting back when he made to swipe for her stomach, before swinging high again and again and again. When she was sure he had bought into her pattern, she swung high, clashing sword and claws together once more, at the same time that she took her left hand off her sword, using it to swipe her dagger from her right sleeve before embedding it in his exposed stomach.

The man let out a sharp cry, but did not stumble to the ground. Having expected him to do so, Coren was not prepared for the swipe that came to her face, leading to her hissing and recoiling as he caught her left cheek.

Choke, she told the Darkness, anger simmering.

They had chosen to attack at night, when darkness was everywhere for Coren to manipulate. Thus, it was no time at all before a collar of black surrounded his throat, squeezing inwards as it stole the air from his lungs.

This time, his knees did give way, and his hands came up to claw at it. Instead of helping, his long, sharp claws slashed at his own jugular, making it so that it was not clear if it was the darkness or a slit throat that had killed him.

With him out of the way, and, from her peripheral vision, knowing that Auryon had been engaging the other two – one already dead and the other with one foot in the Below – Coren glanced at the other assailant, only to realise that rather than just hitting the man's stomach, her Darkness had made a hole through it.

Disgusting, but helpful, Coren thought, reaching down to take her dagger from her former opponent's gut.

A sudden symphony of squawking had Coren looking up, and she watched as an even larger flock of vultures headed in the direction of the southbound camp; her heartbeat sped. *Zarola*, it appeared to shout with every pound.

"We'll head that way," Auryon told her, wiping blood from her sword upon a dead woman's top, "it looks like they'll need the back up."

And so, the Light and Dark Mages set about carving themselves a pathway southward.

In response to every approaching Transformative Mage, Auryon raised her sword and fought with the grace, agility and fury of wind, twisting herself around the back of one opponent like a dancer, before turning again into an executioner as she lopped their head from their shoulders.

The Dark Mage was far clumsier with the sword, but strategy saved her when steel could not. The next Transformative Mage she met was a blonde-haired, well-muscled woman, who posed to be a greater threat than those she had already laid to rest.

Her adversary went high, an attack which Coren forcibly pushed away with her own sword, before the Dark Mage swiped low. She seemed to have anticipated this, as she aimed for Coren's unguarded upper body. Knowing that getting a cut on the Transformative Mage's lower stomach was not worth sacrificing what would likely be her own life, Coren was forced to swiftly bring her own sword up to block, leading to her stumbling several steps back at the force of the collision.

Seeing three others approaching her from various sides, any plans for Coren to use her powers against the woman were thwarted as Auryon was too close for the Dark Mage to blindly allow her powers to explode outwards. And it very much wanted to, considering the threat that she was under.

With half her concentration now on preventing her Darkness from committing a wild massacre, Coren almost lost an arm to her opponent. Falling back several steps, the Dark Mage once more reached for her dagger.

And threw it.

Not unexpectedly, as Coren had still not had any time to master such an art, the dagger missed the woman's foot – for which Coren had been aiming – and instead embedded itself in the ground just in front of her opponent.

The Dark Mage shot it a look of betrayal, whilst the Transformative Mage raised an unimpressed eyebrow. *This could still work*, Coren thought to herself, falling back further and waiting for the other woman to follow her, *so long as I get the exact positioning.*

The Transformative Mage followed her, past the dagger, and so Coren quickly ate up the distance between them, moving herself a little left and then a little further left, before fraction right.

Perfect.

As their weapons clashed together for a final time, Coren, as she had with her last opponent, awarded her a swift kick to the stomach. This time, she barely avoided getting her leg caught by the other woman's tan, well-muscled arm. Though she didn't step in front of the dagger and then topple back as Coren had anticipated, she did step on the raised hilt, and stumbled.

Using that momentary distraction, the Dark Mage

hooked her left leg behind the other woman's as the Transformative Mage desperately tried to bring her sword up to counter Coren's downward strike. The Transformative Mage managed to counter, but fell backwards, so Coren twisted around before impaling the sword through her open mouth.

Then, she continued onwards, sparing but a momentary thought to whether or not she would be asked to hand over the willow mage stake in her possession after the battle, so that all the Transformative Mages could be formally killed.

If not, that woman was going to wake up with one hell of a headache.

By the time Coren and Auryon – their bodies now decorated in bite marks, claw marks and crimson – reached the edges of the south encampment, there was a trail of bodies marking their path. More than three quarters had been dealt with by the Darkness, choked or sliced or possessing holes through which you could see the pale grass beneath, but those who had perished to their swords met no kinder fate.

Even when using her Darkness to choke two adversaries, which, due her uneasy emotions, led instead to their necks being crushed, Coren was looking for Zarola everywhere. Desperately, she fought further and further into the camp, searching for red hair at every corner, upon every body.

When Coren found her, she wished that she hadn't. The redhead was slumped on the ground like a puppet with her strings cut, a slim, tall, dark-haired woman standing over her with their sword raised high. Poised for another strike.

Dead. Dead. Dead.

The Dark Mage screamed at the sight and Darkness shot from her grasp, binding the Transformative Mages' arms to their sides and legs in their current position before it threw her back; incapacitating them completely. With no mind for the other opponents rapidly casting their attention upon her, Coren darted over bodies of both the dead and injured to get to the rebel secondary's side.

"Don't be dead," Coren begged, kneeling at her side as she gazed down upon Zarola, moving her hands to cup the woman's face, where her eyes were closed. Blood. There was so much blood, "please don't be dead. Please. Please. Please. *Please!*"

A sob worked its way out of Coren's mouth as her hands moved down from the other girl's face to instead try to cover the blood seeping rapidly from a rather horrendous stomach wound.

Just looking at it made something vicious take hold of her. Without a thought, Coren took the willow mage stake from up her left sleeve and, for the first time since she had received it from Zarola, it left her possession.

To be embedded in the Transformative Mage's chest. Coren spared no more time for the dead Mage, placing her hands swiftly back onto the stomach wound. She knew it was probably in vain but-

Coren glanced back up to Zarola's face, and found tired brown eyes looking up at her. A sob of relief worked its way out of the blonde's mouth and she, keeping one hand upon Zarola's stomach, crawled her way back up towards the red-head's face.

"You're going to be okay; you hear me?" Coren told her, looking from one eye to the other, "you're going to be fine."

Zarola nodded shakily and, before she could stop herself, Coren found herself leaning down towards the redhead. Closer and closer. Finally, she brushed her lips against the other woman's, closing her eyes at their softness. It was brief, she didn't want to cost Zarola any of the oxygen she dearly needed, but it felt beautiful. The secondary stared up at her with wide eyes and, unable to think of anything else to say, the Dark Mage merely blurted out something similar to what Zarola had said days ago.

"I-I just wanted to try something."

The smile that the bleeding girl awarded her with was blinding.

Unbeknownst to them, the sounds of battle were ceasing. Though they had been taken by surprise, the rebels' numbers were ten times that of the Transformative Mages', numbers of which they were either ignorant of or too arrogant to consider a threat due to the human nature of many of the fighters.

The rebels had won the battle.

But the war was not finished yet.

As the sun reached its peak, Coren was kicked out of the healer's tent. It seemed that they had finally had enough of her fussing, and all but commanded that she go for a walk and destress.

So, reluctantly, the Dark Mage pushed herself past the bright red tent flaps and entered the midst of the south camp.

They said that Zarola's going to make a full recovery, Coren reassured herself every time she looked back at the healer's tent – which was every other step. They had told Coren, and the others, so repeatedly.

The others had consisted of Auryon, Izak and Riah, who had visited Zarola before heading to the west camp to check on Dahlia. She had also been injured in the fighting. They had promised to pass on Coren's well wishes and to tell the Air Mage that she would visit before nightfall.

There had been other visitors too. Almost all of the secondarys had made their way to Zarola's bedside, and Coren had some idea of why they were there. Commander Alyxan was dead, Coren had seen his body with her own eyes, and so had many others. Somebody was needed to replace him, and that somebody would be one of his secondaries: Cilla, Aldric, Zarola or Xian.

Coren was brought out of her thoughts when she tripped over a maliciously placed stone, leading to her gaze falling to her feet.

By the Gods, Coren thought as she examined her clothing and skin, the latter of which was stained scarlet. It was only now that the Dark Mage realised that what had been either a bite or claw mark on her leg had been bandaged. Glancing at her arm, she realised that there were bandages on there too.

Pausing in her step, the Dark Mage took a moment to try to gather her wits, before she forced herself to continue onwards, exhaustion hanging on her every muscle.

She had overexerted herself last night, both physically and magically.

Without the Connection, her magic was still capped. When Coren got to the route that would lead her from the south to east camp, she paused in her step and fought off the urge to retch.

Bodies lay strewn about, some piled on top of one another. Ones that *she* had killed.

Coren turned her head left, and saw the forest that resided near all the camps. She could walk through there, and then make her way to the east camp. That way, she wouldn't have to look at her own victims, or feel that green, sticky, lumpy feeling within her throat.

So, she walked into the forest, moving deeper and deeper, away from the bodies, and then east until Coren knew that she would come out past the bodies, only needing to take a short walk north to her camp.

When the Dark Mage finally reached her tent, all she longed to do was collapse within it, to take a small break from reality until she ventured out once more – through the world of violence and death that she had helped forge – to visit Dahlia.

Her plans were somewhat halted, however, when she entered past her tent flaps to see Auryon with her back to Coren and cloak on. Coren had expected that she would still be with Dahlia.

Regardless, the Dark Mage barely looked at her, choosing instead to collapse atop their sleeping bag, resting her back gently against one side of the tent and shutting her heavy eyes.

"How's Dahls?" Coren inquired, her eyes remaining closed as she fought off the lull of sleep.

"I wouldn't know," replied a voice that was decidedly not Auryon's. It was male, deep. Displeased, "considering that you took her with you when you fled from me."

The Dark Mage stumbled to her feet as fast as she could, her eyes shooting straight to the caped figure. They had turned to face her now, and dropped the hood.

Beneath black-red hair, fiery eyes gazed upon her with all the kindness and mercy of a slow, excruciating death.

"Caradoc," Coren breathed out, fear weaving throughout each syllable.

Inwardly, she cursed herself. How could she not have realised that, if the vultures could transport corpses, they could certainly move those alive as well?

"Hello, sweetheart," he responded, smiling cruelly.

The last thing that the Dark Mage felt was someone gripping her mind, before darkness overtook her vision completely.

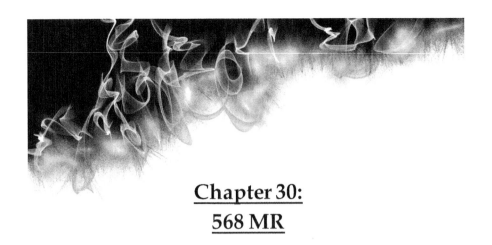

Chapter 30:
568 MR

$\mathcal{T}$hrough the ruins of the west wing, a figure strode
over rubble and ash, their ruby-encrusted gown trailing
behind them, its vibrant colour slowly darkening at the
exposure. To their sides, servants who had been trying
in vain to clear the destroyed area bowed in deference,
in fear. Their legs shook as they lowered their bodies,
eyes never daring to gaze up – to see the pale-faced
woman with golden hair piled atop her head, onyx and
ruby stones weaved within said tresses.
It mattered not, for they were invisible to her. Grey-
green eyes cared only for a set of stairs that lay beneath
one room, the rubble having hurriedly been cleared
out of it the minute it was known that the High Ruler of
Galaris, the Night Queen, sought to enter it.
As she continued her slow, elegant strides, the letter
from earlier ran through Coren's head.
The earth upon the site of the Bloody Massacre is

overturned, one of her Queen's Guard had cited, *and scarce bodies remain beneath it, likely the few of King Caradoc's men the rebels managed to overpower. The Mind Mage was telling the truth.*

Her teeth gritted together at the memory, and she did not bother to restrain her Darkness as it made her displeasure known – lashing outwards into the two remaining marble pillars within the west wing. They fell harshly to the ground, slamming in a way that had servants screaming, running and covering their ears. A small smile formed upon crimson lips at the desperate, fearful sounds that pierced the air.

Power, the Darkness told her, embracing the Queen from behind. She closed her eyes at the comfort, *you'll always have power, Coren. You'll always have me.*

Power. The power to rule the Galarian Empire was hers alone, not Caradoc's, not that bastard Hearne's. No, it was hers, and she would fight to retain it at any cost; it did not matter who or what needed to be sacrificed. The pace of her steps quickened as she grew nearer and nearer to the dark staircase, the spring wind fighting against her valiantly, but never being a recipient of victory against the Queen who would not bow.

Finally, one golden heel was placed upon the top step, and nature was forced to accept its failure for a second time. Another step and then another, spiralling down so deep that Caradoc's fiery temper tantrum the previous day had not so much as left a scorch mark upon the stone.

Before she reached the bottom, the Queen called the shadows to her and they answered – eagerly, as if they were an extension of her opposed to a separate entity. Some snaked their way to her head, forming a dark crown around golden waves, more chose to cling to her shoulders and back like a cape, whilst most seemed to enter her, a black ring forming around her outer iris.

On one side of the deep, hidden room, now completely devoid of Darkness, lay an entire shelf of books, no one book the same. On the opposite side sat a cage in which a prisoner kneeled.

Their head was bowed, hair – the colour of which was brown and crimson, though it was doubtful that it represented their true colouring opposed to the mud and blood of their prison floor – that surpassed their ankles covering any defining facial features.

Despite their slumped over, deathly thin form, the caged person displayed themselves to be fully conscious when they stated, voice croaking, "I know why you're here, Coren."

At first, the Queen did not deign him with a reply. Instead, she took the time to trace her fingers across the spines of her books, smiling somewhat at the feel.

When she reached a certain book, long fingers grasped onto it and pulled, before she brought the cover to her face and blew harshly upon it.

Only then did she turn to the one in the cage, smile growing, "then you already know exactly what I'll do to you if you don't give me what I want."

The slumped figure lifted their head up, hair falling out of the way to reveal enchantingly unusual eyes; jewelled eyes; *jikita* eyes.

The eyes of a Mind Mage with seer abilities.

"You're very imaginative, I'll give you that," he informed her, "I thought that after centuries of torturing me, you may have run out ideas, but no."

"Why thank you. As arrogant as it sounds, I did always fancy myself a bit of a strategist," the Queen began, smirking. She knew that there was nothing the Mind Mage hated more than having to listen to her voice, "you know, I actually think that-,"

"It'll work," he cut her off. Any other person would have been tortured within an inch of their life for having such gall, but, well, he already had been. Coren didn't see the point of doing so again, it would only make her dress dirty.

"Explain."

"What Hearne," the Mind Mage began, not missing the way that the Dark Mage's hands curled into balls, Darkness forming around them in a way that had him flinching back, "has done, it created a tear in the universe. The last sorceress' spell has been destroyed. They are free. All of them. Thus, the ritual will work."

Coren looked down to the book in her hand.

During the first century of her reign, the Queen had collected every book detailing necromancy and Death Mages that she could find. Her goal had been obvious: she had wanted to bring someone back to life. Everybody had known why, and everybody had known that she had failed. That she didn't have the *power*.

By the time the second century of her reign had begun, however, the Queen's search had ceased.

"Good," the High Ruler informed her prisoner curtly, moving back towards the staircase, fingers whitening around the leather that, within it, held the key to victory – to retaining the power that she would not lose.

Before she could advance up the stairs, however, the Mind Mage called out to her, "Coren, if you do this, if you engage in the coming war, all that it will bring is death, destruction and chaos. You'll paint the world red."

"Ahren," Coren purred, turning her head back towards him with a raised brow, "don't you know that red's my favourite colour?"

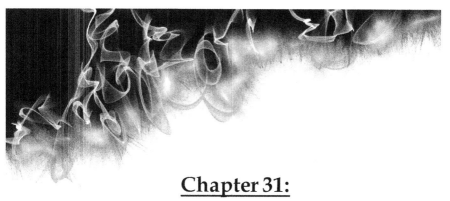

Chapter 31:
216 MR

*P*ain.

It embraced her from every which way, its greedy hands grasping onto Coren and encasing her in its unwanted embrace. If agony were a river, Coren was drowning, being pulled deeper and deeper until the concept of light was naught but a fantasy. Until the lines of reality blurred; until she didn't know truth from falsehood.

Her mouth opened in a soundless scream, a scream that gained volume as a knife dug itself into the skin of her forearm before being dragged down and down, porcelain skin peeling under its influence. She thrashed, she cried, she begged for anything and anyone to save her – for Zarola, for Dahlia, for Auryon, for Izak, for Caradoc and, finally, for her Darkness. But nobody came.

As another knife embedded itself in her opposite forearm, she kicked her legs out desperately, and tried in vain to use her hands but she could not. A set of Mage's Bane clutched her wrists harshly, the chain between the two having been attached to another, stronger steel chain that kept her suspended in the air by her wrists.

It made it difficult to breathe, but that was the least of her worries as another screech-inducing lash landed upon her naked back. She did not know what they were using, but it burned. It burned and burned and burned and burned. It burned to the point that the humiliation of being hung by her wrists, nude in front of a room of spectres, was not felt.

"Please," she begged as another one landed. She just wanted it all to stop. Stop. Stop. *Stop*!

The Dark Mage could no longer remember how she'd got there, who was hurting her, why they were. *What was happening?* She wanted to beg, *what have I done? What do you want?*

The knife in her arm began to move, tearing apart pale skin as it did so. They were writing something. *What were they writing?* Another lash found its home upon Coren, her back arching as she shrieked. It was too much.

Too much. Too much. Too much.

Stop!

Through blurred eyes, Coren caught sight of blonde hair and devastated eyes. *Mum*, Coren thought, *mum stop. I'll learn. I'll learn. I'll be good, I promise. I love you.*

Coren flinched away from her violently, another lash landing, the knife continuing to carve, just as the sticky, warm, lumpy feeling worked its way from her stomach, up and up until it tried to force itself from her throat. Only, the way in which Coren was suspended from the ceiling closed up her throat, making it so constricted that the fluid could not exit. Instead, she began to choke upon her own vomit.

Desperately, the Mage tried to lift herself up above her wrists, to release the pressure on her throat and allow the sick to leave her body. But, as she tried to do so, another burning lash landed on her back, and she fell and fell and fell.

Finally, she took the time to glance down at her arm. Their art was complete.

Within her flesh, through jagged, bleeding letters, they told her exactly what Coren already knew she was. 'MONSTER'.

If she were not choking, the blonde would have laughed. Laughed and laughed until it killed her. *Let it kill me*, she pleaded to whoever was listening – to Nias and Akeros.

"She's dying," a voice may have said, though may not have. Her ears were ringing, her body convulsing, throat full of the lumpy green that was bringing her closer and closer to the both comforting and ominous lull of Darkness.

"It's only temporary," answered another voice. This one was familiar. A voice that she associated with warmth and love. He would save her. He would help her. This man whom she had loved dearly; this man who loved her. "Dying may bring her closer to the Connection. Without it, she is of no further use to me." *Caradoc*, she wanted to say, *help me, please.*

Before long, she was too far gone to understand anything but the delirium of pain. Darkness began to attack her world, taking the light away. *Please. Caradoc.* Then, she knew nothing at all.

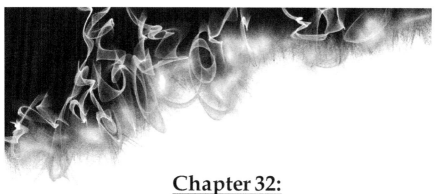

Chapter 32:
216 MR

*S*he was being dragged somewhere, soldiers

crowding all around her. For a moment, the young woman did not know who she was, where she was – it was only pain that she knew, it was the thing that seared at her every limb.

Then, her eyes looked down to her arm, at the words there, and the blonde remembered.

My name is Coren, she thought to herself, the sour taste of bile still within her throat, her tongue connecting with small, spongy lumps that made her want to gag, *and I am a monster.*

They did not allow her to think any further, several sets of hands placing themselves either side of her head. Their influence upon her mind forced her to close her eyes. When she opened them, Coren was somewhere else entirely.

The light that hit her eyes was intense, prompting her to squint once again. They soon adjusted, however, and

Coren found that it was the sun – which she hadn't seen for the Gods knew how long – causing her discomfort.

A frown overcame her face. She was certain that they'd been inside just moments ago. Soon enough, she cast such thoughts aside – it was the pain, no doubt, making her hallucinate. She could barely think straight. To ground herself, she began to trace the words in her arm.

That was, until she saw what lay directly before her. People were gathered around a tall, circular piece of wood, at least a hundred, perhaps more so. To its side, two men stood – hauntingly familiar, and displaying expressions that spoke of cruelty.

"What?" Coren managed to rasp out, turning to one of the soldiers at her side before her entire body froze. The soldiers weren't there any more, in their place were four guards. *Miriam*, she thought with recognition, before glancing to her other side, *Amos*. With growing horror, Coren cast her gaze back towards the crowd.

Mrs. Krenz. Her son. The Patriarch. Garwyn.

With all the strength the Dark Mage had left, she sought to imbed her feet within the ground. She writhed and screamed and tried to throw off her guards in vain. She remembered this day.

It was the day they burned her.

"No," Coren howled out, yanking at wrists that were restrained by the Mage's Bane. When she could not secure the release of her hands, she instead threw herself to the ground, but her guards were not dissuaded. They merely picked her back up by her forearms, dragging her towards the pyre, "no, no, no, *no!*"

Nothing she said or did worked; her gradual approach to the pyre was inevitable. Fear made her throw up no less than three times before they got her to the pyre, but get her there they did.

Coren shook violently as they secured her wrists to the stake, biting the inside of her cheeks to force back the tears that sought to see the day. As she did so, the Dark Mage realised that she was not alone within her own mind, a soothing voice calling out to her: *make the Connection, Coren, and it will all go away.*

It's a trick! She thought desperately, whilst her mind threatened to shatter, *it's not real! It's the Mind Mages!* The soothing voice turned darker, more insistent, as it told her, *you can see it, you can feel it, you can hear it. Just because it's happening inside your head, Corentine, doesn't make it any less real for you. And, should you fail, when the flames come for you, I promise that you will feel **everything**.*

The Patriarch was holding the torch now, the orange flames upon it reaching high towards the clear, blue sky. Coren did not listen to his speech – the same one that he'd given the crowd the first time he'd burned her. Instead, she was begging.

Please, Nias, please help me. I need to make the Connection. I'll pay the price. I'll pay it!

But the Goddess did not care for her plight. Perhaps, she even found it amusing. With silence now reigning inside her head, bar the occasional plea, Coren found herself staring out into the sea of familiar faces – but those in attendance were not all the same as last time. Her father and brothers were there, watching with smiles upon their faces, revelling in the justice being dealt for what she had done to Melrose. Behind them stood Mina and the children. Lucien. Farrah. The others whose names had slipped her mind. Each of their skins were darkly discoloured, bloated in places, with parts of underwater plants trapped beneath their nail beds and in the matts of their hair. In their stomachs or arms or legs or faces, there was willow mage wood embedded.

Coren recoiled in horror and the torch was lowered, further and further down until the twigs around her lit up into a blaze.

"Monster!"

"Murderer!"

"Demon!"

"Dark creature!"

"Witch!"

"Traitor!"

Make the Connection, the voice within her mind whispered once more.

But she could not.

And so, for seven days, Coren burned.

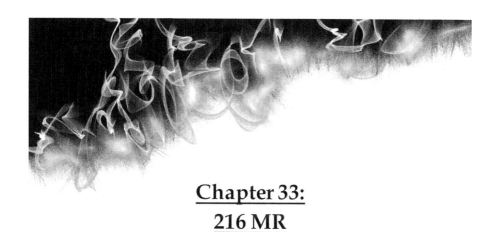

Chapter 33:
216 MR

$\mathcal{T}$ime was subjective.

To the Dark Mage that hung from the ceiling, choking upon her own blood, crimson dripping from every appendage, eyes encircled by black bruises where they resided above a broken nose and split scarlet lips, she had been in the Fire King's care for five days and three centuries all at once. In reality, she had been there closer to five weeks, spending a third of her time as a corpse, and the other two thirds being tortured to the point of insanity.

Coren did nothing but hang there limply, hoping they would think she was dead, wishing she was dead, when large hands lifted her up, allowing the blood to project itself from her throat, landing upon the already bloodied black stones beneath her, before they placed a water cup to her throat.

When she'd awoken after dying for the first time, and been offered water, Coren had spat it straight in their face. Now, she was pliant. There was no fight to be had. One can only lose for so long, before they realise fighting is futile – that it's better just to give in.

When kind hands brushed the hair from her face, Coren saw her.

It was Zarola.

Zarola was here.

Tears worked their way down her cheeks, a sob stuck in her throat, as the beautiful redhead put her forehead against hers. The rebel's hands felt as they always did, soft, yet, in places, calloused from sword fighting. Her beautiful, warrior angel. But they also felt like something else.

They felt like home.

"I love you," Zarola told her, gently twirling a blonde strand around her finger, leaning in to brush her lips against Coren's. Desperately, the blonde tried to lean into her – she was naught but a monster, a thing of Darkness, and Zarola was her salvation. But the chains held her back; held her away from what she sought so desperately.

"Survive this, Coren," she told her. It was as if brown and green-grey were the only colours that existed within this universe, and the next. "Survive this for me. Please."

I don't think I can, Coren wanted to tell her, but could not bring herself to use her throat. *I'm so sorry Zar, I don't think I can fight much longer. It hurts. It hurts so much.*

Zarola seemed to know her thoughts, for she lent her forehead back against Coren's, the warmth of her breath glossing over the freezing woman's face as she whispered, "I know. I know it's hard. But try, please, try and survive it. I'm going to find you."

Then, the door to the room in which she hung opened, and Zarola disappeared. Her home disappeared. Coren thrashed harder than ever – harder than when they whipped her or skinned her, harder than when they'd dragged her out to drown her over and over until she died, harder than when they'd tied her up and burned her for seven days – all the while hearing Mrs. Krenz's little boy screaming at her – *"monster!".*

The crowd watching her never cared for Coren's apologies, for her cries. Her father and brothers had watched it happen that time, with faces that didn't even twitch. She meant nothing to them; to no one. In those moments, all she could do was cling to the memory of soft lips against her own, of a hand embracing hers as they sat in front of a campfire.

"I just want to try something."

It was all that kept her sane, kept her grounded.

But it wasn't real.

Zarola was gone.

Gone. Gone. Gone. Gone.

"Stop!" Someone shouted, as Coren began to scream. "Stop!"

She screamed and screamed and screamed; she screamed herself into unconsciousness. She screamed in her mind; she screamed in her soul – because her home had been taken from her, and she didn't think she could ever return to it.

The next time the Dark Mage awoke, it was to the feeling of a soft hand caressing her face. The hand was loving, it was kind.

"Zarola," the blonde choked out hoarsely, a now unchained hand reaching towards the source. But, at her word, the hand pulled away.

"No," the owner stated simply, "not Zarola."

Desperately, Coren fought to pry her eyes open, just a fraction. But she was tired. So tired. Everything hurt. She didn't want to be here. She didn't want to know what they were going to do to her next – or, worse, what *he* was going to do to her next.

When her eyes did manage to greet the world once more, albeit only being able to take in a blurry picture, Coren found herself gazing up at fiery eyes. Before she could think to stop it – her body, her mind, they were so weak, so weak that she felt as if she was boneless, weightless, nothing but a phantom in the world around her – a sob worked its way out of her throat.

It was violent, more violent than she thought her frail, beaten, naked body was capable of.

"Why are you doing this to me?" She asked of him, her throat screaming in protest as she cried, "I-I *loved* you." For a moment, his eyes flickered.

With the parts of her mind that weren't shrouded in pain, in devastation and defeat, Coren wondered if his sister had said something similar, once. Before he sacrificed her for power too.

When he reached out towards her this time, his hands were not kind. Instead, one hand curled into a ball behind her, blonde strands within it, and he used it to tug her head back harshly. Coren did not even cry out as several strands were pulled from her at the rough movement, as she had been put through worse, so much worse, that she was almost numb to it.

With his other hand, he forced her chin up. His lip curled at what he saw, a broken thing. A broken thing without a home.

"Clearly you didn't love me enough, or else you would have found a way to make the Connection for me. Instead, you're entirely useless. Your father was right, you will mean nothing to no one – you are powerless, you are inferior," his face moved closer to hers, his lips milometers away from her own, "you mean nothing to me."

Her eyes closed of their own accord. They wanted everything to stop.

"But," he continued, and his hands were softer now, unclenched, "you could mean something to me. I could love you. All you need to do is make the Connection, then everything will be okay."

Everything will be okay.

She violently shook her head from side to side, bile rising in her throat once more. Everything would not be okay. It would never be okay.

"Liar," Coren gasped out, gagging as the sick feeling rose in her throat. Ignoring it, she launched herself towards Caradoc, clawing and shaking like a wild animal, "liar, liar, liar, liar!"

Fire leapt from him, burning limbs that screamed in protest, as the room was suddenly flocked with soldiers. They grabbed at skinless arms and matted hair, pulling her from the King whose face was now bloody – and angry. So angry.

"I-I won't," she got out, but barely, her breaths laboured in between each word, "b-be your *puppet*! My strings are cut, you he-hear me? Cut! S-so kill me if you must, because I-I'm not your little manipulated bi-bitch anymore!"

She thought he may kill her for that; end her suffering.

I'm sorry, Zar, but I'll never be as brave as you. As brave as you believe I can be.

But he didn't.

Instead, he nodded at them, and one of the guards shoved her to the ground, another delivering a winding kick to her stomach. Then another to her back. Another stomped upon her knee, and she heard something snap.

"Make the Connection," the Fire King told her, undisturbed by the view in front of him, "and then all of this will go away."

Snap. Snap. Snap.

Ribs, legs, arms.

Caradoc's soldiers attacked all over, breaking, shattering, bruising.

Pain.

Pain.

Pain.

Red blood leaked from her, pooling upon the floor beneath her.

Through eyes that longed to close, Coren stared at it and thought of curly, crimson strands. She thought of the woman they belonged to; she thought of returning to her; she dreamed of the life that they could make together, if they left all of this behind.

Perhaps they would go to warm Azyalai, where the people were kind and the history was grand. Or perhaps to Valark, where snowflakes would fall upon them all year long. Coren thought of pure white snow falling into red hair, she thought of the brown-skinned woman's smile, the one that she had given her as she lay upon the battlefield. But, as a vicious kick to the head was delivered, Coren faced the realisation that Zarola would never run. Could never leave all of this behind. And so, Coren went gladly into the Darkness, allowing the coldness of reality to escape her once again.

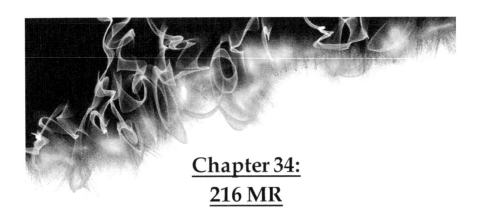

Chapter 34:
216 MR

The Dark Mage was lying, bare, within a circle of her own vomit, urine and blood when the door to her compact room was opened. To her spectator, the woman might as well have been dead. Not a single muscle twitched, head still angled away from the door, legs residing at an unnatural angle that spoke of snapped bones.

The figure moved in slowly, quietly shutting the door behind them before rushing over to the woman, putting an arm beneath pale, crimson, dirty skin and supporting her back. He then placed a cup of water to her mouth, taking care not to jostle her.

Coren's eyes were open, but she did not appear to be taking anything in. One glance into her mind told the Mage that she was retreating inside of it – to a place where a red-haired woman was grinning at her within a field of flowers.

"I'm sorry," the Mind Mage whispered, his throat swelling as he watched her, "I'm so sorry."

Gently, he stroked blonde hair away from her face. Inside of her head, he saw that the redhead had committed such an action instead.

He attempted to reach her, telling the Dark Mage: "Coren, it's Milo. Please, show some sign that you can hear me. Please. You were right about him. I was wrong. I was so, so wrong and I'm sorry. I-I-I'm so, so sorry."

His voice broke as he began to cry. Caradoc had been his friend, but so had she. And yet he had let this happen, let her be humiliated and beaten and tortured. Let her stand on the edge of the cliff of sanity, and watched as she began to tumble. For weeks. All he could do was try to create moments of peace for her – sending 'Zarola' to keep her fighting.

When he looked back down at her, he realised that she had left the utopia of her mind. That she was staring at him, that she knew he was there. That she wasn't gone. Yet.

"I d-d-don't," she tried, and Milo sought to support her back further, trying to get her to drink more water, but she refused. "I d-do-don't for-forgive you."

He felt something within himself tear.

"You don't have to," he said, taking off his coat to lay it beneath her. As Milo lifted her further up, his breath caught when he saw her back.

There were many things that Mages could heal from, and quickly. Over the past weeks, he had seen many a broken bone heal itself, and skin grow back. But the whip they had used upon her back, some lashes wrapping around the side of her stomach, had been

369

dunked in barrels of a liquified version of the metal that the Mage's Bane was made from. Thus, the liquid nullified her healing powers, leaving her back, in parts, as nothing more than destroyed skin; a slab of red, the pale skin underneath barely able to peek through. It would never heal.

When he lowered her back down onto his coat, the Dark Mage cried out and thrashed weakly. The burning guilt threatened to swallow Milo whole.

"Just hold on for a little while longer," he begged, conscious that, due to the pain, the Dark Mage was retreating inside of her head once more, "please." Despite his request, he didn't know if what he asked was truly possible. Milo knew what Caradoc had planned later. His new, torturous solution to forcing the Dark Mage to make the Connection.

She had survived so far, but every part of Milo knew that Coren would not survive what was coming.

A desperate resolve filling him, Milo pulled himself up from the floor and headed to the door, glancing back only once to the crumpled form of Coren.

Milo was not there when Coren faced reality once again. She was not sure that he ever had been. The Dark Mage was not even sure if what she was observing right now was reality, or if it was a fantasy come to life. Zarola had walked through the door, her face changing from one of desperation to relief when she spotted

Coren. Quickly, the redhead rushed over to her, cupping her face as Coren had when she had found the rebel secondary lying on that battlefield – bleeding out. "Coren," she breathed, and the Dark Mage could have sobbed in relief.

Home. She was home.

"Y-y-you should-shouldn't have come," the Dark Mage got out. For the first time in what could have been centuries, she felt warm inside, "I-I'd ra-rather continue l-like this th-than have Cara-Caradoc hu-rt you."

Zarola shook her head vehemently, her hands still caressing the yet-to-heal, bloody skin of Coren's face. The blonde leant into her hand despite the pain it caused.

"Come on," she told the Dark Mage gently, trying to lift Coren up into a sitting position. It took several moments, but, after many agonised cries, the rebel leader managed to do so. Before she could pull her up any further, however, Coren placed one hand over hers, drawing the redhead's attention back to the gravely injured woman.

"I-I want to tell you some-something," she said, her legs, her arms, her chest, her face, all crying out in pain. She ignored them all, "before... before I lo-lose my nerve."

"Coren, we don't have much ti-,"

"I think I might love you," she managed to rush out, crying out at the pain her ribs rewarded her with, "I-I want you to-to know that. In here, it's been y-you that chases aw-away the nightmares of real-ity," she took a shuddering breath, "it should've alw-always been you, Zarola. A-and now, it always will be. I.. I... You're my home."

The redhead's face was unreadable as she scanned Coren's, before the rebel leader let out something akin to a sob, and then buried her face in the Dark Mage's shoulder, clinging to her in a way that – had Coren had any strength at all – she would have returned.

But, when she pulled away, the rebel secondary's face appeared to change entirely. Her lips curled into a mocking smile; her eyes freezing over into something cold and hateful, "pitiful little monster. Do you truly think that I'm looking for you? That I care? You've been nothing but a burden to me from the start. You're the reason the Fire King is attacking my home, my family; you're the reason for Nerah's suffering; you even murdered all those children."

Her hands reached up to encircle Coren's neck, and squeezed, her nails imbedding themselves within the still-healing, burned skin that resided there. Coren didn't care.

"I-I-I'm so... s-so sor-ry," Coren got out eventually, her throat like sandpaper. Zarola could hurt her all she liked, she could tear her skin away with her nails, beat her bloody, if it meant that she would forgive her.

"You're a monster," the woman that she cared for above any other hissed at her.

Coren nodded, "I-I know."

Then, the Zarola clutching her neck suddenly paused, mouth falling open in shock. Coren and the redhead both looked down to see a sword embedded through her stomach; a cry tore itself from the blonde's throat, only to see, once the redhead had been tossed aside, another Zarola standing behind her.

The second Zarola crouched down in front of her, worry painted all over her smooth face and evident in the way that her lips clenched together. She grasped onto Coren just as the last one had, only her hold was kind and considerate.

"We've got to go, Coren," this rebel leader told her, but the blonde could not stop her eyes from wandering to where the corpse of the last Zarola lay, wide brown eyes staring into the distance. Noticing her straying attention, her face was carefully but firmly moved back to face the new one, "that was one of the Fire King's tricks. I would never say that. You need to get up. Quickly. We don't have much time."

The Dark Mage nodded, desperately attempting to pull herself from the ground, unable to stifle the hope and joy that had bloomed within her heart. Zarola had come to find her.

Noticing Coren struggling to get off the floor, Zarola reached under her arm to help her up. The blonde, who could scarcely remember the last time she had experienced a kind touch, leant into her, tears swimming in her eyes, obstructing her vision.

They started to make their way towards the door, one step at a time.

"It's going to be okay," Zarola told her, before pain exploded across Coren's stomach. Her knees slammed to the floor as she screamed, scrambling away from the source of pain, wide eyes looking up to see Zarola standing still, an all too familiar whip in her hands. "This is so you learn, Coren," the redhead told her, but it was another woman's voice that Coren heard instead, a woman that she'd killed, "you need to learn."

Before Zarola could take another step towards her, a gasp left her mouth, and Coren watched as this Zarola's throat was slit. The rebel secondary's body slumped to the floor, blood still spurting from her neck, drenching Coren in the warm liquid, displaying a third Zarola standing behind her.

"Coren," this one began, just as concerned as the others had once been as she rushed towards her, "are you okay? She wasn't real, I promise. But we need to go." All the Dark Mage could do was curl into herself and sob.

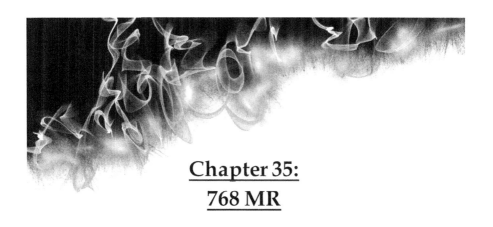

Chapter 35:
768 MR

*O*ff-white parchment held securely within his grasp,

the former member of the Queen's Guard watched
over his camp.

It was thriving.

Not two weeks past, this field had been home to just
two, who had barely escaped Andern intact. Now, at
least five and half thousand resided within it – with
more to join.

A smile gracing his features, Hearne looked down to
the letter held tightly within his hand. Hope gleamed
within him as he recalled its words; how Duke Ardan
had told him of the eager responses minor nobles had
sent him after receiving his and Hearne's
announcement of their intention to rebel. This did not
surprise the human man; people were always looking
to advance in life, and now their imaginations were rife
with their own visions of a world without the Night
Queen – one where they could garner more land and
influence.

Their announcement had also been sent to every major city in Galaris, and word had naturally made it to the more rural towns and villages as well. From that, Hearne had seen more immediate results, with humans making their way from the north, south, east and west, all to gather at the declared location – Caythrys – where discrete messengers would give them the location of the campsite.

Hearne had no doubt that some of the Queen's people had managed to hide themselves amongst his recruits, but he cared little for it. There was nothing he could do, other than wait for them to be rooted out in time. Of course, Thaddeus' talents would have come in useful in weeding out the unfaithful, but he had not seen his Mind Mage since the ritual. No doubt the ambitious dolt was lying dead in a ditch somewhere. *At least that's one less Mage I need to rid the world of,* the former Comrade thought to himself, glancing to his left when he heard the tell-tale sounds of leaves crunching underfoot.

It was Greer that was approaching him, sandy brown hair being blown to her right by the warm summer winds, her expression serious.

He did not need her to speak to know what she had come to tell him, but she did so regardless. "They're awake, and they want answers."

"By 'they'," Hearne began, stuffing the parchment brutally into one of his many pockets before striding past Greer and towards where the camp lay, "I assume you mean Commander Zarola."

"She's definitely one of the most insistent, yes," the

brown-haired Elemental Mage agreed, rushing to keep up with the man's long strides, "what are you going to tell them?"

He did not even pause before telling her simply, "the truth."

After all, with a woman like the Night Queen, there was no need for falsities. Perhaps he may embellish parts of the tales, if necessary, but even that seemed needless for the woman who had laughed as innocents all around her choked upon the Darkness that was a part of her. Who had once cut off a man's limbs and fed them to him whilst he was still breathing.

She had laughed even then.

"What do you call a legless cow?" he remembered her jeering at the man, a twisted smile pulling at those deep red lips as she watched parts of his freshly amputated leg be forced down his throat, *"no guesses? What a shame. They call them ground beef! Tell me, do you taste like beef?"*

At her final inquiry, he remembered her knees caving in as she laughed and laughed and laughed. When she rose her head from the ground, she had barred her teeth at the man, and laughed all the more as his mouth emitted a symphony of pain and fright.

Gods, he hated that woman. Cruel and twisted were far too kind words to describe her.

Shaking his head, the dark-haired man sought to gather himself before he appeared in front of the weary Winter Rebellion – who had earned their legendary nickname from the weather at the Massacre, when snow was said to have blanketed the battlefield, before

377

it was stained red with their blood – knowing that he needed them on his side.

It was easy to tell exactly where they were as all Hearne had to do was search for an obscenely large group of people attempting to huddle as much together as just under four thousand could. At their centre, a red-haired woman stood on shaky feet, mud and blood still caking her face and hair, as she argued with a blonde-haired man who Hearne could not recognise.

"What in the Below are you talking about?" he heard the Commander snarl, "Coren would never do what they're thinking! You're wrong."

Ah, a Mind Mage, Hearne thought in realisation, preparing himself to attempt to shield his thoughts as his Aunt Auryon had taught him, but – to his ire – he'd never been very good at it.

As expected, the Mind Mage had clearly heard his previous thought, because he looked away from the furious woman and towards Hearne and Greer, who were fast approaching and quickly gaining the attention of the whole group.

Realising that the dark-blonde Mage's attention was elsewhere, Zarola followed his gaze to Hearne.

"Commander," Hearne greeted with a charming smile, "it's a pleasure to meet you at last."

The redhead did not smile back. "Perhaps I would say the same, if you could explain where and when we are, along with what on the continents your people are thinking about Coren."

"You noticed the 'when' part?" the former Queen's Guard asked, adopting an impressed tone in the hopes that it would make her more amenable. People loved being complimented, "Colour me impressed. I'd sit down if I were you, Commander, it's a long story." She did not sit.

Hearne's smile fell, ever so slightly. But he recovered it soon enough.

"The year is 768 of the Mage Rule," he ignored the flicker of shock across the Commander's face, and the murmuring of those in the group that could hear his words, "and I orchestrated all of your resurrections because we are in dire need of your help. For over five hundred years, we have suffered-,"

"I d-died?" a young voice inquired to his left. Irritated, Hearne turned to see a boy no older than sixteen staring up at him, "w-what about my mum and dad a- and my little brother? They w-weren't at the battle... Are they dead?"

Just what he needed. A mopey child. Plastering a sympathetic smile upon his face, Hearne informed him, "I'm afraid so, though, with the way that humans are suffering at the moment, it's probably for the best." That did not appear to console the boy, whose expression twisted into something broken and terrified, a sob leaving his lips. Another rebel moved to comfort him, as Hearne turned towards the now silent Commander.

At last, she asked, dark eyes fiercely staring into his own, "where's Coren? Is she alive?"

From the wavering tone of her voice, and from the Mind Mage's earlier words, she already knew the answer.

"She's ruling," Hearne informed the woman simply, revelling in the shock of the crowd; the people who the Night Queen had once fought alongside.

"You're lying," Zarola spat out, and went to move away from Hearne. But he just grabbed her arm, ignoring those who had stood from the ground, ready to defend their Commander should he harm her.

But he wasn't planning to.

Not physically, anyway.

"I'm not, and your Mind Mage can even confirm it if you'd like," he said, "because it's the truth. Coren in my world, in this future, is not a good person. She's not the woman you loved. She's the Night Queen, the High Ruler of Galaris, who you either cower before or are killed more brutally than any of you can possibly imagine!"

"What about Caradoc?" A voice spoke up from the Commander's side. A tall, brown-haired man, who looked to be in as much denial as the Commander about his words concerning the Queen.

"Coren killed him," Hearne said, his gaze moving away from him and back to the dark brown eyes of the redhead, "she shoved a stake through his heart."

For you, Hearne added on mentally, for that was the way that most tales from the days after the Massacre were told. Unfortunately, the Mind Mage caught onto his thoughts even with Hearne's flimsy barriers up, thus he had to explain further. They would not help him if he was thought to be a liar, even if he was merely excluding unnecessary parts of the story.

So, he continued: "Most people believe that she went

380

mad when she saw your dead body," the Commander's eyes widened. She hadn't known Coren had been there; the Dark Mage must have arrived too late. Tragic. "That was when she was said to have made the Connection anyway, before she took off towards the capitol with my Aunt Auryon right on her tail; they say that she murdered the King in retribution for you. But these are merely tales. If you ask me, I think she was too out of her mind to care about anything but power by then. The bitch is crazy."

He clearly should have not let himself get carried away in his hatred, as a fist was sent flying for his nose before he could even think to block it.

A crack sounded and pain exploded across his face, but Hearne merely gritted his teeth and turned back to the redhead, whose eyes appeared to be glazed over with something that looked suspiciously like tears.

"Aunt Auryon?" A different person asked; high up in the leadership if their proximity to the Commander had anything to say about it.

"Yes," Hearne confirmed, hoping that his relation to the former rebels – Auryon and his ancestor Riah – would garner him some trust and amiability from the rebels, "she is head of the Night Bi- Queen's Guard."

"If Auryon has stayed with her, then surely Coren cannot be as bad as you say, perhaps-,"

"Bad doesn't even begin to describe her!" Hearne yelled, his patience brutally snapping as he watched the short, brown-skinned woman in front of him trying to humanise her, "do you know how many humans she has enslaved? How many families she has broken? How many governments she has torn apart? How many people she has tortured? How many people she has killed not just because she felt the need to, but because it was fun? I've spent all twenty-eight years of my life in the capitol, bearing witness to public executions and brutality and disorder on the streets, and then fourteen of those as a member of the Queen's Guard. Fourteen years I have witnessed her tyranny and cruelty; fourteen years I have had to stand by, powerless as that psychotic bitch laughs as she rips people apart; four-,"

"Stop it," the rebel Commander looked weak on her feet; her face pale, "just stop it."

"I can't 'stop it'," Hearne told her, his face twisting into a scowl as he moved closer to the Commander, using his height to leer over her, "nothing will stop until that bitch is dead! And I can't do it alone."

When he felt a knife being pressed threateningly into his side, Hearne took a step back, giving the Azyalian woman with the knife a short glower before he turned, pushing his way through the group with the intention of leaving to cool off, Greer following directly behind him.

Before he exited her hearing range, Hearne moved his head back around to face the Commander whose face was twisted with sorrow and disbelief.

"Welcome to the future, Commander," he said, and then continued to walk away.

Once they were a suitable distance away from the rebels, his shadow informed him, "the Commander will not fight against her. Nor will the other three around her."

"Not yet," Hearne corrected her, continuing to stride swiftly towards his tent, an idea already forming within his mind.

If Commander Zarola would not believe his words, then he would simply have to show her the truth. Trying to get her, and the other non-believers, close enough to the Night Queen to fully cement her position as a monster in their hearts would be both dangerous and difficult, but there was no use in him having gone through all the trouble to resurrect a rebellion if they would not help him fight.

Gritting his teeth in frustration, he shoved his tent flap aside and strode in, heading straight towards his writing desk. As much as he hated to rely upon the Duke, he would need to in order to be able to use the man's contacts to get themselves into the capitol, which the Queen would have no doubt severely increased the security of.

She was insane but, unfortunately, not an idiot.

By the time he had pulled an ink pot and quill out of his draws and placed them upon the desk, Greer perching herself on a nearby armchair, his tent flap was being swiftly opened by a hurried woman – a new addition to the rebellion – who gulped several quick gasps of air before informing him, "one of the rebels, they knocked some of our people out and are leaving on a horse."

Slamming his palms into the desk in front of him, he pushed his chair back and got up.

"And nobody's stopping him?" He inquired angrily.

"He's a Mind Mage, sir," the young woman informed him, worry painted across her pale face, "nobody can."

He hastened his pace, exiting the tent.

"What about the Commander?"

"She's also aiming to leave, I saw her-,"

Hearne could see the Commander ahead of him now, already atop a horse, with a blonde-haired man well ahead of her on a different one, now disappearing amongst the trees.

But that wasn't the only thing that he saw.

Fire.

At the bottom of the generous hill that Hearne had taken residence upon, the small city of Lythan was aflame, smoke reaching its desperate fingers up towards where they resided. Along with the screams. Screams of excruciating pain, of terror and death.

The flames were growing. Higher and higher until Hearne could feel the heat upon his face; until his sweat made his top cling to him like a second skin.

"What..." Greer managed to get out, her voice conveying the shock that Hearne felt in every bone of his body.

Elemental Mages didn't grow to this kind of power, not second generation nor third. There was only one Fire Mage in all of history that had achieved this kind of power.

Caradoc.

Within his own mind, it was not him who whispered the word but the eyeless, limbless being that was Tana, the last Death Mage.

Just as denial desperately attempted to take over, he saw a figure through the flames, the figure of a man. Even from here, he could see the way that his eyes glowed – just as the legends had said – like a living flame.

"You brought him back too?" It was the horror filled voice of the Commander that cut through the silence, as Hearne cursed the Death Mage's name under every God there was – human and Mage.

What have you done? He thought at the image of the dying woman that was replaying within his head over and over, as she uttered the Fire King's name with her last breath, *How can I fight them both now?*

So distracted by his rage, he missed the most peculiar sensation that startled all those around him. It was as if the very air around them had thinned, the very atmosphere giving way to something, or someone.

It was only when Greer nudged him that he took notice, and disbelief rose within him. Surely things cannot get any worse, he attempted to comfort himself, looking around for any sign as to what had caused the sensation.

He did not have to search for long.

"Well," an unfamiliar voice from behind him spoke at last, and Hearne violently twisted around, grasping for a weapon. When he was fully facing them, sword in hand, his stomach sunk deeper and deeper. *Oh Gods, what did that Death bitch do?* "Haven't you gotten yourself, and this world, into a pickle? Luckily for you, I can help with that."

In front of him, with near-white hair and almost matching eyes, stood a figure unmistakable from his tapestry. But, if any doubt remained, the way he appeared to glow certainly made his identity clear. Lexin, the God of Light, was no longer shut away in the Ascended City with the rest of the Gods, but instead had both feet firmly upon the ground of the continents.

As he continued to stare in bewilderment at the God, unbearable heat embracing his back, a more pressing question jostled its way into Hearne's mind: *if the God of Light was here, then where were the rest of the Gods?*

And where was the monster of legends: the First Hybrid?

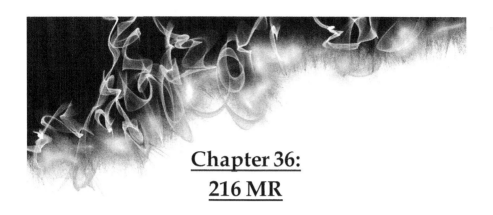

Chapter 36:
216 MR

$\mathcal{F}$ifty Zarolas had saved her, tortured her, and died by

the time that a different presence graced her compact
room – Izak, followed shortly by Auryon.
Initially, Izak recoiled in surprise and she heard his
breath hitch in horror, before he displayed the exact
same look of concern that each and every Zarola had
borne. Auryon, when she managed to gain a full view
of Coren once she emerged from around the Earth
Mage's back, looked as if she wanted to be sick.
Coren didn't even bother to move, nor had she done so
for the last twenty redheads that had entered. Her head
remained slumped to the side, displaying the simple
word – *'MONSTER'* – that Zarola number thirty-two
had carved into her cheek, with her immediate
predecessors having taken the time to carve it into her
arms, legs, and chest. From her stomach and back, the
aftermath of whippings allowed blood to seep onto the
floor. Also upon the floor were nails, and then stumps

of flesh. Zarola number eleven had ripped all of her fingernails off, before number thirteen had chopped each finger off in turn.

She wondered if these two would take her hands, or perhaps her toes. Maybe, when they were killed by their replacement set, her fingers would have grown back, and they would chop them off all over again. *Call me stumpy*, Coren thought to herself.

Such thoughts allowed a hysterical laugh to bubble from her throat, which led to her coughing up blood, something behind her ribs seizing up in pain.

One of the Zarolas who had beaten her must have punctured her lung again, the Dark Mage decided, not bothering to wipe the smile off of her face.

At the sight of the blood rising from her throat, Auryon pushed past Izak and ran to her side, beginning to use her sleeve to wipe the crimson, sticky substance from around Coren's mouth and chin. Her efforts were largely in vain, as it dripped from the carved letters on her cheek and from her nose still.

Whilst 'Auryon' attempted to tend to her, another figure pushed itself past the still-frozen 'Izak'. This one was very, very familiar, and Coren felt the dread rise up into her once more.

Now in front of the Earth Mage, staring down upon Coren, Zarola paused in her step. A look of pure agony rippled through her dark brown eyes, as if something had been torn out of her. The redhead's voice was no more than a whisper when she said, "Coren," and then started forwards.

"No," the Dark Mage begged, and the rebel leader faltered in her step.

She moved her head so that it was angled away from her. Coren did not want to see her face contorted with hatred once more. Could not.

More blood trickled out of her mouth as, facing away, she muttered to herself, "you're not real. None of you are. Not real. Not real. Not real."

The blonde hoped that if she kept on repeating the phrase, then she would feel as if it were true, but it was just as the voice had told her when she burned: she could feel it, the pain they caused; she could hear it, the hate Zarola spewed. It was real to her.

The voice that spoke up was familiar, and miserable. "I thought I'd be able to get you here before they started," he said.

"What," it was Zarola's voice. Coren flinched. If the long, devastated pause the other woman allowed before continuing to speak was anything to go by, then she noticed, "w-what did they do to her?"

Faintly, Coren heard the other voice answer her, but the majority of her attention remained upon the Auryon trying to clean her face, bracing herself for the first hit. "Caradoc had realised that physical torture wasn't working, so he hoped that, if she was under enough physiological pressure, then she'd break. So, he used Mind Mages to uncover what she cared about the most, to weaponize it against her. And that person was you... To Coren, you did all of this to her."

Within the silence of the room, pity was a heavy weight. Coren hated it.

"We need to get her out of here," the Mind Mage's creation of Izak stated, his voice breaking slightly in between words. Coren supposed that, if he were real, she'd remind him of Jakan. After a moment, he continued. "The guards will not stay under your trance for much longer."

Carefully, Auryon moved her hands down so that they were under Coren's arms, her face soft as she told her gently, "come on, we've got to go. I'll help you up."

It was the kindness upon her face that broke Coren, before the cruelty had even begun. A cry forced its way out of her throat as she tried to push the other woman away, shoving herself further down to the floor in the process.

She screamed at the pain, her back, her chest, her legs, her arms, her face – everywhere – flaming up in agony. Still, Coren tried to back away, shoving herself closer to the wall as more worried hands rushed towards her.

"N-n-no," she refused desperately, her voice cracking and broken, "please n-no. I-I can't give you wh-what you want. I can't. Ju... Just kill m-me. Please. I-It's like you said. I'm a-a useless mon-monster, so-so please do i-it."

When her back finally made contact with the wall, Coren saw white as she cried out. It was too much too much too much too much.

Helpmehelpmehelpmehelpmehelpme.

Coughs wracked her body, and some of the blood that was coming out with them stuck in her throat. She began to choke once more, oxygen evading her. In that vulnerable state, she was powerless to fight the hands that grasped onto her, some gentle, others rough, some soft, some calloused.

Nobody else in the room seemed to see the plain faced woman that stood behind them, with dark hair and even darker eyes. The one that, no matter how desperately Coren had begged before now, only appeared in this moment.

Soon, the Goddess of Darkness mouthed, before Coren finally surrendered, hoping that, this time, she wouldn't wake up again.

To the Dark Mage's dismay, she did become conscious once more, blinking harshly at the intrusive attack that light launched upon her eyes, a groan forcing itself from her throat.

When her eyes were partially opened and she was at least semi-alert, Coren noticed that she was no longer within her prison. That, instead, she was within a tent that – bar being a lot more disorganised – mirrored the one that she and Zarola had stayed within at the rebel camp.

The realisation made her shake. What would they do to her here? Were they going to taint or destroy the memories that she held dear from her time in this tent? Tears threatened to prick at her eyes at the thought, but she ignored them. There was nothing she could do to stop it from happening; she had never been trained to evade Mind Mages, and thus her own mind was their playground, to summon and manipulate what evil they could.

Coren closed her eyes when she heard voices close to her tent, hoping to evade her fate for a little longer. "We have to leave, Commander," she heard an unfamiliar male voice state, frustration leaking into his words, "we've already dallied far too long."

"Three more days is all I ask for," another voice tried to reason, though her tone bordered on begging. It was Zarola. Coren did not believe that she had ever heard her so desperate, nor exhausted.

A sympathetic voice joined the fray, and Coren knew that she recognised it, but her mind was still a jumble of pain and denial, so she failed to place it, "I know you want to be here when she wakes, Commander, but whilst we sit idly by, Caradoc is amassing his forces. The more soldiers he gathers, the slimmer our chance at victory becomes. We must leave in the morning. Our forces are ready."

There was a long pause, and Coren could imagine the redhead's curt nod as she reluctantly agreed, "we leave at dawn," before the Dark Mage heard footsteps heading towards her tent. From the sound of them, they belonged to the rebel leader.

Coren kept her eyes shut as she entered the tent, and continued to do so even when the first sob made its way out of Zarola's mouth. From the sounds of things, the other woman had sunk to the floor, and was pressing something over her mouth in a desperate attempt to muffle her cries.

It is a trick, the Dark Mage told herself as another heart-piercing sob left the beautiful woman's mouth, *one designed to hurt me even more.*

And it worked.

Coren would rather take the beatings than listen to this. Finally, the rebel leader began to speak.

"You have no idea how sorry I am," she said, her voice hoarse, hiccups piercing between every other word, "I failed you. I tried... I tried so hard to find you. When I realised you were gone, you have no idea how awful it felt. Fear is not enough to describe it I-I... I've cared for you for a long time, Coren. Perhaps even from the beginning. The first time I felt that kind of fear, t-though maybe not as intense, was when I realised you were out in the walls and-and the feeling was so foreign. I didn't understand it then, or even when I kissed you for the first time, but I understand it now. I u-understood it when I went to bed every night, worrying about you, thinking about you, wishing you would choose me over that bastard of a King. I-I... Seeing you like that, knowing that it was my fault, I'd never felt pain like it. A-and I know that when you wake up, you'll probably fear me. I-I know that maybe you'll blame me, b-because I blame me. I should've protected you, I should've-I should've..."

The sound that Zarola emitted, the cry of a person who had something precious taken from them, something that they could never hope to recover, had Coren turning her head towards her, grey-green eyes opened fully. She didn't care if this was a trick, there was no world in which she ignored Zarola in her pain, no matter the repercussions.

The redhead had sunk down close to the grey sleeping bag upon which Coren was lain and had no doubt stained red, allowing the Dark Mage to stretch her hand out towards the other woman.

Zarola, once she looked up, reached back, entwining Coren's fingers with her own, though she did not try to move any closer to her.

"You're my home," Coren said as if that were the answer to all. From the way that Zarola smiled through her tears, it was.

Without removing her hand from Coren's, she carefully reached over to her other side, her right hand grasping onto a flask of water. Using slow movements, she finally placed the flask to the blonde's mouth, hesitating slightly when the other girl flinched as she lifted her head up so that she could drink.

Taking several gulps, Coren moved her head away, electing to stare tearfully, hope shining within her eyes despite everything, at Zarola as she hesitantly asked, "are you real?"

The hand that had remained at the back of Coren's head gently stroked her hair as the redhead told her, salty tears dripping down her face, "I'm real. I'm real. And you're safe now, Coren. I promise."

Safe. The very concept had been so foreign to her for all this time, yet it was now offered to her once more. But they weren't safe. Not yet.

"A-after all this is over," Coren began, still not allowing herself to accept this as reality and not a part of the fantasy world she sometimes escaped to, nor a cruel trick by Mind Mages, "can we go? To somewhere w-with a meadow of flowers; to somewhere safe where th-there's no Dark Mage and Commander."

"There's nothing I could want more," the rebel leader told her, and Coren couldn't push back the tears at that. After all of this, they would get their happily ever after. Ignoring the red stains upon it, Zarola climbed into the sleeping bag with Coren, careful not to jostle her.

"Tell me if anything hurts," she said, before cautiously moving her arm over Coren's body and gently lowering it over the Dark Mage's middle. Though some wounds stung at the movement, the blonde did not allow a single noise to pass from her lips. She wouldn't trade this moment for the world.

With the rebel's arm around her, who may be the true Zarola, Coren forgot anything else but her warmth. About the looming war, about Caradoc, about some of her pain, about Zarola's upcoming departure.

Tonight, the universe was theirs. And theirs alone.

As the sun rose, so did Zarola, jostled from her dreams by the feeling of somebody watching her. Looking up, one hand already reaching for the dagger that lay beside the sleeping bag, she saw one of her Secondaries gazing upon her – Cilla.

The Mind Mage, after sending a pitying look to the blonde that slumbered on within Zarola's arms, inclined her head towards the exit.

Regret filling her, the redheaded woman slowly began to retract her arm from Coren, wincing at the sounds of pain the sleeping woman made when she brushed past one of her injuries. Having slept beside Coren for months, Zarola knew that it was a miracle that the light-sleeper did not wake. No doubt it was a testament as to just how pained and exhausted she was.

After grabbing a fresh set of clothes, another cloak, her dagger and her sword, Zarola turned to the ratty armchair. Upon it, she had kept the twin dagger – Coren's version of it – and the willow mage stake that had been left behind.

Knowing that she would need it to successfully kill the King, but refusing to leave Coren behind defenceless, Zarola broke the stake in half. Then, by Coren's side, she set down the twin dagger and one half of the stake, before leaning down to kiss the sleeping woman's forehead.

"I'll be back soon," Zarola whispered to her, then she collected her own dagger and stake and made her way out of the tent.

All around her, people were gathering weapons and donning armour, those who would make up the cavalry also readying their horses.

A sense of finality settled over the rebel as she watched it all occur, knowing that she would either come out of this battle as a liberator or a corpse. She was determined that it be the former, already imagining herself travelling the world with Coren at her side. Veering towards her left, she knocked on the plank of wood outside Auryon's tent, entering when she heard a voice call out in acceptance of her.

When Coren had disappeared and the rebel hierarchy was restructured, Zarola had Auryon moved to her camp, along with the few that were zealous to find the Dark Mage. She had needed all the support she could get against the protests of her Secondaries.

When the Commander opened up the tent flap, she saw that Auryon already had half her armour on. Zarola frowned at the sight, telling the other woman, "I want you to stay here with Coren. You're one of the best swordswomen we have, and I won't allow her to be taken again."

The Light Mage, to Zarola's slight surprise, did not look reluctant in the slightest. In fact, she appeared relieved. The redhead knew that this was not her shying from a fight, Auryon was far too talented for that, she had come on leaps and bounds recently in showcasing her talent confidently (especially with her father gone, Zarola had noted privately). Instead, the rebel Commander knew that it was out of concern for Coren's wellbeing.

"Yes, Commander," the dark-haired woman said, and Zarola gave her a curt nod in response.

"You'll need to stay outside of our tent for now, as she is sleeping," Zarola informed her strictly, "I'm trusting that you won't let anything happen to her until I return."

Auryon nodded, "I'll protect her with my life, Commander. I promise."

With that, the Light Mage left for Zarola and Coren's tent with her sword in hand.

The redhead stayed where she was, changing her clothes swiftly before heading back into the chaos that was the final battle preparations. She weaved her way through it all to reach her horse, a fine grey mare, and then pulled herself atop it.

As the Commander of the Rebels led her horse away, she allowed herself a final look back in the direction of hers and Coren's tent.

I love you, she thought back at the woman who laid in there, still deep within the peaceful realm of sleep, *I hope you know that.*

Suddenly, something cold and wet hit her nose, and the redhead looked up to the pale skies.

Snow had begun to fall.

It was time.

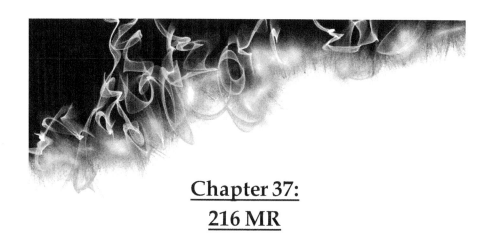

Chapter 37:
216 MR

*W*hen Coren finally awoke, cold and alone, it appeared

as if it were still night. From the conversation she could recall overhearing the previous day, she knew that this was not true – that dawn must have passed, and that the sun was merely hiding.

Slowly, painfully, she began to pull herself up from the ground. Every inch she moved, a small pause was needed in which agony flashed over her, before she could keep on pushing.

She needed to know if anyone had heard any news about Zarola.

Coren had hoped that she would wake up when the redhead did so she could insist on going with her. But she hadn't. And now Zarola was out there fighting – possibly in pain – and here she was, lying in a sleeping bag like the useless waste of space she was.

It made her want to throw something, but that wouldn't help her in the slightest. Straining her injuries would only make it so that she reached the rebel Commander slower.

As she moved so that she could stand on both feet, her back arching in the process, Coren could not stop the yell that left her throat. In response, the tent flap opened and Coren was greeted to the sight of a worried Auryon, who swiftly moved to her side.

"You shouldn't be getting up," the warrior told her, though didn't attempt to push Coren back down.

The Dark Mage merely continued to rise from the ground, and Auryon quickly decided to help her rather than watch her struggle. When she was up, and gripping onto the Light Mage like she was her life line, Coren gasped out, "Zarola. Have you heard anything?"

As she asked, the sides of the tent were rocked and shoved by the harsh winds outside, drawing both Mages' attention to it. Looking back to Auryon, Coren saw that she was still watching the rapidly flapping tent with a grimace.

"I'm sure everything's fine," the dark-haired woman told her, "They've probably already won and are on their way home, but are delayed by the storm."

The swordswoman's face was filled with hope, but Coren could not force herself to feel the same way. Instead, anxiousness and doubt swelled in her stomach.

"I need to go to her. I need to know that they're all okay," Coren told the Light Mage decisively, pushing away from her to make her way towards the tent exit.

Auryon's grip on her arm was strong. "Nobody's going anywhere, not with a snow storm like this one. The cold would probably cost us our limbs."

The Dark Mage couldn't bring herself to care what happened to her own limbs. She just needed to be there. "You stay then. Mine will grow back."

Auryon shot her a disbelieving look as Coren lifted her hand towards her, and then wiggled her fingers about, before telling her, "These certainly have," then she turned her hand around a couple of times, studying it, "in fact, I'd say they've improved. Longer. Do you see what I mean?" before she moved to go past the Light Mage.

It was no surprise that she was stopped once again. "Give them half a day. If they're not back, I will happily ride through that storm with you. But they'll be back. I know they will."

The last part was muttered rather than spoken, fear flicking across the warrior's face.

Coren wasn't the only one with people to lose on the battlefield – Auryon's sister was out there too. Possibly hurt. Possibly dying.

"They've got to be," the Dark Mage said, *because I don't know what I'll do if they're not,* was heard yet unspoken.

The Light Mage managed a small, hesitant smile, before she reached into her pocket and took a swing from her water flask, then sat down in the ratty armchair. When she opened her mouth again, Auryon hesitated for a moment, and Coren knew exactly what she was about to ask.

No.

She couldn't – she... Not about that. Not now. Possibly not ever. What had happened to her under Caradoc's care she had locked in a box already, and buried it deep, so deep that even she would struggle to touch such moments.

And she would not allow it to reach the surface.

There's no need for her to know, Coren told herself, already imagining the Light Mage's encouraging smile as she did what she could to make the Dark Mage feel safe, whilst hiding her own horror and pity just beneath the comforting surface, *there's no need for anybody to know.*

"So," Coren said, pretending as if she had not read Auryon's intentions, "what chaos have you all gotten up to whilst I've been gone?"

It was a weak attempt to change the conversation, she supposed, but Auryon allowed it to work.

"What, because you're the rational one out of all of us?" she teased back. Relaxing, Coren allowed herself to smile, as if nothing had happened to her at all. "Sometimes. So, come on. Spill."

As the day progressed, the sun never deeming them worthy enough to witness her light, Auryon's hopeful eyes trekked down the slow path to despair. As much as she could, Coren attempted to busy herself – she viewed her injuries, which were extensive and ghastly. She had never considered herself a particularly vain person, but the feeling of shame that staring at her

402

mutilated stomach and back gave her proved Coren wrong.

They'd painted her in blood and flesh.

At least, she supposed, it was her own, rather than the blood and flesh of those she had killed. Perhaps this pain, this... this... awfulness was her penance.

Auryon had watched her as she viewed them, no doubt hoping that her presence would give the Dark Mage some form of comfort, but instead it just made her feel embarrassed, ashamed.

"Milo was the one who led us to you," the Light Mage had said suddenly, breaking the silence as one stewed in shame and the other in pity, to answer the question that Coren had never asked. The one that she had chosen to forget, "and he joined us afterwards. He's gone with Riah and the Commander."

Coren hadn't responded. She didn't know how to.

The Mind Mage had betrayed her before he had saved her. Did that mean she was supposed to forgive him? Forget what it felt to be carried in the arms of a friend – her first friend since Mina – who had deceived her and then delivered her to the man who had pretended to love her, all so that he could sacrifice her to better his own power? Could she forgive a man who had stood by, knowing children were being locked away and drained of blood for said King's power?

No. Time. She needed more time.

The atmosphere had tensed further when the storm had died down and, in the hours following, there was still no sign of anyone. No rebels holding up a flag of victory, nor a few thousand returning with their heads hanging in defeat.

When a waxing gibbous moon took to the sky, Coren took a stand.

"We're leaving."

Auryon merely nodded and disappeared into her tent, reappearing with her sword in hand, and some additional armour adorning her. She tossed a chestplate at Coren, which the other woman swiftly placed on, before continuing to tack up their horses. When both horses were readied, Coren darted back to her and Zarola's tent, where she grabbed one of the twin blades and one half of the willow mage stake, the counterparts of which were hopefully still in the hands of a very alive and very safe Commander Zarola.

Exiting through the tent flap, she caught that same look of fear from earlier upon the Light Mage's face. But she wouldn't acknowledge it. She couldn't.

Instead, Coren slowly and painfully pulled herself atop a horse, letting out a gasping breath with each movement and slipped her feet through the stirrups.

"Are you sure you'll be okay?" Auryon asked from behind her, already atop her own horse.

Coren's eyes were squeezed tightly shut as a shooting pain in her chest threatened to cripple her. She quickly angled her face away from Auryon. After a moment, the Dark Mage turned her head with a half-hearted smile, telling her, "I was out for eleven days before now, I've rested enough. Let's go."

She squeezed her legs together tightly and the horse set off into a light canter, Auryon trailing just behind. Village after village passed by, with the two only changing direction to avoid the major towns and cities. According to Auryon, the location of Caradoc's camp (where they had found Coren) was almost directly east from the rebels' settlement.

By the time they had begun to approach the general location, the moon was setting in the south. Coren watched as it did so, tuning out the sound of yet another villager telling Auryon that no, he had neither seen or heard any battle, in favour of considering the story behind it.

In one of the many books that Coren had been given at Milo's request regarding the tall tales of Galaris, it had explained that the moon had once set in the east, and risen in the west. However, when the First Hybrid had come into his powers, the balance of the continents had become so untethered that the moon and sun would rise and set in different places each night – they could even sometimes be seen in the sky together.

Then, when the future Gods and Goddesses defeated him, balance was restored. At the time, the moon and sun had been rising in the north, so they continued to do so even though their direction no longer changed each night and they no longer appeared in the sky together.

The Dark Mage was imagining what it must have been like to see such a thing when a hand rested upon her shoulder, before steering her back towards the horses. That familiar feeling of defeat, of hopelessness, threatened to embrace her once more. So, Coren shut her eyes and tried to imagine it – tried to take herself away from this reality.

It looked so beautiful, the sun and the moon being beside one another. Perhaps it was painful for them when they were forced apart.

"Coren," Auryon gently prompted, before she braced her hands together beside Coren and bent down a little to give the Dark Mage a leg-up onto the horse. Clearly, the Light Mage had not been as ignorant to Coren's pain as she had previously thought.

Coren held back any gasps in the hopes that it would give Auryon one less thing to worry about. She was no doubt struggling to hold herself together as much as Coren was.

Now atop her horse, she muttered, "thank you."

The other woman merely nodded, neither of them feeling particularly talkative, and then they moved onto the next village.

"I'm sorry, I haven't seen or heard anything."

"No armies have passed through here, love. Have you been drinking?"

"Armies? No. Saw a couple of festival goers a couple of days ago though. Does that help?"

"I haven't seen anybody, I'm sorry. I wish you every luck in finding them."

"No."

Each place was met with rejection after rejection, and each word from their mouths made Coren feel sick. *Imagine the sun and the moon, reunited*, she had told herself more times than the Dark Mage could count. And then the traitorous thought had come along: *but what if they never find each other?*

They approached yet another village, this one just at

the bottom of a tall, tall hill. Coren looked to her right towards Auryon, who had done the majority of the asking, but she was immobile, gripping onto the reins of her horse so tightly that her knuckles were turning white.

Painfully, Coren drew her left leg over to her right side, before pushing herself off the horse, ignoring Auryon's sudden protesting when the Light Mage realised what she was doing.

The short drop left her dizzy at the throbbing pain it prompted, but Coren forced herself to walk as straight as she could towards the first villager she could find.

It was a woman. She must have been in her late sixties with a face scattered with wrinkles, yet she possessed a kind of aged beauty that women in Coren's old village would have envied. At her side, a small boy stood, probably her grandchild, with curly blonde hair and bright blue eyes, who was staring towards the brow of the hill with anticipation.

When she noticed Coren's approach, her expression became one of an almost motherly concern, but the Dark Mage ignored it.

"Have you seen any armies passing through here? Heard anything about a battle?"

After the words left her mouth, Coren felt some regret for being so rude and abrupt in her questioning, but she couldn't bring herself to summon anything good to her mouth. It felt as if it had been drained out of her by all the possibilities running through her head – that Zarola could be gone. Gone. *Gonegonegonegonegone-*

"Yes, I have," the woman said to the Dark Mage's

407

surprise, her concern appearing to grow, "it was all atop that hill over there, my grandson saw flames a couple of hours ago and-,"

Before she had even finished, Coren was turning to face the steep hill, and was stopped in her place at what she saw.

There was a woman running down it.

Covered in blood.

Soon, the woman was falling, tumbling down the hill. Coren was frozen in place as Auryon, who Coren had not realised had been following closely behind her, rushed towards the crimson body.

When they had reached the bottom of the hill, having made the journey mostly by her fall, the woman lay with her face towards the two Mages.

Auryon, much closer and able to see the woman's features far better, let out a gasp and surged towards her. Finally, Coren also began to run towards them, with the woman behind her shouting for them to be careful; that she didn't think going up there was a good idea.

To the Below with good ideas, Zarola might be up there, Coren thought back at her, moving closer and closer to the person. Soon enough, her facial features became distinguishable, and Auryon's reason for her desperate sprint towards the woman became obvious – it was Riah.

The Light Mage was cradling her younger sister's head by the time Coren came to kneel beside her. By some miracle, the dark-haired woman was awake, though her breaths were coming out in short gasps.

"It happened s-so fast," she got out, her eyes wide and far away, though they appeared to be fixated upon Auryon, "h-he knew. He knew what was going to happen s-so he... he did to us what we were g-going to do to him. C-c... circled us from even further afield and-and-and-,"

The coughs that Riah let out were violent, shaking her whole body as she looked up at her sister with a kind of desperation for something. For reassurance, for comfort, for something to ease the pain. Emotional and physical.

Auryon shushed her gently, moving one hand to stroke the other girl's hair.

"It's okay," Coren heard her whisper, tears falling down the Light Mage's cheeks, "it's okay now. You're okay now."

For a moment, the devastation in Riah's eyes appeared to lessen. That was, before she caught eyes with Coren.

"C-Com-Commander... Dahlia... T-they," Coren's blood went cold at the look of pure guilt and regret in Riah's eyes, "i-it was Caradoc. H-he did it. He k-kill-illed her."

Not true, not true, not true, not true.

She must have said one of them out loud, if the looks of pity she received were anything to go by.

It's not true. Notnotnotnotnotnot-

"Coren!" Auryon shouted as the Dark Mage began to run up the hill, pushing herself to the limits of her enhanced speed. Still, she wasn't going fast enough. The snow was making her slide, filling her boots with wet sludge. But she didn't stop. She couldn't. She needed to get to the top, she needed to prove that Riah

was wrong, that she had merely misunderstood.
Perhaps Zarola was a little hurt, but she wasn't dead.
She couldn't be.
Not Zarola. Not Dahlia. Not Izak. Not even Milo.
None of them could be dead.
Zarola and her still had places to go – lives to escape
from.
Zarola couldn't be dead because Coren loved her, and
she had never told her that.
The Commander wasn't allowed to be dead, because
they were supposed to be happy.
Coren was nearly at the top of the hill, her view of the
land seated atop it still just obscured; Auryon was
racing up the hill behind her, screaming for her to wait
– to come back. Telling her that she didn't need to see
this.
She wasn't going to see anything, didn't Auryon
understand? Because Zarola was fine. She was healthy
and alive and Coren was going to tell her she loved her
and they were going to be happy.
It was with this belief held tightly within her soul that
Coren made the final steps to the top of the hill, and
her knees gave way.
In front of her was a field of red, upon which bodies
lay, some burned beyond recognition, some with heads
and arms and legs missing, some with faces screwed up
in horror, some with eyes closed and weapons through
their stomachs.
Dead. Dead. Dead. Dead.
Perhaps they were all dead but Zarola – she couldn't
be. Dahlia and Milo and Izak – they couldn't be.

And so, Coren, whose legs refused to stand, began to crawl. Her pale palms and knees gradually began to stain crimson as she placed them upon flesh, moving herself over body after body.

She recognised some of them as she placed a hand or a knee upon their chest. Secondary Cilla, a young boy who she'd bumped into when collecting water, an older woman who she'd seen in the training grounds on occasion.

Coren did not cry when she pushed herself over Milo's body, nor when she stared down at Dahlia's closed eyes, the other woman's lower body severely burned and a sword through her chest. She did not allow herself to mourn when she saw a body that could have been Izak's, which was burned beyond true recognition everywhere bar his forehead, where the word *TRAITOR* was able to be seen.

And there, in the centre of it all, when Coren had stained herself red with the blood of the people that she had helped to kill, because there was no doubt in her mind that Caradoc's Mind Mages had found out the rebels plans from her head; that Zarola hadn't thought to change the plan based on that possibility because she was too busy worrying about her, was the Commander herself.

She looked as beautiful as ever, with bright red-orange hair strewn about and her skin glowing beneath the moon, highlighting the five small freckles that Coren had managed to find upon her nose.

Perhaps Coren could tell herself she was still sleeping, sleeping beneath the moon as they had done in their long travels to the rebel camp, if not for the fact that her dark eyes were wide open, staring towards Coren, but at nothing at all.

"Zar," Coren said in a broken whisper, crawling towards the girl with every ounce of strength she had left, "Zar." After what felt like an age, Coren finally reached the rebel Commander, her hands moving to balance her lower back upon her knee, so that Coren could cradle her.

"Zar, it's time to wake up... You've got to wake up. We-we've got a boat to catch t-to that p-place with the med-meadow. The-the one that we talked about. Zar... Zar!" When she would still not do anything – not blink, not move a finger, Coren tried to shake her into responding, all the while shouting to her, "Zar! Zarola! Zarola! Zarola, please... Please."

This time, there was no way to force back the tears. No way to hold herself together. Everything was unravelling. Everything was being drained from her. She had nothing. Nothing but the tears that streamed down her face, nothing but her voice as she screamed in agony, her head falling down to the other woman's shoulder.

"I s-s-still nee-need you Z-Zar," the Dark Mage tried to tell her, hugging her arms around the other girl as she cried and cried and drowned herself in her own tears, "you can't leave me! You can't! You can't! You can't!" There were arms around Coren's middle, and a tugging force from behind. It was saying something to her, but Coren didn't care. She fought the force with all her strength, never releasing her grip on Zarola.

The Darkness answered her desperation, and shoved the force away, allowing Coren to fall back down to the ground with the body of the woman she loved. To hold her and imagine that she was warm, not cold; to hold her and imagine that she was hugging her back, not laying with her arms stiffly by her side; to imagine that she was smiling that beautiful smile of hers, not staring expressionlessly into the distance.

The force came back.

It pulled her away with more strength now, but Coren still refused to yield.

"No!" She howled at it, elbowing shoving backwards and still not releasing her grip on the redhead who was just sleeping. She wasn't dead. She must have learned to sleep with her eyes open. She must have-

A sudden burst of blinding light shocked Coren into releasing Zarola, whose body fell back to the ground. As it did so, Coren found herself staring lower, to a place that she hadn't yet looked.

The middle left of Zarola's chest had been messily cut into, her pale ribs on show to both Mages, the nearby flesh barely hanging on. Some of the ribs, and the breastbone, had been broken, and it was easy to see why.

There was something missing.

Caradoc had ripped out Zarola's heart, and taken it with him.

The one pulling her away – Auryon – had clearly realised it too, her hands stilling where they had fought to keep Coren still.

Bile rose in the Dark Mage's throat as she clawed and

she screamed and she threw Auryon away from her, falling back to the ground upon her knees.

In Coren's own chest, behind and to the left of her breastbone, it felt as if there was nothing there at all. It felt hollow.

Zarola was dead. She was dead because of her. Her only chance of happiness was dead. She was gone and there was no hope for her now; there was nothing for her now.

Everything had been taken away from her.

The next time agony threatened to rip her apart – because even if Coren didn't have a heart anymore, she had a soul and oh Gods it hurt – a scream wasn't the only thing that Coren let out.

No.

Instead, a kind of pale emptiness filled the east of Galaris as the Darkness that had once been night came rushing towards her, rushing home. Somewhere inside of her, Coren felt that black line that she had once followed so diligently for Caradoc ignite, and so Coren tugged upon it, took from it, before she sent Darkness into the world as she cried out, where it covered the setting moon and the just-rising sun, bathing her entire continent in a deep, endless black.

The sun had died.

And the moon had no home.

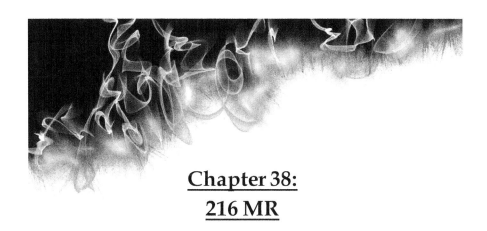

Chapter 38:
216 MR

$\mathcal{A}$uryon had never known a darkness like this one. It

was consuming her; embracing her; drowning her and hating her. It pushed her down and down beneath it, closer to the earth – the pressure was too much. It was all too much. Too much darkness. Too much pain. Too much nothing. Too much everything.

Somewhere in the centre of the Darkness, a woman was screaming.

It was the kind of scream that would make Gods weep to hear, one of exploding pain and dying hope. Of a star that had fallen from its place in the sky – hurtling helplessly down to earth.

"Coren," the brown-eyed woman choked out beneath it, hands grabbing for purchase as the black appeared to shove her away, "C-Coren."

Against the Darkness, the Light Mage pushed. The ground ruthlessly forced her nails back into her skin as she clawed her way through the earth, blood trickling from their beds. Her friend. She had to get to her friend.

The warrior tried to speak again, but her words merely came out as a gasp. The Darkness was stifling, and Auryon felt with utmost certainty that it was going to kill her – that she would be yet another rebel lying on this crimson field beneath the obscured, cold sun; more food for the ground to eat.

She supposed it wasn't the worst way to go. Dying whilst trying to save a friend. And so, she pressed her hand into the ground once more, and battled to just move, even just an inch.

And then, with a kind of sudden, cracking sound that made your ears ring and your head feel as if it would cave in on itself, the Darkness possessed the world. What had once been day was now night; what once had been light was cast in shadow. It was as if the world itself was a widow in mourning, and if one was to wonder who the world was mourning for, they only had to look as far as the centre of the battlefield, no more than ten metres from where Auryon had managed to claw herself to.

A blonde-haired Mage kneeled there. Her head had fallen to the ground, presumably exhausted by the exhibition of power unlike anything Auryon had ever seen.

She had heard that a Dark Mage's magic was great, but something about this felt unnatural. Wrong. Nobody should have the kind of power that forced nature to cower.

"What have you done, Coren?" Auryon asked, the words coming out far louder than she had intended now that the crippling pressure of her friend's magic had decided to beat the skies into submission instead of the Light Mage herself.

The breath in her throat caught as Coren turned.

Her eyes.

They were entirely black.

The other woman did not acknowledge Auryon as she pushed herself off of the ground, not even as she strode past the black-haired woman towards the hill edge.

The Light Mage tried to scramble up from the ground and follow her, but the Light Mage's legs barely made it two steps before they gave way, not yet recovered from the earlier pressure.

All Auryon could do was hopelessly call out, "Coren, stop! Where are you going?"

For the first time since discovering Zarola's corpse, the Dark Mage acknowledged her. When black eyes made contact with Auryon's own, she almost wished she hadn't.

"I'm going to find him," her friend informed her, voice far too gentle for the message they were delivering, "and I'm going to kill him, slowly, painfully. And the last thing he will hear is Zarola's name."

"Coren! Stop! This isn't you," Auryon called out desperately, attempting to crawl when she found she could not stand. But her legs refused to obey even that. And so Coren's journey down the hill continued, and all Auryon could do was listen out as, when the Dark Mage finally reached the bottom, snow crunched beneath the hooves of the other woman's horse.

As soon as the pressure gave in, Auryon would follow. Until then, all she could do was hope that she was not too late to save Coren's soul.

Unbidden, her mind brought to the surface the image of Coren's all-black eyes from moments ago. *If there's anything left to save,* it thought.

Auryon shook that idea away.

There was. There had to be.

Chapter 39:
216 MR

*O*ver and over, a horse's hooves found their home in the deep, settled snow of northern Galaris. When the horse's legs kicked up, the snow went with them, leaving a trail of white in the wake of the strong mare and its turbulent rider.

Red marked the path of hot, salty tears down the rider's pale face. But they were old tears. The rider wasn't crying any longer, not as the cold air nipped harshly at her features, nor as, every now and again, her darkened eyes would glance towards where her hands had been stained by the blood of the woman she loved.

Each glance had her squeezing her legs around the horse harder, urging her on with only one destination in mind; one person.

All around her, a formidable deep darkness had formed. It was blacker even than the night that had settled across the lands. It flickered and expanded; it seemed to pulse. The erratic movements of it were not in tune with the rider's harsh breathing nor with the shaking of her hands. Everything about it screamed uncontrolled. Unrestrained.

When they had first headed north, Zarola dictated that they would journey upwards alongside the River of the Dead, as she had believed the King would either follow the Golden River or the Alyda River. They hadn't wanted to be found by him.

Coren had no such concerns.

Instead, when she found a river that was so bright a gold it managed to glow in the newfound darkness of day, the Dark Mage directed her horse atop of its ice and watched in satisfaction as each harsh pounding of her horse's hooves saw it fracture.

The Darkness is coming for you, Caradoc, she thought to herself as she imagined the cracking of the ice being that of his skull. Then, the golden-haired woman looked up and saw the Dark new world she'd created. Her lips twitched up into a smile. *And there's nowhere to hide.*

Nearly three weeks of eternal night had passed by the time the lone rider made it back to the Golden City and the palace that presided over it. Upon arrival, there were no subtle disguises or meticulous plans. No. Instead, the woman whose face was painted with grief and anger, whose eyes were twinged with something twisted and so wrong, simply approached the fiery moat.

In front of it stood no less than four dozen soldiers. Some held bows, others swords, and some held nothing at all. All were Mages.

And all would fall.

Behind her, the Darkness rose up like a tsunami wave, casting the Golden Palace into shadow. She could feel their fear from where she sat, still atop her horse. It made her feel powerful.

Though they shook, though some could not prevent the helplessness that seeped into their gazes, the King's Guards stood their ground. To those who watched on from the houses nearest to the Golden Palace, it seemed as if all the continents, as if the Gods themselves, were baiting their breath.

Then, the Dark Mage raised both her hands high in the air.

And brought them down.

The tsunami hit. It surged towards where the guards stood, putting out the fires of the moat as it did so, and trapped them all within its awful current. Several King's Guards screamed as the Darkness pulled them down into its depths; a few blindly shot arrows in the direction of the blonde Mage; many tried to use their abilities. The power of the Elementals did not reach her, the Darkness containing them; the Transformative Mages who turned themselves into birds to escape the flood were soon recaptured when Coren raised her hands once more, transforming the Darkness into something of a tornado. Any magic from Light Mages was easily snuffed out.

A Mind Mage attempted to break into her head, she could feel their clammy hands grip around it and their attempts to squeeze, but they could not. They clenched and clenched in vain. Coren smiled and sought to test out a theory. Like she had been taught with the Connection, she searched for some kind of thread. Some kind of a connection.

She found it. It was a thin but strong chord of dark purple. Outside of her realm of focus, her shoulder gave a burst of pain. Coren ignored it. Instead, she focused on the chord. Mentally, she latched onto it, and shoved all the Darkness she could summon from within her down and down and down.

Somewhere within the flood, she heard a man's torturous screams rise above the rest. When the screams stopped, the dark purple chord disappeared from her grip.

Something swelled within her. Adrenaline. Intoxication. Bliss. She laughed, and wished she could latch onto it; to keep feeling like this forever.

If she couldn't have Zarola, she decided, then she would have this.

Power.

When no more sounds were emitted from the flood, she shoved at the Darkness, and it soon moved away to allow her a clear view of where the soldiers had once stood. Now, there was nothing but a pile of bodies.

She did not pity them. She did not mourn for their families, nor for what they could have been. They had chosen their side, and so they were all guilty. They had all helped kill her.

I want a bridge, she told the Darkness, staring at the moat that separated her from the Mages' bodies.

A layer of black rushed to cover the dip that had once been a moat of fire. Still dressed in her bloodied clothes and chest plate, Coren shoved herself from the mare and began to walk towards her creation. Though the Darkness over the moat appeared smoke-like in appearance, it was solid beneath her crimson-soaked boots.

One step. Another.

Already, there were more King's guards waiting to greet her at the other side. Another two dozen. They observed their comrades' bodies mournfully, before turning their determined gazes upon her.

They barely had time to prepare to exercise their powers when Coren shoved both of her palms forward, and the six guards closest to her crashed brutally into the hard walls of the palace behind them.

Within her left hand, Coren allowed a ball of Darkness to grow whereas, with the other, she lifted her hand upwards and downwards at a slow pace, forcing the six guards up into the air as she slammed them onto the bottom of a balcony and then into the hard ground over and over, before releasing the now large ball in the direction of another group of guards.

One guard attempted to sneak up on her, approaching slowly from her left and raising his sword high when he judged himself close enough. Coren merely turned to him, letting the others drop to the ground for a final time, and caught the sharp edge of the sword within her palm.

With a strength she hadn't had before, the Dark Mage wrenched the sword from his grip, staining the steel a dark red as it cut deeper into her hand, before she grasped the hilt with her opposite hand and turned it, then plunged the sword through the guard's chest. She watched him die. And then she continued on.

One step. Another.

When Coren finally reached the small podium that stood before the gates, she brought the bloodied sword down upon the cooling arm of a dead guard. Picking the arm up from the floor, she then placed the woman's palm against the podium.

The gates opened.

One step. Another.

More guards were waiting inside the gate, and she delivered upon them the same treatment as was given to the rest. When only eight were left standing, she demanded of them, coldly, "where is Caradoc?"

An exhausted woman glanced up with just her desperate eyes, unable to move her injured head from where it remained hanging low. Breathless, she told the Dark creature before her, "he'll kill us if we tell you."

Coren offered her a humourless smile. "I'll kill you if you don't."

Still, her opponents remained voiceless. Eyes narrowed; Coren closed her eyes. She reached deeper and deeper into the well of Darkness that seemed to never end – did it end? What would happen if she reached the bottom? They were questions for another time – and pulled. Once she felt scores of Darkness just below the surface, she pushed it out.

The guards screeched as the Darkness attacked them brutally; scarring and scratching, brutalising and burning. One fell. So did the next. Two more followed suit.

"The throne room!" It was the woman from before, her voice raw with pain, "the King and his Mind Mages are holed up in the throne room!"

Coren smiled.

"Thank you," she said, before the Dark Mage clenched her fists. Four snaps sounded simultaneously, and the last of that group of guards fell to the floor.

One step, the Dark Mage thought as she moved her right leg, *another*.

All she could do now was keep on moving; all she had now was herself, her Darkness and the vengeance coiling in her stomach.

The Dark Mage threw the doors to the throne room open, entirely incautious as to what lay behind them. After all, Caradoc could hide himself away with all the Mind Mages he liked; after the display earlier, their powers seemed to have no effect on her.

True to the guard's word, the doors revealed more than twenty Mind Mages standing in front of a dais, their eyes all trained upon her and poised for attack. Behind them, the dark-haired King lounged on his throne with a goblet held precariously in his grasp. If he was afraid, King Caradoc did not show it.

"Coren," he greeted, his tone perfectly neutral, if not amiable, "I see that you decided that my throne was worth taking after all."

He took a moment to look her over. It was only then that she truly felt the harsh throbbing in her shoulder. Though she refused to look down, she angled her eyes in such a way that the blonde could keep an eye on Caradoc and yet still see the arrow protruding from it.

"Do you need to sit down?" He inquired mockingly, "that looks like it hurt."

"Where is her heart?" Coren asked instead. Her voice was smaller than she had intended and laced with far more pain and desperation than she had wanted to give away.

The Fire King laughed. "I have no idea what you're talking about."

From the way he smiled, from his tone of voice, Coren knew that he was aware of exactly what she was talking about.

"I said," Coren began slowly, taking several threatening steps towards the dark-haired man, shadows growing behind her, "where. Is. Her. Heart?"

Perhaps Caradoc had decided he'd had enough of their conversation, or perhaps the Mind Mages had seen her growing Darkness and decided they had to act now, either way, numerous hands sought purchase around her mind, trying to harshly clutch at it.

Coren shut her eyes and focused on those threads. The

first nine were easy to locate, and so she grasped onto them, ready. The next eight were more difficult, obscuring themselves in the smallest of shadowed corners, but she managed to grasp them too. There were a few that she could not find, but she would simply have to deal with them in the outside realm. So, summoning the Darkness within her as she had done previously, Coren harshly pushed it down all of those dark purple threads, opening her eyes to the sounds of harsh screams in time to watch as their minds quite literally exploded with a cloud of black vapour.

The Dark Mage was unaffected when some of the consequences of the explosion covered her.

The four remaining Mind Mages paused for a moment before continuing to move towards her, so she swiftly threw them back, sickening cracks accompanying their meetings with the ground.

When Coren looked back towards the Fire King, she saw him staring back at her with wide eyes, blood and what she could only assume was brain matter dripping down one side of his face.

"How did you," he tried, before beginning again, "no other Dark Mage can... Unless-,"

The King stopped his final train of thought, staring at Coren as if she were something akin to a deity rather than a mere Mage.

"Where is her heart?" She asked again, uncaring as to what he was prattling on about. She needed to do this; for herself, for Zarola. She couldn't let this man keep her heart. She couldn't let this man live after what he'd taken from the world.

Out of her cloak, she took her half of the Willow Mage stake.

Caradoc stilled.

"Killing me would be a mistake," he said when the Dark Mage did not move from where she stood, her knuckles whitening due to her harsh grip, "I know what's happening to you. I know why you have this much power. It's not natural, Coren, but I can help you, I-,"

"I don't want your help," the Dark Mage all but shouted, ashamed at the way that tears had begun to track their way down her cheeks. She felt weak, when she so desperately needed to be powerful, "I just want her heart. W-where is her heart?"

The King scowled as he told her, "she's dead, Coren. She's gone and she's not coming back. Zarola was nothing but a human. Do you think the two of you would have lasted? Do you think you still would have been together in fifty years, when you still looked nineteen and she was seventy odd? When she'd be dead at eighty? Or, if you hadn't managed to make the Connection, do you think that she would have stayed with you when your magic was out of control and you were killing people by the dozen? You may have even killed her yourself."

When Coren didn't move or answer, Caradoc rose from his throne and began to stalk towards her, stepping carelessly over the bodies of his fallen Mind Mages. "With me," he continued, offering her a wide smile, "you could have been so much more. You even could have been my Queen. We would have married, shared our powers. You would have been the Queen of Fire and Darkness. You still could be. You could still have all that power."

Her grip on the stake began to wane. "Where's her heart?" She asked again, brokenly.

"Burned," he tells her at last. He was nearly before her now. "In the moat. Fire purges all."

The Dark Mage's legs weakened, threatening to drop her to the floor. Before that could happen, Caradoc grasped onto the underneath of her arm to keep her standing, whilst his other hand caressed her face. "Be with me," he said with a smile, "marry me and we can share our powers with one another. And you can start anew and forget all that once was. Forget her."

For a moment, Coren was back in the forest by the River of the Dead. Beside her, Zarola lay; her hair shining beneath the light of the moon. She turned to Coren, red curls flying about recklessly, and smiled. The Dark Mage held onto this picture of her, of the woman that she would never forget, as the Fire King leaned in and embraced her. Just as he had that day in his office.

Deep within the realm of her mind, Zarola was saying those three words that neither had the chance to say to the other as, outside of her fantasy, Coren altered her grasp on the stake.

Having leant down, the King was at perfect height for Coren to whisper, "you should have learned the first time," before moving her wrist in a quick motion towards his back.

Caradoc caught her right arm without even looking. "I did," Caradoc responded as he moved away from where he had rested his head on her shoulder. Now, the King put his forehead against hers and stared at her with those familiar flaming eyes. They looked mournful.

She felt a fire building up behind her and knew that the King was going to burn her just as he had done to Febronia.

But he wouldn't have the chance.

"Goodbye," she told him in nothing but a murmur, before shoving the Willow Mage stake straight through his heart.

He'd caught the wrong wrist.

Her right hand had held her dagger, but her left had held the stake.

The Fire King's brilliant eyes widened as all the veins in his body began to show up as a bright orange colour against his tanned skin. She felt the fires at her back cease at the same time as the flames in his eyes died, turning them to a dark brown colour.

The Dark Mage felt a part of herself wither up and die as they did so, listening as Caradoc let out a final, shuddering breath before he slumped against her. The weight of his body threatened to push her to the ground and Coren allowed it to do so.

When they hit the ground with a resounding thump, she eventually rolled the body off of her and sat up on her knees, staring at his now dark eyes.

She didn't move, didn't speak, for the two days that it took before the doors to the throne room were shoved open to reveal a frantic, dark haired woman.

"Coren!" The woman called out, her voice thick with fear. When her eyes finally fell upon the blonde Mage, drenched in blood and other substances, her eyes dancing with shadows as she stared down at the man she had once loved, she repeated her name once more. But this time it was in horror.

The warrior took several moments to gather herself, forcing her eyes up from the corpse of the Fire King, before she tentatively asked Coren, "are you okay?"

The Dark Mage ignored her question, getting up from the ground and staring towards Auryon.

Towards. Not at.

Terror filled the stomach of the rebel as she realised just how removed from reality her friend seemed to be.

"Coren!" Auryon called out again. That seemed to break the other woman out of her state somewhat, for her green eyes darted away from the Light Mage's direction and back towards Caradoc.

The rebel watched as her friend leaned down and took the golden crown from atop his black-red hair. The Mage seemed to take a moment to stare at it, before placing it atop her own golden hair.

As soon as it sat upon her head, Darkness appeared all around it, covering the gold to make a crown of shadows in its place.

Then, Coren looked back towards Auryon and began to walk in her direction.

As her friend approached, the Light Mage remained entirely still. She didn't know what to do; she didn't recognise the woman in front of her, who wore a Dark crown and was covered head to toe in the blood of her victims. This wasn't Coren. It wasn't.

She stopped just shy of Auryon, still not looking her in the eye as she told her, quietly but coldly, "throw his body in the moat."

Then, the Dark Mage continued to walk away, and Auryon was helpless to do anything but watch.

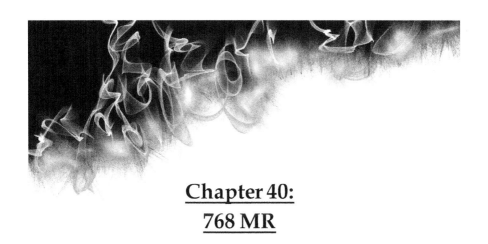

Chapter 40:
768 MR

*T*he hall was empty, bar for a solitary figure who sat,

straight-backed, within a tall, imposing throne. Under the candle's flames, her gold hair seemed to glimmer like something beautiful – something alive. But all it took was one close look into those green-grey eyes to come to the true conclusion.

The Night Queen was a dead thing.

There was no life behind her eyes, no warmth in her heart. Darkness shifted upon her head; a crown of shadows. Throughout her entire body, suffocating silence reigned just as it had for five-hundred years. Since one body fell upon a crimson field, and the other was fed to the moat.

And now, both of those bodies had been reclaimed by life; they walked the earth, as if none of that had ever happened. Only it had, and the girl turned monster was the living proof of that.

Her crown of shadows fell, the Darkness moving to cover her ears, whispering to her, before returning to their place atop her shining curls.

By the time three heavy footsteps were within earshot, the Queen already had the oak doors opening, revealing her form. She was covered by a low-cut, tight, chiffon dress. It was black in colour with a choker that circled the centre of her slender neck before the material parted. At her hips, the material flared out. The dress had a slit from her upper right thigh to the bottom; it was a wide slit that was held together by what appeared to be threads of alternating opals and pearls. A Queen of Darkness in body as she was in heart.

One of the men audibly gulped upon seeing her. They never did like to be in her presence, much preferring to report to the strong-willed, sympathetic Auryon to, well, her.

"I hear you've finished the preparations for my ritual," the Night Queen said, one side of her blood-red lips quirking upwards, "tell me, are you ready to meet the ruler of the Below?"

If it were possible to smell fear, her Queen's guards would positively reek of it. But, fortunately for them, one guard gained the confidence to nod before bowing his head, and began to lead the Queen through the darkened halls of her castle.

If you want a war, Coren thought to herself, recalling Caradoc's grand displays of fire both outside her castle and throughout her kingdom, *then I'll give you one.*

In the centre of a dark room, deep within the lower halls of the Black Castle, lay an eight-pointed star. At each point lay a different stone: diamond, emerald, fluorite, blood stone, alexandrite, amethyst, opal and black diamond. Each represented one of the categories of Mages.

In the centre was a large stone pedestal upon which the Queen set her aged, leather-bound book.

When she had first approached it, two guards had tried to take the book from her; to place it on the pedestal in her place. But she allowed no one else to touch it.

This was to be her greatest weapon.

Around the podium, a small, almost pipe-like object slithered downwards before connecting to the eight-pointed star that had been harshly carved into the ground.

As the Night Queen took in the set-up, ensuring everything was in the correct positioning, eight adults took several steps forward until they paused, trembling, just behind each of the eight points.

"Dejit adir un kir hyses Gods, jhar yslen sacra un lyfe. Dejit solen hyitt dejit hava lorceen aditta; bynd, bynd, bynd jhar kira hyitt. Dejit hyitt God. Dejit hyitt God. Dejit hyitt God."

"Jhar yslen sacra un lyfe."

With the blade from beneath her sleeve, Coren tore into her skin, watching as the red substance trickled into the tube and down. Its final position was filling the eight pointed star completely.

Then, she advanced upon the dark-haired woman who stood before the diamond point of the star. A small whimper emerged from the woman's lips as the Night Queen repeated, *"Jhar yslen sacra un lyfe, Lexin."*

Then the fine blade, one that had fought on behalf of the rebels so long ago, pierced the woman's heart before it surged back out of her body. She fell forwards, into the star, the diamond a crushing force against the dead woman's stomach.

The Night Queen then retreated back to the centre of the circle, before following the line to the second point – adorned with an emerald at its end – to where a fair haired man waited.

He did not shake like the woman, but nor was he fearless in the face of death. His brown eyes seemed to widen with each step Coren took towards him.

"Jhar yslen sacra un lyfe, Aliona."

The Elemental Mage tried and failed to dodge the knife that advanced upon him.

Another body fell into the star.

"Jhar yslen sacra un lyfe, Minerra."

And another.

"Jhar yslen sacra un lyfe, Venrin."

And another.

"Jhar yslen sacra un lyfe, Jakar."

"Jhar yslen sacra un lyfe, Remi."

"Jhar yslen sacra un lyfe, Nias."

Now, seven corpses lay at seven points of the star; their faces were angled downwards, never to look up to see the sun nor the stars again.

I guess now I really did kill all of the Dark Mages, the Queen thought dryly, knowing well what accusations her court threw at her. *Shame.*

Finally, Coren advanced upon the eighth person.

"Jhar yslen sacra un lyfe, Akeros."

Having spent over a century in captivity, this woman was not afraid. No. She watched the knife eagerly as it found a home in her heart. As the ritual neared completion.

Her suffering was done, yet the suffering of so many more was just beginning.

Coren retreated back to the centre of the circle.

"Rhynd lor kir on mak dejit hyitt victa."

For the first time in five centuries, the Queen felt anticipation burning in her stomach.

"Dejit hyitt God."

It burned brighter.

"Dejit hyitt God."

She smiled.

"Dejit hyitt God."

Cold filled the room. Not a chilling breeze but a bone-freezing cold. A kind of cold that made you wish you were dead. The Darkness shielded Coren as it made its attack, but the effort was unnecessary.

The powers of the God of Death could not harm her; she had seen to that.

Her guards would not be so fortunate. Coren frowned as she briefly considered the nagging she would be subjected to by Auryon over their loss.

After the cold came the screams; the loudest of all was a
man's, deep and tortured. Behind his was that of many,
a woman sobbing, a man begging for it all to just stop,
another woman crying out and asking why can't she
just *die die die!*

It felt as if all of the Below might emerge into this
dingy castle dungeon, but it did not. The voices, the
cold, it all retreated as swiftly as they had come.

And all that was left of the Below's little show was a
rather pitiful-looking figure.

How disappointing, the Night Queen mulled, moving
to circle the figure with a cocked head.

The man had dark-hair that was in dire disarray, and
she noted that they must not have clothes in the bowels
of the Below for he wore none. He was on the floor, his
head to the ground and arms held roughly behind his
back by invisible bounds. The skin of his back shown to
her was pale, unhealthily so, and scarred cruelly.

Briefly, she wondered if he had gained those scars in
the war against the First Hybrid.

Another aspect Coren observed was the broad set of his
shoulders. Good. She could use a warrior in addition to
his party tricks.

She moved her head to the side, angling it so that she
might see whether the face matched the downtrodden
warrior-like figure.

While she inspected, the creature was silent.

"Are you going to keep me down here forever?" he
asked, his deep voice filled with such utter loathing
that, had he been able to use his powers at will, Coren
had no doubt she would be nought but a memory to

438

this world.

Her lips curled and she jabbed the God in the side with her heeled foot, "you should be more grateful towards the person who just rescued you from the Below."

The man was silent then, but she could positively feel the hatred emanating from him.

Gods, he will not make this easy, she thought to herself, before deciding the best cause of action was to kick him in the side roughly again.

This time, he angled his head to the left – still being unable to lift it – and looked at her.

His eyes put those of Nias' to shame. Their dark red shade was unnatural, inhuman, *Godly.* They struck even the Queen silent for a moment, pushing an ounce of true fear within her heart, which only grew by the malice that shone within the crimson.

"Didn't you hear, master?" he taunted, "the Gods are free."

"But you are not."

She had found the book that had given her this ritual four centuries ago, when she had been searching for something else. For something she no longer desired. Back then, she had soon realised that what she held was the ability to enslave a God to her will, but Coren had never bothered with it. She didn't want anybody credited for the way she rose to power and maintained it; no man had given her a throne, she had taken it alone. She had made her power alone.

The Queen had considered burning it so that no other may figure out how to command the same power, but she had been too paranoid to do so. What if there was a threat to her power so large that it was a necessity? And her paranoia had come to fruition.

Now, she had a God and his powers bound to her whims. The most powerful of them all.

The Night Queen leaned over to her left where the God of Death's scythe lay, having materialised alongside him, pulling it towards her and then hooking the blade over his neck. She willed the invisible force holding him down to lighten, allowing her to guide his head level with hers using his weapon.

The power she held to have a God at her mercy. Coren positively revelled in it.

Akeros did not look afraid. Instead, he continued to gaze at her; his eyes merely beds for his hatred within his otherworldly, sharply-structured face.

She leaned in closer, her breath no doubt tickling at his ear.

"When we're done with this word, my darling Death, my enemies' blood will run the streets and there will be a crown upon my head. You and I, we're going to destroy *everything.*"

Coren, Zarola, Caradoc, Auryon, Hearne, Akeros, Milo and others will return in **QUEEN OF RAGE AND RUIN**.

ACKNOWLEDGEMENTS:

When I started writing this book, I was simply a 17 year old A-Level student who'd considered the question: what would make me turn evil? It was a shower thought, of all things, and I had been greeted in my mind with the image of me, sobbing over the body of the person I loved the most.
From that image, Kingdom of Wrath and Ruin was born.
I want to thank every single one of you for your commitment to my story, following Coren's journey from a kind-hearted, naïve girl in 216 MR to the cold-hearted Queen she becomes. It means the world to me that people have the opportunity to read and enjoy my story.
Thank you so much to my wonderful Editor, Lindsay, whose belief in me and this book meant the world to me. Thank you for all you've done! And to the fabulous Amara who designed my cover, her talent is simply amazing and I look forward to working with you again in the future!
A special thank you goes out to one of my A Level teachers, Ms Hamilton-Cooper, without whom this story would never have been finished. You were my first and most dedicated reader, you made me feel confident and talented enough to continue with this to the end, and for that I can't thank you enough. I wish all the best to you and your family, and that you'll enjoy being the first reader of books two and three as well :)

To my mum, who always encouraged my dreams, I thank you for never telling me there was anything I could not do, and giving me the confidence to be the person I am today.

To the rest of my family, I thank you for all your support and for listening to me ranting about storyline ideas I had at every other family get together... In other words, thank you for putting up with a teenager who poured all of her energy into dreaming :)

Lastly, and perhaps vainly, I want to congratulate myself. Well, more accurately, the five year old girl who proudly showed books she'd written about the Adventures of Marmalade the Cat to her grandparents. You did it. I'm proud of you.

FOLLOW ME ON:
Instagram – vmstiller
TikTok - cynicalsloth